THE DAY LINCOLN LOST

The Day Lincoln Lost

A NOVEL

Charles Rosenberg

HANOVER
SQUARE
PRESS

**HANOVER
SQUARE
PRESS™**

ISBN-13: 978-1-335-14522-2

The Day Lincoln Lost

This edition published by arrangement with Harlequin Books S.A.

Hanover Square Press
22 Adelaide St. West, 40th Floor
Toronto, Ontario M5H 4E3, Canada
HanoverSqPress.com
BookClubbish.com

Printed in U.S.A.

For Sally Anne

THE DAY
LINCOLN
LOST

I

Kentucky
Early August 1860

Lucy Battelle's birthday was tomorrow. She would be twelve. Or at least that was what her mother told her. Lucy knew the date might not be exact, because Riverview Plantation didn't keep close track of when slaves were born. Or when they died, for that matter. They came, they worked and they went to their heavenly reward. Unless, of course, they were sold off to somewhere else.

There had been a lot of selling-off of late. The Old Master, her mother told her, had at least known how to run a plantation. And while their food may have been wretched at times, there had always been enough. But the Old Master had died years before Lucy was born. His eldest son, Ezekiel Goshorn, had inherited Riverview.

Ezekiel was cruel, and he had an eye for young black women, although he stayed away from those who had not yet developed. Lucy has seen him looking at her of late, though. She was thin, and very tall for her age—someone had told her she looked like a young tree—and when she looked at herself naked, she could tell that her breasts were beginning to come. "You are pretty," her mother said, which sent a chill through her.

Whatever his sexual practices, Goshorn had no head for either tobacco farming or business, and Riverview was visibly suffering for it, and not only for a shortage of food. Lucy could see that the big house was in bad need of painting and other repairs, and the dock on the river, which allowed their crop to be sent to market, looked worse and worse every year. By now it was half-falling-down. Slaves could supply the labor to repair things, of course, but apparently Goshorn couldn't afford the materials.

Last year, a blight had damaged almost half the tobacco crop. Goshorn had begun to sell his slaves south to make ends meet.

In the slave quarter, not a lot was really known about being sold south, except that it was much hotter there, the crop was harder-to-work cotton instead of tobacco and those who went didn't come back. Ever.

Several months earlier, two of Lucy's slightly older friends had been sold, and she had watched them manacled and put in the back of a wagon, along with six others. Her friends were sobbing as the wagon moved away. Lucy was dry-eyed because then and there she had decided to escape.

Others had tried to escape before her, of course, but most had been caught and brought back. When they arrived back, usually dragged along in chains by slave catchers, Goshorn—or one of his five sons—had whipped each of them near to death. A few had actually died, but most had been nursed back to at least some semblance of health by the other slaves.

Lucy began to volunteer to help tend to them—to feed them, put grease on their wounds, hold their hands while they moaned and carry away the waste from their bodies. Most of all, though, she had listened to their stories—especially to what had worked and what had failed.

One thing she had learned was that they used hounds to pursue you, and that the hounds smelled any clothes you left behind to track you. One man told her that another man who had buried his one pair of extra pants in the woods before he left—not hard to do because slaves had so little—had not been found by the dogs.

Still another man said a runaway needed to take a blanket because as you went north, it got colder, especially at night, even in the summer. And you needed to find a pair of boots that would fit you. Lucy had tried on her mother's boots—the ones she used in the winter—and they fit. Her mother would find another pair, she was sure.

The hard thing was the Underground Railroad. They had all heard about it. They had even heard the masters damning it. Lucy had long understood that it wasn't actually underground and wasn't even a railroad. It was just people, white and black, who helped you escape—who fed you, hid you in safe houses and moved you, sometimes by night, sometimes under a load of hay or whatever they had that would cover you.

The problem was you couldn't always tell which ones were real railroaders and which ones were slave catchers posing as railroaders. The slaves who came back weren't much help about how to tell the difference because most had guessed wrong. Lucy wasn't too worried about it. She had not only the optimism of youth, but a secret that she thought would surely help her.

Tonight was the night. Over the past few days she had dug a deep hole in the woods where she could bury her tiny stash of things that might carry her smell. For weeks before that, she had foraged and dug for mushrooms in the woods, and so no one seemed to pay much mind to her foraging and digging earlier that day. As she left, she planned to take the now-too-small shift she had secretly saved from last year's allotment—her only extra piece of clothing—along with her shoes and bury them in the hole. That way the dogs could not take her smell from anything left behind. She would take the blanket she slept in with her.

She had also saved up small pieces of smoked meat so that she had enough—she hoped—to sustain her for a few days until she could locate the Railroad. She dropped the meat into a small cloth bag and hung it from a string tied around her waist, hidden under her shift.

Her mother had long ago fallen asleep, and the moon had set. Even better, it was cloudy and there was no starlight. Lucy put on her mother's boots, stepped outside the cabin and looked toward the woods.

As she started to move, Ezekiel Goshorn appeared in front of her, seemingly out of nowhere, along with two of his sons, and said, "Going somewhere, Lucy?"

"I'm just standing here."

"Hold out your arms."

"Why?"

"Hold out your arms!"

She hesitated but finally did as he asked, and one of his sons, the one called Amasa, clamped a pair of manacles around her wrists. "We've been watching you dig in the woods," he said. "Planning a trip perhaps?"

Lucy didn't answer.

"Well, we have a little trip to St. Louis planned for you instead."

As Ezekiel pushed her along, she turned to see if her mother had been awakened by the noise. If she had, she hadn't come out of the cabin. Probably afraid. Lucy had been only four the first time she'd seen Ezekiel Goshorn flog her mother, and that was not the last time she'd been forced to stand there and hear her scream.

2

They had moved her to a waiting wagon, which was enclosed by wooden slats, with crude benches built in along each side. A gate hung open at the foot. Lanterns on the four corners cast a ghostly light.

As Lucy stood at the bottom of the wagon, Goshorn pulled her shift up and held it above her head.

"Perhaps I should keep you after all," he said. "You'll be ripe soon." He paused, as if thinking it over. "But I need the money, and you'll bring a right fine price."

She held her breath, hoping he wouldn't notice the bag strung around her waist.

She heard Amasa say, "I wish you'd keep her, Father."

"You can sow your oats elsewhere," Goshorn said. He dropped the shift and stared into Lucy's eyes, trying, she thought, to make her avert her gaze. She stared back and tried to fix his ugly face in her memory.

"Get in the wagon," Goshorn said.

She climbed in and saw that there were six other Negroes already sitting on the benches, each of them manacled, the manacles tied by rope to railings atop the slats. They all appeared to be asleep. Two white men were also dozing on the benches. She assumed they were guards of some kind.

At the foot of the wagon, Goshorn was talking to a man, who handed him a sheaf of papers. Goshorn looked through them, and said, "This is a sale on consignment, right?"

"That's right, Zeke. You keep title to her until I actually sell her. That's when you get your money. If she doesn't sell, I bring her back."

"She'll sell," Goshorn said.

Lucy didn't understand the fancy words, but she did understand that they were talking about her like she was a cooking pot. It made her so angry she began to tremble.

"She's perhaps cold," the man said. "She's shaking violently." He went over and touched her neck. "Nope. Warm as can be. Hope she's not got the fever. That'll bring down the price right quick."

"She'll be good once you're underway," Goshorn said.

"I don't know…" the man said.

"She's young and strong. If she gets the fever, stop a day or two, and she'll recover. They almost always do. Or if you think she's faking, whip her until she stops. That works, too."

Lucy felt a deep fear settle over her. She needed to hide her anger. At least for now.

The man seemed to think about it, then nodded. "Alright. I'll take her."

Goshorn signed one of the pages and handed it back, whereupon the man dropped some coins into his hand. "Here's a small amount of earnest money, so I'll have something at risk, too," he said.

She heard Goshorn say, "Thank you. When do you think I'll see the full price?"

"Assuming the weather holds, we should be in St. Louis in

three days. So Thursday if we're lucky. The sales are usually on Saturday, and the paperwork will take a day after that to finish up. Then three days back here. So you should have the rest of your money in ten days if all goes well."

"That sounds good," Goshorn said.

"Or you could take 70 percent of the estimated price right now," the man said. "That way, I'll take title now, and you won't have to worry about my having to come back. And I'll be taking the risk she'll sell low."

"Thanks, Luke," Goshorn said, "but I think she'll sell high, so I'll stick with the current deal, just like last time."

"I don't know," Luke said. "She don't look like she can pick a lot of cotton."

"Well then she'll sell as a pretty house slave. For one of them fancy mansions they have down in Mississippi."

"Have it your way," Luke said. He closed the wagon gate up and headed for the front, poking one of the dozing guards as he went by. The man looked up, startled.

"Tom, tie her up like the others," Luke said.

"I think we should put 'em in ankle fetters," Tom said. "Now there are seven of them, and just three of us."

"No, that will give 'em cuts and bruises down there, and folks will argue the price down for that. They ain't going nowhere, and you both got what you need to keep them in line."

Lucy looked more closely at the guards and saw that each carried a short whip in his belt and had a heavy club at his side.

Tom picked up a piece of rope from the wagon floor, looped one end around Lucy's manacles and tied it off with an elaborate knot. He tied the other end to the top rail, but left enough slack so that Lucy could move her hands freely.

"There you go, sugar," he said.

"My name is Lucy."

"Look like sugar to me." He grinned and she saw that half his teeth were missing.

As the wagon began to move, Goshorn and Amasa stood there, watching them go.

"Bye, sugar," Goshorn said. "Enjoy Mississippi."

Lucy imagined putting her hands around Goshorn's throat and squeezing until the life went out of him.

At the end of the second day of travel, Lucy knew they must be getting near St. Louis. The man called Luke had said it would be a three-day trip.

Her grandmother had been to St. Louis once, and had told her about it. She said it was in a place called Missouri—a *state* she called it. And to the north was a *free state* called Illinois.

Lucy didn't understand what a state was or what made one state free and another slave, but she did remember what her grandmother had said to do. "If you can get near St. Louis and you can get free, go north 'til you get to Illinois, but watch out for slave catchers. You got to get to the Underground Railroad. They will take you to Canada, where slaves are free."

Her grandmother had seemed to know a lot about the Railroad, except how to contact it.

Lucy remembered asking, "Yaya, how will I know where north is?"

Her grandmother had taken her outside and showed her how to find the Big Dipper and the North Star. "Just follow that star," she said. "There will be north."

Lucy spent a few minutes thinking about her grandmother, who had died right before Christmas. She missed her. Then she turned her attention to how to escape.

Lucy had noticed that her manacles were too big for her wrists. Her wrists were unusually thin and her hands quite small despite her height. To avoid anyone noticing, she had tried to keep her forearms up so the manacles slid back onto a thicker part of her arms. When they were given thin blankets to keep themselves warm at night—hardly necessary in the humid August air—the other slaves had let theirs drop to the floor. Lucy had kept hers spread across her wrists and midsection, frequently complaining about being cold.

The first night that had almost been her undoing, when Tom said, "I can keep you warm, sugar."

She had said, once again, "My name is Lucy," which seemed, for some reason she could not fathom, to keep him at bay. Or perhaps he was simply afraid of what Luke would do to him if he damaged the "merchandise," a term Luke had used several times to refer to the slaves.

On that second night, with the wagon stopped near an inn, she saw her chance. Luke had gone in some hours ago but had not returned. The two guards had been drinking—despite Luke's constantly yelling at them that he wasn't paying them to imbibe. They seemed to have fallen into a deep slumber, as had the other slaves.

Lucy looked up, found the North Star and tried to fix in her mind where it was. Then she waited for the moon to set. Once it did, she looked around and saw that everyone in the wagon was still asleep.

Her first problem was the rope that tied her to the railing. It was loose enough that she was able to twist around in her seat and reach the knot. It was poorly made and she had it undone in seconds.

With the rope gathered up into her hand, she climbed quietly over the tailgate and lowered herself to the ground, trying to keep the manacles from jangling. It was hard because she had begun shaking from fear again. She willed it to stop, and, to her surprise, it did.

She walked slowly and quietly north until she reached some scrub woods. She turned into the woods, walked some more and finally began to run when she thought that the noise she was making would no longer reach back to the wagon. She had also brought two blankets with her: her own, and one from one of the other slaves, which she had picked up as she fled.

Once she had gone a ways, she dropped the other slave's blanket where she hoped it would be easily seen. Perhaps the dogs would find it, and the smell would lead them to circle back to the blanket's owner, who was still back in the wagon. It probably wouldn't work, but she smiled at the thought.

She needed to get the manacles off her wrists. She folded her thumbs into her palms and tried to work the metal off. It proved more difficult than she thought it would be. Finally, after much pushing and shoving, including using a thin tree as a lever against which to pull, she managed to get them off. The effort had left her wrists and hands scraped raw.

What to do with the manacles and their trailing rope? She unknotted the rope and kept it, thinking she might have need of it later. When she came upon a stream, she threw the manacles into a deep pool.

Now all she needed to do was to find the Railroad. She checked the North Star, set off and thanked Yaya for her help.

3

Lucy's first two days on the run had been terrifying.

The terror had begun not long after she dropped the manacles into the stream. When, after a few more minutes of running, she looked up to check the North Star once again, it had disappeared. The thickening forest canopy had blocked out the sky, and she no longer knew in which direction she was running. Was she perhaps heading back toward her captors? She stopped for a few seconds, then started running again. Not long after that, she heard dogs barking and men yelling. They sounded close.

One of the returned slaves, whose wounds she had tried to soothe, had told her, "If they're close, get in the water and walk as far as you can. Then get down in it. They won't be able to smell you."

Within minutes of hearing the dogs, she found a stream, jumped in and walked down it, stumbling at times on the bottom stones, but managing each time to catch herself. When she could walk no farther, she collapsed and let the water wash over her for what seemed like forever. It must have worked, she thought, because no dogs found her.

She hadn't counted on the insects—what seemed like thousands of mosquitoes, each and every one looking for its next blood meal. Or the chiggers and ticks and other things that bit deep. She tried to stop scratching, because she knew from what she'd seen on the men who worked the fields back home that the bites she picked at would soon begin to fester. "Stop it!" she said aloud to herself. "Stop! Stop!" It did little good, and by the second day some of the bites were starting to ooze.

She tried to comfort herself by imagining herself in Canada, although she had trouble picturing exactly what that would be like or what she would be doing there. But it made her smile and, briefly, stop scratching.

On the third day she found a tree whose oozing sap, leaking from holes that bird or insects had drilled in its bark, soothed her bites.

That night she woke up screaming. A snake had crawled right across her face before moving on.

In the morning, she woke up and said to herself, "I have to get out of these woods and use the roads."

But she figured she could only trust the roads late at night. As each day dawned, she retreated back into the woods, found a hollow spot to sleep in and covered herself with leaves. It not only obscured her from sight but seemed to keep at least some of the bugs and all of the snakes away.

By the start of the fourth day, she had exhausted the smoked meat she had brought. At one point, growing hungry, she ate some berries, but it didn't help. Later, she leaned over a stream, waited for what seemed like forever and finally flipped a small fish onto the bank.

Her grandmother had shown her how to clean a fish with a knife. This time she did it with her fingers, and ate the flesh raw, gagging at first at the thought of putting it in her mouth uncooked. When she had finished every morsel of flesh she could find amid the small bones, she said, aloud, "Thank you, Yaya."

Despite the fish, by the end of the fourth day she was weak from hunger. That night, as she trudged along a road in the dark, she came upon an abandoned cabin, its door gone and one wall half-caved-in. It looked dangerous to go inside, but looking in, she thought she saw a jar of something sitting on a high shelf and decided to risk it. She went in, stepping carefully across the rotting floor lest it cave in. She reached up to the shelf and found what turned out to be a jar of preserves.

As she stepped out of the house, the rotted wall collapsed inward, and she realized she was at a point where she would do almost anything to get food.

She managed to eat only a little bit of the preserves at a time, making it last for more than a day.

Still, she was brutally hungry. On the next night, as she walked along a darkened road, she saw, in the far distance, a lone house that seemed to be out in the country, away from any town. She could see a family of two adults and two children getting into a carriage in front of the house. She hid in the woods until the carriage moved out of sight.

When she got to the house, there were no candles burning inside. She hoped that meant everyone was gone. She felt herself trembling as she walked up to the front door and pushed on it. It yielded and swung open. With her heart pounding loudly in her chest, she walked in.

Soon enough, though, she discovered that whatever food there was in that house had been put in a cupboard and shut fast behind a sturdy lock. She had neither the skill not the strength to pry it open. She broke into tears and left.

4

Over the next several days and nights, she managed to flip a few more fish out of streams. She also came upon two more abandoned cabins and took from them the small amounts of food that had been left behind. But it was not enough to stave off her growing hunger. One day she lifted her shift and looked down at her torso. Where before there had been a thin layer of fat, she could now see each and every one of her ribs.

Finally, toward the end of still another seemingly endless day on the run (Lucy had long ago lost track of how many days it had been), she came to a large river. It was the widest she had ever seen. She had no idea how to get across. Because she couldn't think of anything else to do, she walked downstream, keeping near the bank until she came to some big boats tethered to a pier. She heard men talking and watched them loading something onto the boats. Long past dark, after the men had left, she sneaked aboard one of boats, went down a ladder to the hold and hid under a large pile of smelly rags and tarps. Early in the night, she had to pee, and peed where she was. She worried someone would smell it when they came back in the morning. Eventually, her worry gave way to sleep.

She was awakened by the sound of men coming back down the ladder and talking among themselves, saying it was time to shove off. She was shaking in fear about the smell of her pee, which was sharp in her nostrils, but no one said anything about it. She was terrified her shaking would make the pile of rags move, but if it did no one noticed.

She felt the boat start to move and, later, bump when it hit something. She waited until she heard the men leave again, then moved out from under the rags and crept back up the ladder to the deck, where the light that temporarily blinded her told her it was morning. She could see that the boat was now at a dock. The men were nowhere to be seen, nor was anyone on the dock. She looked behind her and could see that they had crossed the river. She saw no choice but to make a run for it.

She moved down a gangway onto the dock and sprinted toward a road she could see in the distance. She heard men shouting, but none came after her. She reached the road and ran along it for a minute or two, then plunged into the woods, trying to run as fast as she could without stepping in a hole. She could feel her heart pounding in her chest. Eventually, she could go no farther and collapsed.

As she lay there panting, she realized that sooner or later she was going to get caught. And sooner or later, if she didn't want to be found and sent back in chains, she was going to have to throw herself on the mercy of some white person and hope they would take pity on her and lead her to the Railroad. Otherwise, she was going to break an ankle or a leg and die in the woods. Or be eaten by something. Along the way, she had already avoided a few bears and stepped away from several snakes, all of whom had, luckily, seemed uninterested in her.

After her breathing returned to normal, she got up and continued to make her way through the trees, avoiding the road for the time being. When she was finally too exhausted to go any farther, she lay down, covered herself over with leaves and fell asleep again.

She was roused by a foot poking her side and a voice saying, "Well, well, what have we here?"

A hand brushed the leaves away from her face and she found herself staring up at an old white man with bone-white hair and blue eyes.

"You must be that slave girl what escaped from Riverview Plantation down in Kentuck. They had posters up about you all over the towns near there."

She said nothing in response.

"Lucky none of them posters got put up hereabouts. Slave catchers be on you in a second."

And then, as if to answer a question she wanted to ask but was afraid to voice, he said, "Guess there ain't no posters 'round here because they think you died in the river or got yourself ate by one creature or the other."

She still said nothing.

"I know your name, too," he said. "From the posters. Lucy Battelle."

There seemed little point in denying it so, finally, she spoke and said, "Yes."

"And I suppose you're looking for the Underground Railroad," he said.

She shook her head up and down.

"Well, I can take you to 'em. Usual, I charge the Railroaders for delivering the slave to 'em. But seeing as you are so young, I'm gonna do it free." He grinned and she saw that there was something wrong with his upper lip. Odd as it was, she felt sorry for him.

"Thank you," she said.

"Stand on up," he said.

She did and when the leaves had fallen away, he looked her

up and down and said, "Here's the thing. I can't hardly take you anywhere looking like that. We gotta get you cleaned up."

He thought for a moment. "There's a town right close. I'm gonna get you some better things to put on so you don't look like no escaped slave. You stay here while I get 'em and come back." Almost as an afterthought, he said, "I'll bring food."

With that, he walked off.

After he left, Lucy thought, *I should get up and run away.* Then she thought, *Well, why would he leave me here to run away if he wasn't really gonna help me?* She burrowed back under the leaves and fell back asleep. After some time—she had no idea how long it had been—the man came back with clothes for her—a green, cotton dress that more or less fit—and some shoes.

He turned around while she changed into the dress.

When they walked back to the road, she saw that he had brought a one-horse carriage and there was bread, cheese and a small piece of meat in a basket on the seat. "Please get in," he said. "Eat what you want."

After she was seated, he said, "Here's the thing. We are in Illinois, a free state. People here can't legally have no slaves. But folks 'round here is used to people with Negro servants. So that's what you gonna be. Get it?"

"Yes," she said.

"We're still three days' ride from a house I know is on the Railroad. I got friends along the way we kin stay with, won't ask no questions. But you got to shut up, understand?"

"Yes."

"Good. We run into anyone, I talk. You say nothing."

"Alright. What's your name?" she said.

"Robert Hacker. Friends call me Bobby."

He flicked his whip at the horse, and the carriage moved forward. Lucy picked up the piece of meat out of the basket—it was chicken—and bit into it. It tasted like the best thing she'd ever eaten. In Canada, there would be endless chicken, she was sure.

5

Springfield, Illinois
Late August 1860

Abby Kelley Foster knew she had become famous, even though her Quaker upbringing required that she pay it no heed, and she did not—except when she needed something done for the cause of the slave. In those cases, she was always willing to take full advantage.

She also knew that she was beautiful. Well, she had *once* been beautiful. Now, at age forty-nine, she had become what people called handsome. Her eyes were still deep and blue, but her hair, once flaxen, was going gray, and the bloom of youth had left her cheeks. And yet...

"Do not be vain." She said it aloud to the mirror. "It does not become you." Even twenty years after her mother's death, she could still hear her mother reproving her for her vanity.

If she were honest with herself, the mirror reflected back to her more than just the lost bloom of youth. She looked downright worn-out. Perhaps it was because she was bone-tired, not just from the long train ride, but from her entire career. This month would see the twenty-second anniversary of the day she had first gone out on her own, near her hometown of Lynn, Massachusetts, as an abolition lecturer, asking people to "consider the poor slave." And asking them to do something about it, lecturing to the few who might've been willing to listen way back then. If they had not instead been throwing things at her.

In some ways, she realized, that day was a more important anniversary to her than the day she had gotten married or the day her daughter had been born. Because it was the day, as her Quaker parents would have said, that the way had opened to her.

The mirror she had been staring into was on the wall of her room in the Chenery House Hotel, in Springfield, Illinois, where she had just checked in. Abby had never been to Illinois before. She had come at the request of a good friend, whose abolitionist husband had been taken seriously ill on a trip to Springfield and needed someone to accompany him back to Boston. It would be a multiday trip with many changes of train and difficult for an invalid traveling alone.

In the old days, the idea of a woman of her social class traveling openly with a man to whom she was not married would have been a scandal. Now, at least among the more progressive of the abolitionists, it was routine. It was—mostly—not like the old days when her appointment to a committee of the American Anti-Slavery Society had split the organization down the middle, as some of the men walked out in protest at serving with a woman, and went on to form their own antislavery organization.

Somehow, the Reverend Albert Hale, the pastor of Springfield's Second Presbyterian Church, whom she had met several times at antislavery meetings, had learned she was coming to town. He had sent her a telegram importuning her to give a lecture at his church, the largest abolitionist congregation in Springfield. He had added that she could expect to address a large, fervently abolitionist crowd, from whom she could raise a lot of money for the cause. The latter point had attracted her because *The Bugle,* the antislavery newspaper she had founded in Ohio was, as always, in need of funds.

The only downside to speaking at Hale's church was that she would be speaking in the hometown of Abraham Lincoln, the Republican candidate for president of the United States. She supposed that people would expect her to say something about him. She hoped they would not be disappointed because what she had to say about Lincoln was not going to be anything good.

She sighed, put on her plain Quaker bonnet and went down to the hotel dining room to join Reverend Hale for an early supper. In the lobby, she instantly recognized Hale from their last encounter, years before. He had hardly changed—still thin and balding on top, with a graying thatch of hair on each side that gave him a slightly impish look.

He clearly recognized her, too, because he strode forward and held out his hand. She took it and they shook. "Mrs. Foster, it is so good to see you again after so long a time. Welcome to Springfield."

"Thank you, but please call me Abby."

"Of course! Let us go in to supper. I have made a reservation at the hotel's very fine restaurant."

She noted that he had not in return invited her to call him Albert. She had noticed, over the years, that ministers—she had met hundreds of them—tended to be a rather formal lot. She would call him Albert or not, as it pleased her.

The restaurant was indeed fine, although its menu seemed focused on clearing the prairie of cows, so that they might be turned into beefsteaks, beef stews, beef potpies and a dozen other beef dishes, with a few chickens thrown in for good measure. Without explaining her dietary preferences, she asked for a double order of a chicken noodle casserole. She ate the noodles but not the chicken, and when Hale asked about it, just said the train ride had upset her stomach.

During dinner, they spoke mostly about the abolition movement in Springfield.

"It is like a contagion here," Hale said. "Ten years ago, it was still hard to find ten true abolitionists in a crowd of fifty. Now, it might well be a majority if people felt free to state their beliefs openly."

"Why do they not feel free?" she said.

"There is such bitterness in our politics now that people want to avoid arguments with their neighbors, their families and the people they work with. Or, if they are merchants, with the people they sell goods to."

"Does Lincoln living here make the bitterness worse?"

"I think not. Most people here, whether they agree with his politics or not, are proud that someone from the West—and from our very city—has been nominated for such a high position."

"He is popular, then?"

"Politically, perhaps not. I do not know if he will even carry Sangamon County—that's our county name—in the election. But he is personally popular because he is such a nice man." He paused. "But so much more than that, as I hope everyone in this country will see when he becomes president."

She had on the tip of her tongue to tell Hale what her opinion was of Lincoln, but then thought better of it. She had long ago learned to deliver her strong opinions while standing at a lectern, where they tended not to be taken quite so personally as when delivered face-to-face.

While they were talking, a young man, clearly in his early twenties, accompanied by an older, well-dressed woman, walked in and were seated at a table not far from them. Hale looked over at them and said, "Ah, that is young Clarence Artemis and his mother. They're from Boston, and he has relocated here."

"Why?" Abby said, and as soon as she said it realized that her tone was such as to suggest that no one in their right mind would want to relocate from Boston to this place from which the frontier had only recently departed.

Hale laughed. "There is a lot of opportunity here if you know how to seize it. Especially for a young man with money, which his parents apparently have in abundance."

"Do you know what he's planning to do here?"

"He's starting a new abolitionist newspaper called *The Radical Abolitionist*. In fact, its inaugural edition is coming out tomorrow I believe."

Abby raised her eyebrows. "I suppose there cannot be too many such papers if we are to liberate the slave. Having started two myself, I might be able to give him some advice." She paused. "If he wants it."

"Oh, I suspect he would love to have it. So far, he has only gotten advice from his mother, who is here in person the better to provide it directly. Although I believe Clarence would be happy to see her depart sooner rather than later." He laughed. "Or even yesterday."

"So you have met him?"

"Yes."

The rest of their dinner conversation moved away from politics to more mundane topics. When they had finished coffee (which she declined) and dessert (she took a small bite out of a giant piece of cherry pie), Abby said, "I would like now to retreat to my room for an hour or so of rest before my lecture. It is at eight, correct?"

"Yes, and you need not be there far in advance. Everything is ready, and please let me thank you again for agreeing to do it."

"It is my pleasure."

"Oh," he said. "I almost forgot. There is another event, so to speak, taking place right before yours, but I don't think it will interfere."

"In the church?"

"No, in the square in front of the courthouse. You see, a

runaway slave has been captured, and the so-called master is planning to go to a federal court sometime today to prove his ownership under the Fugitive Slave Act. If he wins, which he most certainly will, he will take his human property, as people like him vilely call their enslaved Negroes, back south."

"What is the event, then?"

"The enslaved girl is being held in the county jail in the courthouse because the federal government doesn't have its own jail. The rumor is that she will be moved tonight from there to the train station."

"There will be a protest?"

"Yes, there always is when this happens, which it does perhaps twice a year. But other than a lot of shouting, not much ever comes of it."

"Perhaps I should go myself and protest."

"If it turned violent, you could end up being in harm's way."

She laughed. "In harm's way? I think I have been there before. Have you ever had stones thrown at you while you were giving a sermon?"

"No, can't say as I have."

"How about manure?"

"Not that either."

"Well, I have had both thrown at me, and worse, while I lectured about the evils of slavery."

"I doubt anyone will throw anything tonight. These demonstrations are almost never violent."

"Good, I argue with all my might against this horrible Fugitive Slave Act, but as a pacifist I am opposed to violence to liberate the slaves. Violence will beget violence and the people who will suffer the most will be the enslaved."

"I am not a pacifist, really," he said, "although I would not countenance violence to free this slave."

They stared at each other for a moment, until finally Abby said, "I hate it when people so remove slaves from their humanity that they talk of them only as 'the slave.' Does this enslaved woman have a name?"

"Yes, Lucy Battelle. She is but a girl. Only twelve years old."

"Twelve. Good gracious. Do you know her story?"

"Only that she escaped from somewhere in Kentucky weeks ago, and somehow made it this far before being captured."

"That is a sad story," Abby said. "But I am far too weary from the trip to go to the demonstration. Much as I would like to. I will instead retreat to my room for a while."

"I'm pleased you could join me, Abby."

"It has been a great pleasure. Thank you for dinner, Albert."

6

As Reverend Hale and Abby Kelley Foster were finishing their meal, a federal legal hearing was concluding inside a room on the first floor of the Sangamon County Courthouse. The room was small, windowless and bare of furniture except for a battered wooden desk and five equally decrepit wooden chairs gathered in front of it.

Lucy Battelle was sitting in one of the chairs, manacled, fettered at her ankles and tied to the chair by a thick rope around her waist. The other chairs were occupied by Ezekiel Goshorn, by United States Marshal Thaddeus O'Connor (a beefy man with a full head of red hair, known around town as Red) and by Thomas Stromberg, the sheriff of Sangamon County. The final chair was occupied by a white man who had earlier identified himself but asked not to have his name written down in the record of the proceeding.

The hearing was being presided over by Nathaniel Harper, a United States Slave Commissioner for the Southern District of Illinois. The only indications that Harper was a judge of some sort was the small name plaque placed on the desk in front of him and the fact that he was wearing a black robe, albeit darned in several places.

The only hint that the room was a courtroom was the thirty-three star United States flag that someone had stuck into what had once served as a tall brass candleholder. It was an ill fit, and the flag was tilting at a precarious angle. As the hearing droned on, Lucy had been watching it and willing it to fall. She had seen that flag before, inside Ezekiel Goshorn's private room in the big house—a place he called his study.

Goshorn was addressing Commissioner Harper. "You already have my written Property Claim, Your Honor. And here is my duly executed affidavit, certified by a court in my home county in Kentucky, affirming that the slave girl is my property. I had it prepared as soon as I got the telegram telling me she had been captured." He handed the affidavit to Harper.

"Thank you, Mr. Goshorn. Do you see your slave property in this courtroom?"

Goshorn pointed to Lucy. "That is her, sitting in the chair right there. Name of Lucy Battelle, as the affidavit affirms."

"Do you swear under penalty of perjury that she is the one?"

"Yes."

Goshorn wasn't worried in the least about the outcome. Everyone understood that, under the provisions of the Fugitive Slave Act, Commissioner Harper would be paid ten dollars if he ruled in Goshorn's favor, but only five if he ruled against him.

Harper puffed himself up and said, "After considering the material presented, it has been duly proven by substantial and persuasive evidence that one Lucy Battelle, present before me in this courtroom—" he pointed at her "—is a fugitive slave duly owned by Claimant Ezekiel Goshorn, also present, and that no evidence has been presented that she has been manumitted or otherwise given her freedom. She is hereby returned to him."

Lucy didn't understand the meaning of every fancy word the

man had uttered, but she did understand this was about send-ing her back. She also knew that, according to something her mother had called the law, she *did* belong to Goshorn. Still, she thought she should not belong to anybody, and she wanted to say so, even if she'd be beaten for it later, assuming she survived the beating for running away.

"I want to say something."

"Girl, you can't talk here," Harper said.

"Why not?"

"The Fugitive Slave Act doesn't permit the slave in question—that would be you—to give evidence. In fact, you're just a piece of property, and property doesn't talk. You should read the *Dred Scott* case. It clearly says that there is no difference between you, as slave property, and property like a wagon." Then he said, "Oh, but I forgot, in your stupidity and ignorance, you can't read." He laughed uproariously, joined by everyone else in the courtroom.

"I can too read," Lucy said. "Some."

The room fell briefly silent.

"That is certainly not true," Goshorn said. "I don't permit my slaves to learn to read, not even the house slaves."

Lucy said again, "I can too read. That-there thing on the table says, excuse me... I gotta work it out." Then she read it aloud slowly, "*Nat-han-i-el har-per.* That next word says, *com-mis...*" She stopped and said, "I don't get that word."

"This is some kind of joke," Goshorn said. "She just heard your name said and mimicked it."

"My yaya taught me," Lucy said.

It had been a secret between them. But now that her grand-mother was dead, she could tell it. The old woman had used a stick and a patch of dirt in her small garden behind her cabin for the lessons. They had always pretended to be planting or weeding or picking. It was the most thrilling part of Lucy's growing up.

"What is a yaya?" Harper said.

"It's slave talk for grandmother," Goshorn said. "And I don't believe this. It's a trick."

"Well, it is neither here nor there as far as my ruling goes," Harper said.

He puffed himself up again and said, "The slave catcher, who has asked not to be named—" he glanced at the white man "—shall turn over the slave Lucy Battelle to Petitioner Goshorn forthwith."

He looked at Goshorn. "Sir, if you have made some monetary arrangement with the gentleman, I leave it to the two of you to settle that matter outside the hearing of the court."

"Of course," Goshorn said. He was holding several gold coins in his hand, rubbing them together.

"Finally," the commissioner said, "all federal and local officials in the State of Illinois and the County of Sangamon and whosoever else may come upon Claimant Goshorn and his slave property are hereby ordered to render all reasonable assistance to claimant in returning the slave to Riverview Plantation in Kentucky, on pain of severe penalties for failing to assist. Claimant to cover costs."

With that, he signed a stack of papers on his desk and passed them over to Goshorn.

Watching this, Lucy thought that her life of late seemed to be taken up with Goshorn and other white men signing papers that treated her like she was a pair of shoes. Mostly, though, her hatred was aimed at Bobby Hacker, the unidentified-in-the-record white man who was sitting two seats down from her and grinning.

The secret station on the Underground Railroad he had promised her had turned out to be the Sangamon County jail. But if Goshorn wanted to keep her from running away again, he would have to cut off her feet.

"What is your pleasure, Mr. Goshorn?" Harper said. "Do you want the slave jailed overnight again and then leave in the morning with her?"

"No, I've arranged for a carriage to take us from here to the railroad station for the eight o'clock train south tonight. The carriage is waiting in back of the jail."

"Do you want her left manacled and in fetters?"

"Yes. No point in risking her getting away again."

The sheriff spoke up. "Let me see what is happening outside." He got up and left the room.

When he came back he said, "Somehow, the fact that we were going to have this hearing here this evening was found out, and there is a crowd gathering outside. It might be best to wait until the crowd disperses some."

"I'd really like to get started now," Goshorn said. "Assuming y'all think you can protect us."

The sheriff looked at the marshal. "This is really a federal matter. We can assist, but…"

"We can handle it," the marshal said. "The crowds here, for things like this, have been loud, but they've never turned violent." He paused. "I'll have to line up my deputies. Give us an hour to get ready, and then you can bring her out."

"I would not go out the back way," the sheriff said. "The rear door leads to a narrow alley, and the crowd there is already unruly. We can protect you better if you go out the front door into the square, where we can form a phalanx if we need it."

"I agree with the sheriff," the marshal said. "Can you arrange for the carriage to be waiting out front instead, Mr. Goshorn?"

"Of course."

"I wonder who found out about this," the marshal said. "This is a public hearing, but we tried very hard not to publicize it."

7

The person who had found out about it was in fact Clarence Artemis, who had heard a stray remark made to the sheriff by one of his deputies as he and his mother walked across the courthouse square earlier in the day. Clarence had promptly told everyone he could, and his mother had told still others.

Upon his return to the square later in the day, Clarence was both astonished and delighted at the size of the crowd that he beheld. Hundreds of people were milling about, some shaking their fists at the courthouse while others shouted at a carriage that was parked off to the side of the front door. He could see a bald man sitting inside it.

Suddenly, the courthouse door flew open, and Marshal O'Connor, kitted out in full uniform, walked out and planted himself in front of the crowd, arms folded, legs apart, a gun belt draped prominently around his waist.

Seconds later, five of his deputies, each cradling a long gun, also emerged and formed a human wall behind him, their silver badges glinting in the flickering light cast by torches being passed hand to hand in the crowd.

Then the courthouse door opened again and three more people walked out—two additional deputies and a chained-up young Negro girl, who was being dragged along. When she was finally allowed to stand up, she was trembling.

The crowd, which had already blocked the path between the front door and the carriage, began to curse and shout.

Clarence had an excellent view of the whole thing because he had earlier found a wooden riser that someone had left at the very back of the courthouse square. He had climbed up to the top and started to try to count heads. His best guess was that there were already close to a thousand people pressed into the square—amazing in itself when you considered that the city had a population of under ten thousand. And people were still streaming in.

Clarence watched Marshal O'Connor, his voice rising, attempting to calm the crowd. "My friends," he said, "my only job tonight is to move this young woman to that carriage over there—safely—so that she can be returned to her proper owner. As officially ordered by an official of a court of the United States of America."

He's afraid, Clarence thought, to use the term *slave commissioner.*

The marshal waved a document in the air. "So I ask you kindly to move aside and give way."

"Slavery is a sin!" someone screamed. "The slave commissioner be damned! You, too, Red!" The cry was picked up by others, growing louder with each repetition. "The commissioner be damned! Red be damned! The commissioner be damned!"

The crowd pressed ever closer.

Marshal O'Connor tried again, shouting to try to be heard above the din. "I am, my fellow citizens, just trying to do my job. Enforcing the law and the Constitution." He paused and added, "A Constitution that we all love and support." There was a split-second pause in the crowd noise, and then it hissed at him, hundreds of protestors pulling their lips back, baring their teeth and hissing as one, like a giant snake.

The sound sent a chill down Clarence's spine. It took him back to Boston six years earlier, when an even larger crowd of abolitionists—some said it had been ten-thousand strong—tried to block the return south from Boston of the escaped slave Anthony Burns. The crowd had fixed itself in front of the Boston Federal Courthouse and hissed loudly at the police guarding the prisoner. Clarence had only just turned eighteen then, standing next to his father and shaking off his attempt to hold his hand amid the mob, but feeling then, as he did now, a revulsion that the law permitted human beings to be held in bondage.

But this wasn't Boston in 1854. It was instead Springfield, Illinois, in 1860. It was a small town perhaps, but one with the nation's attention focused squarely upon it because the Republican Party's candidate for president of the United States lived there, not eight blocks from where Clarence was standing.

Nor was the slave the marshal was seeking to return to her owner an enslaved Negro man in his midtwenties, like Anthony Burns. She was instead a mere girl, rumored to be only twelve years of age.

Nor was Clarence any longer eighteen. He was now twenty-four and hoping to make a success of his new newspaper and show his parents that they were wrong about it being a foolish venture. If he could write the story of tonight's mob and get it to his printer before midnight, it would appear in the paper's inaugural edition. But if he left now to write it, he might miss the real story—any attempt to somehow avoid the mob and move the slave girl to the carriage.

The marshal saved him the decision with a sudden announcement, "Ladies and gentlemen, you can all go home. The slave girl will not be moved tonight."

"When then, Red?" someone yelled.

Instead of responding, the marshal just waved his hand at the waiting carriage, and Clarence watched as the driver snapped his whip at one of the horses and began to drive slowly off the square. The bald-headed man was still inside.

Clarence watched as the deputy marshals took the Negro girl back into the courthouse, and the crowd began to disperse.

Clarence pulled out his pocket watch—a gift from his mother—and checked the time. He had at least two hours left to write his report of the event—which would be plenty of time. The hardest part would be rendering for his readers the bone-chilling hiss, using mere words. If only there were some way to record the sound of such things.

Just then a man standing next to him, a stranger who looked to be about his own age said, "Are you heading to the church?"

"What church?"

"Second Presbyterian." The man pointed to a squat brick tower that could be seen poking up above the surrounding buildings, itself perhaps two blocks away. "Abby Kelley Foster is speaking."

"I've heard her before," Clarence said. "In New England. What's she doing here, so far from home?"

"Don't know. This Lucy business perhaps."

Clarence hesitated. If she spoke long, he would miss his printer's deadline, even with his two-hour leeway. But if luck were with him, she would be brief and he could put both the hiss and her speech in the same article, on deadline.

"Alright," he said. "I'll go. Although I'll not likely hear anything new. Abby Kelley Foster always says the same damn things, 'Pity the poor slave' and 'I speak for my slave sister.' And then she passes the collection plate to support all the abolitionist publications that are laid out on the tables, as well as her newspaper in Ohio."

"Come with me, then," the stranger said. "Friends have promised to save seats in the back, from whence we can escape if it turns tedious and should it prove advantageous to do so."

Clarence cocked his head at the man's flowery speech, then said, "What's your name?"

"John Hay. And yours?"

"Clarence Artemis."

"Ah," Hay said. "If I am not mistaken, you are the one who is launching the new radical abolitionist paper."

Clarence grinned. "Yes, the very one. Tomorrow if all goes well!"

"I will sign up for a subscription!" Hay said.

"Why, thank you."

As they walked away from the square, Clarence glanced over his shoulder and noticed that while most of the protestors were dispersing, a knot of twenty or thirty had stayed put. He'd have to check on them on his way back.

8

Second Presbyterian was on Fourth Street, only a few blocks away. It was, Clarence had learned several weeks earlier, an avowedly abolitionist church. Indeed, it was rumored about town that several of its parishioners were active in the Underground Railroad. Indeed, some were quite open about it.

When he'd first arrived in town, Clarence had made the rounds of the various churches to introduce himself. It was in the churches where arguments about abolition were most heated, and where he hoped to find some of his stories. The two stories in particular that he hankered after were that Lincoln, despite his public disavowals, was himself an abolitionist, and that he was an infidel to boot.

It had taken him many days to pay his respects to the pastors of all of the churches. Even with its relatively small population, Springfield boasted more than a dozen formal congregations. A few had permanent buildings and paid pastors, while others met only in people's homes and made do with volunteer preachers, some of them itinerant.

Clarence had first gone to pay his respects to Reverend James Smith, the pastor of First Presbyterian, where the Lincolns themselves worshipped. Smith had been politely welcoming, but quite guarded about the Lincolns.

He'd gone next to Second Presbyterian, presided over by Reverend Albert Hale, whom most people, Clarence had learned, addressed as Father Hale.

Hale had greeted him warmly and took him on a whirlwind tour of his church, including the large chapel, which the reverend claimed seated three hundred (perhaps, Clarence thought, if the people were really skinny and sat pressed shoulder to shoulder).

When they were done, Clarence said, "May I see the church's bell? I'm told it's the largest one around."

Hale seemed to hesitate. After a long pause, he finally said, "Alright. Follow me." He led Clarence toward an arched wooden door that was made of vertical planks studded with brass nails. Hale opened it with an iron skeleton key that he extracted from a pocket inside his vest and pulled the door open by the brass ring at its center. Clarence half expected the door to creak, but instead it slid open on well-lubricated hinges.

Behind the door Clarence saw an empty room with a plank floor. A thick, knotted pull rope hung down into the middle of the room. He had to duck to keep from hitting his head on the door frame as they went in.

"Let's go up," Hale said.

To Clarence's distress, "up" meant climbing onto a long, rickety ladder. He steeled himself and followed Hale, trying hard not to reveal his intense fear of heights, made worse by the fact that with two men moving on it, the ladder shook. Worse, the rungs had been worn smooth by the passage across them of so many hands and feet over the years. He regretted asking to see the bell.

When they reached the top they emerged through an open trap door into a small belfry, perhaps ten feet by ten feet square.

It had no windows, but only vertical louvered slots, through which many blocks of Springfield could be seen. The only piece of furniture in the room was a small wooden chair with a broken back, which had been pushed into a corner. Despite the louvers, it was quite hot inside.

In the middle of the room a very large bronze bell, perhaps two feet across at the lip, hung down from a polished wooden yoke, its clapper protruding slightly. Clarence could see that there were raised letters circling the top of the bell. He walked slowly around it, reading the inscription aloud as he went: "Cast by George H. Holbrook, East Medway Massachusetts 1839."

"That was indeed the year it was cast," Hale said. "But it didn't arrive here until 1840, then took another year to install. I'm proud to say I was already the pastor here when it pealed for the first time on Easter Sunday, 1842. The bell was a gift to the congregation by Elder Joseph Thayer, and he pulled the rope that day."

"It's quite beautiful."

"Yes, it is. Now that you've seen it, though, it's too hot in here for someone my age, and we should head back down."

Which was the last thing Clarence wanted to do because his hands were still shaking inside his pockets.

"It *is* hot," Clarence said. "But before we go back down, I have a question. I know the town of East Medway. It's not far from Boston, where I grew up. But how *ever* did they manage to move it out here?"

"By ship down the Atlantic coast, around Florida, up to New Orleans, and then by steamer up the Mississippi to St. Louis," Hale said. "From there to Springfield by rail. Although at first the railroad didn't want to haul it. At over seven hundred pounds they worried it might crash through the floor of the rail car."

"But in the end it made it here."

"Yes. And it's still, almost twenty years later, the largest bell in Springfield and still used as the town's fire bell."

"Yet the only inscription it bears is the bell maker's name," Clarence said, still hoping to delay a trip back down the ladder.

Hale grinned. "What would you suggest it be, young man? Something religious? Something abolitionist?"

"Perhaps something philosophical," Clarence said. "What about a couplet. I think there's room for this one—'Send not to know for whom the bell tolls. It tolls for thee.'"

Hale raised his eyebrows. "John Donne?"

"You're familiar with Donne?" As soon as the words left his mouth, Clarence realized how condescending it had sounded.

"Mr. Artemis, you seem to think we here in Illinois are somehow less well educated than someone…like yourself."

"Well…"

"This is the capital of Illinois. It is not as if we are in Kentucky or Indiana."

"I apologize. I just didn't realize… You're clearly a learned man. Where were you educated?"

"Yale. And you, Mr. Artemis?"

"Being from Boston, I rather naturally went to Harvard."

"Abe Lincoln's oldest son, Robert, is enrolling there this fall. Or so I have heard."

"I see. Well, thank you for showing me the bell."

"Ah, but come to think of it, you have not heard it sound yet."

"Surely you are not going to have it rung with us standing here?"

"Of course not! The bell peals only on Sundays before and after church and on special occasions, like weddings." And with that, he drew from his pocket a small hammer with a ball-shaped wooden head and struck the bell gently. Even with that light tap, the vibration was so intense that Clarence wanted to put his fingers in his ears. But that would have meant taking his still shaking hands out of his pockets.

"A very beautiful tone, Father Hale," he said.

"Indeed. But let us now return to the church proper," Hale

said. "I hope you will find the trip down the ladder a bit less scary than the trip up." He grinned. "In any case, Mr. Artemis, you'll need to take your hands out of your pockets."

"How did you know?" Clarence said.

Hale smiled an impish smile. "If you have been the pastor of hundreds of souls for many years—twenty-one years for me in this very church—you learn to read many things about people by just observing them. And recognizing that someone's hands are shaking inside their pockets is not one of the harder things to spot."

"I see."

"You perhaps find yourself with the same observational powers as a journalist, Mr. Artemis."

"In all candor, I have not been one for very long." Even as he said it, he thought if he were to be candid he ought to admit that he had been a journalist for only a few weeks, and self-trained for all of that.

"Well, in any case, down we go," Hale said. "It will work better if you go first. That way I can hold the ladder at the top to keep it from swaying."

"Ah, thank you. Then I shall hold it for you, Father."

"If you wish, although there is no real need. I have long ago gotten over my fear of the thing and stopped thinking about having it replaced."

With that, they started back down the ladder.

9

Clarence went first, his hands shaking even more than they had on the way up. Once or twice, his foot slipped on one of the polished rungs, but he managed to catch himself.

He stopped halfway down and yelled up at Hale, "Isn't there any way to make this more stable?"

"Afraid not, son. I don't know why it's always worse on the way down. It just is." He paused. "I guess I should have mentioned that to you earlier, but I feared if I did you would still be up in the tower."

When he finally reached the bottom, Clarence stood there, shaking badly and waiting for Hale, who arrived quickly, seemingly unfazed by his descent.

Standing next to Hale in the little room, Clarence asked what he imagined to be a crack journalistic question. "What is the real reason you haven't had this ladder fixed, Father?"

"Ah, an excellent question. It's because the bell loft is one of the few places I can go in this church and in this city and not be found. Most of my parishioners are afraid to climb up, even if they suspect I am up there."

"I see."

"Did you notice the chair in the corner, Mr. Artemis?"

"Yes."

"It is mine. I can sit up there and read the Bible without interruption."

"Or John Donne."

He smiled. "Yes, that, too."

Suddenly, Clarence realized he had yet to inquire about Lincoln. He was about to broach the subject when Hale provided him the opening.

"So, Mr. Artemis," Hale said, "What is your view of the political question of the day? Do you favor freeing the slaves?"

"I think the name of my new newspaper, which will be out with its very first edition soon, should answer your question."

"What is it, pray tell?"

"*The Radical Abolitionist*."

Hale laughed. "Ah, I suppose that does indeed answer my question."

"I thought it might."

"But there are other questions," Hale said.

"Such as?"

"Do you favor immediate abolition, Mr. Artemis, or are you one of those wishy-washy folks who would see it happen someday, without saying when that day might come?"

Clarence realized that he was being tested, and tested by someone whose own views he didn't know. The word *abolitionist* had come to have a thousand shades of meaning, from those who wanted to go south and personally liberate the slaves, while perhaps garroting their masters, to those who simply hoped against hope that slavery would go away, with nary a clue how to bring that about. He decided to answer honestly.

"I do not know exactly how or when it should happen, Father Hale. I only know it should be very, very soon, and that it will take a great deal of hard work—and probably state and federal monies—to bring it about."

"That hardly seems very radical, Mr. Artemis."

"I know. Perhaps a better way to put it is that we are hurtling toward a confrontation between North and South on the issue, and that some radical solution must be found if we are to avoid more violence or even a war. I hope not to spend my youth on a battlefield."

Hale shook his head up and down, as if satisfied with Clarence's answer. Clarence decided to use the opportunity to change the topic and ask directly what he wanted to know.

"Father, do you know Abraham Lincoln?"

"Of course. Almost everyone in Springfield knows him. He has lived here almost twenty-five years, and he is quite the friendly fellow—hardly one to keep to himself. And as a lawyer, he has represented many of us."

"Do you consider him a friend?"

"Of course, as do many. But I am not an intimate."

"Do you know if he is an abolitionist?"

"Ha! He contends he is not. His very careful position is that slavery is a sin, and that it should not expand beyond where it now exists. But that the federal government should take no role in abolishing it where it currently exists."

"Do you believe him?"

"Walk with me to the pulpit."

They walked to the front of the church, mounted the steps to the pulpit and looked out on the rows of empty pews.

"When I preach here, and we are full, I look out on three hundred souls," Hale said. "Because they have chosen to join this church instead of First, many are abolitionists."

"In favor of immediate abolition?"

"Well, if you walk up to one of them after the service and ask that question point-blank, most will hem and haw and not give you a firm answer, for fear of offending someone—their husband or wife, their employer, their best friend. So even though I favor outright abolition of slavery and favor it right now, I must speak carefully so I can keep my post."

"What does that have to do with Lincoln?"

"Mr. Lincoln wants to be president of the United States. Like me, he does not want to offend, but unlike me, he has to worry about more than three hundred people. He wants to avoid offending the millions of voters."

"Even in the Southern states?"

"No, of course not. Just the three million or so in the Northern states, where there are as many views about slavery as there are in my congregation, even among those who dislike the *peculiar institution*, as our Southern friends call it to avoid calling it by its ugly name."

"But Father Hale, Lincoln has called slavery evil."

"Indeed, he has. But Mr. Lincoln has adopted a tactic to try to get himself elected."

"Which is?"

"To call slavery evil, and say it will eventually fade away, but to avoid saying exactly how—or when—that will come about."

"And insist he is not an abolitionist?"

"That is correct, Mr. Artemis."

"But my question to you was not subtle. I asked simply whether you believe him."

"I do, and if Lincoln believes differently, he shares it only with God."

Clarence decided to save for another day asking Father Hale whether he thought Lincoln even believed in God. With only a little over two months left until the election, and with the increasing belief that Lincoln was likely to win, his opponents had begun insisting with more and more vigor that Lincoln was a nonbeliever—an infidel.

There was a more urgent topic, though, that Clarence wanted

to raise. "Do you think there is any way I could get an interview with Mr. Lincoln? Could you help?"

"The answers, sir, are no and no. What efforts have you made yourself?"

"I understand he has been given a small office at the statehouse in which to answer mail and receive visitors. So I've tried to find him going from his home to or from there or from his home to his law office. I've not been able to spy him on either route."

"Is that all you've done?"

"No. I have also left notes at his home and his law office, and with the guard at the statehouse."

"None of this is surprising. As I am sure you know, once they are nominated, by tradition candidates do not campaign. And they certainly don't give interviews to journalists."

"Senator Douglas is out campaigning."

"That's because, as of now, it looks like he is going to lose. So he is desperate. Lincoln is not."

"Can you think of anything else I might try?"

Hale looked thoughtful. "Try talking to the baker."

"The baker?"

"Yes. The one on Fourth Street."

"What shall I ask him?"

"You are a smart young fellow, I'm sure you'll figure it out."

As he was about to leave, Clarence felt emboldened to ask something he had been wondering about. "Father Hale, if I might be so impolite as to ask, why are you called Father? In my perhaps too limited experience, that term is usually used to address Catholic or Episcopal priests."

Hale laughed. "At some point I had been here so long that many of my adult congregants had been children when they first met me. So they began to call me Father. I'd like to think it's intended as a term of affection, but it could just as easily be because I now seem increasingly ancient to them."

Clarence thought Hale's answer had a certain amount of disingenuousness to it. However old Hale was, he had been the leader of a major church for over twenty years and, Clarence had heard, one of Springfield's most influential men. So rather than respond directly to Hale's answer, Clarence just said, "Thank you for the tour of your church, Father Hale. It is a beautiful place, and I am most grateful."

"I don't know your religious inclinations, Mr. Artemis, but even if you are not of a Presbyterian frame of mind—or not yet anyway—you are most welcome to come and join us for worship on Sunday. And given your education and your fondness for both the abolition cause and John Donne, I would welcome your comments on my sermons."

To avoid offending, Clarence said only, "I was brought up as a Unitarian, but my beliefs are not fixed. I'd be very pleased to attend, but not likely until after I get my new newspaper launched."

"I would consider Unitarians to be close to unbelievers, Mr. Artemis, but perhaps if you came here on a regular basis, you could find your way to belief."

"I will keep that in mind, Father. As I said, my beliefs are not yet firm in any direction."

"Of course," Hale said. "If I might inquire, Mr. Artemis, how old are you?"

"Twenty-four."

"Are you married?"

"No."

"Well, do keep in mind that we have a large congregation. Most of our young women marry at an early age, but in these modern times some do not. With your education and prospects, you would be welcomed into the very best families in Springfield."

"I will keep that in mind, too."

"Let me add that should you come upon someone you think

comely, I'm sure my wife, Abiah, could arrange a proper and chaste meeting."

Clarence thought he detected a twinkle in Hale's eye, and responded in kind. "Father Hale, I would love at some point to be married. But I'm not currently looking for female attachment—again, all of the work involved in starting my paper. But were I to meet and marry someone through your agency, my mother might well be persuaded to donate a second bell!"

They both laughed together.

"I must add," Clarence said, "I didn't know men of the cloth were also matchmakers."

"There are many paths to bring people to God, Mr. Artemis."

10

When Clarence and Hay reached Second Presbyterian, the sanctuary was not full, but very crowded. Perhaps, Clarence thought, it really did seat three hundred. Hay's friends were, as Hay had said they would be, in the back row, and had saved several seats. He and Hay clambered over the back of the pew and took two of them.

Hay did quick introductions. Three of the men, Bobby, Tom and Harry, were, like Clarence and Hay, in their early twenties. A man whose name Clarence didn't catch in full—Billy something or other—seemed quite a bit older and was sitting farther down the row.

"Why is Abby Kelley coming here to speak?" Hay asked, aiming his question at no one in particular. "I thought she was an abolitionist lecturer in New England and New York."

"Pennsylvania and Ohio, too," Harry said. "I don't know why she is now here, so far out west."

The man called Billy had folded his hands behind his head and propped his boots up on the top of the empty pew in front of him. "I bet she is here to urge disunion," he said. "For that is her position. If Lincoln is elected, and the hotheads in South Carolina and elsewhere secede, as they have threatened, then 'good riddance,' she says. 'Let us form a new Union without them.'"

"And one without slavery," Hay added.

"Indeed," Billy said. "Without any vestige of the *peculiar institution*."

Clarence felt he needed a more proper introduction to the man. He leaned across Hay and Harry and said, "I'm sorry, but I didn't catch your name." He held out his hand. "I'm Clarence Artemis, editor of *The Radical Abolitionist*."

"Billy Herndon," the man said, shaking his proffered hand. "Pleased to meet you."

Clarence was transfixed. "Lincoln's law partner?"

Herndon laughed. "The very one."

"Perhaps I can interview you afterward," Clarence said.

"I regret not, sir. I am no fan of slavery, but I am also involved with Mr. Lincoln's campaign for the presidency. We are in a period of quiet. He is not campaigning, nor I on his behalf. He has other surrogates you might speak with, but not me."

Clarence was about to press him further when there was a stir toward the front of the room, and a thin woman in plain clothing, her hair pulled back into a severe bun, started to walk slowly up the stairs to the pulpit where Reverend Hale awaited her.

As soon as she reached the stage, Hale walked to the lectern and said, "Ladies and gentlemen, let us pray for an end to slavery." He then led the assembled group in a brief prayer, followed by a boisterous amen from the audience.

During the prayer, Clarence had kept his eyes focused on the woman, whom he knew to be Abby Kelley. Not only had he heard her speak before, but his mother had pointed her out to him in the hotel restaurant, earlier. He had expected her to bow her head during the prayer, but she did not. Instead, she stared out at the audience as if sizing them up. For a brief second, Clarence thought she was staring directly at him.

After Father Hale introduced her as Abby Kelley Foster, choosing to use her married name, she walked slowly to the lectern, shook his hand, but without great energy, and turned to the audience.

"Brothers and sisters, thank you for coming this evening. I know some of you wonder why I am here, when most of my life has been spent well to the East." She paused, as if waiting for someone to shout out the answer. When no one did, she went on. "The reason is pedestrian. One of my close friends, another abolitionist lecturer, came here to visit his ill sister and then fell ill himself. I came by train to take him back to his family in Boston."

There was a murmur in the crowd. Clarence knew it was because women did not normally accompany unrelated men anywhere, whether they be ill or well. But then this audience itself was a mixed one of both men and women, and that, too, was unusual. So unusual that such an audience was referred to by many as *promiscuous*.

Having explained her presence in Springfield, Abby continued. "Those of you here who know me can no doubt attest that I do not participate in politics. I do not advise people whom to vote for, and I do not cast ballots myself. For that would be to approve the Constitution, which is pure and simple an evil slave document— written *by* slaveholders *for* slaveholders. And yet those slave masters who wrote it did not have the courage even to write the word *slave* into their holy document. Instead they referred to slaves with words of evasion. Too ashamed to call slavery what it is.

"Father Hale has kindly asked me to speak today on a topic of my choosing—" she smiled over at him "—and he may well expect that I will break my practice of over twenty years and recommend for whom you should vote in this election of 1860, which so many call crucial." She smiled again. "But I will not.

"I will also not, as some have urged me, say at least that Abraham Lincoln is a good man. I will not because he is not. As my friend and fellow abolitionist Wendell Phillips has said, Lincoln is rightly called the *slave hound of Illinois*."

"What do you mean?" someone shouted out.

"It's simple," she said, raising her voice. "He has said that if elected he will enforce the Fugitive Slave Act. And if he does, he might as well run with the slave hounds himself, helping to sniff out the poor souls who have had the undaunted courage to run away from their so-called masters."

If she had been listless earlier, she seemed suddenly to find an energy that filled her body.

"Let us pause for a moment to talk about that revolting Act."

"It is an abomination!" someone yelled.

"Indeed it is!" she said. "It allows a supposed owner of a slave to drag that person bodily into a courtroom of the United States—a courtroom sanctioned by the very Constitution so many claim to hold dear—and present a sworn affidavit that he owns that particular human being. Owns him like you can own a mattress!

"And is it before a real judge?" She went on to answer her own question. "No, hardly ever. It is instead before a man called a slave commissioner.

"Can you imagine that in this supposed land of liberty there are government officials called slave commissioners?

"And does the enslaved person get to contest his status in a trial and prove that he is a free Negro?"

Some people in the audience shouted, "No!"

Abby echoed them again. "No, absolutely not!

"Well, does the slave get to argue that slavery is an abomination that ought not to be recognized by any court of law that pretends to be civilized?"

Again, the audience answered, with even more voices raised. "No! No!"

"No, the enslaved man or woman or child certainly does not. Instead, a United States marshal is charged, after this summary proceeding, with assisting the cruel slave master to transport that enslaved man or woman—even a child of tender years—back to slavery.

"So why not Lincoln anyway, you ask? Perhaps you think Lincoln really is an abolitionist but can't admit it because then he won't get elected. You think he's hiding it out of electoral necessity. If that is so, can he not at least bring himself to oppose the Slave Act? Can't Honest Abe, as some call him, find in his heart that small amount of human decency needed to oppose that heinous Act?

"No, he cannot."

Clarence looked over at Billy Herndon to see his reaction, but Herndon was completely stone-faced.

"Now let us now talk about what is happening this very night, mere blocks from here," Abby said. "A young woman not even thirteen years of age—a girl, really—is about to be returned to bondage in Kentucky. Which is being done, not in hiding, but in the open, not two blocks from Mr. Lincoln's law office and not many more blocks from his home. Yet Mr. Lincoln has not found it in himself to walk down to the courthouse and protest."

She looked out at the audience. "How many of you were there tonight, standing witness?"

Clarence heard at least a dozen voices shout, "I was."

Abby Kelley raised her voice higher. "Was Honest Abe there?"

"No!" shouted even more people.

"Raise your hand if you were there!"

Clarence stood up on the pew for a better look, and saw at least a hundred hands waving in the air. He half expected Abby Kelley to urge her audience to take action, but she did not. She was, he recalled, a pacifist who eschewed violence.

Instead, Abby said only, "Well, if you are a *political* abolitionist and you therefore decide to vote in this election, you may think to vote for Mr. Lincoln because you imagine he is the best of the four candidates."

A few voices responded, "He is!"

"I have heard the argument before," she said. "That two of Lincoln's opponents—Breckinridge and Bell—have actually owned slaves themselves, and Senator Douglas, who would have men vote on whether to expand slavery, might as well own them." She paused again, letting the tension build. She was, Clarence realized, a person who had learned to hold an audience in her hands.

"Do not delude yourself into thinking Lincoln is any better. If he wins, as the newspapers have begun to say he will, he will do *nothing at all* for the slave. Nothing... Not one set of iron manacles will drop away the night he is elected. Not one pair of fetters will fall from a slave's ankles. Not one master's whip will still the day Lincoln takes the oath."

She paused for a second. "Four years hence, nothing will have changed."

She was breathing heavily. "So go and vote if you must. But do not delude yourself that it will make a difference to the more than three million slaves who toil in this supposed land of liberty.

"Now let me return to what I truly wish to speak to you about tonight—the actual fate of the poor slave who is held in bondage not two hundred miles south of where we sit tonight. And what we can do about it without the frivolity of elections."

Clarence looked at his watch. If he was to make his deadline, he needed to leave. And he already had his story. Abby Kelley's usual speech would make it into the story only as a brief mention. Most everyone had heard it all before, if not from her, then from one of the other abolitionist lecturers who barnstormed the country.

He wished his seatmates farewell and said, "It was a pleasure to meet all of you." He clambered over the back of the pew and headed for the front door.

II

On the way back to his office, Clarence passed again through the square. Several armed deputies were still guarding the courthouse entrance. The small knot of people who'd been there half an hour before were still milling about. Despite the fact that it was August, someone had even dug a small hole in the dirt and built a wood fire in it.

Clarence stopped to talk to them. Perhaps a brief interview could somehow liven up his story about the escaped slave, which by now was seeming of not much interest.

"Excuse me, sir," Clarence said, addressing a man he guessed to be of middle years who was, despite the warmth of the evening, bundled inside a large coat, with a scarf that hid much of his face, but left his bald pate exposed to the air. "I'm Clarence Artemis, the owner and editor of *The Radical Abolitionist*, the first *truly* abolitionist paper in Springfield."

"Ah, yes," the man said, whipping his scarf back off his face so he could be heard. "Still one more abolitionist paper. Every time you turn around there is another, all reporting the same news. Which is that there has been no progress on ending slavery. None!"

"I understand your frustration," Clarence said. "But, as the politicians say, we have surrounded slavery with a ring of fire, and like a scorpion, it will eventually die in the middle of the fire."

The man snorted. "Ha! Have you ever seen a scorpion in Springfield?"

"Well, I've not been here long, but no. It's just a saying, it's not…"

"It's a worthless saying. Those who use it—they are just politicians trying to gull us abolitionists into inaction. They claim that slaves are escaping in ever larger numbers from the Border states and that those states will eventually have no choice but to abolish slavery because there will be no slaves left in them."

"Is that not true?" Clarence said.

"I know only that slave catchers are thick as fleas hereabouts and most slaves who escape are seized and sent back. It is to prevent that that we are here tonight."

Clarence realized that he was arguing with the man instead of interviewing him. He shifted his approach.

"If they try again to move the enslaved girl, are you prepared to block the attempt?"

"We are. We succeeded earlier this evening in driving them back inside. We will not let them move her."

"Who is *we*? There are perhaps only a dozen of you left, if even that many." Clarence gestured at the four or five people around them and a few more in front of the courthouse, talking to the men guarding it.

"We have people ready to ride out and let people know they must come," the man said.

"May I have your name?" Clarence said.

"I will keep that to myself."

"Thank you for the information," Clarence said. "Perhaps I can work it into my story."

"What you should work into your story is that all the politicians in this town, be they Republican or Democrat or Whig—what's left of the Whigs—are cowards. And that includes Mr. Lincoln."

"What about the enslaved girl, sir? Do you have any thoughts about her?" Clarence realized that in posing the question to the man it was a way of asking the same question of himself.

"I feel great pity for her," the man said. "As I do for all of those who are enslaved." With that, he walked away.

Was pity what Clarence himself felt for the trembling girl? He had not actually seen a captured slave since he had watched the mob try to free Anthony Burns back in Boston. Now he was struggling to reconcile the politics of it, which he'd heard from his parents all of his life, with the reality. That poor girl had been terrified, and he felt for her in a way he would not have predicted. Mixed with the pity was rage. What kind of country was he living in?

Clarence hurried back to his office, which consisted of a small room above a store and doubled as his living quarters. Its only furniture was a bed, a dresser with a washbasin on top and a small writing desk.

He sat at the desk, pen in hand, inkwell and paper in front of him, trying to think how to work the man's biting comment about politicians being cowards into his article. But he made little progress. Then he had an epiphany. The piece should begin with that little girl shivering in fear. That was the heart of the story, and he began to fill the page.

After not very long, he heard shouts outside. He looked out the window and saw men running, carrying torches. He ran down the steps and into the street. "What's happening?" he shouted to one of the men.

"They have brought the carriage around for the girl again!"

Clarence took the steps back up to his office two at a time, grabbed his notebook, stuffed several pencils into his pocket, then ran back down, almost losing his footing in his haste. He sprinted at full tilt back to the jail.

When he got there, it was clear the action was already mostly over. In lieu of the dozen or so people who had been there before, there were perhaps fifty or sixty people, but they were all leaving the square, some of them running fast. A highly polished, black, two-wheeled cabriolet was lying on its side, still attached to a single horse. The horse was dragging the carriage along the ground, making a great grinding noise.

There was blood on the side of the carriage and on the ground next to it, too, along with a man's leather hat. A small fire was burning inside the courthouse, casting flickering patterns on the windows that faced the street. Clarence could hear the fire bell sounding.

He looked around for the man he'd been talking to earlier, but he was nowhere to be found, even though the small fire he'd been tending in the pit was still burning. In his place was a young boy, perhaps eleven or twelve at the most.

Clarence walked up to him and introduced himself. The boy did not respond with his own name, just grunted. Clarence plowed ahead. "What just happened here?"

"They was tryin' to sneak that slave girl out again. That carriage there came in real sudden—" he pointed to the cabriolet "—and they rushed that girl out of the courthouse, with the master, and put 'em in the carriage."

"Didn't the people who were here try to stop them?"

"There wasn't near enough of us. But then at least a hundred people came tearing 'round that corner there—" he pointed just behind the carriage "—and dragged out the girl and the master, too, and took them away somewheres."

"Didn't the marshals do something about it?"

"They weren't near enough to take on the mob."

"Where did the mob come from?"

"From Second Pres. They just come from hearing that jezebel Abby Kelley speak."

"What did she have to do with it?" Clarence said.

"One of them guys that come to rescue the slave girl said Abby told them, "Go do somethin' 'bout that poor slave girl.""

"Are you sure that's what he said she said?"

"Near as I can remember."

"Did you see where they took the slave girl and her master?"

"No. Too many people between me and them," the boy said.

"Did you know any of the people?"

The boy paused. He pursed his lips "No, mister, I didn't know none of them."

"What did the marshal and his deputies do?"

"Soon as the mob come, they went back in the courthouse. I woulda, too. That mob was right scary."

"Can you tell me anything else you think's important?" Clarence said. It was his cleanup question for interviews.

"Well," the boy said. "I got somethin'." He reached into his pocket and took out a folded piece of paper. "I drawed what I saw."

He showed Clarence a pencil sketch of the square. It was in three parts. The first part showed people boiling around the corner into the square. It was amazingly lifelike. The second part showed the mob rocking the carriage, with the master peering out from the window, a terrified look on his face. The third part showed the carriage on the ground, with a spot next to it of what was, he assumed, supposed to be blood, and next to that a discarded hat.

"You drew this?" Clarence said.

"Yes, sir. I want to be an artist. Do you like it?"

"It's great. I want to buy it from you. I will give you three dollars for all rights."

"What does that mean?"

"It means I will own the drawing and can publish it anywhere or have other people publish it."

"Three dollars. Let me think."

"I'll give you five. No more."

"Alright."

"Please sign and date it."

"Uh, alright." He took the drawing, pulled a pencil from his pocket, signed it *Robbie Culp*, and dated it *August 24, 1860*.

"There's one more thing I need from you, Robbie," Clarence said.

"What?"

"A bill of sale." Clarence tore a piece of paper from his notebook and wrote out a bill of sale, providing that Robbie was selling him all rights.

Robbie read it, shrugged and signed.

"I have to go now," Clarence said. "If I want to reach you again, where do you live?"

"With my parents, near the corner of Cook Street and Spring."

"Alright. Hey, by the way, did you see who lit the fire in the courthouse?"

"No. But I got other drawings, sir."

"Oh, like what?"

"Well, I made some-a Mr. Lincoln."

"Does he know you did them?"

"I ain't sure."

"We'll talk about those later, Robbie. But right now I gotta go." As he left the square, Clarence contemplated the great story he had stumbled upon. And although there was no printing press in Springfield that could put the drawing into his own paper, he suspected magazines in the East like *The Atlantic* and *Harper's Weekly* would pay dearly for it. If he could only get it to them in time. Although he'd heard about experiments in Europe to transmit pictures over the telegraph, none of that had as yet come to the frontier of Illinois, so the drawing would have

to go by train to Chicago and then on to New York and Boston. On the way back to his office, Clarence took a short de-
tour so that he could pass by Lincoln's house, a large, two-story
structure at the corner of Eighth and Jackson. If the lights were
on, he would be bold, knock on the door and ask Lincoln for
a comment on the night's events. When he arrived, there were
no lights on, but he decided to do it anyway. He walked up the
steps to the veranda that surrounded the house. There was no
guard on the veranda. Nor, so far as he could see, were there any
guards anywhere else. Which surprised him. Wouldn't someone
have thought to guard the man?

The door was high, made of brown oak, with thin glass panels to either side. Where a knocker might have been there was
instead only a narrow sign that said "A Lincoln". He rapped on
the door.

After not too long, he heard a noise inside. A few seconds
later, the door was opened by a small boy. "Hello," the boy said.
"Do you want to talk to my papa or my mama?"

Clarence prided himself at being able to talk to small children, so he said, "Perhaps I want to talk to *you*."

The boy just stared at him and said, "You must want my papa.
I'll see if he wants to talk to you," and closed the door.

The minutes ticked by and Clarence wondered if the boy was
ever coming back. As he was about to give up and leave, the
door opened again, and the boy said, "Papa will be here soon."
Then he reached up, grabbed Clarence's cap off his head and
scurried away.

"Come back with that!" Clarence shouted.

No sooner had the words left his mouth than Abraham Lincoln appeared. He was so tall and his face so craggy that Clarence
could not have mistaken him for anyone else. What Clarence
had not expected, however, was to meet Lincoln when he was
wearing a long, checkered nightshirt and brown leather slippers.
Still, Clarence was awestruck.

Lincoln, however, seemed not to be surprised to find a stranger on his doorstep. "Good evening," Lincoln said. "I'm sorry about your cap, Mr...."

"Artemis. Clarence Artemis."

"The boy is a bit of a scamp. Perhaps we can retrieve it a little later. But in the meantime, what might I do for you?"

Clarence explained who he was, where he was from and what he hoped to accomplish with his new paper. "It would be a wonderful thing if my paper's first edition, which is coming soon, could be graced by an interview with you, and particularly about the events at the courthouse tonight."

Then he suddenly remembered that he was bothering the man at his home well after supper and said, "I'm so sorry to bother you in the evening, but..."

"Please don't be concerned about that," Lincoln said. "Unfortunately, I'm not giving any interviews, but following the tradition that, once nominated, candidates for the presidency do not campaign. I'm sure you're aware of that."

"I am. I thought perhaps you'd make an exception for a new publication."

"I'm afraid not. Now let me see if I can retrieve your hat." He turned but left the door open. Clarence peered in, hoping to see something he could report, but it was too dark to make out any details.

Eventually, Lincoln returned. "I'm sorry, Mr. Artemis, but Tad has hidden it somewhere. Perhaps I could lend you my hat in the meantime." He held up a tall top hat.

"I'm afraid I'd look ridiculous in that hat," Clarence said. "I have other caps. I'll get that one back from you another time. Again, forgive my intrusion."

"Good luck with your new paper, Mr. Artemis."

"Thank you," Clarence said, went down the steps and headed home, disappointed at not getting the interview, but exhilarated at having managed to make the acquaintance of the man he hoped would be the next president of the United States.

12

The White House
September 8, 1860

He had contested for the presidency three times before—1844, 1848 and 1852—and failed. On the fourth try—1856—he had finally captured the Democratic nomination and been elected. The day of his inauguration had been joyous. Now, nearly four years later, the final days of his administration were running through his fingers like grains of sand, and joy was nowhere to be found. If things went as predicted, the nation he loved—and love it he did, despite what the critics said—was about to come apart.

The cause was that man running for president on the Republican ticket, Abraham Lincoln. And who was he, really? A man with no formal education, a hick from Kentucky now transplanted to Illinois and someone who couldn't even speak properly. Rumor had it that when he had addressed the august Cooper Union the year before in New York he had begun by saying "Mr. *Cheerman.*"

Buchanan had been drinking all day, although in moderation, as he always did. Or so he liked to tell himself. He picked up the bottle and peered at it. He had begun in early morning, as usual, but the bottle was not even half-empty. And, of course, he could hold his liquor. He poured himself another. He suddenly noticed an usher hovering in the doorway, and it reminded him that he was about to have company. "Mr. Washburn, we are expecting Jeremiah Black, the attorney general. When he arrives, please show him to the cabinet room."

"Of course, Mr. President."

Buchanan peered out the window at the Washington darkness and thought, not for the first time, that he wished he had married. Then he would have had a wife, and perhaps even children, to talk to about his plight. After the death of his fiancée, so many years ago, he had had other opportunities to wed, but had not taken any of them up. Now, as the newspapers were so fond of pointing out, he was the first and only bachelor president of the United States.

He could, of course, talk with his wonderful thirty-year-old niece, Harriet Lane, who had so ably served as the White House hostess since he had taken office. Despite the growing political crisis, she had turned the White House into a place of style and gaiety. Her parties were the talk of the town and a much sought-after ticket. Her beauty was topped by a good political head, which he prided himself on having created and nurtured by admitting her into his political and social circles starting when she was only fifteen years old.

But Harriet was away for a few days, and in any case, she had begun to diverge from his views on the abolition issue. While she did not favor immediate abolition as some did, she thought it should become compulsory, to take place on a definite schedule. Indeed, he suspected she was going to return to their home in Pennsylvania on Election Day and vote for Lincoln, even though she had said she would not.

He did, of course, have his cabinet members to consult with. They were all good friends, or had become so, and almost all had stuck with him since the beginning. He would lean on their advice and counsel. Perhaps there was some pathway he had not yet discovered to keep the country from unraveling. If it did unravel, he had no doubt it would be blamed on him.

"Mr. President," the usher said, interrupting his reverie.

"Yes, Mr. Washburn?"

"The attorney general is in the cabinet room, as you requested. Will you want any refreshments during your meeting?"

Buchanan held up the bottle. "Just two clean glasses, please. There's no need to announce me. Please just put the bottle and the glasses on the table. That will be announcement enough."

"Very well, sir."

The president unlimbered himself from his chair and walked to the cabinet room, where he found his attorney general waiting.

"Good evening, Mr. President."

"Good evening, Mr. Attorney General. Thank you for accepting my invitation to come by this evening. Would you perchance like some refreshment?"

"Thank you, but I've only recently dined. I see, however, that you are working your way through a bottle of my favorite libation, and I would gladly share in that if you're offering."

"Oh, indeed I am. I'm drinking Old Overholt, to which I'm partial because of its Pennsylvania origins. But if you like we could switch to Madeira. I have a nice supply of the best."

"No, rye will do just fine."

Buchanan poured each of them a tumblerful, and said, "Jeremiah, have you seen the greenhouse that Ms. Lane has built?"

"No, I have heard tell of it, of course. But I've always understood it was reserved for the family."

Buchanan laughed. "You have been with me since the beginning of this burden that the presidency has become. Which counts you as family. It will be a pleasant evening to sit awhile in the greenhouse. The heat of summer is gone, but the damp of winter is not yet upon us. Follow me."

They walked together to the western wall of the main White House building and came to a low doorway that led into a glassed-in tunnel. They were both tall men, and had to duck to avoid hitting their heads. After perhaps twenty feet they emerged into a large greenhouse with walls made of square glass panels that reached up to high, slanted ceilings, also paneled in glass. Small trees in pots, exuberantly flowering plants and wide ferns planted in baskets were everywhere.

"It is quite beautiful," Black said. "I would never have expected such a thing."

"Yes, Harriet has done a marvelous job of creating a space that is away from it all. Let us sit." Buchanan pointed to a small wrought-iron table with two matching chairs.

"To get right to the point, Jeremiah, we are not far from the election," Buchanan said. "Of the four candidates, who do you think is most likely to win? I have my own opinion, but would like to hear yours."

"Lincoln, with a mere plurality of the popular vote but a majority of the electoral college."

"That is what I feared you'd say. Sadly, it is my opinion, too."

They sat for a while, swishing the liquor around in their glasses, but saying nothing. Finally, Black broke the silence. "Some of the flowers and plants in here look quite exotic."

"Yes, Harriet has tried to collect all she can, and has had the State Department let visiting foreign delegations know that they should bring plants as gifts."

"And do they do so?"

"Yes. Let me show you something recently arrived." Buchanan arose and walked down one of the long aisles to its midway point. Black followed.

The president pointed at a small tree. "That is a gift from the

Japanese delegation that was here last May to ratify the Treaty of Amity and Commerce between our two countries."

"It looks like an orange tree," Black said. "But the oranges are tiny."

"That is indeed what they are. Harriet has tried one and reports it quite bitter. Would you care to taste one, Jeremiah?" He reached forward as if to pick one.

"Oh no, that is quite alright! Perhaps another time."

Buchanan went ahead, picked one and tucked it into a pocket of his jacket.

As they headed back to their chairs, Buchanan said, "To return to our conversation of earlier, tell me more of your thinking on the election, and let's see if it's the same as mine."

"I'll start with Senator Douglas. He has killed his once good prospects with his popular sovereignty nonsense of letting people vote on whether or not to permit slavery in territories that want to become states. Southerners don't want a vote, just the right to take their human property with them into the new areas. In the North, most want no slavery at all, anywhere, vote or no vote."

"I agree," Buchanan said. "I'd even wager you Douglas will end up without a single Northern state in his column. I'll give you ten-to-one odds on it." He dug a ten-dollar gold piece out of his waistcoat pocket.

"Put it back, Mr. President. I wouldn't take that bet even at one-hundred-to-one."

They had again reached the little table and resumed their seats. Buchanan filled their tumblers once again, this time to the brim. He raised his glass, spilling a small amount, which he ignored. "To anyone but Lincoln."

They clinked glasses, and Buchanan said, "What about my vice president, Mr. Breckinridge? He seems to be running a robust campaign." He asked, despite knowing full well what the answer was going to be.

"Ha!" Black said. "He's a Southerner who owns slaves."

"Owned. Past tense."

"Then or now, doesn't matter. He'll probably carry all of the Southern states, but that will be it, and not enough to win." They didn't even bother to discuss the fourth candidate, John Bell, the aging candidate of the recently formed Constitutional Union Party, who had ludicrously chosen a former president of Harvard as his running mate. Their platform urged that the country just ignore the slavery problem and focus on strengthening the Union.

"So we are going to be stuck with Lincoln," Buchanan said, and took a long swallow from his glass.

"Yes. The crude Westerner will be coming to town and sitting in your chair, along with his loud wife. Who everyone says is a shrew."

Buchanan smiled. "Perhaps he can retreat to this lovely spot to get away from her."

"You will likely be introduced to her at the inauguration and can judge her for yourself, Mr. President."

Buchanan took the tiny orange from his pocket, held it up and laughed. "Perhaps I will offer her this orange, tell her it is from the White House garden and laud its sweetness. By the time she bites into it, I will be well on my way back home to Lancaster, where I will be but a spectator to the coming catastrophe."

Black drank down the last of his rye. "If the hotheads in South Carolina secede…"

"There's no *if* about it, Jeremiah."

They sat quietly for a moment, each thinking his own thoughts.

Black broke the silence. "Perhaps Lincoln will let them go without using military force to stop them."

"I don't think a president has the authority to use force to stop them," Buchanan said. "As you know."

"I doubt Lincoln agrees with you about that. And he will be

the one sitting in this house as commander-in-chief. The military will do what he tells them to do."

Buchanan refilled their glasses again. "If we keep this up, Jeremiah, we will both soon be drunk."

"I think we long ago proved we could hold our liquor, Mr. President."

"Well, I don't think there's much to do now but drink. The nation we love is either going to be split asunder or racked by war. And there's apparently nothing much I can do to affect Lincoln's choice of which that will be."

"I think perhaps there is something we can do," Black said. "I've come up with an idea that might stop Lincoln from being elected."

13

"Do you read *Harper's Weekly*, Mr. President?" Black said.

"Who does not? Although they have disappointed recently by supporting Douglas."

"Have you seen the most recent issue?"

"No."

"I had meant to bring one, but forgot."

"I would hazard that there must be multiple copies here in the White House," Buchanan said. He picked up a small bell that was sitting on the table and rang it. Washburn appeared within seconds.

"What can I be of assistance with, Mr. President?"

"Mr. Washburn, could you locate the current issue of *Harper's Weekly*? I am sure there must be one about somewhere."

"Of course, Mr. President. I will return with it as soon as possible."

"Why are you wanting me to see it, Jeremiah?"

"Have you heard about the riot in Springfield that prevented the return of a slave to her master?"

"Not that I recall. Those events are now so common—the abolitionists become bolder with every passing day—that I pay little attention and permit others to deal with it."

"This one is perhaps a bit different because the riot is said to have been caused by a speech by a radical abolitionist named Abby Kelley Foster."

"Ah, I have heard of her. Long before I became president, Harriet attended one of her antislavery harangues. In Pennsylvania I think it was. Harriet was impressed by her willingness to endure what came her way."

"What came her way?"

"Why, according to Harriet, rotten eggs. And worse."

Black drew back and his eyes widened. "Is Harriet an abolitionist, then?"

Buchanan paused, wanting to think carefully before answering. "She hates slavery and would see it end. But I do not think she is an abolitionist, at least in the sense people use that term now."

Just then Washburn returned and handed a stack of papers to Buchanan. "I think the one you want is on top, Mr. President."

"Thank you, Washburn." Buchanan took the stack from him and handed it immediately to Black.

"Yes, here it is," Black said. "Right on top. The issue of September 8, with Senator Douglas on the cover." He leafed through the issue and opened it to an interior page. "Here, Mr. President, is the drawing that caught my attention."

He handed it to Buchanan, who examined it and said, "I see a turned-over carriage and a hat on the ground. Is that spot on the ground supposed to be blood?"

"Yes."

"What does it have to do with defeating Lincoln? Was he involved?"

"Not so far as we know. But this event is reliably said to be the aftermath of Mrs. Foster's speech, in which she harangued a crowd in a Springfield church to interfere with the return of a slave to her lawful owner. The slave was recently escaped from Kentucky."

"Where is the slave now?"

"No one knows. Nor does anyone know where the slave owner is. He left only blood and his hat behind. Or at least I've been told the blood is his."

"Is there anything special about the slave?"

"She's only twelve years old."

Buchanan shuddered. "This is such bad business, but it is the law." He took another sip from his glass, which was near to being empty.

"Whether it be bad business or good business, it appears Mrs. Foster interfered with the return of a slave to her lawful owner, in violation of the Fugitive Slave Act," Black said. "The slave was in the custody of the United States marshal. We can prosecute her for that."

Buchanan didn't respond but instead rang the small bell again. When Washburn reappeared, the president said, "Mr. Washburn, would you bring another bottle of Old Overholt, please?" He paused. "And, uh, please dispose of the empty bottle here where Miss Lane is not likely to see it."

"Of course, Mr. President."

Buchanan tipped his glass back and drained it, then said, "I don't follow how prosecuting Mrs. Foster will help us defeat Lincoln."

"It is a bit complicated—and uncertain—Mr. President, but let me describe it to you."

Before Black could continue, Washburn reappeared with a fresh bottle and, without being asked, filled both glasses near to the top.

"Thank you, Washburn," the president said. "Please continue, Jeremiah."

"In a nutshell, Mr. Lincoln has been very careful to say he is *not* an abolitionist," Black said.

"I know, I know. Lincoln claims, every day it seems, that he will leave slavery as it is in the states that have it now, while trying to bar it from new territories. And that he will even enforce the Fugitive Slave Act."

"Exactly, but at least some of the abolitionists are moving toward voting for him anyway, in the belief that he is not telling the truth about his intentions. Because when he was in Congress he sponsored a bill to abolish slavery here in the District."

"Which is why the South will not vote for him at all," Buchanan said.

"Correct. But if abolitionists—many of whom have up 'til now refrained from voting at all—turn out for him in large numbers, it will help Lincoln carry New York *and* Pennsylvania, where they are now thick as flies. And that will get him elected."

"That is all very interesting," Buchanan said. "Yet I still don't see how prosecuting Mrs. Foster will help to defeat him."

"It's simple, Mr. President. If we prosecute her, the abolitionists are sure to ask Lincoln, 'If she is convicted and you are elected president of the United States, are you going to pardon her?'"

Buchanan sloshed the liquor around in his glass. "So…if he refuses to answer, the abolitionists will abandon him, is that your theory?"

"Yes. But if he even hints that he *will* pardon her, the voters in the North who think he is the only reasonable candidate—who have taken him at his word on enforcing the Fugitive Slave Act—will instead abandon him."

Buchanan took a long swallow from his glass.

"It is brilliant, Jeremiah. Brilliant. In the bitter politics of our time, he could lose both sets of voters. Is there time to get it done?"

"The election is still almost two months away. I think we can easily get a grand jury to indict her in that time."

"What if she is acquitted? After all, when we've prosecuted people who interfered with the return of escaped slaves, they've mostly been acquitted."

"I think we can arrange for the trial to start before Election Day, but the verdict, whatever it turns out to be, to come only after Election Day."

"Putting maximum pressure on Lincoln to say *something*."

"Exactly."

"Do you want me to refill your glass, Jeremiah?"

"Uh, no. I have to go home soon, and Mrs. Black has been threatening to join a temperance society if I don't let up some."

"Pity, that. Well, where is Mrs. Foster now?"

"Still in Springfield, tending to an ill friend."

"Even better," Buchanan said. "She can be indicted and tried right in Lincoln's backyard. Is this something you can order directly?"

"No. United States attorneys are under the control of the Solicitor of the Treasury Department. But I'm sure it can be arranged." He paused briefly. "The current solicitor is a Southerner."

Buchanan raised his glass. "To success in this!" Then he put his glass back down. "Oh, I forgot. Yours is empty. I insist, no matter what Mrs. Black might think." He filled Black's glass to the very brim.

Buchanan raised his glass again. "To success." Black raised his own glass, which was sloshing over slightly, and they clinked.

"By the way, do we know what has actually happened to the slave and her master?" Buchanan said.

"We don't know, and I think we might be better off not knowing," Black said.

Buchanan thought for a moment. "I'm not sure you're right about that."

"How do you mean, Mr. President?"

"If you manage to make this into a national issue, the mystery of what happened to them will no doubt enthrall the public."

"I still don't see…"

"If they're found—and especially if the slave master is found dead—the outcry to convict Mrs. Foster by those who support the South will be much greater. Southerners have a tremendous fear of slave uprisings fomented by abolitionists."

Black wrinkled his brow. "This wasn't an uprising, and it wasn't in the South."

"Close enough. Do you have someone you trust who can be sent to try to find the slave master?"

Black shrugged. "There is really no official person to send, Mr. President."

"Why not?"

"We have no federal police force, and the State of Illinois doesn't have one either. Out West, there is only the county sheriff and his deputies. And possibly a constable or two in the town."

"What about someone from the United States attorney's office in Springfield?"

"There is only one lawyer in that office—the US attorney himself—and I doubt very much he has anyone who could investigate this sort of thing. Our United States attorneys tend to focus on federal financial crimes, like counterfeiting."

"Perhaps the United States marshal?"

"It's a possibility, although the marshal is controlled by the district court there, which tends to guard its independence. I have been in touch by telegram with the district court judge there about it, however."

"And?"

"He is reluctant to have the marshal get involved in 'slave chasing,' as he put it. Plus the marshal and his deputies were made to look foolish in this riot, and they are apparently not wanting to risk further embarrassment if either the master or the slave is found dead."

"Perhaps I could send a staff member from here."

"Not a good idea. I will find someone who can do the job, Mr. President. I promise."

14

Springfield, Illinois
Law Offices of Lincoln and Herndon

Herndon had been watching Lincoln for a while and finally couldn't stand it anymore. "Lincoln, if you go on tipping your chair back while you read that newspaper, you'll topple over and break your neck."

"Billy, I been doin' it all my life and it ain't happened yet."

"Well, if it *did* happen this time, the party would have to find a new candidate for president, and it'd likely be Seward or Chase."

"They'd do just fine, I'm sure."

"No, they would lose the election, because they are both avowed abolitionists, which you are not."

"Very carefully not."

"Which paper are you reading?"

"The latest issue of that new local one, *The Radical Abolitionist*. They're still trying to sell copies by writing stories about the enslaved girl, Lucy Battelle, and the mob that freed her a month or so ago."

"I'm surprised that story hasn't gone away. There've been so many attempts by mobs across the North to prevent the return of slaves that it doesn't seem like much of a story anymore."

"The story continues of interest to people, Billy, because those two people have disappeared. Everyone loves a mystery."

"Can I see it?"

Lincoln handed it over, and Herndon started to read it.

Just then, the door into the office slammed open—reminding Herndon, who tended to take care of such things around the office—that he'd neglected to fix the broken doorstop. John Hay, whom they'd recently hired to work part-time on correspondence for the campaign, burst into the room, out of breath from, apparently, having run up the steps to the office. "Have you heard?"

"Heard what?" Lincoln asked, finally lowering the front legs of his chair to the floor and sitting fully upright.

"The United States attorney here in Springfield has impaneled a grand jury, and they indicted Abby Kelley for, among other things, interfering with the return of that runaway slave when Red was trying to transfer her back to her so-called owner. She's charged with a federal felony under the Fugitive Slave Act. It carries a prison term."

"Abby Kelley interfered with Red?" Lincoln said. "However did she do that? Was she there?"

"No. They say Kelley fomented the riot that freed the enslaved girl and carried off her master."

"*Fomented.* Well, there's a fancy word," Lincoln said. "What are the details?"

"The indictment supposedly says—I've not actually seen it yet—that she gave an antislavery lecture in a church here, Second Presbyterian, and at the very end, urged the crowd to 'go and do something about' the enslaved girl who was about to be returned south."

"Do we know anyone who was there?" Lincoln said.

"I was," Hay said.

Lincoln raised his eyebrows. "I don't know you well, Johnny, but I would have expected you to be out drinking and carousing of an evening, not attending antislavery lectures." He laughed.

"I was there by happenstance," Hay said.

"Well, never mind why you were there," Herndon said. "Did Abby Kelley do the kind of urging the indictment says she did?"

"Um, I don't know because I left before the end."

"Why?" Lincoln said.

"I was bored," Hay said. "But up until the point I left, it was just the usual antislavery talk. No urging, except perhaps to contribute money to the cause. Oh, and saying she did not support Mr. Lincoln."

Lincoln rose from the chair and walked to the tall window that looked out over a rooftop. The window, Herndon noted, was even more stained and dirty than usual—one more thing he'd neglected to take care of.

"So, right here in this office, we don't know whether Abby Kelley urged anyone to do anything violent, do we?" Lincoln said.

Herndon spoke up. "I was there, too." He looked momentarily abashed. "But I, too, left early. Same reason."

Lincoln folded his hands behind his back, still staring out the window. "Whether she urged or didn't urge, the press will be here by the dozens for the trial, on the top of the national press already here for the election. I will need to find somewhere to hide out."

"Why do you need to hide out?" Hay said.

Herndon saw that Hay had sat himself down in the chair Lincoln had just vacated. It was well understood in the office that it was *Lincoln's* chair, and by unspoken agreement, no one else ever sat in it. Herndon saw Lincoln flick an eye toward the chair, but he said nothing.

Lincoln turned around, rested his rear end against the windowsill and folded his arms. "Johnny, you've not been at this politics thing very long, but, as sure as God made little green apples, the abolitionists are going to demand I promise to pardon Abby Kelley if I'm elected president, and they will be enraged if I don't so promise."

"But if you do promise, it will enrage the people who think you are neutral on the slavery question," Herndon said. "And plan to vote for you on that basis."

"I'm not neutral," Lincoln said. "I want slavery to go away, but I have pledged not to disturb it where it already exists. My political problem with this Kelley prosecution arises only if she is convicted. If she is acquitted, the jury will have removed me from the horns of the dilemma."

"Unless the trial is still pending on Election Day with no verdict," Herndon said. "In which case it will make the worst of both worlds for you."

"A true point, Billy. You are in touch with the world of abolitionists, are you not?"

"Yes."

"The government has prosecuted many people for interfering with the return of fugitive slaves. How have those prosecutions fared?"

"Poorly. Juries have refused to convict them."

Lincoln lowered his head and stared at the floor for what seemed to Herndon like minutes. Finally, he said, "My instincts tell me that if the enslaved girl is found alive hereabouts or can be proved to be alive and well in Canada, the wind will go out of the sails of this prosecution."

"Won't the government want to find her, too?" Hay said.

"Johnny, the government will want to find her, if at all, only dead. Then they can lay her death at Abby Kelley Foster's feet— no matter what she actually urged anyone to do—and hope for a conviction."

"Do you fear they will kill her if they find her alive?" Hay said.

"That may depend on whom the government sends to look

for her," Lincoln said. "Or—" he sighed deeply "—whether the owner's family promises a reward for finding both of them, which will put the entire state to beating the bushes searching for them."

"We must find them first ourselves," Herndon said.

"Billy, let's get in touch with Pinkerton as soon as we can," Lincoln said.

"You know Allan Pinkerton?" Hay said.

"Yes, Johnny, for lo these many years. His detective agency has long done work for the Illinois Central Railroad. I have represented the Central as a lawyer, so our paths have frequently crossed."

Herndon was already at the door. "I will telegraph him immediately."

"Yes, but he cannot come here," Lincoln said. "Or respond to you by telegram. The fact that we are looking for the girl ourselves cannot be learned by anyone. Instead of sending a telegram, go to Chicago and see him. His headquarters are on Washington Street."

"And if he sees Pinkerton, then what?" Hay said.

"He will know what to do. But as I think about it, Johnny, why don't you go, too. Have you ever been to Chicago?"

"Not yet."

"You'll find it fascinating, I dare say. But now, Johnny, I need a word in private with Mr. Herndon, if you don't mind."

"Oh, of course," Hay said.

He promptly left and, unlike the clatter with which he had arrived, closed the door quietly behind him.

"What is it, Lincoln?" Herndon said.

"You know, Billy, that you and I differ on some things."

"We do."

"And one of them is abolition. We both detest slavery, but you would have it end immediately, although I've never quite understand how you would make that work. I respect your position, though."

"And I respect your position, Lincoln, although I've never understood how you could detest slavery and allow it to continue."

"Well, be that as it may, here is what I wanted to say outside of Johnny's presence. Whatever your own inclinations might be in the matter, please do not take any position on my behalf as to what I might or should do if Mrs. Foster is convicted. Say nothing one way or the other. Hint nothing one way or the other."

"I understand."

"And please be sure that your young charge, Johnny Hay, also understands."

15

Herndon, unlike Hay, had been to Chicago several times before, including briefly at the Republican Convention in May that had nominated Lincoln. He was not in any way fond of the place. It was crowded, noisy and, worst of all, smelly, even in its finer parts.

They took the Toledo, Wabash and Great Western to Urbana and changed there to the Illinois Central, which took them on to Chicago. The accommodations on the Wabash had been primitive. On the Central, Herndon managed to wangle their way into a first-class car by mentioning Lincoln and his connection to the railroad's president, William Osborne.

They each enjoyed a cigar after an opulent dinner served on fine china.

The train from Urbana to Chicago was an express, so it took them only a little over eight hours to cover the entire two hundred miles. They disembarked at Chicago's Central Depot station, a large wooden building fronted by high masonry arches.

As they walked under the arches and emerged onto Water Street, Hay wrinkled his nose. "What is that execrable smell?"

"It's sewage," Hay said. "They recently built a sewage collection system, but the discharge, both human and industrial, pours directly into the river. My friends here tell me it has made the smell worse than ever."

Hay held a handkerchief up to his nose. "How many people live here to deposit so much smelly detritus?"

"My friends claim the 1860 census will count more than one hundred thousand Chicagoans, which is threefold what it was just ten years ago."

"That is big," Hay said. "But not New York City big."

"Did you spend a lot of time there?" Herndon said.

"I went to Brown, as you know, so we went over to New York frequently for a little..."

Herndon finished the sentence for him. "Drinking."

Hay laughed. "There was some of that, yes."

"Let's take a hackney cab to Pinkerton," Herndon said. "Their office is at 80 Washington Street. It's only a few blocks."

"Can't we just walk there? Our carpetbags are quite light."

Herndon pointed to the dirt roadway in front of them, which was still wet from a recent rain. The running water had raised damp furrows. "We can if you would like to be covered in mud by the time we get there."

"I take your point," Hay said, and held up his hand to wave down a cab.

They climbed in and Herndon gave the driver the address. The man snapped a whip at his horses, and they were off.

"Are there always cows being driven through the streets here?" Hay said, as they dodged a bellowing line of the animals.

"Yes. This city has become a major transit point for cattle and pigs being sent to market. It was another good reason not to walk."

In not very long, they arrived at a nondescript two-story

building. The cabdriver came around to open the door for them and said, "You gentlemen are quite fancy-dressed. I apologize there's a large puddle between the cab and the curb. You might want to hold up your pant legs as you go so as not to soil them."

They climbed down from the cab and, hiking up their pants as suggested, made it over to the wooden sidewalk with only a bit of mud getting on them.

A very large sign hung from the second story of the building: Pinkerton National Detective Agency, showing an open eye and within it the slogan We Never Sleep.

Unlike most office buildings with which Herndon was familiar, this one had a uniformed guard posted at the front door. He wore a shield-style silver badge that had Pinkerton National Detective Agency embossed on it in gold.

The guard politely inquired as to their business. Herndon explained that they had been sent by Abraham Lincoln to see Mr. Pinkerton on an urgent matter. As proof of their bona fides, Herndon handed the man Lincoln's calling card, along with his own.

The guard examined them with care and raised his eyebrows as he inspected the one from Lincoln. "Please wait here. I will return shortly," he said, and disappeared into the building. Herndon heard the distinct snick of the lock being fastened from the other side after the man had shut the door behind him.

After they had cooled their heels on the sidewalk for almost ten minutes, while being stared at by each and every passerby, the guard finally reappeared and said, "Mr. Pinkerton will see you. Please follow me."

16

The outside of the building had been plain, but the inside was opulent—polished wood everywhere, elegant gas lamps on the walls and spittoons of gleaming brass to the sides. Pinkerton's office, on the second floor, was reached by a wide stairway of dark wood.

When the guard ushered them into the office, the man they assumed to be Pinkerton was sitting at a large square table that was inlaid with parquet. He rose to greet them and, after introductions all around, shook their hands. He was a short man, going a bit stout at the waist, with dark hair that was receding some and piercing blue eyes.

"I bring you greetings from Mr. Lincoln," Herndon said.

"I send my greetings back to him," Pinkerton said. "We have worked together on railroad matters for quite a few years now. In fact, Mr. Lincoln drafted my first contract with the Central. But I assume you are here on campaign matters."

"Yes," Herndon said. "I've been helping Lincoln manage the

huge volume of correspondence he has been receiving, and Mr. Hay has been doing similar work."

"It is a pleasure to meet you both," Pinkerton said. "How might we here at Pinkerton be of service?"

Herndon gave him a quick summary of the situation and Lincoln's desire to have the enslaved girl and, if possible the master, found. He noticed that while he was talking, Hay was looking about the office, gazing in particular at various certificates on the walls and guns of various kinds on the shelves.

When Herndon had finished, Pinkerton said, "Do you have a description of either the girl or the man?"

"Not a good one," Herndon said. "As you know, to retrieve a slave that an owner contends is his, under the Fugitive Slave Act that man needs only to file a sworn affidavit with a slave commissioner, magistrate or federal judge, identify the slave and attest that the slave is his property. There is no need for a trial at which the alleged slave gives evidence, and the slave cannot contest the allegation."

"And hence no one has seen either of them?"

"Only the slave commissioner and the sheriff of Sangamon County, who held her in his jail," Herndon said. "Oh, and the United States marshal, too. Thus, what we know, we know only from the sworn affidavit the master filed."

"What does it say?

"That Lucy Battelle is approximately five feet six inches tall, with curly hair, and very thin."

"I suppose that makes her taller than average for her age," Pinkerton said.

"Yes, and the description we have gleaned of the master is not much better. He is said by a newspaper article to be both tall and thick. Several people who were in the mob are quoted as saying that he looked like a human bull."

Pinkerton rested his chin in his hands and said, "As you no doubt know, I am involved in the Underground Railroad here.

That would make it awkward, and perhaps make Lucy more likely to be recaptured, if I were to become personally involved."

"So you cannot help us?" Herndon said.

"No, no. I just cannot do it personally. But I think there *is* someone here who can help. I have recently taken to hiring female detectives, and they are at times as good, or better, than men."

"A woman?" Herndon said.

"Yes, a woman, Mr. Herndon. Her name is Annabelle Carter. She has proven herself one of my best. Better yet, she is born and bred in Kentucky. So she is able to pretend to be a Southern sympathizer."

Hay suddenly returned to the conversation. "Is she in fact a Southern sympathizer?" he said.

"No, not at all, Mr. Hay. She is an abolitionist, but one who thinks—as many do—that abolition must be gradual or it will lead to chaos. She would begin with the Border states. But she is able to hide her true feelings in order to be of better service to our cause. And—" he paused "—she is quite good with a gun."

There was a silence in the room as they all considered that. Finally, Herndon said, "She sounds good. Let us go forward with her."

"Alright, consider it done," Pinkerton said. "I will arrange for you to meet with her tonight for supper."

"There is one more thing," Herndon said. "Lincoln has authorized me to spend a certain sum on this project, so we should turn to that."

"There will be no need, sir. Anything the Pinkerton Detective Agency can do to assure the election of Mr. Lincoln to the presidency will be on the house. I will consider it a sacred honor for Pinkerton to participate."

"Thank you so very much," Herndon said.

"Mr. Herndon," Pinkerton said, "before we part, I noticed that Mr. Hay has been eyeing the guns on the shelves. Mr. Hay, would you like to look them over? You might have need of one in this adventure."

"I would," Hay said, jumping up and heading over to the shelf that seemed most burdened-down with weaponry.

While Hay went over the guns, Pinkerton got up and began to pace about the room.

"I don't know if I should tell you this," he said. "Because the information was given to me in confidence. And maintaining confidences is one of the things that makes Pinkerton quite different from our competitors."

"What is it?" Herndon said.

"Yesterday, a Major Robert Hedpeth came to see me."

"From our own army?"

"Yes. The army of the United States of America. He wanted to retain us to find the very slave you have come to see me about, as well as her master. But I declined."

"Why?"

"I had the sense that he wanted to find the slave so he could return her to bondage. As an abolitionist, I will take no part in that. I sent him away."

"Did he say who sent him?" Herndon said. "Officers in the army don't assign such missions to themselves."

"He didn't say."

Hay, who was still examining the guns, said, "I think I know who he is."

"Who?" Herndon and Pinkerton said it almost as one.

"My college roommate at Brown had the same last name. His father was an officer in the army, a major. I never met him, but I'm pretty sure his first name was Robert."

"Do you know anything else about him?" Herndon said.

"Only that, according to his son, he was assigned to the Military District of Washington, and that his unit was sometimes sent to protect the White House."

"Why would the White House need protecting?" Herndon said.

"Throughout the more than seventy years this republic has been in existence, there have been various threats against presidents," Pinkerton said. "President Jackson was shot at. And it has been the military's job to step up when those kind of threats arise."

"That means that, one way or another, the president sent him," Hay said. "Sent, not to protect the president against a physical threat, but against a political one."

There was silence in the room as they all considered what Hay had just said.

Herndon broke the silence. "We will simply have to keep a lookout for the major."

Pinkerton laughed. "That won't be hard. He's very short, walks with a limp and has a right arm that is more or less useless to him."

Hay had come back to the table, toting a pistol. "Why is he still on active duty if he has all these physical problems?" he said.

"I asked him that," Pinkerton said. "He replied that he did not want to retire and was being kept on active duty as a reward for his heroism at the Battle of Guadeloupe in the Mexican War."

Pinkerton changed the subject. "Where are you gentlemen staying?"

"At the Tremont," Herndon said.

Pinkerton smiled. "Ah, yes, a very Republican hotel."

"We wouldn't stay anywhere else," Herndon said.

"Of course. In any case, there is a very fine restaurant only a few blocks from there, The Versailles, and I believe I can arrange a private room in which we can meet confidentially. I will see you there at 8:00 p.m. if that is convenient. I will bring Mrs. Carter with me."

17

They checked into the Tremont, then took a horse cab to The Versailles and arrived promptly at 8:00. On emerging from the cab, Herndon took one look at the restaurant's entrance and found himself disappointed. He had expected something grand, and instead beheld only a small wooden door, without even a doorkeeper. A small sign on the door said "Knock. Loudly!"

He did so, and the door was opened almost immediately by a middle-aged man who sported a graying goatee and a high collar.

The man looked them over, glanced at Hay's boots, which, despite Hay's best efforts, still had a bit of dried mud clinging to them from the morning, and wrinkled his nose ever so slightly. "Welcome, gentlemen. Do you by chance have a reservation?"

"No, we don't," Herndon said. "We are, however, joining Mr. Pinkerton here for dinner, and I assume he has made one. I am Mr. Herndon and this is Mr. Hay."

"Ah, yes, of course. Mr. Pinkerton did let us know you would be joining him. He has reserved a private room. I am Mr. Belmont. Please follow me."

As they walked through the restaurant, Herndon realized that the impression he had gained from the plain front door was misplaced. Inside, the eatery was the most splendid he had ever set eyes on. It had high ceilings, from which descended multiple chandeliers, each featuring a half dozen white, gas-fed globes. It had equally high windows, curtained with rich velvet drapes of a deep maroon color. Round tables draped with white tablecloths were set with bone-white china with a red rim, and to the side of each plate, gleaming crystal. Wrought-iron chairs, with matching maroon backs and seat pads surrounded each table.

Belmont led them to a private room whose entrance was a door next to the huge, carved wooden bar that flanked one side of the room. The room was small, with a single round table in the middle. There were no windows. There were four chairs.

"Mr. Pinkerton will be joining you very shortly," Belmont said, and left.

No sooner had Belmont left than a door in the back wall opened, and Pinkerton came through, preceded by a tall woman in a black dress. Her most arresting feature, though, was a toile hat decorated with three brilliant feathers, one red, one blue and one white.

"Messrs. Herndon and Hay, may I introduce Mrs. Annabelle Carter. Mrs. Carter, the gentleman on the right is William Herndon, Abraham Lincoln's law partner. The other gentleman is John Hay, who is working on the campaign."

"A pleasure to meet both of you," she said.

"And a pleasure to meet you, Mrs. Carter," Herndon said.

"Please call me Annabelle," she said.

"Let's make it first names all around, then," Herndon said.

Once they were seated, Pinkerton said, "My apologies for our late arrival. Being a Scot, I like to be on time lest I be mistaken for an Englishman."

"I thought the English were always punctual," Hay said.

"Only in comparison to the French, Mr. Hay. Only in comparison to the French."

A waiter brought the bill of fare and left. Each one consisted of three pages, one for soups, fish, oysters and poultry, one for roasts, steaks, chops, game and boiled meats, and one for puddings, pies and ice cream.

After paging through it, Herndon said, "No restaurant in Springfield has anything to compare to this."

"Welcome to Chicago," Pinkerton said. "The metropolis of the West."

"I've seen as good in New York," Hay said.

After they'd decided what they wanted, Pinkerton got up and pulled a cord on the wall. The faint tinkling of a bell on the other side could be heard. Almost instantly, the waiter reappeared and took their orders.

As soon as the waiter departed, Annabelle said, "Allan, you know that I enjoy working for you. But for the most part I have gone after thieves and burglars and a few counterfeiters. What is it you would have me do in this case?"

"I want you to take at least a week off and return to Logan Hill, the plantation on which you grew up. It is, I believe, not far from Riverview, from which the enslaved girl Lucy comes."

"What do you want me to do there?"

"Find out everything you can about the girl, including why she left when she did."

"How will that help?" Hay said. "Lucy is long gone from Riverview."

"I believe that in any investigation, it is best to start at the beginning," Pinkerton said. "The more we know about the beginnings of all of this, the better we will be able to know where to look for her."

"That doesn't make a lot of sense to me," Hay said. "Given how long she's been gone."

"I suspect Allan has further plans for detections I might under-take when I return from Kentucky," Annabelle said. "Because of my political positions, I can travel in many circles without too much suspicion. I might even be able to find out what hap-pened to the master."

"What political positions are those?" Herndon said.

"I'm a gradual abolitionist. I favor abolition, but not right away and not without compensation to the owners of slaves. Both slaveholders and abolitionists will talk to me without ran-cor, even though they may not agree with me."

Herndon was indignant. "What? Use taxpayer money to pay those who hold human beings in bondage?"

"It would be far better than the war I fear is coming if Lin-coln is elected," Annabelle said. "And much cheaper compared to what will be spent on both sides for a war."

Hay smiled. "Are you aware that Southern newspapers have said that if the Southern states secede, not one thimbleful of Southern blood will be spilled? Because all Yankees are cow-ards?"

Annabelle laughed. "My daddy would say that is God's truth. That the yellow-bellied Yankees will all run for the hills at the first whiff of gunpowder."

"That is certainly not true!" Hay said.

"I think she is trying to get a rise out of you, John," Pinker-ton said.

"Only a little," Annabelle said and smiled a very broad smile. "In any case, what do we know about Lucy? Especially, what does she looks like?"

"I can help with that," Hay said. "Before we left Springfield, I went to the federal courthouse and looked up the petition filed there by the slave owner."

"What did it say?" Annabelle said.

"I copied the key parts," Hay said. He pulled two pieces of paper from an inside pocket of his jacket. "Here, I'll read it to you. 'That petitioner, Ezekiel Goshorn, is personally acquainted with Lucy Battelle, aged about twelve years, and knows her well; that she was born on his plantation of Riverview in Kentucky and is enslaved for life. Petitioner is her lawful owner.'"

"What a chilling way to describe someone," Herndon said. *"Enslaved for life."*

Hay resumed reading. "'Petitioner has not recently measured Lucy but believes that she is approximately five feet six inches tall. She is of very light complexion, a mulatto he would say, with gray eyes. She is slender and very handsome for a mulatto. Her head is what is called wooly, but petitioner believes that she has likely shaved her head and now wears some type of wig that has been supplied to her by others.

"'Petitioner has not seen the slave naked in recent years but believes that her breasts have not yet come in and her hips have not yet widened, so she might be taken for a boy.

"'The slave girl was being taken to St. Louis to be sold to a legitimate slaver there when she absconded from the wagon in which she was being transported.'"

"What is a *legitimate* slaver?" Herndon said. "Are there illegitimate slavers?"

"It means a slaver who is bonded," Pinkerton said. "Someone who won't take your slave on consignment, sell her south and not pay you what you are due when the sale goes through."

Hay continued. "Here's the rest of it. 'Petitioner believes Lucy is now in custody in Springfield, Illinois.'"

"The file also contains the final court order," Hay said. "The judge found that the petitioner had proved ownership and ordered everyone, including the United States marshal, to assist him in the slave's repatriation to Kentucky."

"There is one more thing to discuss," Pinkerton said.

He was interrupted by the arrival of the waiter and an assistant, their arms stacked high with plates of food.

"The owner instructed that your order should go ahead of all the others," the waiter said. "It appears you are important." He said it in such a flat tone that Herndon couldn't tell whether he approved or disapproved. Or didn't care.

"Please thank the owner on our behalf," Pinkerton said.

After the waiter and his helper had departed, Carter said, "What was the one more thing you wanted to discuss, Allan?"

"Whether we want to try to find out what has happened to the slave owner, too."

"I vote not to bother," Hay said.

"I am not so sure," Herndon said. "Lincoln instructed us to try to find them both. He must have his political reasons."

"We have little choice," Annabelle said. "I grew up with Ezekiel Goshorn's sons. All five of them. I'm sure that at least one of them has already gone north to look for him."

"How well do you know the sons?" Herndon said.

"We went to the same church, attended the same schoolhouse and then had the same tutor, who taught me, them and my sisters together at one plantation or the other. And we attended the same social events. I even had to dance with them." She wrinkled her nose at the memory.

"What are they like?" Pinkerton said.

"All thugs, wealthy due to the efforts of, really, their grandfather, but none of their own. But that fortune is fading fast because their father is so bad at business."

18

Annabelle was not enthused by her assignment. She had come to like investigating more ordinary crimes, in part because it was apolitical. Lately, all people talked about was the election, which meant that all people talked about was slavery. Yes, they also talked about the deep corruption of the Buchanan administration, but in the end, it was endless talk about slavery.

She also didn't like going home. Lately, she had been more dutiful about it because her father was ill. But that didn't make going back any better.

She telegraphed her mother that she would be coming and packed for a one-week trip. Before she left for the station, she went to see Pinkerton.

"Allan, I really don't fully understand my assignment. Am I simply to find out, if I can, where these people are, or am I to go and locate them?"

"You are to get as close to them as you can without putting yourself in danger. And you can always ask the local police for assistance. Your Pinkerton badge—if you want to reveal who you work for—should help with that."

"Yes, usually the police welcome our assistance," she said. "Unless, of course, they are themselves the crooks."

"There is that, yes. But in case you need it, here's a letter of introduction from me addressed to 'Whom It May Concern.'" He reached inside his jacket pocket and handed her an envelope. "This introduces you as a trusted Pinkerton detective and requests their assistance. I am well-enough known that it should work for you almost anywhere and especially with the police."

"Thank you, Allan."

"I'd take a gun during this investigation if I were you." He walked over to a cabinet against the wall, opened a drawer, pulled out a small revolver, handed it to her and said, "I know you're expert with weapons, but have you practiced lately?"

"Yes. They said I am still a very good shot." She turned the gun over in her hand. "I suppose it will fit in my handbag."

"You should also draw the cash you need from Mr. Striker. Take a lot. You never know when you might need to..."

She finished his sentence for him. "Grease the wheels of justice."

He laughed. "Something like that."

"I have a question," she said. "Why does it make any sense to try to find these people? How will it help Lincoln?"

"I might agree with you, Annabelle, but Abraham Lincoln has very good political instincts—against great odds he captured the Republican nomination for president from much better-known men. I have to trust his view that finding these people will help."

"One more thing. If Lucy's not dead, isn't it likely she's already in Canada?"

"That is possible."

"Since it's no secret you're a station on the Railroad, Allan, can't you just make an inquiry?"

"Would that I might, but one of the guiding principles is for each person on the Railroad to know as little as possible. Hence, I have helped deliver travelers to a station near a steamer that will take them across Lake Michigan, but I don't know where that steamer goes. And I don't know a single soul in Canada who is involved. So I have no one to ask."

"Alright, then. I will go forth and try my best."

"Good luck, Annie!"

"Don't call me that."

He smiled. "Good luck, Annabelle."

Her trip to Logan Hill, by train, ferry and, finally, by coach, took three days. She had telegraphed her mother that she was coming, so when the coach clattered noisily up the long gravel driveway, her mother and two of her sisters who still lived at home had lined up on the veranda to greet her. The mansion's six stately white pillars rose up alongside them. The pillars were peeling and looked to Annabelle as if they needed a fresh coat of paint. She also noticed that the servants who worked in the house—she tried to avoid calling them slaves—were missing. Her thoughts on all of that were quickly swallowed up by the hugs and kisses of her family.

She didn't initially see her father and thought for a second that the news was going to be very bad, but then she spied him sitting in shadow on a straight-backed wooden chair, somewhat back from the doorway into the house. He was staring straight ahead with no expression on his face.

She glanced over at him, and then at her mother with a questioning look. "Is Daddy...?"

"No, dear. He still has his mind. He's just within himself a lot these days." Her mother looked over at her father and said, "You're still with us, aren't you, Jed?"

Her father grunted, in what Annabelle took to be a yes. She walked over and gave him a hug and a kiss on the top of his nearly bald head, which caused him to grunt again. "I love you, Daddy," she said. He didn't respond.

After her mother got her settled in her old room—it didn't look much different than it had when she'd left, eight years before—she said, "What's really wrong with Daddy?"

"No one knows, dear. He's been like this for months, and the doctors have no idea what it is. He doesn't say much, but every once in a while he gets going, and it's usually an incoherent babble about politics, and slavery, and that damned Abraham Lincoln and so on. Then, on rare occasion, he's totally lucid. But not today, obviously."

"Is there anything I can do to help, Mama?"

"I don't think so. But just you being here is a big lift for me. In fact, I want to have a party in your honor. I've already invited the neighbors, and the children your own age who are still at home. Perhaps now that you have no husband, you'll even find an eligible young man among them."

Annabelle ignored her mother's comment and said, "I hope you haven't invited the Goshorn boys. You know how much I dislike them." In saying it, she felt a bit guilty because that is exactly whom she wanted her mother to invite.

"Of course, I've invited them, Annie. They are friends of many years."

"I've asked you a thousand times, Mama, not to call me Annie."

"That's your name! Annabelle was just something we put down on the baptismal record because it was the name your father's grandmother went by."

"Alright, the Goshorn boys are coming, then. So be it. All of them?"

"Just four. The oldest one, Amasa, has gone north to look for his father, who's missing. Let us go downstairs and have some cake and coffee, and I'll tell you all about it."

19

Her mother's tale of what had happened to Ezekiel Goshorn, while elaborate in the telling, added little to what Annabelle already knew. She ended by saying that the eldest son, Amasa, had left several days ago to find his father. But when Amasa departed, he had admitted to his mother, Mrs. Goshorn, that he had no idea where to start looking.

Annabelle listened quietly, clucked occasionally as if in sympathy and, when her mother had finally finished, said, "Well, I hope Amasa finds him alive and in good health."

"May that wish sound in God's ear, Annie."

Annabelle stifled her complaint about her name. It was hopeless. "Yes, Mama, let us hope God will hear all of our prayers."

Throughout, they had been nibbling on small cakes and sipping coffee. Annabelle noticed that some of the plates and cups were chipped, which surprised her. Normally, if even a few plates became chipped, her mother banished them out to the slave quarters, and a whole new set was promptly ordered.

"Mama, does anyone know what happened to the slave who escaped?"

"Lucy?"

"Whatever her name is."

"It's Lucy. Maybelline Goshorn told me that girl'd been nothing but trouble. She was insolent and couldn't be made to work even in the main house, where the work's a lot easier. Mr. Goshorn finally decided to sell her south, although Maybelline didn't think they'd get much for her if they were honest about the merchandise."

"Was she on her way to be sold when she escaped?"

Her mother gave her an appraising look. "I would hardly know. Where did you hear that?"

"It's a rumor in Chicago, where people seem very interested in the whole affair. In the office I work in, the girls like to gossip about that kind of thing."

"You know I don't like you working as a clerk."

"I like my job. And working in an accounting firm is very safe."

"Perhaps so. But to be blunt about it, you're already twenty-six, which means before you know it you'll be thirty and no one will want you. No one. You need to get married."

"Thirty is still four years away, Mama. And I've already been married, remember?"

"How could I forget? That man was a worthless son of a bitch."

"Mama! Such language."

"Anyway, you need to come on back here to live and get married again to the right kind of man."

"The only way I'm coming back here is to be buried."

"Well, then, come back to be buried beside a husband."

Annabelle sighed deeply. "Mama, I would be delighted to fall in love again, this time, as you put it, with the right kind of man. But men don't seem much interested in me these days. Could be a lot of reasons, but they just don't seem to be."

"Like what reasons?"

Annabelle paused. Her mother was utterly unaware of her detective job. "Most likely because I'm divorced. Now let's change the topic."

Her mother poured a heavy dose of cream into her coffee, something that would normally have been attended to by a maid.

"Mama, where are the servants? Did you go all modern and give them a day off?"

Her mother didn't immediately answer, but just stirred the cream in her coffee around and around. Finally, she said, "Unless we really need them in the house, they are working now in the tobacco drying sheds. We've been really shorthanded there."

"Polly isn't working there, is she?" Polly was the slave who had really raised Annabelle and her sisters from infancy. She had to be in her late sixties by now and the last time Annabelle had seen her, she was bent over by age.

"No. Of course not," her mother said. "She was the one slave we have kept in the house. She is upstairs resting right now. She is not well."

"If you ever send her to the sheds…"

Her mother's face grew red. "What, Annie? You'll come back here from your wage-paying job in Chicago and help us run this place?"

"You're right, Mama. I'm sorry. But why are you shorthanded in the sheds?"

Her mother sighed deeply. "Truth be told, we've been having a hard time. Your father doesn't manage very well these days and his overseer left, so things slip."

"That can't be the only problem. What else?"

"A blight in one large field. And you'd think shortages would drive up the price. But for some reason the price paid for tobacco is dropping like a stone in a pond."

"So you're cash short."

"Yes."

"What about the bank?"

"They're not lending. Afraid of what that Abraham Lincoln person is going to do if he's elected. If he frees the slaves, everyone around here will be ruined."

"Lincoln says he has no intention of freeing the slaves."

"I don't believe him."

"I do. But what does being cash short have to do with being shorthanded in the tobacco sheds?"

"We sold some of the men who used to work there."

Annabelle sat bolt upright. "Did you break up families?"

"No, we didn't."

"But they thought about it!" The voice was that of her youngest sister, Suzanna, who had just turned sixteen. She had apparently sneaked into the room at some point.

"Suzanna, I have told you more than once that it's rude to sneak into a room like that," her mother said.

"But such fun, Mama!"

"Fun or not, stop telling your sister stories that aren't true. We *never* thought about breaking up families."

"Yes, you did. I heard you and Daddy talking."

There was a sudden silence in the kitchen. After a few seconds, their mother said, "Well, I never," got up from her chair and marched out, slamming the door behind her.

"Annabelle, Mama and Daddy are in desperate financial condition," Suzanna said. "I know. I listen."

"I didn't know."

"They have kept it from you, but it has been over a year since you were last here."

"I know. I've been busy, and I really had no idea."

"Why are you here anyway?" Suzanna squinted her eyes and held her sister's stare without blinking.

Annabelle looked away and shrugged. "I just needed to get

away for a while. Work has become taxing. I thought I could relax here for a few days. But it appears not."

"Perhaps the party Mama is planning for you will be fun. It's tomorrow night, and there will be dancing." She twirled around.

"Perhaps. But she has invited the Goshorn brothers, whom I despise."

"They can be fun."

"Perhaps for you, Suzanna."

"The one you dislike most is away, looking for his father, who disappeared while chasing after an escaped slave named Lucy."

"The story of Lucy and the riot in Springfield is all over the Chicago papers. Did you know her?"

"A little. You know how slaves and white children from the plantations sometimes play together some when we're all young?" She twirled again and kept going.

"Uh-huh."

Suzanna stopped twirling, looked at Annabelle and said, "That's why you came back, isn't it?"

Annabelle realized she had a decision to make. Suzanna had always been her favorite sibling. She had been ten when Suzanna was born and she had helped raise her. So they shared a bond more like mother and daughter than sisters. And a lot of confidences.

"Can you keep a secret, Suzanna?"

"Of course. Tell me, tell me!"

"Cross your heart and hope to die?"

"You taught me that when I was six. And you were..."

"Sixteen."

"Have I ever gone back on those words, Annabelle? And notice I didn't call you Annie." She started spinning again.

"I did notice, and no, you haven't."

Suzanna grinned, showing a crooked tooth, and put her hand over her heart. "Cross my heart and hope to die, I won't tell anyone what you tell me."

"Alright, I need to find Lucy."

"To help them get her back?"

"No. The opposite. My employer is part of the Underground Railroad and wants to help her escape to Canada."

"Oh. Well, I don't know where she is. But I think Polly does. She's friends with Lucy's mother." She twirled once again and fell down from the dizziness, laughing.

20

Annabelle had gone to visit Polly that very afternoon. When Annabelle found her, she was no longer upstairs, like her mother had said. Instead, she was sitting in the old, ladder-back wooden chair in the small room off the kitchen that she'd always sat in when she wasn't working. Annabelle saw Polly before Polly saw her, and the same thought went through her head that passed through it every time she came back and laid eyes on her: Polly had been more a mother to her than her own mother, except that, as Annabelle passed out of childhood, they had become separated by the impenetrable wall of slavery, woven over centuries by law and custom.

Polly turned her head at the noise of Annabelle coming in and smiled a broad smile. She rose to greet her, but made it only halfway up before grabbing on to the arms of the chair. As Annabelle rushed to help, Polly said, "I will do it myself, child!" and pushed herself to a standing position.

Annabelle hugged her and was shocked. Polly had always been thin, but now she was not just more bent than the last time she'd seen her, but almost bony. Her face was gaunt, and her once jet-black hair was now totally gray. "Polly, you are clearly not well."

"It's my age, Annie. I will be seventy next month. If they got my birth month right, and my mama thought they did. Anyway, I am old, child. Old. It is so good to see you."

"Please sit back down."

Polly did, but made a grunting sound as she more or less fell back into the chair. Annabelle had lunged forward to help, but too late. And she thought, as she had the last time she'd been there, that she had now saved up enough money to buy Polly's freedom. But to what effect? Where would Polly go? Who would look after her? Somehow, she would figure those things out, too. She had to.

"You still working for that detective, Annie?"

"I told you what I really do is a deadly secret, Polly. You haven't told anyone, have you?"

Polly looked at her, clearly offended. "Right now, I'm only telling you. I ain't told nobody else."

"Alright. I still work for the same man, Allan Pinkerton. The best detective in the country."

"What do you detect?"

"You ask me that each time I see you."

"I do, 'cause I still don't understand what you do."

"I try to track down criminals, Polly. Bad guys. And sometimes good guys who have gone missing."

"Your sister done tell me you be looking for Lucy, too."

Annabelle realized that Suzie had not kept her secret after all and wondered if she would keep the more important one. But she might as well admit it. "Yes, I am looking for her."

"Why don't you stop lookin'?"

"Why? Do you think she's dead?"

"No, no, I got nothing 'bout where she is. I just think you will do her no good if you find her."

"I can help her be liberated. Help her find her way to Canada."

"She be finding her own way."

"But she may need help."

"I am gonna say somethin', Annie, that woulda' got me whipped by your daddy back in the old days."

"Daddy never whipped you!"

"Oh, he did. He surely did."

There was a silence as Annabelle contemplated what Polly had just said. It was probably true. It had just been kept from her by the enveloping myth of her childhood. That their plantation was just her peaceful Old Kentucky Home, and all the Darkies were happy, just like in the popular song.

"What were you going to say, Polly? No one will whip you for it, least of all me."

"When Lucy really needed you to help her—over on that plantation run by that evil Goshorn man—you weren't no way there to help."

"I didn't know."

"Did'ya try to find out?"

"No."

"Let her go. Don't go finding her. She has took her own life in her own hands. For the first time. Don't be one of them white people always tryin' to help out."

Annabelle suddenly realized that Polly didn't know. "You don't know, do you, Polly?"

"Know what?"

"Lucy was being sold south when she escaped. And then she was taken by slave catchers in Illinois. She was about to be returned back here when there was a riot in Springfield."

"Then what?"

Annabelle told her the rest of the story and finished by saying, "So you see, I *can* help her. Because half the slave catchers in Illinois are looking for her right now, but with Pinkerton's help—*if* I can find her—I can be sure she gets on the Railroad."

After that, Polly relented and told her the little she knew.

Which was that the year before, a man named Winston Green, perhaps seventeen years old, had escaped from Riverview and made it to Springfield, Illinois. The news that filtered back was that someone there had bought Winston's freedom.

In any case, Lucy had told someone, who had told someone else, who had told Polly that Lucy was going to head for Springfield to find Winston Green.

If any of that was true—and Annabelle had her doubts—she at least had some things to talk about with whichever one of the Goshorn boys showed up at the party.

As she was about to leave the room, Polly said, "Have you found love again, child?"

"No. Not yet."

"You so needs to. Or before you knows it, you will be an old lady."

As Annabelle departed, she wondered why *everyone* seemed to be after her to marry again. If truth be told, she was happy just as she was, although they all had a point that it was in many ways easier for a woman to be married. But what husband, even in this modern age, would let his wife be a detective?

For the next day and a half, Annabelle tried to forget about the world outside and focused instead on the plantation. She attempted to bring her father out of his trance, but without much success. She met with the new overseer and went over the plantation's finances. She helped him think through putting one of their pieces of land up for sale, and got his agreement that they would sell no more slaves to make ends meet. She also persuaded him to let at least some of the house slaves leave the sheds.

Annabelle also tried to do what she could for Polly. As she suspected he would, the local doctor refused to treat her. "Black bodies are very different," he said. "I wouldn't know what to do."

Then the doctor said the thing that upset her the most. "Do

let me know if she gets even worse, though, to where she really can't do any useful work."

"Why?"

"I could buy her from you—not for too much you understand—and try out an experimental treatment on her."

"One that might be too dangerous for white people until you see if it works?"

"Exactly. But if it works it could benefit everyone."

Annabelle just stared at him.

Finally, the doctor said, "I can tell you think that's evil. I just think it's practical. Which is what medicine is mostly about."

Annabelle wanted to throw him bodily out of the house, but she needed information from him, so she buried her feelings and said, "Doctor, my mother also has a little bit of the same thing that Polly does. What would you recommend for her?"

"Ah, there is a tea brewed from willow bark that can be quite helpful. You can find it in most pharmacies."

She went to the small town nearby, found that very tea at the apothecary and bought a month's supply. She showed Suzanna how to brew it and persuaded Polly to take it. She hoped it would help.

By the evening of the second day, all was ready for the party. Annabelle looked deep into the armoire in her old room and found a red party dress with a ruffled top that she'd last worn when she was twenty. Her mother permitted the seamstress to come back from the tobacco shed to adjust it, and together with a too-tight corset, it looked good.

Suzanna was going, too, even though her mother's usual rule for girls was that you had to be seventeen to attend a "grown-ups party." But she had cajoled and wheedled, and her mother had finally relented.

21

When Annabelle arrived—somewhat late, on purpose—the plantation ballroom (a separate structure her father had had built for her mother to celebrate their tenth anniversary) was already filled with people standing, sipping champagne and talking. Her mother had gone all out. Six long tables, each one able to seat ten people, were arrayed around the sides of the room. The tables were draped in elegant white damask cloths and set with the plantation's special china—bone white with a blue edge. The service, Annabelle knew, had been imported from England when the plantation had been at the height of its prosperity. Tall candelabra on each table completed the look.

In the middle was a wooden dance floor. There was no one on it, though. Her mother's strict rule was "no dancing before dinner." Well, there was actually one person on it—Suzanna—who was waltzing, sort of, by herself over in a corner, to the piece being played by the pianist, who was hammering out the newly popular *Mephisto Waltz*. It would not have been her pick, but her mother loved Liszt, and it was at least lively.

Over in another corner, she saw two fiddle players and a banjo player talking and guessed the music would become more to plantation taste in Kentucky later. She had a request in mind.

The music stopped not long after she arrived, and she spotted Slim Goshorn walking along one of the tables, clearly trying to find his place card. Annabelle knew exactly where it was because she had earlier rearranged them so they would be seated together.

She walked down the tables, pretended to locate her own, and called out, "Slim. We're together. Over here!"

He turned, and a look passed across his face that Annabelle read as at first dread and then anticipation: dread being the part that came from her having tormented him all through their childhood with her superior intelligence; anticipation from, perhaps, the thought that she had come back to belatedly accept his proposal of marriage. She had turned him down by explaining that she was enjoying seeing the wider world and had no desire to come back to Kentucky. That had been seven years ago.

After they greeted each other and had gotten seated, she said, "I am so sorry to hear about your father."

He looked startled. "What have you heard?"

"Well, that he was attacked by an abolitionist mob in Springfield and that they haven't found his body yet."

"You think he's dead?"

"That's what I heard."

"Where did you hear that?"

"You know I work at a bank in Chicago, right?"

"Of course. You're the one girl who got out of here."

"One of the girls in the office is married to a detective of some sort, who has a friend who has a friend who works for an agency that looks for escaped slaves."

"And you heard he's likely dead?"

"Yes. I'm so sorry." She put her hand on his shoulder, as if to comfort him. "But it's far from certain. You know how rumors are."

He didn't say anything in response, but she thought she saw a tear on his cheek.

"Slim, my mother said Amasa went to look for your father. Have you heard anything from him?"

"He's got a lead, but that's it."

"That's good. Perhaps that means he's still alive. What about the slave girl?"

"We assume she's dead or gone to Canada. We don't care anymore. She was a useless piece of dirt in any case. Amasa is using the lead to look for our father, nothing more."

Now was the time Annabelle needed to use all of her wiles.

"Well, I hope it's a good one." She took his chin between her fingers and turned his face gently toward her. "I know how close you are to your father." She wiped the tear from his cheek. "If there's anything I can do to help when I'm up in Chicago, please let me know."

"Thank you."

"Has the lead worked out at all?"

"Not yet, Annie."

She gritted her teeth and baited the hook. "I'm going to tell you a secret, but you have to agree to keep it strictly to yourself."

"Alright."

"I've applied for a job at Pinkerton National Detective Agency. Have you heard of it?"

"Of course!"

"Well, it's just a job as a clerk, but if I get it I could always ask one of the detectives there to follow up on your lead. They may have contacts you don't have that could make it go somewhere."

"I will keep that in mind. And again, thank you."

"My mother knows how to reach me."

She had taken a risk, of course, in mentioning Pinkerton. She worked on her salad for a few minutes, waiting to see if Slim would bite.

After a while, Slim looked at her and said, "I've been thinking about it. Much as I like you, Annie, I'm unlikely to tell you the lead we've got. You seem much too interested. And I know you're an abolitionist of some sort."

"That I am."

After that, she and Slim chatted amiably through dinner without further discussion of the lead. She even agreed to dance with him when the fiddles and the banjo took over from the piano. Mostly, they were playing a Stephen Foster medley, and one of the men was singing. It was hard to dance to, but they did their best.

At some point, people began to sing along. She cringed when they got to "Oh Susanna!" because she was so deeply offended by the lyrics in the second verse. But it gave her an idea.

When the party was nearing its end, she went over to the man who was singing and said, "I have a request."

"Of course, miss. The party is in your honor, after all."

She knew that what she was about to request would totally destroy her plan with Slim, but he'd made clear that the plan wouldn't work anyway, and she couldn't resist.

"Can y'all play 'My Old Kentucky Home, Good Night'?"

The man looked at her, clearly startled. "We know your mother, and we don't reckon she will appreciate that."

"Why ever not?"

"Because it's an abolitionist ballad."

"It is? I never knew."

"It is."

"Please play it anyway. As you said, this party is in my honor, and it's my special request."

"Alright, miss, but if your mother comes over here, furious, it was *your* idea."

"It certainly was."

As the first fiddle picked up the tune, and one of the men began to sing the lyrics, Annabelle watched heads snap up all over the room. Seconds later, Slim stormed over to her. "Was this song your request?"

"Yes. I love the tune. Is there a problem?"

"It's an abolitionist ballad. In fact, it's Fred Douglass's favorite song."

"You call that famous man *Fred*?"

"Frederick is too fancy a name for a former slave."

"Well, I still like the tune."

"I suppose all you radical abolitionists do."

"I'm a gradual abolitionist."

"What the hell does that mean?"

"It means that sooner or later, slavery has to end."

"Why?"

"Because it's immoral. And because every civilized nation but this one has already ended it on their territory."

"So what?"

"*So what* means—can you imagine, a hundred years from now, when all the world is free of slavery, this will be the only country that still permits it? A country whose founding document talks about all men being *created equal*?"

"The Declaration doesn't have the force of law. Only the Constitution does. And it doesn't talk about any of that stuff. Not one word."

They stood, facing one another; both had stopped talking.

Finally, Slim broke the silence and said, "Well, to go back to what we were talking about before, why should I give you our lead, even if you're only a *gradual* abolitionist? Why would you want to help my father? He is certainly not in favor of any kind of abolition. Nor am I."

"Because I don't let my politics get in the way of my friendships," she said. "And because you're a lifelong friend and neighbor. Isn't that enough?"

"No."

"Well, do let me know if you change your mind." She gave him her best smile and a tight hug, of which her mother would certainly have disapproved had she chanced to see it. Women in Kentucky didn't hug men they weren't related to. "Take good care, Slim."

As she was about to leave the party, Annabelle noticed that Suzanna was dancing with Georgie, the youngest of the Goshorn brothers. He was about Suzanna's age. They were dancing closer than her mother would approve, but her mother had apparently gone back to the main house. Annabelle caught Suzanna's eye, winked, left and went back to her room.

About an hour later, Suzanna knocked on her door, and she let her in.

"It's late. Why aren't you in bed?"

"I have something to tell you. I know what the Goshorns' lead is to where their father might be."

"You do?"

"Yes. I was sitting right down the table from you, but you were so intent on charming Slim that you didn't even notice me. Anyway, I overheard you talking about the lead. When I danced with Georgie, I wormed it out of him."

"Was that hard?"

"He was hard, but it wasn't hard to find out." She grinned.

"Suzanna!"

"I'm a modern girl, Annabelle."

"So it appears. What is the lead?"

"Their father—Ezekiel—has a brother who lives in a tiny town called Berlin, about fifteen miles west of Springfield. They think their father may be hiding there."

"Why does he have to hide anywhere?"

"I don't know. I wasn't smart enough to ask that. Darn."

"Don't worry. You did great."

"Thank you. I have a question, though."

"Alright. What?"

"Why did everyone get so upset when they played 'My Old Kentucky Home, Good Night'? I remember everyone played it for a little while when I was a kid, and then they just stopped."

"It's because it's an abolitionist ballad."

"It is?"

"Yes, it's about a Darkie—a slave—who misses his old Kentucky home far away. And the reason he misses it, and that it's far away, is because he's been shipped south to work in the cotton fields. Where he expects to die of backbreaking work."

"Are you an abolitionist, Annabelle?"

"Yes." She decided not to add the gradual part. "And you should be, too. Just don't mention it to Mama. Or Daddy. They won't cotton to it."

"Was that a pun?"

"Indeed it was."

"Annabelle, before you go, I need to ask. Do you have any feelings at all for Slim?"

"No. Should I?"

"He's a nice man, and if we were to put together their plantation and ours, we might be able to make it. Right now, they're both going to fail. And, well, if that happens I will have no prospects."

"He is only the second-oldest brother. He won't likely inherit."

"He says Amasa wants to leave and try his luck in Atlanta and will sell him his share on credit. So will the others. They all want out."

"Suzie, if you love Slim and he loves you, you have my blessing. Although you're only sixteen, and Mama won't let you marry 'til you're at least seventeen."

"I will be seventeen before you know it! And if you find someone, too, we can have a double wedding!"

Annabelle rolled her eyes. "Go to bed, Suzie!"

22

The White House

The weather had turned chillier, but the president was again sitting with Jeremiah Black at a small table in the greenhouse. Both were wearing overcoats, buttoned to the neck. They had been talking for over an hour.

"It will soon be too cold to meet here, Jeremiah," Buchanan said.

Black laughed and rubbed his hands together. "It is already too cold, Mr. President."

"Yes, but I am savoring the place. Next year someone else will be sitting here."

"Perhaps Lincoln will prefer the mansion to the garden."

"You still think it will be Lincoln, Jeremiah?"

"I do."

"Why? Vice President Breckinridge tells me his surrogates, who are out campaigning, have been drawing large crowds."

"Mr. President, excuse me, but unless my plan works it's going to be Lincoln."

"What about the crowds that Breckinridge tells me about?"

Buchanan had already drained half a bottle of liquor and was slurring his words.

"The crowds have been in the South and in the Border states," Black said. "In Pennsylvania and Ohio, his surrogates draw more boos than people, if anyone comes at all."

"What is your source for this?"

"I have dozens of newspapers and magazines brought to me from all over the country every week. They are the pulse of the nation."

"Speaking of pulse, would you like a refill?"

Black looked at his glass, swirled the little bit that was left in the bottom and said, "The day is almost done. Another won't hurt, and it *is* cold in here."

Buchanan took the bottle and filled Black's glass near to the brim. Then he did the same with his own.

Glancing at the bottle, Black said, "We'll soon need another."

Buchanan held the bottle up to the fading light, examined it carefully and said, "You are right! Yes you are, sir!" He looked over to Washburn, who was standing by the doorway into the greenhouse. "Mr. Washburn, could you please bring us another Old Overholt?"

"Of course, Mr. President."

Buchanan took a large sip from his glass and said, "So, Jeremiah, now that we are refortified, with more supply soon on the way, how do you read the pulse of the nation, as you put it?"

"Exactly the way I read it several weeks ago. Lincoln is going to win."

"And only God knows what he will do."

"He likely does not know himself, Mr. President."

"How is the effort with the radical abolitionist coming along?"

"Abby Kelley Foster?"

"Yes, her. You were going to have her indicted and also try to locate both the escaped slave and her owner, dead or alive."

"You preferred the owner dead, if I recall," Black said.

"Yes, but only because, to my way of thinking, that will rile up our voters more."

"Well, the slave owner has not been found, but Mrs. Foster has been indicted, as planned. People are losing interest, though. The newspapers talked of nothing else for a week, but are now largely silent about it."

Buchman was silent for a while, then blurted out, "If the slave is found dead, it will rile up the abolitionists. But if her master is found dead, it will put people, North *and* South, in fear for their lives."

"You said that several weeks ago, Mr. President."

"I will say it again! Southern women are huddled around their hearths afraid of a slave uprising. A slave owner murdered in Springfield by an abolitionist mob will make them even more afraid. And *Northern* women will be afraid, too, and will get their husbands to vote for anyone but Lincoln."

Black paused for a moment. "I am not sure that finding the slave master dead will accomplish that. In any case, the War Department seconded me one of their own to look for both the slave and the master. His name is Major Robert Hedpeth."

"Did he find them?"

"Not yet, and his report is not encouraging. I've taken the liberty of inviting him here so you can hear from him directly. He is in an anteroom."

Buchanan turned to the usher and said, "Mr. Washburn, please locate Major Hedpeth and bring him in."

"Here to the greenhouse?"

"Yes."

While they waited, Black briefed Buchanan on Hedpeth's background. When Hedpeth came in, resplendent in full dress uniform, with all of his medals showing, he saluted Buchanan, who stood up and returned the salute. "Major, welcome to the White House. Mr. Black tells me you are a hero of the Mexican War. And I see you have the decorations for it." Buchanan pointed to the gold Palmetto Medal on Hedpeth's chest, which he knew had been awarded by the South Carolina legislature to its officers who served in the war.

"I would not say a hero, Mr. President, just someone who served his country—and his state—in battle."

"I say you are a hero to us all," Buchanan said.

"Why, thank you, sir."

"Please sit down, Major. We're drinking Old Overholt. Will you join us?"

"I'd be pleased to, Mr. President."

Buchanan turned to Washburn and said, "Mr. Washburn, will you bring another glass for the major?"

"I will be right back with it, Mr. President."

They chatted about nothing in particular until the clean glass arrived. Buchanan poured a full glass for Hedpeth, freshened his own and Black's, and raised his glass. "To you, Major, for your service to our country."

They clinked, and the president said, "Major, I understand you went out to Illinois. What did you find?"

"In truth, Mr. President, almost nothing of use. I interviewed many people in Springfield, but could not find a single person who said they were in the square when the riot occurred."

"What else did you do?"

"I spent several days in small towns around Springfield, trying to find out where either the slave or the slave master might be hiding. Once again, no one had seen them."

"So you found nothing."

"Not quite. I am planning to return to Springfield and interview a young newspaper reporter, who is also the proprietor of his own newly minted newspaper. I brought a copy with me."

Using his left hand, Major Hedpeth reached into an inner pocket of his uniform jacket, extracted a folded-up copy of *The Radical Abolitionist* and handed it to the president.

Buchanan examined it and said, "This lead article is an account of Abby Kelley's speech, am I correct?"

"Yes. The reporter was there for part of it, and so the first section of the article is his own recollection. The rest he collected in interviews from those who stayed for the entire thing."

Buchanan looked over at Black. "Will we be able to use this in court when we try her?"

"Only indirectly, but yes. And in any case we can call the reporter, whose name is Clarence Artemis, to the stand to testify to what she said while he was there."

Buchanan wrinkled his brow. "Major, but why are you going all the way back to Springfield to interview this Artemis person?"

"Because as I was leaving Springfield, one of my companions on the train, to whom I had disclosed my frustrations at not finding the slave owner—I was not hiding my search—told me this Artemis fellow might know where the slave owner is."

"So you're going back to get Artemis to lead you to him?"

"Yes, Mr. President, right away. Whether the slave master is in hiding or holed up somewhere because he is injured, I plan to bring him back to testify to the horror of the mob that swept him up."

Buchanan was silent for a moment. Finally, he said, "Perhaps you will find him dead."

"I should hope not!"

Buchanan glanced over at Black, then looked back at Hedpeth and said, "Well, either way, it will be useful to find out what has happened to him."

"Yes, of course."

Buchanan stood up abruptly, which caused Black and Hedpeth to stand, too. "Major, thank you for coming. And again, thank you for your service to our wonderful country."

"I hope to serve our country again in the coming war, Mr. President."

Buchanan was taken aback. "Why do you think there will be a war, Major?"

"Well, sir, if Lincoln is elected—and pardon me for saying that looks likely, even though he will not have my vote—then at least several Southern states are going to secede."

"At least South Carolina has so threatened," Buchanan said. "But they might yet be dissuaded if Lincoln—or whoever is elected—offers them a plan that protects both slavery and their honor."

"Perhaps, Mr. President, but if they do secede, I assume whoever holds this office will use military force to prevent it. Indeed, I believe you yourself have said that there is nothing in the Constitution that permits secession."

"I did say that, Major, but my attorney general—" he pointed at Black "—has told me that there is also nothing in the Constitution that permits me to use military force to prevent it."

"May I speak candidly, Mr. President?" Black said.

"Of course, Jeremiah."

"My position is more subtle, Major. There is nothing in the Constitution that permits the president to send soldiers to make the South Carolina legislature, for example, rescind a declaration of secession should it issue one. It is a quasi-sovereign entity."

"Exactly," Buchanan said.

"But," Black said, "*if* the South Carolinians were to interfere with federal tax collectors in the ports, or interfere with federal naval activities in the ports and so forth, *then* yes, a president could use military force to upend that treason."

Hedpeth looked back and forth between Buchanan and Black, then said, "Either way—soldiers to make the legislature recant or soldiers to ensure that federal law is followed—seem likely to have the same outcome—a war between the states."

"Exactly!" Buchanan said. "And that is why I will not send troops to do as Mr. Black suggests. Nor, I hope, will any future president."

Buchanan looked at Hedpeth and could see that he was becoming uncomfortable at witnessing a disagreement between his commander-in-chief and the attorney general. "Thank you for coming, Major," Buchanan said.

"It has been an honor to meet you, sir." He saluted. "And Godspeed."

"Mr. Washburn will show you out."

After Hedpeth had left, Buchanan turned to Black and said, "I am not using force, Jeremiah, to prevent a state from leaving. The major is right. Your solution inevitably leads to war. It is too clever by half."

"It's nevertheless my view," Black said. "To which you are entitled."

"Well, let Lincoln start a war if he wants to. Then he can endure history's wrath for the utter foolishness of having done so."

The two of them sat in silence for a few minutes. Finally, Buchanan said, "Would you like another, Jeremiah?"

"No, Mr. President. Thank you, but I need to get home for supper. So I will bid you a pleasant evening." He raised his glass in salute.

Buchanan turned to Washburn. "Has Miss Lane returned as yet?"

"No, sir."

"Well, please see who else is in the house who might join me. I prefer company tonight."

23

Springfield
Late September

Clarence was at his desk in his small room above the store, trying to think what to try next. The articles he'd written for *The Radical Abolitionist* about the Abby Kelley riot, as it was being called (people seemed often to ignore her married name), had been a sensation. But interest had quickly faded. And subscriptions to the paper had not increased much. He did take notice when William Herndon, Lincoln's law partner, came by to subscribe. When he'd tried to feel Herndon out (Herndon was a known abolitionist) as to whether Lincoln himself was reading the paper, the man had been noncommittal. In fact, he had been noncommittal about almost everything having to do with Lincoln, the campaign, abolitionists and everything else Clarence asked him about.

Even the publication of the boy's drawing of the overturned coach in *Harper's Weekly*, with an attribution to *The Radical Abolitionist*, had failed to increase interest in his publication. Or at least not in Springfield.

He had considered that renting a small office for the paper, with its name over the door, might help to raise its profile—*if* his parents would pay for it and if an office could even be found. With Lincoln now the Republican candidate for president of the United States, every large newspaper in the country had sent someone to report from Springfield, and the national Republican Party apparatus had taken up residence, as well. Not to mention the hangers-on who'd arrived by the dozens, hoping to obtain for themselves one of the hundreds of positions in the federal government that would be changing hands if Lincoln were elected president of the United States, as now seemed ever more likely. As a result, it was hard even to find an empty storeroom to let.

Even as he uttered the words to himself—*president of the United States*—it seemed to him astonishing that a hick from nowhere (because that's what Springfield seemed to him and almost everyone from the East) might soon assume the highest office in the land. On the other hand, Lincoln was clearly an enormously clever hick to have achieved what he had so far. Clarence hankered to talk to him when he wasn't wearing his nightshirt.

He had one other thing to ponder, as well. Two weeks ago, he had received a tip as to where the missing slave owner might be hiding—in a small town several miles away. He wanted badly to go there and interview the man. But he didn't want to go alone. Several people he'd approached about accompanying him had turned him down.

His reverie was interrupted by a knock on the door. When he opened it, a very short man stood there, decked out in full military uniform, his chest covered with campaign medals.

"I'm Major Robert Hedpeth," he said. "Are you Clarence Artemis?"

"I am indeed."

"May I come in?"

"Of course. To what do I owe the pleasure of your visit?"

"I am conducting an investigation."

"On whose behalf?"

"I cannot tell you that, Mr. Artemis, until I receive your pledge of compete confidentiality."

Clarence paused to think about it. It was in truth a new request for him. Up until that point, everyone he had talked with had been most anxious to be quoted by name in his newspaper. Or at least they had raised no objection.

"I suppose I could agree to that," Clarence said. "So long as I can tell you at some point that I cannot go on. That what you have told me is so important that I must report it. I am a reporter after all."

"That is agreeable," the major said. "I can now tell you that I was sent here by the president of the United States."

"President Buchanan?"

"He is, for the moment, our only president." He smiled. "So far as I am aware. Do you know of another?"

"No, of course not. But he will not be in office very much longer."

"Mr. Artemis, even when President Buchanan's successor is elected on November 6—a date still well over a month away—whoever it turns out to be will not be inaugurated as our new president until March 4."

"I am quite confident it will be Lincoln taking that oath," Clarence said.

"Well, whoever it is, you must be aware that, until March 4, President Buchanan's powers remain fully intact." He paused. "Fully."

"Yes, of course. And so, Major, what does our President Buchanan, through you, wish to ask of me?"

"May I sit down while we talk? I have been somewhat diminished by my war experiences."

"Yes. Please excuse my not having offered you a seat earlier."

"That is of no consequence."

"Ah, but it is to me because my mother taught me the importance of being polite to all. As you can see, I have but two chairs. The big stuffed one, and the one with the cane back. Please take whichever one might please you the most."

"Thank you. I think I will rest my weary bones in the large one." And with that, he sat down in it and let out a sigh.

Clarence took the other chair and said, "You were, I think, about to tell me what you want to know."

"I am looking for the escaped slave, Lucy Battelle, and for her missing master, Ezekiel Goshorn."

"Why do you think I might know where they are?"

"Because someone who knows you has told me that you may know at least where the slave owner is."

"Who told you that?"

Hedpeth threw his hands up in the air and laughed. "This may sound odd, but a man on a train told me. And I neglected to ask him his name."

"What did he look like?"

"Very thin, almost bald, piercing blue eyes."

"Ah, that would be my printer. He apparently cannot keep his mouth closed."

"So it's true."

"Yes. I have some supposed information on the slave owner's whereabouts."

"If you could find him before others do, it would make a great story for your paper."

Clarence didn't reply immediately. Here was a man who could accompany him to find the missing man, and was an army officer to boot. And yet.

"Mr. Artemis," Major Hedpeth said, "you haven't responded to my offer to help you."

"To be candid, Major, I'm not sure that I want to help out President Buchanan."

"Why ever not? He is, until March 4, the president of all of us."

"Perhaps so, but he is an apologist for slavery."

Hedpeth did not respond. After a long silence that was on the edge of becoming uncomfortable, he finally said, "He is my commander-in-chief, and I am therefore loath to get into a discussion of his politics, just as I will be about Mr. Lincoln's politics should he be elected."

"So you are asking me to help out a slavery-loving president?"

"I don't think it's fair to call him slavery-loving. Unlike many of his predecessors, he has never owned slaves himself. And he has condemned slavery."

"He has also supported the Fugitive Slave Act, praised the *Dred Scott* decision and attempted to bring Kansas into the Union as a slave state."

Hedpeth stood up and said, "Mr. Artemis, I think I am wasting both your time and mine. I will have to continue my investigations without your assistance. But I thank you for your willingness to see me."

"Wait a moment, please, Major. Are you familiar with what we in the West have recently come to call a newspaper scoop?"

"No."

"It is a term that means for a paper to get an important story no one else has gotten yet, and publish it first."

"I see. And?"

"I will give you a lead as to where you might find Goshorn if, in exchange, you will let me know, before you tell anyone else, what you find out."

"Before the president?"

"Exactly."

"But, Mr. Artemis, if I find Goshorn and need to involve the sheriff, for example, then he will know first. And I won't likely be able to prevent him from telling others."

"There is an easy solution to that, Major. I will go with you."

"That would be most unusual, Mr. Artemis."

"To be blunt, take it or leave it."

"Alright, you can come. But what about the slave, Lucy, Mr. Artemis? Do you also know where she might be?"

"I have no information about her. She is likely dead or already in Canada."

"I see. Well, where do you suggest we look for the slave master?"

"In a small town not too far from here. I have learned from reliable sources that Goshorn has a brother there."

"What is the name of the town?"

"I'll tell you when we're ready to depart. Tomorrow morning at 7:00?"

"Do you have a carriage, Mr. Artemis?"

"No, but I'm sure you can locate one to hire, Major."

24

Berlin, Illinois

They left for Berlin, which was about fifteen miles west of Springfield, at the crack of dawn the next day, riding in a rented two-horse carriage. Before they climbed aboard, Hedpeth stuffed a large satchel into the storage compartment behind the seats.

"What's in there?" Clarence said.

"A shovel, among other things."

"Why do we need a shovel?"

"All well-equipped soldiers carry a shovel on a mission like this. They're useful for many things."

"I've never seen anyone carry one in Boston" was all Clarence could think of to say, and he forgot to ask what else might be in the satchel.

The road to Berlin was terrible—ruts and bumps everywhere—and it took them all morning and then some to get there. When they finally arrived, they jumped down and spent several minutes rubbing their butts to try to soothe the pain that the constant bucking of the contraption had caused them both.

Berlin qualified as a town, but only barely. It consisted of perhaps a dozen small houses, laid out on two streets that crossed at right angles. Where the roads met, there was a tiny general store and a weathered sign for a blacksmith, hung high on the side of the building next door. Not a soul was to be seen.

Fields spread out in all directions from the town's center. Most had been harvested, leaving only a few tattered cornstalks and, here and there on the ground, some scattered corncobs. There were also two large barns, one in good repair, painted bright red, and the other unpainted and near to falling down.

"There doesn't appear to be anyone here," Major Hedpeth said to no one in particular, but since Clarence was within earshot, he answered. "Perhaps they're out in the fields."

Hedpeth gestured at the empty fields around them. "I don't see anyone."

They walked together into the blacksmith shop, whose doors stood open. Inside there was the usual equipment, as well as a banked fire in the forge, but no blacksmith. A back door led to a small stable, but there were no horses in it.

They walked back out to the road and had resolved to go house-to-house and knock on doors when a voice from somewhere up above shouted, "Are ye gentlemen looking for the blacksmith?"

Clarence looked up and saw a woman with blond pigtails leaning out a second-story window above the blacksmith shop.

"No," Clarence said, "we're not looking for the blacksmith, or at least not specifically."

"Well, then, what are ye doing here?" the woman said.

"We are looking for a man whose last name is Goshorn," Clarence said.

"Ye don't know his first name?"

"No."

"Well, that's passing odd if ye ask me," she said.

"It's just because we know his brother, Ezekiel Goshorn—"

Clarence considered that just a small, inconsequential journalistic lie in aid of getting a story "—and we think Ezekiel may be visiting his brother here in Berlin. But we don't know the brother's exact address."

"Odder still," she said. "Why do ye want to find this Ezekiel?"

"We have urgent news from his family back in Kentucky," Clarence said. It was true, he figured, in a certain sense.

"Alright," she said. "The two of you look harmless enough, even the one in uniform. Clem Goshorn has a farm about two miles that way." She pointed down the south-facing road. "He calls it Good Luck Farm."

"We thank you," Clarence said, and tipped his cap.

"Good luck finding Good Luck Farm," she said, laughing. She withdrew and closed the shutters with a bang.

They got back in the carriage and headed south. After they'd gone only a short distance, Clarence looked at Hedpeth and said, "It's lonely out here. Perhaps we should have brought a gun."

"The satchel behind us holds a long gun, two pistols and plenty of ammunition."

The road to Good Luck Farm was even worse than the road from Springfield to Berlin. The ruts were at times so deep that they had to urge the horses off the road and onto the field and then back onto the road again some distance later. After an hour of painful travel, they finally came upon a split-rail fence with a gate. A sign in the shape of a four-leaf clover was attached to the gate with rope. Someone had written *Good Luck Farm* on it in crude lettering.

They opened the unlocked gate and drove down the long driveway, at the end of which stood a small white house with a steep roof. There was no answer at the front door when they knocked, and no sign of anyone being inside.

"I guess we will need to try the barn," Clarence said, gesturing across a pasture at a large barn that was painted red.

"We will," Hedpeth said. "But I'm guessing we'll have no luck there, either. These fields are clearly pastures, but there are no animals about—no cows, no pigs, no goats. Not even any chickens."

"Let's go take a look," Clarence said.

"One moment."

Hedpeth went back to their carriage, opened the satchel and extracted two identical pistols, with barrels Clarence judged to be about eight inches long. He took powder and ball from pouches in the satchel and loaded one of the guns, which he held on to. He handed the other to Clarence, who held it awkwardly.

"You can load your own," Hedpeth said.

Clarence just stood there, not sure what to do. He was embarrassed to admit that he'd never held a gun before.

"Have you ever loaded or fired a gun, Clarence?"

"No."

"Seen one up close?"

"Uh, not really. People in my part of Boston tended not to have them."

"Alright. I'll bring my gun, then, but not give you one. If you have no experience with it, you're as likely to shoot yourself as anyone else." He put the second gun back in the satchel and slid his own into a holster on his left side, under his jacket.

"Let's go inspect the barns," Hedpeth said.

When they reached the barn, they were confronted with a single door in the side. Hedpeth started to reach for the handle when Clarence said, "Aren't you going to take out your gun?"

"No. If someone inside means us harm, they've no doubt already heard us coming, and will shoot us, likely with a long gun, as soon as we walk through the door. Having my pistol out won't help much, whereas if they don't mean us harm and they see the gun, they may take it as a threat and act on it."

"That's a risk."

"There are risks in many things in life, Clarence." He paused for a second, pulled open the door and walked right in. Nothing happened.

"Come on," Hedpeth said. "There's no one here that I can see."

When Clarence went inside he saw that the barn was filled with wagons, farm machinery and a variety of tools, including scythes, hoes and rakes. Up above, the loft was full of hay, and it smelled freshly cut.

At the end of the barn, against a far wall, there were three doors.

"Let's check those rooms down there," Hedpeth said.

"Do you think we should check out the hay loft first?" Clarence said.

"No, I would think that if anyone was up there, they would have heard us come in and made themselves known."

"Unless they are hiding."

"Why would they hide, Clarence?"

"Um, I don't know. I'm new at this."

They walked over to the wall and Hedpeth opened the first door, but the room was empty. So was the second room.

"Why don't you open the third door," Hedpeth said.

"Why?"

"Fair is fair."

"Alright." With his heart pounding, Clarence grabbed the handle of the third door and pulled it open. Nothing happened, so he poked his head into the opening.

"I think we have found what we are looking for," he said. "Come on in. No need for the gun, I don't think."

What Clarence saw inside was a man lying on a bed, his head propped up on pillows, his body covered with multiple blankets and his face swathed in bandages. In the corner of the room was a small dresser, with a pitcher and washbasin on top. More pillows and blankets were piled in the corner.

He and Hedpeth moved fully into the room, but the man on

the bed did not try to rise up to greet them. Instead he said, in a low and whispery voice, "You men them abolitionists what beat me in Springfield come to finish me off?"

Hedpeth laughed. "Not at all. I am Major Hedpeth, of the United States Army. This other gentleman is Clarence Artemis. We have come to find you because many people have been concerned to learn your fate, including the president."

"Of the United States?"

"Yes, and he is hardly an abolitionist."

"Alright. I'm Ezekiel Goshorn…" His voice trailed off as if he had something to add but couldn't quite get it out.

"We know what happened to you," Hedpeth said. "We can, if you like, take you back to Springfield for medical care."

Clarence winced. The trip back to Springfield on the bucking carriage would surely kill this man. But he said nothing because he didn't know where Hedpeth was going.

"Or," Hedpeth was saying, "we could bring a physician here to treat you."

"My brother, who is caring for me, already had a physician come."

"What did that doctor say?"

Goshorn took a deep breath, clearly marshaling the energy to speak. Finally, he said, "He said nothing broke. Just beat up real bad. Must lay here and heal."

"Is it working?" Clarence said.

"No. Been a lot of days. Still can't walk without help. Worse every day. Sometimes I lose my way in my thoughts."

Hedpeth put his hand on Goshorn's forehead. "At least you don't have a fever. And you know, if you're injured badly, healing often takes more time than you wish. I know that so very well."

"I fear I am not long for this world, Major."

Hedpeth leaned down closer to him and pulled his collar away from his throat. "You have marks on your throat, too. Like someone went after you there with something. Do you know how that happened?"

"I don't remember. Some part of the attack in the riot probably."

"Where is your brother now?" Clarence said.

"Said he had to go out. Didn't say where. Said he'd be back soon."

Clarence heard a noise out in the barn. Hedpeth clearly heard it, too, because his head snapped around at the sound. "Clarence, go out and see who that is," Hedpeth said. "Perhaps it's just his brother returning."

Clarence went out the door to check. What he saw, at the end of the barn, was a woman sitting on a horse. She sat tall in the saddle with a pistol holstered at her hip.

She saw him, drew the pistol and rode closer as he strode toward her until both of them stopped a few feet apart.

"Who are you?" she said.

"Clarence Artemis. I'm a journalist, come to find Ezekiel Goshorn." He held out his hand.

Annabelle ignored his proffered hand and said, "Is he here?"

"Yes. And there is no need to wave that gun around. I'm here with Major Hedpeth of the United States Army, and we mean no harm to anyone."

"I didn't know journalists rescued people. I thought all your kind did was stir up trouble. So why are you here at all?"

"We have been talking to Mr. Goshorn and trying to see if we can help him. He is in very poor condition."

"That doesn't answer why the two of you are here."

"Major Hedpeth is sent by President Buchanan."

She raised her eyebrows. "Really?"

The truth was that Clarence had no idea if Buchanan had actually sent Hedpeth, but he just answered, "Yes."

"And you, Mr. Artemis? Why are *you* here?"

"Like I just said. A journalist."

"From where?"

"Springfield." It did not seem to Clarence the right time to announce the name of his newspaper.

"Alright," she said.

"If I might ask, who are you, ma'am?" Clarence said.

"I'm Annabelle Carter. I'm a neighbor of Mr. Goshorn in Kentucky. His family has sent me to look for him."

"I see. Well, you have found him. But he is in no shape to travel, I'm afraid."

"Is his brother here?"

"Out somewhere briefly, supposedly. We have not yet met the man. We are only just arrived, and have been talking to Mr. Goshorn about what has happened to him."

"I see. Is his son here?"

"He has not mentioned his son. Do you know his brother, ma'am?"

"I met him once. But I don't really know him."

"He will be back, I assume."

"I will see Goshorn for myself," she said, holstering her gun and dismounting. She looked for a place to tie up her horse, found a post and tied the horse's lead around it.

"Goshorn is in that small room there," Clarence said, pointing.

They crossed the barn and walked into the room together.

After introductions, Hedpeth said, "It is a pleasure to meet you, ma'am. If you are looking for Mr. Goshorn, I fear you are too late. He seems to have expired just a moment ago. Not surprising in some ways. Injuries like his take their toll."

"Dead? Are you sure?" Annabelle went up to Goshorn and lifted his arm to take a pulse at his wrist. "He indeed has no pulse," she said.

"Ma'am, if I may, my military training is to take a pulse at his neck." Hedpeth stepped forward, put his finger against Goshorn's neck and said, "No pulse there, either."

"Major, if he was alive just a few moments ago, and talking to you, how could he be dead so suddenly?"

"Ma'am, it is my experience in battle that a man who is badly injured can be talking one moment—even making jokes—and be stone dead the next moment." They all stepped back and regarded the corpse for several minutes, saying nothing.

"If he was a friend of yours, my condolences," Hedpeth said.

"Mine as well," Clarence said.

"Not exactly a friend," she said. "More like a longtime acquaintance."

"We will await his brother's return," Hedpeth said. "But for now, let us leave this man in peace." He walked over and closed Goshorn's eyelids. Then he took two coins out of his pocket and put them on top. "Keeps them from popping open," he said.

"Let us pray," Hedpeth said. He then recited the Lord's Prayer.

When they were done, Annabelle walked back to the corpse and touched his cheek. "Still warm," she said.

As Clarence was getting ready to leave the room, he looked carefully around, the better to be able to describe the scene in his newspaper. Readers, he knew from having worked briefly at a paper in Boston, ate up such details. He even leaned over the body to see what coins Hedpeth had used. They were copper-colored Indian Head pennies. It was a new type of coin, issued for the first time the year before. Clarence had read that they were in surplus. The mint had overestimated demand.

25

The trip to Berlin had been, from Clarence's point of view, a spectacular success. Upon his return, he had put out a special edition of *The Radical Abolitionist*. It contained his first person account of finding Ezekiel Goshorn and the man's subsequent death. It had sold out in Springfield.

He had sent the text to his contact at *Harper's Weekly*, and a story crediting him and his paper had appeared there not long after. Coveted annual subscriptions to his paper had begun to pour in by both mail and telegram. He had put his paper on the map.

He knew, though, that the fame would be short-lived unless he could come up with more, and quickly. He sought out Robbie Culp, the boy who had sketched the overturned carriage. He paid him ten dollars, based on Clarence's recollections, to prepare two drawings. The first showed Clarence and Major Hedpeth standing over Goshorn's body. The second was a close-up of the dead man's face, complete with Indian Head pennies. Clarence used the drawings to illustrate a second edition and sent that, too, off to *Harper's*.

Meanwhile, the federal government had given him a gift. It had earlier indicted Abby Kelley Foster for violating the Fugitive Slave Act by supposedly inciting a riot that interfered with a United States marshal returning a slave to her owner. The indictment even managed to mention Goshorn's death, without exactly accusing Abby of having caused it.

The indictment was brought in the Southern District of Illinois, and since the United States District Court for that district sat in Springfield, journalists from all over the United States had begun to arrive. And Clarence was the man to see. Embarrassed at his paltry quarters, he had telegraphed his mother and gotten a commitment of funds that enabled him to find and rent a real office, tiny though it was.

The first visitor to his new office was a man named Harry Jones, who identified himself as a journalist from New York who wrote *occasionally*, as he put it, for *Harper's Weekly*. And what he wanted to know was how to get in to see Abraham Lincoln.

"I wish you good fortune in getting that interview," Clarence said. "I have tried many times to get in to see him, but except for one passing encounter, I have failed. He readily sees politicians and office seekers who come to town, but not journalists."

"So you can be of no help to me, Mr. Artemis, a fellow journalist?"

"I would if I could, but I am holding nothing back. I can think of no trick that would help."

"Well, I thank you anyway. Here is my calling card." He handed it to him. "The next time you are in New York, please look me up."

"I will most surely do that."

As he watched Jones leave, Clarence wondered at the man's audacity. If he had not himself been able to get in to see Lincoln, why ever would he give away any remaining tricks he might have to Jones? Perhaps that was just the way people from New York were.

Then he remembered something he had nearly forgotten about, perhaps because it had seemed so absurd. Father Hale had told him, weeks ago now, "Try talking to the baker on Fourth Street."

Clarence put on his overcoat and went out into the chill. A cold fall was coming on with a vengeance.

He arrived at the bakery toward three o'clock, as the proprietor, a man named Hotchkiss, was just closing up. Clarence introduced himself and said, "I am surprised you are closing so early."

Hotchkiss looked at him with a kindly expression on his face— one Clarence imagined he might have shone upon an unusually slow four-year-old—and said, "Mr. Artemis, people come to buy their daily bread in the early morning. If they want sweets or pies, they come after lunch. So that I, who arise at 4:00 a.m. to start baking, can go home and enjoy my own dinner."

"Yes, of course," Clarence said. "I am sorry to be so ignorant of these things. In Boston, where I'm from, it seems things are open all the time. Except on Sundays, of course."

"Well, be that as it may, to what do I owe the pleasure of your company? I know who you are, of course. You have of late garnered quite a reputation as a journalist." Clarence tried to keep the smile off his face. His increasing fame—well, not really fame exactly—but being known around town, pleased him more than he would have imagined, but he didn't want it to get in the way of his journalism. He fell back on commerce.

"Why, thank you, sir. Perhaps I can offer you a free subscription to my newspaper."

"That would be most welcome. I have been an avid reader of it, but had not thought to subscribe."

"I will see to it. But I came to ask you about something Father Hale said to me quite a few weeks ago now."

"Ah, yes. A man both kind and wise. What is it that he said?"

"I told him I wanted to find a way to interview Abraham Lincoln, who since he became the nominee of his party, does not speak to journalists. Father Hale told me to talk to the baker."

"I am not the only baker in this city."

"True, but you are the only one on Fourth Street, which is the address he gave."

The baker looked genuinely puzzled, and Clarence thought for a second that Father Hale had been playing a practical joke on him. Then Hotchkiss lit up and said, "Ah, he is likely referring to the fact that Mr. Lincoln often shopped for his family's bread here of an early morning."

"Lincoln shopped for his family's bread? In person?" Clarence was truly shocked. Even his mother sent servants out for bread and he didn't imagine the Lincolns were too poor to afford them.

"Yes, he did. He would come here with his basket over his shoulder, buy a few loaves, and we would talk of this and that—rarely I might add, of politics."

"Why did he do it?"

"He never said, but I suspect it was as much to have an excuse to get out of the house as anything. Mrs. Lincoln...well, I should not speak ill of someone who I hope will soon be living in the White House."

"I would never quote you without your permission, Mr. Hotchkiss."

Even as he said it, Clarence realized he was gulling the man. There were a hundred ways to avoid quoting someone directly but nevertheless leave it quite clear to the reader exactly who had said what.

"Well," Hotchkiss said, "I need more than that from you, sir. I need you to promise to say nothing that could lead anyone back to me."

"Alright. I agree."

"Fine, then. I assume Mr. Lincoln did the shopping because

Mrs. Lincoln is a shrew. People have even seen her shoo him out of the house with a broom. So he no doubt enjoyed the freedom of shopping."

"You have used the past tense. Does he no longer shop?"

"Not usually. After he became the nominee of his party, he was persuaded that it was beneath him. So he hired a young black boy to come in his stead."

"He no longer comes himself?"

"Not quite. Today, the boy had taken ill, and Mr. Lincoln came himself for the first time in many weeks. Perhaps he will come again tomorrow. Or perhaps not."

"What time did he come today?"

"When I opened at 6:00, when the loaves were still hot."

"Would I be welcome to come by tomorrow about that time?"

"Yes, just don't…"

"Tell Lincoln you suggested it."

"Precisely. They are good customers."

"I will see you tomorrow, Mr. Hotchkiss, and thank you." Clarence left quickly, lest Hotchkiss change his mind.

26

Clarence arrived at the bakery at 5:30 a.m. There was no point in missing Lincoln should he come early—assuming he came at all.

Clarence positioned himself about a block away, in the opposite direction from Lincoln's house. That way, if Lincoln came from home, he would be walking toward Clarence, and Clarence could walk casually toward him. He had dressed nicely, but not too formally, and was carrying his own bread basket.

Shortly before 6:00, Lincoln appeared down the block, walking—sauntering really—and whistling. He was wearing a top hat and had a cloak pulled around his shoulders against the early morning chill. Clarence waited a few seconds, then set off himself at a pace he judged would take him abreast of the bakery at about the same time Lincoln arrived there.

It worked. Lincoln was starting to open the door to the bakery just as Clarence got there. Lincoln at first seemed startled to find someone at the same doorway at the same time, but quickly recovered. He opened the door fully and said, "After you, sir. I see we both come early to this excellent establishment." As he threw the door wide, the aroma of fresh baked bread poured into the street.

Hotchkiss was standing behind the counter and, on hearing Lincoln's praise, beamed. "Mr. Lincoln, good morning, and good morning to you, too, Mr. Artemis." Then he introduced the two of them, but neglected to mention that Clarence was a journalist. He found no need, of course, to mention who Lincoln was.

"As I'm sure you well recall, Mr. Artemis, we have met briefly once before," Lincoln said, smiling. "In fact, I have brought you your cap back, with apologies that it has taken so long." He reached into his basket and handed the hat to Clarence.

Clarence was taken aback—Hotchkiss must have told Lincoln that Clarence was likely to be there—but he recovered quickly and said, "It is no problem. Thank you for the cap's return." Then he looked at it more carefully. "But I'm almost embarrassed to say that it's not my hat. So it wouldn't be right for me to keep it." He handed it back to Lincoln, who took it and, without a word, put it back in the basket.

Hotchkiss, clearly uncertain about what had just happened, ignored it and said, "I must now decide which of you to serve first. I suppose I shall choose age before beauty, and serve Mr. Lincoln first."

Lincoln laughed and said, "Well, it is a good thing, Mr. Hotchkiss, that I have age on my side because if I had to contend with only beauty to support me, I suspect that I would never receive service anywhere."

Clarence looked at Lincoln and realized that the man was right about himself. His face was long, thin and rough, and his skin was, if not quite sallow, at least not in the bloom of health. He realized that Lincoln's quip called for some clever riposte on his part, but he was once again dumbstruck that he was standing next to the man he expected to be the next president and could find nothing to say—a rarity for him. His mother was fond of remarking that he had not had an unexpressed thought since he first learned to speak.

Lincoln, seeming to wait for a response but apparently realizing that none was going to be forthcoming, turned to Hotchkiss and said, "My boys seem quite hungry of late, Mr. Hotchkiss. So in lieu of the usual two large loaves, I will take three today. Please just add them to our account. Mrs. Lincoln will take care of it at month's end."

"Very well, sir." Hotchkiss swiveled around to face five shelves, all laden-down with loaves of bread. He took three and handed them to Lincoln, who slipped them into his basket.

"Thank you, Mr. Hotchkiss," Lincoln said. "Good day to you." He turned briefly toward Clarence. "And to you, Mr. Artemis."

Before Lincoln could make it back out the door, Clarence finally found his voice. "Mr. Lincoln, as you already know, I am a journalist. And although I am here with you by happenstance." He paused. "Well, not exactly happenstance. I wonder if I might again trouble you for an interview."

"Ah, yes, I recall that you introduced yourself at my house as the editor of that new newspaper, *The Radical Abolitionist*."

"Yes, and some of my pieces have now also appeared in *Harper's Weekly*."

Lincoln smiled. "I have read a couple of them."

"And so would you grant me a brief interview, sir? I would be most obliged."

"Mr. Artemis, I am still not campaigning and as a result not giving interviews. But I admire your persistence." He glanced at Hotchkiss. "And your cleverness."

"Senator Douglas is campaigning," Clarence said.

"So I have heard. So I have heard. I am sure he has his reasons, but I know not what they are and therefore cannot comment on them."

Lincoln turned once again to try to leave.

Clarence saw no harm in trying one more time. "But, sir, I

could limit my interview to the mundane, to just asking you, for example, what it is like to be here in Springfield as others campaign on your behalf."

Lincoln laughed uproariously. "Would it be called 'Marooned in Springfield'? You know, there is a wonderful story about a hedgehog who was marooned on an island, but I don't have time to tell it, alas."

"No, the interview would not be called anything like that."

"It doesn't matter, Mr. Artemis, because I'm not prepared right now to give you an interview on any subject. But I will offer this. If the American people do me the great honor of electing me as their chief magistrate, I invite you to come to Washington for an interview after I am inaugurated."

"That would be a great honor."

"There is one condition."

"Yes?"

"You will not write up this interaction we have just had. I'm sure a clever fellow like you could make an article of it, even though I have said nothing. If you do, I will never be able to go into any store in this city in peace. There will always be journalists who are there at the same time...by happenstance."

"I can agree to that."

"I should add, Mr. Artemis, that if I should lose, and if you prove still interested in asking me questions, which I tend to doubt you will be, come here to Springfield and ask me all you want. And I'll tell you the hedgehog story."

"I will do that, certainly, although I think you are going to win."

Lincoln turned to leave and said, over his shoulder, "Do try the bread. You've stumbled by happenstance on the best bakery in Springfield."

After he had gone, Clarence said to Hotchkiss, "Thank you for making that possible."

"You're quite welcome, young man. How many loaves would you like?"

"Just one. I feed only myself at this point."

As he said it, it hit him. The extra loaf that Lincoln bought could be for Lucy. Could Lincoln himself be hiding her? But that would make no sense whatsoever since it would put the election at risk if it were discovered. He pushed the thought out of his mind.

Hotchkiss handed him a loaf, still warm. "Don't forget my free subscription to your new paper."

"I won't."

As he left, Clarence noticed a Negro man walk up to the bakery and go in. Clarence lingered a bit in front of the general store that was down the street and pretended to examine items in its window. Several minutes later the man emerged carrying a loaf of bread.

After the man had departed, Clarence went back into the bakery. Hotchkiss looked surprised to see him again and said, "Need another loaf? Or perhaps a pie? Although you'd need to wait awhile since they aren't quite ready yet."

"No, I came with a question," Clarence said.

"What is it, pray tell?"

"The man who was just here. Is he someone's servant or a free black?"

"Well, even if he were a servant, he'd still be free. We do not permit slavery here in Illinois, as you well know."

"Let me ask my question a different way. Is it the case that you have no problem selling to Negroes?"

Hotchkiss reared back slightly and said, "Why ever would I have a problem, sir?"

"I must apologize. I have simply noticed that at least some merchants in Springfield will not sell to Negroes unless they are accompanied by a white person who is their employer. But you clearly do sell bread to them, from what I just observed."

"Yes, they are God's people, like the rest of us."

"Are you an abolitionist, then?"

"That is a political question, and I am a simple baker, not a politician."

"Mr. Hotchkiss, do you believe free blacks should be able to come into Illinois if they want to?"

Hotchkiss was becoming visibly upset. Indeed, despite the chill of the early morning, beads of perspiration had appeared on his forehead. "Mr. Artemis, is this an interview for your newspaper? I am a quiet baker. I have my opinions, but I keep them largely to myself."

"I'm not trying to interview you, just trying to understand the sweep of opinions in the city as the election approaches." Clarence knew that was a half-truth, but it was a convenient half-truth because it seemed to calm Hotchkiss.

"Good," Hotchkiss said. He took a kerchief from his pocket and wiped his brow. "I have many customers, who hold many different opinions. Were my views, one way or the other, to appear in your paper, I might lose fully half of them. These are bitter times." He paused. "In case you haven't noticed."

"I have of course noticed. But let me be candid, sir. The reason I was asking you about the status of free blacks in Springfield is simply that I am looking for my next big story."

"Which is what?"

"Where the escaped slave Lucy Battelle is."

"Likely in Canada via the Railroad, wouldn't you guess?"

"Perhaps she is. But I am nevertheless looking for an entrée into the community of free blacks hereabout. They might know something more. I was hoping you might provide that entrée."

"Alas, Mr. Artemis, aside from the few free blacks who buy bread here, I know no one in that community. Now, if you have nothing further, I have baking left to attend to."

Clarence thanked him and left. He would have to try to find Lucy some other way.

27

"Are you sure he was dead?" Pinkerton said.

"He had no pulse and his skin was already slightly blue by the time I finally left. How much deader can you get?" Annabelle said.

"Did you stay to see him buried?"

"No. We waited for his brother to come back and when he got there, he said he would take care of things. Since you still pay me by the hour, Allan, I didn't want to waste your money watching someone stuck in the ground." She put on her best smile.

"Alright, alright. I take your point. Have you learned anything at all about where Lucy Battelle might be?"

"Nothing, despite much asking around. I assume she is either dead or in Canada by now."

"Did you ask the newspaper fellow if he knew where she was?"

Annabelle paused before answering, as she realized she was about to admit a failure. "I didn't. I guess I tend to think of people from the press as useless." She shrugged. "The few times I have been involved with something that appeared in the papers, they always got the facts wrong. Sometimes wildly wrong."

"That was a beginner's mistake," Pinkerton said. "Reporters can often be very useful. They may have different motives than detectives, but they sometimes know things. Important things."

"I'm not a beginner," she said.

"No, you're not, which is what makes it particularly disappointing." Pinkerton pointed his finger at her—something she'd never seen him do before—and said, "Go befriend him."

She was not sure if she was shocked by the idea or titillated by it, but in response said only, "Do you mean socialize with him? Women don't ask men they hardly know to dine with them. Or even go for a walk down a city street."

Pinkerton grinned. "Here I thought you were a modern woman. And, as I recall, you have been married, so it's not as if you need a chaperone."

"He's not the type of man to whom I am attracted, Allan."

"Not handsome?"

"In a New England kind of way, perhaps. But not what I'm looking for."

"Give it some thought."

"I will," she said. "But before I sidle up to that reporter—if I do—there is another possibility to explore about what happened to Lucy."

"Which is?"

"That slave catchers may already have found her and taken her directly back to Kentucky," she said. "Without worrying about complying with the Fugitive Slave Act—first taking her into court and all of that."

"Do you have a way to find that out?" Pinkerton said.

"Perhaps. If Lucy has been taken back to Riverview, my mother would surely have heard about it and let me know. She always writes to me about the local gossip. But since letters take a while, I could send a carefully worded telegram to my sister and find out what she knows. She's close to one of the dead man's sons."

Pinkerton looked skeptical. "If the slave catchers found Lucy they could instead have just gotten a bill of sale from the owner—that would be the eldest son now that the father's dead—and taken her directly to a slave market somewhere and sold her south without ever taking her back to the plantation."

"That could be. What do you want me to do now, Allan? Other than befriend that reporter?"

"I want you to go on looking for Lucy."

"Dear God, why? Isn't it obvious, like I just said, that she's either dead or in Canada by now? Or sold south, which is pretty much the same as dead."

Pinkerton got up from behind his desk and began to pace the room. Annabelle sat, watching him, saying nothing. After a minute or two, he stopped, faced her and said, "I will tell you something, but I must ask you to swear to keep what I tell you secret."

"I swear that I will."

"So... I am the Railroad Stationmaster in Chicago."

"That is widely rumored, Allan, so hardly a secret."

"I know. However, I do want you to keep my confirmation of that fact secret. But that is not the only important part."

"What is?"

"That we keep a list of passengers. I think it will be useful to show it to you, but I must first ask you to leave the building and come back in a few minutes."

"Alright." She left and busied herself outside, talking to the guard by the front door. Eventually, Allan poked his head out and bade her return.

When they were back in his office, he handed her a piece of paper and said, "This is the list of those who have reached Chicago on the Railroad in the last several weeks. It contains their names and a description of each. In not too long, we will destroy it and start a new list."

She took it and read through it, noting that it contained around a dozen names.

"It seems risky to keep this list. Why do you?"

"Because we need to make sure that those who came through here were transported on to the next station without being captured along the way. This area is thick with slave catchers, and if they succeed we try to learn how they did it and change our routes."

"So you check the names off when you hear that they have gotten through?"

"Yes, and since we dare not use telegrams or the post office to check, we must wait 'til a worker from the Railroad's next station shows up here and tells us that such and such a slave made it at least that far."

"To Canada?"

"To wherever they were going."

"And if a lot of them do not make it to wherever that is?" Annabelle said.

"Then we need to figure out how to change our methods or our routes."

"What do you want me to take away from seeing this list, Allan?"

"Did you see Lucy Battelle's name on it?"

"No. But she might have given a false name."

"Do you see any description that might fit what we know of her from the affidavit her master filed, the one we all discussed during dinner? Young? Tall for her age? Thin?"

"No."

"What that means, Annabelle, is that she has not come through here in the last few weeks."

"Perhaps she took a different route."

"This is the main Railroad route from the Springfield area."

"She could have taken a branch."

"If there is a branch, I don't know about it."

"So she is either…"

"Dead, sold south or still in Springfield or nearby, but almost surely not in Canada."

"As I said, Allan, what do you want me to do now?"

"Go on looking for her. I have traded telegrams with Lincoln, using an alias with which he's familiar, and he still wants her found if at all possible."

"I may not be the best person to do that. I had thought my abolitionism, even though not absolute, would help open doors, but as soon as they hear my Kentucky accent, the doors slam shut."

"You are clever, my dear, and I am sure you can figure it out."

"That is not very helpful, Allan."

He thought for a moment, opened a desk drawer and pulled out a blank sheet of paper. Then he wrote something on it, folded it and handed it to her.

"Shall I read it?"

"Of course."

She unfolded it and read it to herself. It said simply, "This woman is to be trusted." It was signed "Henry."

"What am I to do with it?" she said.

"Fold it back up and hide in on your person in a place that most men would hesitate to search. Then go to Springfield and go to see the baker, Mr. Hotchkiss. His bakery is on Fourth Street."

"And show him the note?"

"Yes, and tell him what you are trying to do. He might help you."

28

Sangamon County Jail

The jail, which was in the back of the courthouse, had seven cells in all. Four were off the corridor leading directly to the sheriff's office and were usually filled with drunks—those who'd gotten violent—spending the night. The final three, always referred to as the "far set," was on the other side of the building, guarded by an armed deputy. Those cells were used for real criminals.

When the federal magistrate requested Sheriff Stromberg to house Abby Kelley Foster while she awaited trial—the federal court lacked its own jail cells—the far set was empty. Which enabled them to put Mrs. Foster over there without housing her alongside men.

Not that the sheriff had been at all happy about it. In fact, he had tried to talk the magistrate out of jailing her at all.

"Bert, why are you doing this?" he had asked after Mrs. Foster had been settled in her cell. "They didn't even lock up that woman last year who was accused of hacking up her husband with a hand ax."

"Mrs. O'Brien?"

"Yes, her. We all knew her, and she was a hellcat. And yet she went free until her trial."

"She was a state prisoner, Sheriff," Bert said. "The state has its own policies about such things. Mrs. Foster is a federal prisoner, and Judge Treat wants her held under lock and key."

"Why don't you grant her bail? As the magistrate, you have the authority to do that, and Judge Treat be damned. Set a high bail and one of her fancy abolitionist friends from back East will surely post it."

"Do you recall what must be done before someone can be bailed out, Sheriff?"

He knew it was a trick question, and he hated to be tricked, so he just said, "Uh, not exactly. What?"

"They have to *apply* for bail, and she hasn't done that. And even if she were to do so, I wouldn't grant it. She has no local ties and she could easily flee."

"I thought she came here to look after a close friend who is ill. Wouldn't that be ties enough, Bert?"

The magistrate smiled a very broad smile. "He died two days ago. So I guess he ain't a local tie anymore, eh?"

"I still don't like the idea of holding her, but I guess I am stuck with her."

"Yes, you have an agreement with the federal court to house our prisoners, and I assume you'll keep on honoring it."

The sheriff shrugged. "It's good money, I suppose."

"So you'll honor the agreement?"

"Yes. And perhaps I'll go and pay her a visit. She's the most famous prisoner we've had here in a long time."

The sheriff had intended to visit Mrs. Foster right away, but one thing led to another and he didn't get around to it until her third day in his jail, when a crisis of sorts arose and he felt he had to go and see her.

When he got near to the far set, he stopped for a moment to observe Abby from a place where he could see her but she couldn't see him.

They had given her the nicest and largest of the three cells. It was perhaps eight feet square, with bars on the front and a worn-looking wooden bench running along one side. A small wooden table sat in a corner and held a washbasin and pitcher. There was even a small painting of Jesus hung on a nail.

The Jesus picture had been placed there a couple of years before by an itinerant preacher. The preacher had spent a few nights in the cell after punching a man at a camp meeting who had taken issue with his theology. No one had objected to it, so he had just left it up.

Mrs. Foster was primly dressed—high white collar atop a long black dress, with her hair pinned up.

As he drew near the bars, she was sitting stiffly upright on the only other piece of furniture in the cell—a straight-backed chair placed at the very rear. She looked both older and more severe—it was perhaps the gray hair—than he had expected. He could tell that she had once been quite beautiful, perhaps even stunning.

She had apparently heard him approaching, because she looked up and said, "Good afternoon, Sheriff."

"Good afternoon, Mrs. Foster. I'm Sheriff Tom Stromberg. I apologize that I've not come to visit you before this."

"I'm sure you have many duties to keep you busy, and your deputies have been tending to me."

"I've heard you are not well, and, if I may be so bold, you look quite pale."

"The problem is the food, sir. I cannot eat it and I do not have enough of my own."

"I am surprised because my wife has been cooking specially for you, and she is quite the good cook in my opinion." He smiled. "Which could be biased, but is attested to by others, as well."

"It is of fine quality, Sheriff, I'm sure. The problem is that I am a follower of Sylvester Graham's diet."

"I'm not sure I know what it is."

"I don't eat meat."

"What else is there to eat?"

"Fresh fruits and vegetables and Graham cakes."

"What are they?"

"They're made of wheat or corn that is coarse-ground."

He wrinkled his nose.

"They taste better than you might think, Sheriff. Perhaps you'd like to try one."

"Well…"

"I have only two left, but am happy to share one." She opened a small satchel—prisoners were allowed to bring personal items into the jail as long as they were searched first—and took out two stiff-looking, brown, square cakes with rounded corners.

She broke off a piece, walked to the bars and held it out to him.

He shrugged, took it from her and bit into it. It tasted to him like sawdust might. But, not wishing to offend, he said simply, "Not really to my taste, but I can see how one might come to like it."

"I have."

"What about cheese and milk?" he said. "Do you eat those?"

"Only if they are very fresh."

"Were you able to find the makings of the Graham diet here in Springfield before you were jailed?"

"With some difficulty, but yes, although only a small amount."

It seemed a solution to his desire not to hold her in his jail. He hadn't worked out the details, but he said it aloud anyway.

"Suppose, Mrs. Foster, I were simply to let you go, on the

ground that you need to be able to seek out your own special foods or it will imperil your health."

"What would I be required to do in exchange?"

"To appear for your trial on the date it will be set for."

She was silent for a moment, drumming her fingers on the arm of the chair, to which she had returned. Finally, she said, "If you let me go, I cannot promise to come back since I consider the government that has imprisoned me to be illegitimate."

"You would not agree to stay in Springfield?"

"I am most likely to get on a train and go back to Massachusetts."

"I just don't understand, Mrs. Foster. I am offering you an opportunity to get out of this cell—in which you are clearly suffering—and you are turning it down based on some high principle."

"Sheriff, I am an abolition lecturer. Have you ever gone to an abolition lecture?"

"Can't say as I have."

"If you were to come—and I invite you to come—you would learn that, very close to here, for Kentucky is not far away, slaves are suffering this very day. They are being forced to work in the blazing sun. They are being whipped and beaten. And they are being paid not one nickel for their hard work."

"I know that, of course. I am something of an abolitionist myself. In my own way."

"What way is that?"

"I know that it has to end someday, somehow."

"Abolitionists want slavery abolished instantly."

"I don't see how that is practical."

"That is always said. And it becomes an excuse for doing nothing."

There was a small silence, during which he felt embarrassed, because what she said was true. He was opposed to slavery, but not in any way that mattered. Finally, she broke the silence. "Do you have children, Sheriff?"

"Two surviving."

"How old are they?"

"Ten-year-old twins."

"Ah, that is a good age. I recall when my daughter was that age. But do you know what happens to slave children at the age of ten?"

"No."

"That is often when they are taken from their families and sent to the fields for the rest of their short lives. Or sold."

"Not all of them surely."

"Most of them, quite surely. And that is why I am staying here in this cell. So that when the trial comes, I will emerge, haggard and thin, to fight the ludicrous charges against me. And stand witness to the terrible scourge of slavery. It will be the best platform I have ever had."

29

Law Offices of Lincoln and Herndon

Lincoln was, as usual, tilted back in his chair, reading. This time, he was perusing a telegram that Herndon had just handed him.

"Billy, this an unwelcome complication. Do you think anyone at the telegraph office who has read it has told others about it?"

"Telegraphers are sworn to secrecy by the telegraph company, and the ones here in Springfield have for the most part honored their oaths these last few years."

"Well, perhaps it doesn't matter. It is unlikely that Frederick Douglass will keep his position on the matter a secret for long. I assume the telegram is just him letting me know his position in advance, out of politeness. They say he can at times be a very polite man."

"If rather fierce," Herndon said. "And at times blunt to a point that could hardly be called polite."

"You might be impolite, too, Billy, if you'd gone through what he has. Or gone through what those on whose behalf he speaks suffer every day. If you have not already done it, you should read his most recent autobiography."

"I have, Lincoln. I have. At times you forget that it is I who am the abolitionist, and you who are not one."

Lincoln smiled. "True."

"You have heard, I assume, that Abby Kelley is not doing well in jail," Herndon said.

"Yes. But who does do well in jail?"

"I mean more than that. Apparently, Mrs. Foster was already in ill health when she arrived in Springfield. The jail confinement has made it worse."

"Is she in such ill health that she might die?" Lincoln said.

"I don't think so, but I really don't know. The information I have comes from the sheriff's wife, who has been looking after her in the jail."

Lincoln got up out of his chair, walked to the window and looked out, saying nothing.

After a while, he said, "We are truly in a pickle, Billy. I cannot do what Frederick Douglass demands—promise to pardon Abby Kelley if she is convicted and I am elected. Because while it *might* gain me more abolitionist voters, it will surely lose as great or greater a number of other voters. In particular those who are opposed to immediate abolition and believe me to be someone who will not rock the boat."

"Quite a pickle indeed, Lincoln."

"It would also be presumptuous of me to take a position on a pardon for Mrs. Foster before I have even been elected, not to mention before I have studied the facts of her indictment."

"You can't continue to do nothing about it and say nothing about it."

"Perhaps you are right. But I continue to think that the solution is to find the slave—now that we know the master is dead—before Mrs. Foster's trial. It will take the heat out of the thing and allow some sort of resolution short of trial."

"Unless President Buchanan wants a trial."

Lincoln turned from the window to face him. "Why would he want a trial?"

"To put you on the spot. A famous abolitionist would be on trial not five blocks from your own home and you would not only be doing nothing about it but saying nothing about it."

"I see your point, Billy. But I see no easy solution. If I come out against the prosecution or say, as this telegram demands, that I will pardon her if elected, I fear I will not be elected. And what good would that do Mrs. Foster? Or the slaves, for that matter?"

"You may also not be elected if you stay silent."

Lincoln shrugged. "My estimation is that it is not the abolitionist vote that will boost me into office. Frankly, they have nowhere else to go."

"And if they choose to stay home?" Billy said.

"Many of them stay home anyway. Or at least they have in past elections."

"So you hope to rely on whom?"

"I must rely primarily on Republicans who are opposed to slavery but don't want to blow up the Union over the issue. And on Democrats who, in the privacy of their thoughts, don't care a fig about slavery, but are fed up with the corruption of the Buchanan administration and will vote for me."

Lincoln returned to his chair, sat back down, picked up the telegram again and studied it. "Billy," he said, "now that we know the slave master is dead, have you heard anything about where the missing slave might herself be?"

"Not one thing."

"Do you think you might be able to find her?"

"I could try."

"May I suggest you start by talking to the young editor of that new newspaper?"

"Which one?"

Lincoln walked over to a stack of newspapers that was teetering on a small table and extracted one from the middle of the pile, keeping his hand on top so that the whole thing wouldn't topple over. "This one." He handed it to Herndon. *The Radical Abolitionist.*

"Ah, yes. I met that young man the night of Abby Kelley's speech. Clarence Artemis is his name."

"Yes. He has accosted me twice. Once at home and once at the baker's this morning, hoping for an interview."

"I hope to God you didn't give him one."

"Of course not. But I told him if I'm elected he can come to Washington and I'll let him interview me there."

"Why do you think he might know where Lucy Battelle is?"

"He managed to track me down at the bakery, which took some sleuthing. And I suspect he is looking for Lucy Battelle himself."

"I'll talk with him."

30

Herndon had never liked running errands, as he called them, for Lincoln. Sometimes it involved handling cases Lincoln didn't want to handle, sometimes it meant making sure the firm's bills were paid on time (which he still wasn't all that good at) and sometimes it meant researching the law for Lincoln since he didn't much like doing that himself.

Herndon had been doing those kinds of things now for sixteen years, ever since they had formed their law partnership in 1844. In those early days, it had made sense, of course, because Herndon was the very junior partner. When they'd begun he'd had effectively zero years of experience—he had just been admitted to the bar—to Lincoln's eight.

Over time, though, he had grown in stature, at least in his own mind, arguing his own cases in all the important courts in Illinois, including the Illinois Supreme Court. In 1854, he'd even been elected mayor of Springfield. With Lincoln's nomination for president, he had hoped for a robust role in the campaign. Which had not been forthcoming due to Lincoln's fear that Herndon's strong abolitionist sentiments would come to the fore and damage Lincoln's careful balancing on the slavery issue. Herndon knew that his praise of John Brown's raid on Harpers Ferry—he had said that Brown would "live among the world's gods and heroes"—had not helped Lincoln's opinion of his political judgment.

Now he'd been given something to do that rose well above an errand—to find the missing slave girl. He was not certain what good finding her would do. But Lincoln had proven to have superb political instincts (he had managed to get the nomination for president!), so if Lincoln thought it important, it must be so.

But where to start? It seemed obvious that the Underground Railroad had her. But to his shame, while he had been willing to defend fugitive slaves in court, he had shied away from helping them escape. It was, after all, a federal felony. He was a lawyer with children to support, and with his beloved wife of twenty years dead from consumption not much more than a month ago, it was too great a risk.

Instead of going to see Artemis, he started with the baker. Wanting to avoid confronting him while others were around, Herndon waited until late afternoon, as Hotchkiss was about to close up shop for the day.

"Mr. Hotchkiss," he said, walking into the store, "can you spare a few minutes?"

Hotchkiss looked up from the glass case from which he had been emptying the few items that had not sold.

"Of course, Mr. Herndon. Would you like to buy a few loaves? I can sell them to you at a steep discount. End of day and all of that."

"No, thank you. I came on other business."

"Ah, and what business might that be?"

"I am hoping to find out where Lucy Battelle is being hidden."

Hotchkiss went back to clearing out the glass case without

looking up again. "There seems to be a run today on people hoping to find that out. You're the second person today."

"Was the other one Mr. Artemis?"

Hotchkiss paused a moment, as if considering whether he wanted to give up that information. Finally, he said, "Why, yes, as a matter of fact it was."

"I hope I'm not too late, then, to find out where Lucy is," Herndon said.

"Mr. Herndon, I can tell you what I told Mr. Artemis. I have no idea where Lucy Battelle is, and I don't know why anyone thinks I do know."

Herndon made a noise with his lips that he hoped indicated his disbelief in Hotchkiss's answer. "Why, sir, it is because it is widely known that you are the Stationmaster of the Underground Railroad here in Springfield."

Hotchkiss stood up, folded his arms and looked Herndon straight in the eye. "Sir, I do not know where that rumor got started, but as God is my witness, I know nothing at all about the so-called Railroad."

"Really?"

"I do not even know if there is such a thing. For all I know, it has been made up by journalists from the East hoping to tell a good story in order to sell more newspapers."

"I'm a lawyer, Mr. Hotchkiss. I've become quite good over the years at teasing out who is telling the truth and who is not. And I say you are not."

"Tease out all you want. It won't be any more true when you leave my store than when you came in. Now, if you don't mind, I need to lock the door so I can finish cleaning up. I don't mean to be rude, but you need to vamoose."

Herndon left as requested, smiling at Hotchkiss's use of the word *vamoose*. He had apparently been to see the same play as Herndon had, at the recently opened small theater a couple of blocks away.

After Herndon departed, he walked down the street, but lingered in a doorway not far away. He hoped in the gathering darkness that he would not be seen. Soon enough, Hotchkiss came out, carrying a basket.

Herndon followed him for several blocks, pleased at his ability to follow someone without being detected and thrilled at the adventure of it. He noticed his heart was even beating fast. He was disappointed, though, when Hotchkiss arrived at home.

As Hotchkiss opened his front door, he turned and yelled, in a voice loud enough to carry all the way to the doorway in which Herndon was trying to hide himself, "Mr. Herndon, you should stay with lawyering!" He entered his house and slammed the door behind him.

Upon his return to their law offices, Herndon found Lincoln still perusing newspapers from the stack on the table, several of which had, once again, toppled onto the floor. Herndon walked over, picked up the strays and placed them back on the stack.

Lincoln, seeming not to have noticed the disarray, said, "This thing with the arrest of Abby Kelley is beginning to gain more attention." He handed the newspaper he'd been holding to Herndon. "Here's a front page article about it from the *Akron Summit Beacon*."

Herndon read through the article quickly. "They demand you make a statement about it."

"Yes, and given their radical Republican politics, they probably want me to say I'll pardon her if I'm elected. And the drumbeat is even louder from the opposition newspapers, Billy. Here, look at the *Springfield Register*, for example." He dug into the pile and handed Herndon another paper,

Herndon read it and said, "My God, they've written an editorial, condemning you in advance for pardoning her even though she's not yet been convicted and you've not been elected." He laughed.

"Yes, the Democratic papers are trying hard to create an issue for me out of this."

"What does *Harper's Weekly* have to say?"

"I don't think they've yet spoken on the issue. We must keep in mind, though, that they have endorsed Senator Douglas. So they will likely demand I promise *not* to pardon her."

"Have you thought, Lincoln, of just putting out a general statement that doesn't take a position one way or the other? Just gives the arguments on both sides and seems statesmanlike." He laughed. "You are quite good at that."

Lincoln pursed his lips and shook his head. "I still don't cotton to the idea of breaking the long tradition that candidates don't campaign once they are nominated."

"Douglas is doing it. He is campaigning all over the South."

"And looks desperate by doing it, Billy. But enough of that topic. Did you discover where Lucy is being hidden?"

"No. I suspect the baker of being the Stationmaster, but when I followed him, he just ended up going home."

Lincoln raised his eyebrows. "You followed him?"

"Yes."

"In the street?" He raised his eyebrows even farther.

"Yes, in the street." In confirming it Herndon realized how foolish it had been. To distract Lincoln from pursuing the matter further, he got up and walked around the office using a taper to light the gas lamps, since it was starting to get dark.

When he was done, Lincoln said, smiling broadly, "So, are you hoping to abandon law and go to work for Pinkerton?"

"Of course not."

"Good. But speaking of Pinkerton, Billy, I haven't heard from him since the discovery of the death of the slaveholder. Have you?"

"I have heard only that Annabelle Carter is continuing to look for the escaped slave."

"Who?"

"Ah, sorry. I thought I had told you about her. She is a female detective Pinkerton employs. I met her when I went to Chicago. She is very impressive."

"Is she the one who discovered the death of the slaveholder?"

"No. Our friend the radical editor did, at least to hear him tell it."

"Well," Lincoln said, "perhaps we had best put you to work as a lawyer, which, unlike detection, is something that you are quite good at."

Herndon had grown to be suspicious of praise by Lincoln, because it often meant that he was about to be sent on some legal mission that Lincoln himself preferred to avoid.

"What do you have in mind, Lincoln?"

"Mrs. Foster is going to need a lawyer."

Herndon shrank back, and it was not feigned. "Oh no! That is a very poor idea. For one thing, if you don't wish anyone to associate you with Mrs. Foster's cause, that would accomplish just the opposite."

"I don't agree. You are known as a strong abolitionist. So it would make sense for you to want to do it."

"Why don't you ask someone else?" Herndon said. "There are a number of very good lawyers hereabouts."

"I've asked all of the ones I think would be capable of it. They've all come up with various reasons to say no."

"Well, if I agree to do it, who will pay me? I am not doing this one for free."

"I'm sure a wealthy abolitionist can be dug up to foot the bill," Lincoln said.

"When is the trial?"

"October 16. Three weeks before Election Day."

"There is still another problem, Lincoln. We haven't been asked to represent Mrs. Foster."

"I'm going to take care of that right now."

"What about the original mission you sent me on? To find Lucy Battelle."

"Let's leave it to Pinkerton and his men—and women. They are professionals."

"Fine."

"Good. Can you lock up the office, Billy? I won't be back this evening."

"Where are you heading?"

"Home first, and then to jail."

31

Lincoln had known the sheriff for many years, and he knew him to be a man who often worked late. He was not surprised, then, that when he approached the jail there was a light lit in the sheriff's office.

The sheriff looked up as he came in. "Why, Mr. Lincoln, what brings you here this time of evening? Things uneasy at home?" The sheriff knew, of course, of the difficulties of Lincoln's marriage, so it didn't surprise Lincoln that the sheriff thought he might be out for a stroll just to escape from the house.

"No, things are fine at home, Sheriff. I'm here to see one of your prisoners."

"I thought now that you were nominated to the highest office in the land that you had suspended your law practice."

"I have, but Billy has not suspended his, and it is on his behalf that I'm here."

"Is he representing drunks again?" He laughed. "We have two in custody at the moment, but I thought he had long ago moved on from that."

"It is Mrs. Foster I want to see."

The sheriff blinked. "Well… I wonder if she'll want to see you. You know, a friend went to that speech she gave at Second Presbyterian a while back—the one that's gotten her indicted—and he said she didn't appear too fond of you."

"No?"

"No. He said she called you the slave hound of Illinois."

"I see. Well, people have called me a lot of things. But in any case, could you inquire if Mrs. Foster might do me the honor of seeing me?"

"If she says yes, do you want to meet her in her cell or in a room in the courthouse?"

"Oh, her cell will be fine I think."

"I'll be back in a few minutes," the sheriff said.

While he was gone, Lincoln looked around the office. On the wall behind the desk a thick ring of keys hung on a big nail. On the sheriff's desk lay a large, leather-bound notebook. The cover said *Jail Register*. Next to it was a porcelain figurine, which featured a brown-and-white spotted cow on a white stand and, next to it, a calf with the same markings.

The sheriff returned and said, "Mrs. Foster has agreed to see you." Then he seemed to notice for the first time that Lincoln was carrying a small cloth sack.

"I will need to ask you what is in the bag, Mr. Lincoln."

"Apples." He held it open for the sheriff to inspect for himself.

The sheriff peered in. "Harmless enough, I guess."

"I wanted to ask you, Sheriff, before we go on back, why you have those cows on your desk."

"It's because when my father came out here in '30, he intended to be a dairy farmer. I was a child and was made to milk the cows."

"What happened to the business?"

"My mother and father both died of the milk sickness not long after we got here."

"My mother, Nancy, died of that same thing. When I was nine."

They were both quiet for a moment.

Lincoln broke the silence. "How did you go from cows to keys?" He gestured at the ring on the wall.

"Went to live with an aunt and uncle in Chicago, along with my three sisters, got into police work there and then came back here. Got a job as deputy sheriff to start. You know the rest."

"Funny how way leads on to way for all of us."

"True, and I don't need to ask your story. It's all in your campaign biography."

"You read that?"

"Of course. Everyone in town has read it."

"Guess so. Well, time to look in on Mrs. Foster."

The sheriff led Lincoln back to the far set of three cells. Mrs. Foster's cell was the only one that was occupied. She was sitting on the long brown bench. When she saw Lincoln and the sheriff, she got up, although with some difficulty, placing her hand on the small of her back and grimacing as she rose.

Lincoln spoke first. "Good evening, Mrs. Foster. I am Abraham Lincoln."

"And I, as you no doubt already know, am Abby Kelley Foster."

They stood looking at each other for a moment, neither speaking.

Finally, she smiled and said, "Why do they call you Old Abe? You don't look all that old."

"I don't quite know why they call me that. I'm only fifty-one."

"Well, I must say that you look much younger than you did in the one photo I've seen of you. I think it was in *Harper's Weekly*."

"Why, thank you. But please sit down, Mrs. Foster. You look as if you are ailing, and I don't mean to make you stand."

She sat down and said, "Sheriff, why don't you let Mr. Lincoln come into the cell? It would make it much easier for us to talk."

The sheriff shrugged and said, "I don't see why not. I doubt Mr. Lincoln is here to help you escape, and I doubt you will injure him. I will need to fetch the key to the lock. I neglected to bring the keys with me."

While they waited for the sheriff to return, Lincoln said, "I have heard you are on the Graham diet, and so I brought you some fresh apples." He held up the sack.

"I'm sorry to seem impolite, but where are they from?"

"Mrs. Lincoln's brother brought them."

"I have read that her brothers are from Kentucky."

"Yes."

"And so these apples were likely grown by slave labor, in which case I cannot eat them because I have taken the pledge not to buy slave-produced products."

Lincoln thought about it for a moment—he didn't wish to lie to her—and finally said, "I really don't know if that is so. At my wife's family's home in Lexington, there were a few apple trees right next to the house, and I think it was the family children who picked them."

"Did they not also own slaves?"

"Yes."

"Then I cannot eat them."

"Mrs. Foster, I would hazard that the dress you are wearing is made of cotton. And if that is so, that cotton must have been grown and picked by slaves. Unless you know of cotton fields in Ohio, Pennsylvania or New York."

"You may be right. I have oft been accused of being too rigid on these things. And my Quaker upbringing tells me it is rude to refuse a gift. Please leave the apples and I will see."

"If you don't eat them yourself, you can no doubt find someone around here who is a less principled eater," Lincoln said and smiled.

Just then the sheriff returned and opened the padlock that locked the door to the wall. "I will leave the two of you and come back in perhaps fifteen minutes."

Lincoln went into the cell, and Mrs. Foster said, "Please sit down."

Lincoln sat on the other end of the bench and handed her the apples. "I will leave these with you, Mrs. Foster."

"Please call me Abby. Our Quaker tradition is to use first names."

"That will please me just fine."

"Good. May I call you Abraham?"

"Of course."

"When you are elected president, I suppose I will need to address you as Mr. President."

"If I am so fortunate—and I cannot know if the nation will turn out to be fortunate in the event—please come to the White House and call me there anything you want."

"I hope if you are elected that you will keep the fate of the poor slave in mind, Abraham."

"I think of slavery all the time, Abby. All the time. It is evil beyond evil. I would hope that by the end of my term it will be gone from our land or if not, it will at least not have spread beyond where it is now."

"How?"

"At this point I do not know exactly how that will all come about or what my role in it will be."

"President Buchanan is on record as opposing slavery, but all that his term as president has brought us is the *Dred Scott* case, holding that Negroes, enslaved or free, are not citizens. And that Congress may not bar slavery from the territories."

"It is a terrible decision, certainly."

"There are more slaves now than when Buchanan took the oath of office. So forgive me, Abraham, if I do not trust you to make your hopes come true."

"Perhaps you would at least agree that my heart is in the right place. I do not know if you are aware, but when I was in Congress—now so long ago—I introduced a bill to free the slaves in the District of Columbia."

She cocked her head and looked at him as if, Lincoln thought, she had just caught a child in an obvious lie. "But, Abraham, in that bill you stipulated, did you not, that the slave owners would be compensated for their emancipated slaves?"

"Yes, of course. It would otherwise have had no chance at all of passage."

"But that is the very point. The slaves should be freed, not because it is doable or practical or will make some people feel better about themselves, but because it is a pure matter of justice."

They were both silent for a moment, as the word *justice* hung in the air between them.

Finally, Lincoln rose and began to pace the cell. "I understand your position," he said. "But I did not come tonight to debate with you how justice on the slavery issue might be achieved. Much as I suspect I might learn a great deal from you if we had the time to discuss it."

"Why did you come, then?"

He stopped pacing and looked directly at her. "To offer you legal representation in your upcoming felony trial."

She looked surprised. "You?"

"No, my partner, William Herndon. He is an excellent lawyer and a staunch abolitionist of many years standing."

"I am planning to represent myself."

"You are much more likely to be convicted if you do that."

"Then I may become a martyr of sorts and do a thousand times more good preaching from inside a prison than from out."

"You are naive about that, Abby. Women's prisons are as bad as or worse than men's prisons. You are likely to die there. And even if you don't, they are not likely to let you write or speak from inside."

"Prisoners are permitted to write letters. I know this."

"Not of the kind you hope to write. They will be censored or destroyed."

"Perhaps…if you are president…"

He smiled. "Ah, you, too, have a pardon on your mind."

"If you are truly opposed to slavery, Abraham, it would seem a logical thing to do."

"Way leads on to way in politics, and one can never predict the situation at a particular time, Abby. And in any case, I have not been elected yet and it would be presumptuous of me even to contemplate it."

"What is the advantage of having this partner of yours represent me?"

"I have a sense the government's case against you is weak, and that he will get you acquitted."

"Which will benefit you, too, will it not, Abraham? Because you will not need to consider a pardon if I am acquitted. Or answer those who are demanding you take a position on it now."

He grinned. "It's true, Abby, that the acquitted are in no need of pardons."

"Tell me more of this partner of yours."

Lincoln sat back down on the bench, looked her directly in the eye and saw that she did not look away. In his many years in the legislature, trying to persuade men to vote his way on a bill, he had learned that if he could get them to lock eyes with him, he had a chance to persuade them to his side. It was a talent he had. And so, eye to eye, he began the task of selling Billy to her.

"Billy Herndon studied law with me," he said. "And when he was admitted to the bar—sixteen years ago now—I asked him, even though he was newly minted as a lawyer, to be my partner. It was a good choice. Indeed, an excellent choice. He has tremendous skills as a lawyer, and he also has great passion."

"When I was first here in Springfield, Abraham, I inquired

about you, for obvious reasons. It is not often that you find your-self on the home ground of a likely future president."

"And?"

"I was told that *you* are the best jury lawyer in Illinois." She folded her arms across her chest. "Why should I not want you instead of your junior partner?"

"If I cannot speak now to the issue of a possible pardon for you, I think I can hardly be your lawyer and advocate for your acquittal."

"I see."

"I should also mention that Billy can help you find a way to use the trial as a platform for your views. I suspect every major newspaper in the country will have a reporter there."

"If he is such a great lawyer, why do you call him Billy in-stead of William or Mr. Herndon?"

Lincoln blinked. It was a good question, but one he had ne-glected ever to ask himself. Billy had never complained, and Mrs. Foster—Abby as she wanted to be called—had been the first person ever to mention it. He gave her the best answer he could come up with.

"I suppose I would say that it is a term of affection born of long acquaintance."

"What does he call you?"

"Lincoln."

She laughed. "Won't *Billy* representing me make it seem as if you are in accord with my being acquitted?"

"I can avoid that in various ways, Abby. Among other things, and to be direct about it, I suspect I will find a reason to visit some other town during your trial."

"Ah."

"Will you accept his offer to represent you?"

"I don't know that I'd want to afford him."

"I'm sure one of your wealthy abolitionist friends will come forward to take care of that."

"My husband, Stephen, is coming here tomorrow from Massachusetts. I will discuss it with him."

Lincoln was startled. "You're married to the famous songwriter?"

She laughed, loudly. "No, no, that is a different person, and although that man claims to be an abolitionist because he wrote 'My Old Kentucky Home,' the lyrics of other songs he has written tell me that he is no friend of Negroes."

"Oh."

"As I was saying, I will talk with my husband and let you know. Whichever way we decide, I thank you and Mr. Herndon for your kind offer."

"Thank you, Abby. I will wait to hear from you."

"Goodbye, Abraham. Perhaps I will see you in the White House." She picked up the bag and took two apples from inside. "Here," she said. "Take one with you. And here is another for the sheriff."

The sheriff arrived back shortly after that, asked Lincoln to step out of the cell and then relocked it.

As they walked away, the sheriff said, "Did I hear her call you Abraham?"

"You did."

"Isn't that rather forward?"

"She is a Quaker. That is their way."

"A weird way if you ask me."

"Perhaps so, but in any case, she is making you a gift of this apple." He handed it to him.

32

When he returned to the office, Lincoln found Herndon at the big table, surrounded by stacks of case reporters, with his head buried in one. In their division of labor over the years, Herndon did legal research more often than Lincoln, but Lincoln did, too, on occasion. Lincoln's enemies, though, enjoyed spreading the rumor that he'd hardly ever opened a law book, and was just good on his feet, telling stories and persuading juries to ignore the facts.

"What are you doing, Billy?"

"Researching how the Fugitive Slave Act has been interpreted."

"Aren't you already familiar with it? You represented that captured slave, Edward Canter, earlier this year."

"This case is different. There, I was trying to find a way to prevent Canter's return south. Here, we have someone charged with, among other things, attempting to rescue a slave from custody or assisting a slave to escape from her lawful master. Which is a violation of Section 7 of the Act."

"What, specifically, are you researching?"

"Whether mere words can constitute an attempt to rescue or assist an escape."

"What's the penalty if she's convicted?"

"Look for yourself." He handed Lincoln a statute book. Lincoln took it, studied it and said, "Not as harsh as I would have expected—up to six months in prison and a $1,000 fine."

"Correct. But here's the thing," Herndon said. "They are *also* asking for a fine of $10,000 and imprisonment of up to five years."

"Connected with what charged crime?" Lincoln said.

"It's not connected to any charge in the indictment. Perhaps the original draft of the indictment included some other crime that carried those penalties. Then they took it out but left in the penalty. So it's a mistake."

After a moment, Lincoln said, "Do you mind my calling you Billy?"

"Instead of what?"

"*Herndon*, just as you call me Lincoln."

Herndon paused for a few seconds before answering, then said, "I never thought on it before." After a few more seconds, he said, "I've rather come to like it. And quite a few people call me Billy. I don't know if I want you to call me *Herndon*."

They left it at that, and returned to the topic at hand.

Lincoln said, "My guess is that Mrs. Foster might well welcome six months in jail. It would raise her reputation among abolitionists to the highest level and fill her lecture halls to overflowing."

"She wants to be a martyr to the cause?"

"Perhaps. How well do you know the marshal, Billy?"

"Red? Well enough. I've played poker with him a lot."

"Who wins?"

Herndon got up and went over to the rolltop desk that stood against the wall. He burrowed in a cubbyhole and pulled out a sheet of paper. "I've kept track of who has won and lost in that game over the years." He handed the paper to Lincoln.

Lincoln looked it over and said, "Red won a lot more than he lost."

"I made sure of that," Herndon said. "It pays to be on his good side."

Lincoln raised his eyebrows. "Small towns. They are the same everywhere."

"Be that as it may, I will need to interview Red about what he knows."

"I assume he'll be truthful," Lincoln said.

"Or perhaps not."

"Why not?"

"Section 5 of the Act says that if a marshal allows a captured slave to escape, he's liable to compensate the slave owner for the full value of the slave's lost labor."

"Only if the marshal's at fault for the escape?"

"He has to pay either way. Presumably to discourage an abolition-friendly marshal from looking the other way when a captured slave is about to escape."

"Did Edward Canter try to escape from Red's custody?"

"No. He went peacefully once we lost in court."

"Any idea what happened to him?"

"I heard they sold him south to one of the cotton plantations in Mississippi."

"Did he have a wife and family?"

"Yes, a wife and three children. They sold each one of them south, too, but to four different places."

The two of them were silent for a moment. Lincoln realized that he could treat this as Billy's invitation for them to engage in still another conversation about abolition—and Billy's view that now was the time, not later. Lincoln decided not take him up on it.

"That is terrible" was all he said.

★ ★ ★

The next morning, Lincoln and Herndon were again in the office together, and Lincoln was perusing a freshly arrived batch of newspapers, together with a selection of letters addressed to Lincoln that came in every day from men, women and children from around the country.

"The problem with these newspapers is that they're already old news," Lincoln said to no one in particular, although he knew that only Billy was available to hear him. "And the letters don't have much to say about the Abby Kelley indictment. It's too new."

"You also get telegrams from people," Billy said. "And the Republican National Committee has set up shop in town. A lot of them travel around the country and have news to impart when they get back."

"True, true. But it's just not enough. If the newspapers are correct, this issue with Mrs. Foster and her prosecution has the potential to affect the vote in a lot of places, including in Indiana and Pennsylvania, where the voters are a mixture of abolitionists, Know-Nothings, and the German Catholics whom the Know-Nothings hate."

"It's a problem," Herndon said.

"How well do you know Johnny Hay, Billy?"

Herndon looked up from the case reporter he'd been studying. "Well enough. Why?"

"I'm thinking of sending him out to do a little fact-finding, but I need to know if I can trust him."

"What do you want him to do?"

"To go off and meet ordinary people from various walks of life in both Pennsylvania and Indiana and talk to them about the election. But not tell them who sent him."

"I think he can do that. If drinking in taverns is part of the plan, he'll excel!"

Lincoln laughed. "Alright, I may do it, then."

"Just one thing," Herndon said. "Remind John that women can't vote, and so he shouldn't spend too much time talking to them. He has an eye for the ladies, you see."

Before Lincoln could respond, there was a loud knock on the door.

"Now that you're the Republican nominee, we really should post a guard on the stairway," Herndon said, and got up to see who it was.

When he opened the door, a tall man with graying mutton-chop whiskers, well dressed in a three-piece suit, stood there. "Good evening, sir," he said. "I'm looking for Mr. Lincoln and Mr. Herndon."

"I'm Herndon and that's Lincoln over there," Herndon said. "Who might you be?"

"I'm Stephen Foster, Abby's husband."

33

"Do come in," Herndon said, reaching out to shake Foster's hand. "Please have a seat." He pulled out one of the captain's chairs that had been shoved up against the big table. "Our apologies for the clutter," he said, pushing some of the stacks of books aside to clear a space in front of the chair he'd offered Foster.

At that point, Lincoln unlimbered himself from his chair, came over and shook Foster's hand. "A pleasure to make your acquaintance," he said.

When the three of them were seated, Lincoln said, "As I'm sure you know, I had a lengthy conversation with your wife yesterday at the jail. She is a formidable woman."

"Indeed she is, sir. And that is what I came to talk to you about. Because that formidable woman is still thinking seriously of representing herself in her felony criminal trial."

"I thought I had talked her out of that," Lincoln said. "But then, I often overestimate my powers of persuasion."

"She appreciated your offer to have Mr. Herndon represent her for free, but…"

Lincoln interrupted. "Ah, she must have misunderstood. I thought I had made it clear that we would need to find a wealthy abolitionist to foot the bill. Under the circumstances, I could hardly agree that we would do it for free."

"Because it would seem as if you were supporting the abolitionist cause?"

"Yes."

"I think I can remove this problem," Foster said. "I have persuaded Abby that she must not represent herself. But in that case she wants the best jury lawyer in Illinois, and that is you, Mr. Lincoln." He looked over at Herndon. "With all due respect to your own great talents, sir. I don't mean to give offense."

Herndon nodded his head. "And none taken."

"Good," Foster said.

"But there are many other very good lawyers in this city," Herndon said. "If not me and not Lincoln, why not one of them?"

"We will take only Lincoln," Foster said. "It is either him or she will defend herself."

Lincoln listened, calculating how he might now avoid representing Abby without damaging his chances in the election by losing the entire abolitionist vote for his refusal. Finally, he said, "I will consider it, Mr. Foster. But that should not be taken to mean, 'Yes, I am going to represent her.' Nor will I, under any circumstances, represent your wife for free."

"We can afford your fee on our own, Mr. Lincoln. When can you let you let us know if you will undertake the representation?"

"I think we can let you know by tomorrow morning."

"That will be fine." Foster pushed back his chair, shook hands with both of them and headed for the door.

As he was about to open it, Herndon said, "Mr. Foster, I just wanted to say that I have so admired your work as an abolition-ist. I may not quite share your radical views on every point, but you are certainly an inspiration for us all."

Foster turned to face him. "Mr. Herndon, I think my wife is the one to be admired. She is almost fifty years old and has been at this since she was twenty-five. And while it is now in some quarters fashionable to be an abolitionist, when she began it was not. And she suffered not only the slings and arrows of ugly words, but people throwing manure at her."

Foster paused for a moment and no one of them spoke. Then he said, "And now the outrage of our government trying to put her in jail for doing nothing more than giving an abolitionist lecture in a church." He looked directly at Lincoln. "You have the power to prevent that. I suggest you consult your conscience and decide."

Foster didn't close the door behind him when he left, and Lincoln and Herndon stood there, looking at the open door and then at each other, neither one at first saying anything. Finally, Lincoln said, "I am in a pickle to be sure."

"To be sure you are. It's too bad you don't smoke or drink, Lincoln. This is a time when the calming effects of those items might help you see your way through this."

They went back to the table, and Lincoln said, "The problem is that if she defends herself, she will almost surely lose. Which will put great pressure on me to say what I will do if elected."

"And either way, it will cost you votes. And the newspapers will make hay out of it because it will sell newspapers."

Lincoln stood up, leaned against a wall and began tossing a small leather ball up in the air, smashing it against the ceiling, and catching it on its way back down. He assumed the ball had been left behind by his ten-year-old son, Willie, "Perhaps the government's case is weak and she will be acquitted even if she is her own lawyer," he said.

"We don't know much about the government's case, do we?" Herndon said.

"No, except that the woman supposedly never went to the square. So all she is accused of is speech. Can someone, in the words of the statute, 'attempt to rescue a captured slave from custody' by speech alone?"

They looked at each other and said, almost simultaneously, "No!"

"That can't be what the statute means," Lincoln said. He was continuing to toss the ball in the air and to catch it on its return. It did not always bounce true, though, and he could see that he was making Herndon nervous.

"So we could just let her husband know the argument and let them accomplish an acquittal by making their own defense on that basis," Herndon said.

"Or, they can look for another lawyer on their own. There is surely someone in this city—or even from Chicago—who will do it, and it doesn't take a brilliant legal mind to see the argument."

"I'm not sure that solves the problem," Herndon said. "While we wait for someone else to get her acquitted, it will still look to all the abolitionists in the country as if you have abandoned her. And if she is convicted, then..."

Lincoln finished his thought. "I'll move from being in a pickle to leaping into a tub of scalding water."

"And the Fosters will no doubt let it be known that they asked you to represent Abby and you said no."

"So there we are. If I care about the vote of the abolitionists, I must do it," Lincoln said.

"And you must also win the trial, Lincoln, or you will not only make yourself no friends, you will look weak. No lawyer is ever really forgiven for losing."

Lincoln tossed the ball even harder against the ceiling. On its rebound it ricocheted onto the table, not far from where Herndon was sitting. Herndon got up and moved to the other side of the room.

"There is a key question, though," Lincoln said. "By doing it, will I gain enough votes from abolitionists to offset the votes I will lose? And the lost votes will be from Democrats who do not want an abolitionist in the White House, and who will assume, despite my denials, that representing Mrs. Foster proves I am one."

"What are you going to do, Lincoln?"

"Most of the Republican National Committee has set up shop here in Springfield. I am going to visit them, tell them what I've decided to do—represent her myself—and get their advice. Although I most certainly also value yours...*Mr. Herndon.*" He smiled and tossed Herndon the ball as he left.

Before he set out for the state Capitol building, where the Republican National Committee and its staff were occupying three small offices, Lincoln walked next door to the law offices of Stephen Logan. He knew that John Hay was working as a law clerk for Logan, who was Hay's uncle. And John was indeed there.

"Johnny," he said, "I need you to come along with me to a meeting, and then I think I will have a mission for you. My only request right now is that you say nothing during the meeting."

"Alright, Mr. Lincoln. I will do that."

Once they reached the Capitol and found the Committee Lincoln introduced Hay as one of his assistants for correspondence and then got down to business. "Gentlemen, I have agreed to represent Abby Kelley Foster in her upcoming federal trial for aiding and abetting a slave to escape."

As he later told Herndon, the Committee members were collectively aghast. And some were downright apoplectic.

A few, though, like the radical Republicans on the Committee—and once they had calmed down—saw the logic of it. It might well attract abolitionist votes. Others, although Republicans, but of a more conservative mien, argued that the abolitionists were never going to vote for him in any case because they mostly didn't vote. And that representing Mrs. Foster was going to alienate both conservative Republicans and those Democrats who had been edging toward him.

One of the members pointed out one other thing: that Lincoln's support was primarily in rural areas, not in big cities. And abolition lecturers like Abby Kelley were particularly unpopular in rural areas and small towns.

"Reformers are rarely popular," Lincoln said.

One of the other members reminded everyone that although large numbers of people were flocking to big cities—perhaps someday most people would live in such cities—that was a long time away. The last census had shown that, yes, New York City and Brooklyn had over six hundred thousand people between them, but the entire state of New York—most of it still rural— had over three million. So most Republican voters were still to be found outside the cities, not in them.

"I acknowledge your point," Lincoln said. "Indeed, I will be surprised if I even carry the City of Springfield."

When they had all finally had their say—it took almost another hour—Lincoln said, "Gentlemen, I know that some of you were not in favor of my nomination."

"That is certainly true!" one of the members said.

Lincoln nodded his head in agreement and went on. "But whatever your position back in May in Chicago, you are stuck with me now, here in October."

"But we shouldn't be stuck with your foolish decisions," one of the members said.

"I'm the candidate," Lincoln said. "For better or for worse, I get to decide. And I have decided to do this, not only because I think it is right—it is about justice—but also because my intuition tells me that it will also work to our advantage. Especially if Mrs. Foster is acquitted."

"It will lose us votes," one of them said again. "And that just when we're on the cusp of winning. After all, in August—just months ago—we won Congressional seats in Indiana and Pennsylvania that we had lost to Democrats two years before. That means a Republican wave is coming everywhere in the North that will sweep us to victory in the electoral college. But with this decision, Mr. Lincoln, you are about to throw it all away."

"No, Lincoln is right," still another said. "Defending Mrs. Foster may well gain us votes."

"Not anymore due to this nonsensical decision!" someone shouted. It was a man who had until then remained silent.

"And that is just the problem," Lincoln said. "We have no way to be sure."

The argument among the Committee members continued until Lincoln ended it by rising slowly from his chair to his full six feet four—he had long ago learned that suddenly towering over seated people had a tendency to bring arguments to an end—and said, "Voters can change their opinion like the wind on a fall day. We need more information."

"Why?" one of them asked. "Of what use will it be at this late date?"

"Here is my thinking," Lincoln said. "The fact that I'm representing Mrs. Foster will be known all over the country by two days from now. If we can better learn what voters are thinking about that, you can all know what to talk about in newspaper columns, speeches and the like between the end of the trial and Election Day on November 6."

"How do you propose to find out what voters are thinking?" one of the members said. "We have no way to poll them except by counting the votes on Election Day."

"Two ways," Lincoln said. "First, I want each of you, whether by letter, telegraph or in person, to talk to people in your states—

including those who disagree with you—and report back to me what you hear.

"And there is a second thing," Lincoln said. "I am going to send young John Hay here out to talk to voters, particularly in Indiana and Pennsylvania."

"How can he possibly find out anything of use?" one of them said.

"Oh, John is a convivial young man, and I think he can make the rounds of the taverns and there sip some ale with the patrons. And perhaps also attend a few town meetings. How old are you, Johnny?"

"Twenty-one, sir, although I'll be twenty-two in a few days."

"Is there nothing more *we* can do now?" one of the Committee members said.

"Yes," Lincoln said. "If you know any of the mayors of towns in Indiana and Pennsylvania, be they Democrats or Republicans, you can introduce John to them."

"What good will that do?" one of them said.

Lincoln laughed. "They can tell him where the best taverns are."

34

Before boarding the train in Chicago, Annabelle had slipped a gold wedding band onto the ring finger of her left hand. Later on, that had helped her fend off the advances of the man sitting next to her on the train, who seemed quite intent on pursuing a conversation with her, and probably much more if his leer was any indication.

Finally, she had said, "Sir, I am married and I think my husband would feel most uncomfortable with my pursuing a conversation with you."

"Well, he isn't here, is he?" the man said.

"No, but I must again request that you permit me to return to my reading." She had brought with her a copy of the relatively new magazine, *The Atlantic Monthly*, and began to read it again.

"That magazine is an abolitionist tract, you know."

"I know," she said, not bothering to look up. "That is why I read it." Without another word, she got up and relocated to another compartment.

When she disembarked at Springfield's Fourth Street Station, the platform was surrounded by one-horse cabs, jockeying for passengers. She hailed one and asked to be taken to the Chenery House Hotel, where she had telegraphed ahead for a reservation.

The hotel was the nicest one in town. She didn't mind because she was spending Allan's money (or was it Lincoln's?) and so saw no reason to scrimp. Especially because it seemed more and more likely to her that looking further for Lucy was going to be a wild-goose chase.

She checked in under a false name—Mrs. Everett Grant—and explained to the desk clerk that she was awaiting the arrival of her husband, who was expected from New York in two or three days. If anyone should ask (the desk clerk did not), she planned to say that her first name was Jane, which seemed to her to be about as far from Annabelle as she could get.

The problem with operating under a pseudonym was, of course, that she would not be able to use her Pinkerton's calling card. But she had the feeling that calling cards were not going to be important on this particular mission.

She ate alone in the hotel dining room, using her *Atlantic* as a shield against having to talk with anyone. She noticed that the annoying gentleman from the train—he had introduced himself but she had already forgotten his name—was also dining there, but he did not approach her.

Across the room, she also noticed the newspaper reporter, Mr. Artemis, whom she hadn't seen since their encounter in Berlin. He was sitting at a table with an older woman, but was facing away from Annabelle. She spent part of her meal discreetly observing the two of them.

When Annabelle had finished and was about to leave to return to her room, she changed her mind. There was no time like the present to carry out Allan's instructions to try to get to know the reporter better. She realized that she would need to use her real name, since Clarence already knew it. She took a deep breath, got up and went over to their table.

"Good evening, Mr. Artemis," she said. "I'm Annabelle Carter. You may recall that we made each other's acquaintance at that unfortunate event in Berlin several days ago. I wanted to offer my apologies if I was perhaps a bit brusque on that occasion."

Clarence rose from his seat, nodded his head in greeting and said, "There is no need for an apology," He glanced at Annabelle's fake wedding ring, clearly trying to discern what matrimonial title to use for her, and said, "Mrs. Carter. Please allow me to introduce you to my mother, Mrs. Artemis, who is visiting from Boston."

"I'm very pleased to make your acquaintance, Mrs. Artemis," Annabelle said.

"Likewise, I'm sure," Mrs. Artemis said. "We have just called for our coffee, Mrs. Carter. Would you care to join us? I'm sure a third cup can be added to our order with no difficulty."

Annabelle looked back to Clarence, who had an expression on his face that she read as lacking in enthusiasm for his mother's invitation. Which made her all the more interested in accepting it. "I'd be delighted," she said.

Annabelle had not been seated long when Mrs. Artemis said, "If I am not mistaken, I detect a Southern accent in your speech. Do you hail from somewhere to the south of where we sit tonight, Mrs. Carter?"

"I live in Chicago," Annabelle said. "And have for many years." She knew, of course, that Mrs. Artemis, given her son's outlook, was likely an abolitionist, but she saw no reason to hide her origins. She was not ashamed of them. "I grew up in Kentucky, though." She paused a second and added, "On a plantation."

The word fell like a thud into the conversation and engendered an awkward silence, from which they were rescued by the arrival of the waiter with the coffee.

After it had been served, Mrs. Artemis said, looking back and forth between Clarence and Annabelle, "If it is not too intrusive a question, where did the two of you meet?"

Clarence, who had up until that point remained silent, said, "I wouldn't call it 'meet' so much as we both happened to be present at the same place at the same time. Very briefly."

"That's accurate," Annabelle said.

Mrs. Artemis added cream to her coffee, took a sip and said, "I'm unsure why the two of you are being so evasive about it."

"I'm not," Clarence said. "I was visiting the small town of Berlin, outside Springfield, looking for the enslaved girl, Lucy, and her owner. You'll recall, Mother, that my finding the owner there right before he died yielded a great edition for my paper."

"*Our* paper, Clarence."

Clarence ignored her comment and said, "I'm not really sure why Mrs. Carter was in Berlin that day. Something about the dead man being a neighbor in Kentucky."

"I can be more specific," Annabelle said. "I must first ask you, though, to maintain what I tell you in confidence."

She stared at Clarence until, after what seemed to her too long a time, he nodded in the affirmative.

"So long as you're not about to admit to a murder or other horrible crime," Mrs. Artemis said.

"I assure you it's not that," Annabelle said, while wondering if Mrs. Artemis would be alright with keeping secret a *minor* crime Annabelle might have committed.

"I will also keep your secret, then," Mrs. Artemis said. "Pray tell what is it?"

"I'm a detective, working for Allan Pinkerton on a mission to find Lucy if I can. I'm not anxious however, to have it generally known here in Springfield that Mr. Pinkerton is my employer and that finding Lucy is my mission. As a result, I'm registered here under an assumed name." She glanced at her left hand. "And the ring is intended to aid that deception. In fact I'm unmarried—divorced actually." As she said it, she wondered why she had felt the need to clarify that.

"I'm intrigued," Mrs. Artemis said. "How did you come to work as a detective for such a famous man? I didn't even realize he hired women as detectives."

"He has several women detectives on his staff. And once I got divorced, I needed a job, and this one paid better and was more exciting than working as a clerk in a countinghouse."

"A countinghouse," Clarence said. "I haven't heard that phrase since I was a child learning Mother Goose. I think it comes from 'Sing a Song of Sixpence.'" He recited it in a singsongy voice, moving his head back and forth to the rhythm. "The king was in the countinghouse, counting out his money."

Mrs. Artemis laughed, and said, "Do you recall the next line, Hopper?"

"I don't, Mother, and please don't call me that."

She ignored his protest and said, "The next line is, 'While the queen was in the parlor, eating bread and honey.'"

Mrs. Artemis looked directly at Annabelle and said, "I don't suppose they teach children Mother Goose down South."

"Of course they do," Annabelle said. "The rest of the rhyme goes, 'The maid was in the garden, hanging out the clothes. Along came a blackbird and snipped off her nose.'"

The three of them burst into laughter so loud that other guests in the room stared at them.

Finally, Mrs. Artemis said, "Well, I am going to turn in for the evening. I will leave you two young people to continue the conversation. And since you have already been married and divorced, Mrs. Carter, I think you hardly need a chaperone."

Annabelle watched Mrs. Artemis leave and noticed that the rude man from the train had also, at some point, left the dining room.

Clarence, who seemed to Annabelle to relax after his mother left, took a sip from his coffee and said, "Is Mr. Pinkerton looking for Lucy on his own account, or does he have a client who wants her found?"

"He has a client."

"Who is it?"

"I'm not at liberty to tell you…Hopper." She grinned.

"That was a childhood nickname given to me, my mother says, when I was around two years of age and tended to hop around. I'll thank you not to use it."

"Alright, I won't…very often."

"Returning to the topic at hand," Clarence said, "how do I know you're not looking for Lucy on behalf of one of the dead man's sons?"

"I'm not. I'm an abolitionist, even if a gradual one, and I wouldn't work on a case in which one of them was the client."

"I wonder if you're telling the truth, Mrs. Carter."

"If you're going to accuse me of lying, you might as well make it personal and call me Annabelle…Clarence."

At that moment, the waiter came by to ask if they wanted another pot of coffee.

"Bring us a bottle of wine," Annabelle said. "Something good."

"We have a very nice pink Catawba from Ohio," the waiter said. "Sparkling."

Clarence wrinkled his nose. "Something *not* of this region, please. Something French, preferably. Charge it to my mother's room."

The waiter departed.

"You also know about wine, Clarence?"

"I know what I *like*."

The waiter returned with what Clarence called "a fine Bordeaux," and they spent the next hour finishing it.

By the end, although they had become friends of a sort, they had made no progress on how to find Lucy. Or whether she was even findable. Annabelle had continued to refuse to reveal who

Pinkerton's client was, and she had the feeling that Clarence was not telling her everything he knew, either. All they could finally agree to in terms of cooperation was to try to keep each other generally informed as to their progress. And Clarence had put a strong emphasis on the word *generally*.

When they had finally finished talking, they looked around and saw that they were the last people left in the dining room. Five waiters were standing against the wall, each with a towel draped over his arm, staring at them.

"I think, Hopper, we need to go," she said.

"If you continue to call me that, *Mrs. Carter*, we might be able to work together toward our mutual goal, but we are *not* going to be friends."

35

When the next day dawned, Annabelle shook off the furry feeling in her head, ate a breakfast of biscuits and eggs and then walked over to the bakery. One of the things that Pinkerton had taught her, though, was to explore things before rushing in. This mission didn't strike her as dangerous, but she wanted to follow Pinkerton Agency procedure.

So instead of going directly into the bakery, she simply walked by and glanced inside, where she saw a man she assumed to be Hotchkiss standing behind a counter serving customers. There seemed nothing unusual about the place, so she walked on.

When she got farther down the street, she lingered for a few moments, pretending to examine items in a shop window, but actually watching people going in and out of the bakery. The only thing she noticed was that some of the customers were Negroes. Since there seemed to be quite a few Negroes in Springfield, it didn't seem out of the ordinary.

She spent most of the rest of the day doing what she imagined others would expect a married woman awaiting her husband to do—she went shopping. One of the things she bought was a broad-brimmed straw hat with a red bow in the middle. Broad-brimmed hats had recently become popular again, starting to replace bonnets—which she loathed. In the '40s and '50s, she had found it difficult to find anything but dratted bonnets in store windows.

Toward late afternoon, she returned to the bakery. As she approached the front door, a customer was just leaving, carrying a loaf of bread and heading the other way. It was the man from the train, although he didn't appear to recognize her. Probably, it was just a coincidence.

"Good evening, ma'am," the proprietor said. "It is close to closing, and I'm afraid we have no bread left. We do have a few pies."

"I'm not looking for bread. I am here about something else." She reached into the bodice of her dress, extracted Pinkerton's letter and silently handed it to him.

He seemed to evince no surprise at where the letter had been hidden, but simply read it and handed it back. "You may need it again at some point," he said.

"Thank you."

"We need to talk in back." He went to the front window and hung up a Closed sign, locked the front door and led her into a back room. The room featured three tall brick ovens arrayed against one wall, with long butcher-block counters against another. Large wooden spatulas and rolling pins hung from pegs. The room held the yeasty aroma of baking.

"What do you want, Mrs. Carter?" Hotchkiss said.

"I am looking for Lucy Battelle."

He blinked rapidly several times then paused, seeming to think over her request. "You are the third person in as many days who purports to be looking for her."

"Who were the others?"

"Normally, I wouldn't say, but, if the letter you just showed me is to be believed, you are, if not one of us, at least allied with us."

"I am."

"Very well, then, one of those seeking Lucy was Lincoln's partner, Billy Herndon. The other was Clarence Artemis, the young, nosy proprietor of our new weekly newspaper, *The Radical Abolitionist*."

Annabelle felt more than a little annoyed at learning that Clarence had been there first and had not even mentioned it to her the night before. Then she reminded herself that her goal was to find Lucy, not to triumph over Clarence as if they were engaged in a game of whist. But perhaps entering into a more formal alliance with him—something beyond keeping each other generally informed of their progress—would make sense.

"Mrs. Carter?" the baker said, and Annabelle realized she had become so lost in her own thoughts that she had fallen silent. "Oh. I'm sorry," she said. "What did you tell Herndon and Artemis?"

"Nothing. I said I didn't know anything at all about her or the Railroad."

Annabelle laughed. "But in fact you do?"

"Not in any detail. Here is what I can tell you. So far as I know, the girl is not in Springfield. Whoever took her away from the riot—if anyone did—would not have found it prudent to leave her in this city. There are always too many slave catchers here about."

"Why so many here?"

He shrugged. "Very human reasons. Even slave catchers need a place to eat and a bed to sleep in at night. Springfield has comfortable hotels and boardinghouses and many restaurants. Most other towns hereabouts don't."

"A sort of depot for slave catchers?"

"Yes. Those scum, with their whips and nets and hounds, go

out during the day, or even sometimes at night, searching for their prey. Then they return each night to their comforts here in Springfield."

"If Lucy is not here, then where might she be?" Annabelle said.

"Rumor among Stationmasters I have spoken with is that if she is anywhere around here, she is stranded at the station in Pleasanton because it's too dangerous at the moment to move her onward."

"Where is Pleasanton?"

"Not too many miles northwest of here."

"Will the Stationmaster there talk to me if I give him the letter?"

"Most likely, although everyone makes his own decision 'bout that kind of thing."

"Will you tell me his name?"

"No. Just go to the house at Number 3 Crooked Lane, tell whoever answers the door that I sent you and give them your letter."

"I will go there in the morning."

"Beware the roads. They are terrible."

"Thank you for that."

"Would you like a pie? I have several left, all apple."

"Well…"

"I insist, and in any case you ought not to be seen leaving here without something in hand. Else why did you come in?"

As he was handing her the pie, Annabelle said, "By the way, just as I came in a man was leaving. Do you know him?"

"No. He claimed to be a lawyer in town for an important trial. Said he worked for the United States government."

"Did he tell you his name?"

"Yes. G.W. Lizar."

"Well, good night, Mr. Hotchkiss," she said.

"Good night, madame. Don't forget your pie."

She left carrying a fresh apple pie, wondering what she was going to do with it. Then she had an idea.

When she got back to the hotel, she sought out the chef and asked him if he could put it aside for her in the kitchen.

"Yes, of course," he said.

"Good," Annabelle said, and handed it to him. "Do you think it will still be fresh tomorrow evening?"

"Who baked it?"

"Hotchkiss, baked fresh today."

"His pies and cakes tend not to go stale as quickly as those made by others, so your pie should still be quite tasty tomorrow evening." He held it up to his nose and inhaled. "Apple."

"Yes."

"I will have to find a place for it away from prying eyes. People hereabouts love their apple pie."

"Oh no," Annabelle said. "Please feel free to give away or sell most of it to your other guests. Just save two large pieces for me. I will be back tomorrow night to make use of them."

36

Hotchkiss had not exaggerated when he told Annabelle that the road to Pleasanton was terrible. It was worse. It had rained overnight, and the track—for it was really more track than road—was not only deeply rutted, but in places covered with mud from one side to the other. She made very slow progress.

Despite having started out immediately after a very early breakfast, she didn't reach Pleasanton until early afternoon.

Pleasanton belied its name. There were only ten houses, strung out along both sides of a single street that was only slightly less muddy than the road she had come in on. Since there was only one street, she assumed it was Crooked Lane, even though there was no sign. The houses themselves ranged in appearance from dilapidated to falling down. Number 3, which had once been painted red but was now faded to a sort of dull reddish-brown, was in the best state of repair.

She stopped in front of the house, climbed down from the carriage, tied the horse to a hitching post and began to walk toward the house. Looking down, she realized that her boots were caked with mud from the times she'd had to disembark to lead the horse through difficult patches, and that it had also gotten on the bottom of her skirt. She spotted a boot brush nailed beside the bottom of the steps that led up to the house, and used it to scrape at least some of the mud off.

The front door had a large metal knocker, and the door was opened only seconds after she knocked. A large man stood there, wearing a white cotton shirt buttoned to the neck and high-waisted trousers held up by leather suspenders.

"Yes?" he said. "Who are you?"

She thought of using her assumed name, but instead said, "I'm Annabelle Carter. Allan Pinkerton sent me." She pulled the folded letter from her dress and handed it to him.

He took it without comment and read it. He handed it back to her and said, "I can believe that Allan Pinkerton wrote this, but that doesn't tell me that you are anyone I really want to talk to. Your accent alone tells me that." He started to shut the door.

Annabelle put her hand out to stop the door from closing, assuming that he wouldn't shut it on her hand. "I can understand that," she said. "Abolitionists, though, say you should not judge a man or woman by the color of their skin. If you are truly an abolitionist, and I am told you are, then I hope you won't judge me by the color of my speech."

He just stared at her for a while, and she could feel her heart beating as she waited for him to respond. Finally, he said, "A point well made. Do come in. Please take off your muddy boots first and put them over there." He pointed to a row of boots to the left of the door.

Once bootless and inside, she followed him into the parlor, which, to her surprise, was furnished only with wooden benches, wooden chairs, and a wooden table. He must have sensed her surprise because he said, without being prompted, "Easier to keep clean in this godforsaken mud hole. Please sit down."

She chose a wooden chair and sat, while he placed himself on the wooden bench opposite. "Now, who are you looking for?" he said.

"Before I say that, sir, may I at least ask your name?"

"I'm Jared Hostetler. Who did you say you were again?"

"Annabelle Carter."

"Ah, yes, a very Southern name. What can I do for you, Mrs. Carter? Oh, but first, I have forgotten my prairie hospitality. Would you like some coffee or tea?"

"I would very much like some coffee."

"Martha!" he yelled. "We have company."

A few moments later, a petite woman wearing a light blue polka-dot dress with tiny white spots appeared and was introduced.

"Mrs. Carter here is an abolitionist sent by Allan Pinkerton. She is in need of coffee."

Mrs. Hostetler smiled, and it seemed to Annabelle—although perhaps she just imagined it—that Mrs. Hostetler was used to being ordered around by her husband, but that it was done with affection.

"I'll fetch it. I already have a pot on the fire," she said. "Mrs. Carter, would you like something hot to eat as well?"

Annabelle had brought some cured meat and bread in her bag but something hot sounded wonderful. "Yes, that would be lovely."

After Mrs. Hostetler had left the room, Mr. Hostetler said, "What can we do for you, Mrs. Carter?"

"I am looking for Lucy Battelle. I hear she may be a passenger on the Railroad hereabouts."

He laughed out loud. "It is highly unfortunate that someone years ago—I wish I knew who—decided to give our enterprise the name of Underground Railroad and attach to it all these train terms, like passenger, and station and line and Stationmaster and so forth."

"Why?"

"Because it gives people the idea that there is a great deal more organization and precision—and safety—about the whole thing than there is."

"So there is no Stationmaster in Pleasanton, as I was told?"

He shrugged. "There is someone here who often takes care of enslaved people who have escaped and are passing through. He doesn't call himself a Stationmaster, and even if I were to tell you his name, he would not talk to you. Ever. Well, perhaps when the war that is coming is over."

"You think there will be a war?"

At that moment, Mrs. Hostetler came back into the room carrying a cup of coffee in a white mug and a crockery plate piled high with what looked like creamed corn and a chicken leg. She set it down on the table next to Annabelle, and said, "Eat it up, dear," and then sat herself down in one of the other chairs. "Mr. Hostetler does indeed think there's a war a-coming," she continued. "He might be right." She smiled over at him. "He's been right once or twice before. But I think something different is going to happen."

"What's that?" Annabelle said.

"Right now a lot of enslaved people are escaping from the Border states—Missouri and Kentucky and Tennessee and even some from Virginia. Pretty soon, people in those states are gonna tire of their so-called property runnin' away. And they'll have no choice but to make slavery illegal."

Annabelle had been chowing down on the corn and chicken and had to chew a moment before she could say, "And then what?"

"Then what, is the same thing'll happen with the Deep South," Mrs. Hostetler said. "Slaves will find it easier to escape into the newly free Border states, and the whole thing'll collapse!"

"I think this is fantastical thinking," Mr. Hostetler said. "Only a war will set the evil sinners to our south on the road to redemption. If they can ever even be redeemed."

"Of course they can be redeemed," Mrs. Hostetler said.

"Perhaps they will die in the war and only their children and grandchildren will be redeemed," he said.

"You will have to excuse Mr. Hostetler," Mrs. Hostetler said. "He feels about this this quite strongly."

"The chicken and corn are very good," Annabelle said, for although she found the conversation of great interest, she needed to bring it back to Lucy.

"I do feel strongly about it," Mr. Hostetler said.

"May I ask again about Lucy?" Annabelle said.

"I can tell you that she is not to be found in this town," Mr. Hostetler said. "I am not the Stationmaster, but I would know if she is or was here. So the answer is no, she has not been here and is not here."

"She disappeared from the scene of the riot, not far from here, weeks ago now," Annabelle said. "She has not been seen or heard from since. Do you have *any* idea where she might be?"

"Before I answer that, who, exactly, wants to know? Is it really Allan Pinkerton?"

"Yes. I work for him as one of his detectives," Annabelle said. She reached into her purse and handed him one of her visiting cards.

"Pinkerton hires women detectives?"

"Yes, he does. There are several of us."

It seemed to her that Mr. Hostetler actually snorted, but perhaps he was just clearing his throat.

After an uneasy silence, Mrs. Hostetler looked over at her husband and said, "You see, my dear, women really can do things outside the sphere of the home."

When Mr. Hostetler didn't respond to his wife, Annabelle said, "May I ask again, where might Lucy be?"

Mrs. Hostetler sighed deeply and Annabelle had the excited feeling she was finally about to learn where Lucy was.

37

But that was not to be.

All Mr. Hostetler said was, "She is either in Canada or dead. Most likely dead. Or perhaps one of the slave catchers stumbled upon her and took her directly back south. Since there was already a court order to return her, whoever found her may have felt no obligation to go back into court."

"Are you planning to go back to Springfield today?" Mrs. Hostetler said.

"I had thought to," Annabelle said.

Mrs. Hostetler looked over at her husband. "It is getting late," she said. "If she goes back, given the roads, she may not make it before dark."

"I agree. It would be bad for you to be on the road after dark," Mr. Hostetler said. "We can certainly put you up for the night."

Annabelle thought about it for a second. They were right. "That would be most kind of you," she said. "But I hate to be a burden on you."

"It's no burden!" both Hostetlers said, almost as one.

After that, the tension went out of the room.

Mr. Hostetler gave her a tour of their two barns (which required that she put her muddy boots back on), and Mrs. Hostetler showed her around the house, including the bedrooms on the second floor and, finally, the basement, where the Hostetlers were storing cheese and drying apples over the winter. Annabelle had the sense that they were showing her everything so that she could see for herself that Lucy wasn't being hidden anywhere on the property. Of course, they could always have moved her from basement to barn while Annabelle was looking around upstairs and so forth.

Dinner had been pleasant, and Annabelle had been fascinated by the political talk. Mr. Hostetler was a member of the Liberty Party, an avowedly abolitionist party that had, unfortunately in the opinion of both Hostetlers, not fielded a candidate for president this time around. Or at least not in Illinois. They hated Vice President Breckinridge because he had owned slaves. They hated Douglas for introducing the Congressional act that permitted people in the territories to vote on whether to permit slavery, and they hated Bell because he was campaigning on the idea that slavery wasn't an issue worth talking about anymore. As for Lincoln, Mr. Hostetler had thought about voting for him, but he was waiting to see if he would do the "moral thing."

"What is that?" Annabelle said.

Mrs. Hostetler answered for him. "Why, announce he'll pardon Abby Kelley if she's convicted and he's elected. It's the only moral thing to do if he truly cares about the fate of the poor slave."

The conversation then drifted into farm prices as well as tariffs on imports, which the Hostetlers favored. The higher the better.

Not long after dark, they snuffed out the candles, except for the single one that each carried as they went up the steps on the way to bed. Mrs. Hostetler apologized that they had not yet added gas lamps to the house.

After she tucked herself into the feather bed in her room, Annabelle thought about the fact that she was going to fall asleep in a house with two people she hardly knew sleeping nearby— people who might have reason *not* to have her find Lucy. For all their bonhomie, they had not been helpful about that.

She considered moving the small dresser that stood against the wall so that it would block the door. Then again, if they wanted to kill her, a dresser blocking the door was not going to stop them. She also thought about loading her gun and putting it under her pillow. But that would mean charging it with powder and putting a ball in the barrel. Which would risk blowing her head off during the night. She also thought about charging and loading it and leaving it on a nearby table. But that wasn't likely to help, either. That was her final thought as she fell asleep.

She awoke in the morning to bright sunlight filling the room and instantly felt foolish that she had fallen asleep fearing for her life.

No sooner was she awake than Mrs. Hostetler knocked on her door and brought in a rough bar of soap, a towel and a pitcher of warm water so that she could, as Mrs. Hostetler put it, "freshen up." She did so, and then went down to breakfast, regretting that she had brought no change of clothes. But then she hadn't expected to stay anywhere overnight.

For breakfast Mrs. Hostetler put in front of her a robust plate of three fried eggs, a large piece of ham and a big hunk of freshly baked bread, with butter and apple jam to the side. She found it all scrumptious and, trying not to talk with her mouth full (she could still hear her mother in her ear, warning her against that), said, when she'd finished chewing, "Did you make the bread yourself, Mrs. Hostetler? It's quite delicious."

The woman looked at her like she was a bit daft. "Of course. The nearest bakery is in Springfield. So even if we were to buy it there and bring it back here, it would be stale. Did your mother not make bread at home?"

Annabelle felt embarrassed at the answer but gave it anyway. "No, the bread was made by...our—" she had trouble uttering the word "—slaves."

"There is no reason to be embarrassed about that, Annabelle. You didn't choose to have enslaved people attend you. Your parents did, and many sins may be laid by God at our feet, but the sins of our parents are not among them."

"I hope that is true," Annabelle said.

"I am curious how you came to be an opponent of slavery, you having grown up with it."

"It was not an epiphany, but gradual. When I first went to Chicago and went to work for Allan Pinkerton, I had no strong views about it. But he does, and he expresses them. At his urging, I went to several abolition lectures and began to read abolitionist newspapers."

"Like William Lloyd Garrison's *The Liberator*?"

"Yes, although I find that one too shrill for my taste," Annabelle said.

"Have you read the new one published by the young man from Springfield, the one who came out to see us to ask us about Lucy? He left a copy."

Annabelle was taken aback. Clarence had already been there? But she managed to hide her surprise, and said only, "No, I haven't read it. When did he come here?"

"A few days ago. I'll give you the copy he left behind before you leave, but I fear I have interrupted your story. I gather you changed your views about slavery over time?"

"Yes, and now I call myself a gradual abolitionist, although I more and more don't know what I mean by that. Except I still think it will all go more smoothly if slave owners are paid."

Mr. Hostetler had come into the room and, clearly having overheard what Annabelle had said, announced, "I will not see

a penny of my taxes go to reward people for their sinful ownership of human beings. Not one cent." He banged his fist on
the table.

One of the things that Pinkerton had taught Annabelle was—
contrary to her natural instincts—if you want information from
people, it's best, within limits, to appear to agree with them. "I
have come, recently, to see that you are right," she said.

"There is hope for your soul, then," he said.

She wasn't sure about the state of her soul, but didn't want to
lose sight of her goal. "Before I leave, I would like to ask again
about Lucy," Annabelle said. "It is what Allan Pinkerton is paying me to investigate."

"Ask all you want, although, as I said yesterday, we know
nothing about her whereabouts."

"Allan Pinkerton has assured me that she has not passed
through Chicago and that, therefore, she is not in Canada. You
have assured me she is nowhere around here. So where might
she be?"

Mrs. Hostetler answered, "Obviously, my dear, she is still in
Springfield, being hidden."

"If she is not dead," Mr. Hostetler added.

"Ah, then I must look for her there," Annabelle said.

"Why do you so want to find her?" Mr. Hostetler said.

"It is Allan Pinkerton who wants to find her. My assignment
is to help him do so."

"Why does he want to find her?"

Annabelle hesitated. Should she tell them? Would it help or
hurt? She decided to tell the truth. "I would appreciate your
keeping what I am about to tell you to yourselves."

Each of the Hostetlers shook their head in the affirmative.

"It is my understanding that it is Abraham Lincoln who wants
to find her."

The uttering of Lincoln's name created a sudden silence in
the room.

"He is a good man," Mrs. Hostetler finally said. "Even if he is not an abolitionist."

"Do you know why he wants to find her?" Mr. Hostetler said.

"No. But I assume it has something to do with the trial of Abby Kelley Foster for allegedly starting the riot that somehow carried Lucy off."

Mr. Hostetler snorted. "Ha! That will do him no good. Lucy is a Negro, and by law would not be allowed to testify."

"Perhaps there are other ways," Annabelle said.

"Perhaps, Mrs. Carter. Perhaps. But let me say this and say it clearly. If you find Lucy, it may, in some way that is mysterious to me, help out Abby Kelley Foster—and Mrs. Foster is a godly woman who has done much good for the slave. But it will not help Lucy. It will just end up sending her back to Kentucky more quickly."

There was again a silence in the room.

Annabelle broke it by saying, "I have a job to do."

"Then consider not doing it," Hostetler said. "The girl has taken her life into her own hands. Let her take it where she will without you, a white person who cannot possibly help her now and whose help she has in any case not asked for."

"But I…"

Mr. Hostetler interrupted her. "We are all just a lot of white people trying to absolve our national guilt by doing things to, supposedly, help." He was becoming red in the face. "And you in particular. Stop trying to shed your *Southern* guilt by trying to help when you've not been asked to."

"But Mr. Lincoln…"

"Lincoln be damned!"

"You will also endanger others," Mrs. Hostetler said, in a softer tone.

"Who?" Annabelle said. "Those who run the Underground Railroad?"

"Yes. Many of those who run the Railroad are free blacks. Who are barely tolerated here in Illinois."

"I have heard that."

"So if in your zeal to find Lucy, you end up revealing them, they may be tarred and feathered. Or even lynched. But they will find no justice."

"Leave this thing alone, Mrs. Carter," Mrs. Hostetler said.

Annabelle did not agree to leave it alone, although, following Pinkerton's tutelage, she may well have given the Hostetlers the impression that she would in fact let it be. Nothing, however, could have been further from the truth. She had an assignment, and she intended to carry it out.

After polite goodbyes, she headed her horse and carriage back toward Springfield thinking, not about slavery, but about whether the apple pie would still be fresh a day later than she had originally hoped to consume it.

38

Annabelle's trip back to Springfield had gone much more quickly than the trip out. It had not rained the day before, and the mud seemed, miraculously, to have solidified.

She reached the hotel by noon. After changing her clothes and freshening up, she ate a quick midday dinner in the hotel dining room. The chef came out from his kitchen to greet her and assured her that he had diligently guarded her two pieces of pie. Would she perhaps have one piece now, with dinner? She told him she was going to save them for a later occasion. After he left she wrote out a brief note on hotel stationery and dispatched it for delivery by the hotel's messenger "as soon as possible."

The upcoming election had attracted hordes of journalists to Springfield, including many from England and Continental Europe, all come to try to lay eyes on what the London papers called "the crude Westerner" hoping to take the White House by storm. The hotel had decided to take advantage of its new, more sophisticated clientele by setting up an afternoon tea, complete with pastries. Annabelle booked a table, took her seat at 3:00 p.m. sharp by the clock on the wall and waited.

Her table was set with blue-and-white patterned china, with napkins to match. When the waiter came by to take her order, she said she would await her guest.

At 3:15, just as Annabelle was beginning to give up hope that her plan would work, Clarence strode into the room, spoke briefly to the maître d' and walked over to her table. She noticed that he had quite clearly dressed up. He was wearing a crisp white shirt with a starched collar, a string tie and boots that had been polished to perfection.

She was about to stand up to greet him, when her mother's voice in her head said, *A woman never rises to greet a man. Just sittin' there puts him at a fine disadvantage.* And sure enough, it worked. Clarence stood awkwardly in front of her, until she deigned to say, "Thank you, Mr. Artemis, for responding to my invitation. Won't you please join me?" She gestured at the empty chair across from her.

Clarence sat down. "I'm delighted to join you. Although I must say I am puzzled at the words on your note, which suggested we have something important to discuss. If I might jump right to the point, what is it?"

"Oh, Mr. Artemis, that is so like a Yankee and so, well, unchivalrous. Let us do it the Southern way—first we will order tea and cakes, and then we can get to talking business. It's so much more refined that way, don't you agree?"

"Am I to call you, Mrs. Carter, then?"

"No, like I told you the other evening, you may call me Annabelle if you wish."

"It's not Annie?"

"If you call me that, I shall fall to calling you—what was it?—ah, yes, Hopper."

He glared at her. "Alright. Annabelle it is. In which case, as I also said the other evening, please call me Clarence."

After not too long, the waiter came by, and they ordered tea and looked over the cakes on offer, which were laid out on a silver cart that a second waiter had wheeled over.

"None of them looks very appealing," Clarence said.

"Would you prefer apple pie?" Annabelle said.

"Is there some? I was here for supper rather late last night and they said they had none left."

"There are in fact still two pieces left that I had specially put aside."

He gave her an odd look, but said, "Let's have them, then!"

Annabelle turned to the waiter with the cart and said, "Back in the kitchen, I believe you will find that the chef has laid aside two pieces of apple pie for me. If you could bring them to us, we would be most grateful."

When the pie came, together with the tea, Clarence said, "How did you manage to reserve two pieces of pie for yourself? Do you know the chef?"

Annabelle told him the story of her visit to Hotchkiss. When she had finished, Clarence said, "Do I understand, then, that you intended to reserve the pie for me in particular?"

She laughed. He was correct, of course, but instead of acknowledging it, she said, "I'd say I wanted to reserve it more for whoever might prove useful to me."

"Ah, so I am simply useful. A man likes to be thought of as more than that."

"Perhaps so, Clarence, but what I am after right now is the usefulness we could create for one another."

Before he could inquire what that might be, a waiter came by again and, without asking, poured more tea into each of their cups. "I hope the pie is satisfactory," he said.

"Oh, quite," Annabelle said.

After he left Clarence said, "And what is this mutual useful-ness that you have in mind?"

"We are both looking for Lucy, but separately. And although we agreed to keep each other generally informed, we are wast-ing time by doing the same thing. For example, I just went to see the Hostetlers in Pleasanton, only to learn that you had al-ready been there. And I know you had also been to see Hotch-kiss before me, but you didn't tell me that."

Clarence took a sip of tea. "But we were at those places with different purposes," he said. "You want to find Lucy on behalf of Pinkerton—I still don't know on behalf of what client he wants to locate her—but I want to know where she is in order to write a great story for my paper."

Annabelle raised her teacup toward her lips, eyed him over the top of it and said, "A story that puts you, Clarence, at the thrilling center of finding her yourself—just like you suppos-edly did with Goshorn."

He shrugged. "I'm not embarrassed by that kind of story at all. I'm here trying to make my reputation. Once I do that, I'm not planning to spend the rest of my life in this godforsaken place."

"I see," she said. "Well, do you want to cooperate or not?"

"First tell me who Pinkerton's client is."

"Only if you agree to keep it strictly to yourself and not print it."

"Agreed."

"His client is Abraham Lincoln."

"Why does *he* want to find her?"

"I honestly don't know, Clarence."

"If we're to cooperate, we need to have some rules," he said.

"I agree. But we need to work them out somewhere else. I don't know if you've noticed, but the waiters keep passing un-usually close to our table. I suspect they want to try to overhear what we're talking about."

They left the hotel and strolled down the street side by side, arguing out the rules they would need to follow if they weren't to get in each other's way.

To Annabelle's surprise, she saw Lincoln coming toward them. Upon spotting them, he raised his eyebrows in apparent surprise, then tipped his stovepipe hat. "Good evening to you both," he said, and walked on without stopping.

"He will think we're courting!" Annabelle said.

"Why would he think that?"

"In a small town like this one, I suspect men and women don't walk down the street side by side unless they are married or courting."

Clarence hesitated a moment, then held out his arm to her. She looked at it for a second, then took it, and they walked on down the street together, continuing their discussion about how to work in tandem to find Lucy without getting in the way of their differing goals. It was not going to be easy.

39

Washington, DC

The weather in Washington, which had been unseasonably cold, had turned at least a little warmer, and Buchanan felt the need to get out of the White House and go for a walk. Of course, if he went out by himself, he would immediately attract a crowd of hangers-on, who would approach him and try to talk to him. Some would inevitably be people looking for low-level jobs in the administration (even though, with only months to go in his term, there weren't many such jobs to hand out, which you would think they would know).

Some would be people wanting to give him advice on the nation's current troubles. Some would be citizens wishing to thank him for a job well-done. Although in truth there had not been many of those of late.

Today, he wanted to walk undisturbed, so he asked four young officers from the military attaché's office to walk with him. "And please wear your ceremonial swords," he said. "I want people to stay away."

"Yes, sir," one of the young men said.

And so Buchanan, who liked to think of himself as an elegant dresser (although he knew others thought he dressed in clothing that had been stylish twenty years ago), threw on a handsomely tailored dark blue lamb's wool coat. Just in case, he added a patterned red silk scarf that had been a gift to him from Senator King of Georgia. As he prepared to leave the White House via the north portico, he spied his niece standing in the entrance hall. "Harriet, I am going for a walk. Will you join me?"

"Oh, thank you, Uncle, but I am getting ready for the dinner we're having tonight for the leadership of the House and Senate."

"Oh, yes." He sighed. "I fear that since some hail from the North and some from the South we will once again be welcoming into the mansion more yelling and screaming about slavery and secession."

"I have arranged for entertainment that I hope will distract them from that. I've also arranged the seating so as to reduce discussion of sectional politics." She paused. "Or so I hope."

"Alright, well, I will see you at dinner and, once again, I thank you for the wonderful job you have done these last four years in presiding over my White House."

"It has been my pleasure, Uncle."

"Have you decided what to do when my term ends on March 4? It is not far away now."

"I don't think there's ever been any doubt. I'm going back to Wheatland with you to help you write your autobiography."

A smile lit up his face. "I am so pleased to hear that." He would need all the help he could get with his book. The critics were already calling him the worst president in American history, and he would need to explain clearly and succinctly the enormity of the choice he faced—give the South what it wanted, including letting them go in peace, or bring on a fratricidal war.

As he left the White House with his young officers, he looked down Pennsylvania Avenue to its far end and inspected the progress on the Capitol, whose old dome had been removed. The new one, made of iron, was sitting to the side, on the ground. It would replace the old, copper-clad wooden one, which had not only looked too small for the newly expanded building beneath it, but was considered a major fire hazard. Perhaps his successor would see the job completed.

There was an unexpected gust of cold wind, and he hunched up against it. His thoughts had turned melancholy. If Lincoln were elected, and the states of the Deep South seceded, and if Virginia and Maryland followed, wouldn't Washington be the logical capital if they were to form some kind of confederation? Where would the North relocate its capital? He tried to look on the brighter side. Philadelphia, in his own state of Pennsylvania, would be a good choice for a new Northern capital.

As he passed the Treasury building, where still more construction was underway—the Treasury was always expanding it seemed—his guards stopped abruptly. Lost in thought, he almost bumped into the officer leading the group.

"Sir," the guard said. "There is a gentleman who wishes to approach."

Buchanan looked up and saw Jeremiah Black.

"Mr. Attorney General, how nice to see you. Please join me! I am out for a walk."

The guards parted and Black fell in with Buchanan as they walked along.

"What brings you out today, Jeremiah?" Buchanan said.

"I have been at the Treasury."

"Doing what? That is not a usual place for the attorney general."

"I have been consulting with the Solicitor of the Treasury about the trial soon to take place in Springfield. He supervises the United States attorneys around the country."

"Ah, yes, in the press of other business I had almost forgotten about the whole thing."

"I assume you have heard that Lincoln is going to represent Mrs. Foster in her trial."

"No. Why he would agree to do that?"

"If my reading of the newspapers is correct, it is because our plan is working. The abolitionists are demanding to know whether, if Mrs. Foster is convicted and he is elected, he will pardon her. Even Frederick Douglass has demanded to know what he will do."

Buchanan pulled his scarf tight around him against another stronger blast of wind.

"How, then, does representing Mrs. Foster help him?" Buchanan said.

"It's simple, Mr. President. If Lincoln wins the case, he will no longer have to address the pardon issue, pleasing abolitionists, and his great lawyering might also win him votes among other groups."

"And if he loses?"

"He will not only have the pardon issue still in front of him, but will also become a laughingstock—the supposedly great lawyer proven not so great."

The wind was rising, and Buchanan thrust his hands into his coat pockets. He had forgotten to bring gloves. "Perhaps he will not even become president," he said.

They walked on for a while in silence, until finally Black said, "I have also been trying to gain a better understanding of Lincoln as a lawyer so that we can figure out how best to oppose him."

"Don't our chances turn on the strength of our case?"

"Of course, and the government's case is strong. But it is all hearsay, which can easily be attacked on cross-examination. My informants tell me Lincoln is especially good at that. Savage, even."

"What do you recommend be done, then?"

"For one thing, I have been talking about Lincoln with my

friend and yours, Edwin Stanton, who, it turns out, knows him. Stanton was cocounsel with Lincoln on a case last year out in Missouri. Something for the Illinois Central Railroad."

"And?"

"He thinks he is a total rube whose main talent is telling jokes to get everyone to like him. Stanton says if our case is strong and the government prosecutor competent we shouldn't worry about Lincoln."

"Should we not worry about our case, then?"

"Perhaps not. But to be sure, I have talked to the Solicitor of the Treasury Department about certain steps that might be taken to buttress our case, and he has already sent someone to Springfield to start the process. I can explain those steps to you if you like."

"Fine, but I am getting colder and colder. Let us head back to the White House, and you can explain it all to me there while you join me for a drink."

"That sounds excellent, Mr. President."

"Jeremiah, will the steps you have in mind require my approval?"

"No, I don't think so. Not at all."

40

Law Offices of Lincoln and Herndon

"Well," Lincoln said, "the trial starts tomorrow and still no Lucy." He was sitting across a table from Allan Pinkerton.

"We have looked and looked," Pinkerton said. "But we have not found her anywhere. I'm quite confident she is not in Canada or anywhere else along the Railroad's routes. Nor has Annabelle found any trace of her." He gestured at Annabelle, who was sitting beside him.

"I've asked many people," Annabelle said. "And gone to many likely places and snooped around. I've even befriended a few slave catchers and pretended to be a female slave catcher. There are a lot of slave catchers out there looking for Lucy. A large reward has been posted."

"There is indeed a lot of interest in her," Lincoln said, and pointed to the large stack of newspapers sitting on the table beside him. "The upcoming trial and Lucy are the lead articles in almost all the papers I read, national and local."

"There's another reason, too," Annabelle said. She took a

folded-up piece of paper out of her bag, opened it and smoothed it out on the table. It was a reward poster, with, at the top, two drawings side by side. The first showed a tall, thin Negro girl with curly hair, dressed in homespun with the words *Lucy Battelle Escaped Slave* over it. The second showed a tall, thin black boy, his head shaved, wearing a cap and dressed in a suit, with the word *Disguised* over the drawing.

"A two-thousand-dollar reward for her recapture?" Pinkerton said. "That's a lot of money."

"Lincoln, do you still think it's important for us to find her?" Pinkerton said.

"Yes. I continue to think—indeed I am quite certain—that if she is found, the public's interest in Mrs. Foster and this trial will quickly wink out. Instead, people will want to know how Lucy got away the first time, how she got away the second time and so forth. It will be a great adventure story, and she will be the hero. At least in the North."

"How will that help you?" Annabelle said.

"At the very least, abolitionists will stop asking if I'm going to pardon Mrs. Foster if she's convicted and I'm elected."

"I don't understand what you're saying, Abe," Pinkerton said. "Because you will still have to get Mrs. Foster acquitted."

"Of course, Allan. But even though jurors aren't supposed to consider evidence outside what they hear in the courtroom, they always do. And Lucy found will make them less likely to want to convict Mrs. Foster. Trust me on that."

"Isn't it now too late?" Pinkerton said. "Because we haven't found her."

"The trial could last several days," Lincoln said. "Let's keep looking."

"To increase our chances of success," Annabelle said, "I have made common cause with Clarence Artemis. He is looking for Lucy, too. And we both now think she is somewhere in Springfield or nearby. If we can divide up the city in terms of looking, we might make more progress."

"Yes," Lincoln said. "I noticed the two of you just outside the hotel yesterday, as you may recall. You were deep in conversation."

"We were discussing how to further our search."

Lincoln laughed. "Well, after I passed you by, I turned to look behind me and saw that you had taken his arm." He grinned. "It looked as if you were courting."

Annabelle's face reddened. "We are not!"

"I've stayed in that hotel," Pinkerton said. "The sidewalk outside thereabouts is rough, Abe. Anyone would need an arm to lean on."

"True," Lincoln said. "So, Annabelle, what will you and Clarence look for in your search?"

"People who've noticed suspicious activity around a house or business—extra food being brought in, unusual activity at night and so forth."

"Well, let me know if you find her."

"We will," Pinkerton said.

"Thank you," Lincoln said, getting up. "And now if you'll all excuse me, I need to go over to the jail and meet with our client."

When Lincoln arrived at the jail, the sheriff said, on seeing him, "Let me go find out if she wants to see you. She has not been feeling well and has been quite out of sorts of late."

Lincoln watched him leave and busied himself looking around the office. Nothing much had changed since his most recent visit, except that the cows on the desk were gone.

When the sheriff returned a few minutes later, Lincoln said, "What happened to the cows, Sheriff?"

"It's a sad thing, but I dropped them and broke them."

"Beyond repair?"

"Afraid so."

"That's too bad. I liked them."

"Me, too. Anyway, Mrs. Foster will see you. I'll take you back."

When they reached the cell, Abby was sitting toward the back of the wooden bench. She seemed listless, but looked up when Lincoln approached.

"Oh, good morning, Abraham," she said.

"Good morning, Abby. I'm here to talk to you about the trial, which starts tomorrow."

"I know, but I don't know if I am well enough to attend."

"Have you asked to see a doctor?"

"Yes, and he has been here. He says I am not eating well enough. But I did finish the apples." She smiled up at him. "It is impolite to ask, but did you bring any more?"

"No, but I will see that some are brought to you."

The sheriff, who had been listening, said, "I will leave the two of you. Mr. Lincoln, I'm going to unlock the cell door and leave it open. I assume you'll not let Mrs. Foster leave the cell unless you accompany her or bring her out to me."

"Agreed, Sheriff."

After the sheriff had unlocked the door and left, Lincoln said, "What did the doctor think was the problem with your eating, Abby?"

"I have been trying to follow the Graham diet in here, but even with Stephen buying things and bringing them in it has been difficult to get enough to eat."

"Have you gotten any exercise?"

"Yes and no. There is no exercise yard here, but the sheriff has permitted me to go outside, accompanied by one of his deputies, and walk around the square."

"Have you done that?"

"A few times. The problem has been that we attract a crowd

of people who follow us, some in support of me and some not and they begin to yell at me and at each other."

"Do you think you can find the wherewithal to come to court?"

"I don't know. Would it have to be tomorrow?"

"Yes, but not necessarily at the start of the day."

"Perhaps I will skip the trial entirely. Because I consider it an illegitimate process put on by an illegitimate government."

Lincoln thought about it for a moment. "Well, that is a problem. If you tell the judge in open court you are refusing to attend on principle, he *might* be willing to try you in absentia."

"Is that done often?"

"Almost never, but I don't think my friend Judge Treat— he is the only federal judge here in Springfield—is the kind of man who would handcuff you to the chair to make you attend if you wish not to."

"What if I just say I am too sick, which would not be a lie."

"If the judge comes to believe you are too sick to attend, he will likely delay the trial until you are better."

Lincoln looked at her again, more carefully. She was pale and seemed much frailer than the last time he had seen her.

"Would you like to walk up and down the hall for a few minutes?" he said. "I didn't see any other prisoners in the other cells at the moment."

"That would be most appreciated." She rose from the bench and took his proffered arm. They went out into the hallway and began to walk up and down it.

"Let us return, Abraham, to the idea of my being too sick to attend. Would a delay in the trial be good or bad for your campaign?"

"I thought you weren't even going to urge men to vote for me, Abby."

"I'm not, nor to vote for any other candidate. But I would

hate to think that my trial created more problems for you than I have already—albeit inadvertently—sent your way."

"As a lawyer, I am ethically bound to do what is best for you, without regard to my own interests."

"Alright, in that case my desire is get this trial over with as quickly as possible. If I am convicted, I will go to jail for six months and work to bring people I meet there to the cause of abolishing slavery. Perhaps I will start an abolitionist newspaper for prisoners."

"What if you are acquitted?" he said.

"If I am acquitted I will go back to our farm in Worcester, recover there for a few weeks and—" Lincoln noticed a tear in her eye "—spend time with my daughter. She is already thirteen. It is so hard to believe."

"Tempus fugit," Lincoln said.

"So it does, so it does."

"It is unusual for a mother to leave a teenager behind."

"I don't take that as a rebuke, Abraham."

"It was not intended as such."

"Well, I hate to leave her behind each time I go out on the lecture circuit. But I felt, starting many years ago, that I ought not to advantage myself when slave women are often forced to leave their children behind at an even younger age." She paused. "Or, indeed, see them sold away."

"How old was your daughter when you first went back out to lecture?"

"She was five."

They had now traversed the hallway several times, and Lincoln could tell that she was tiring.

"I think it is time to return you to the custody of the sheriff," Lincoln said. "Before I do, are you able to make a decision now about attending the trial tomorrow?"

"I think I will be able to attend so long as I don't have to get there bright and early."

"Alright. I will send Herndon to get you, and he will escort you to the court when you are ready."

After that, Lincoln walked her back the sheriff's office, with her still holding on to his arm.

When they got there, Lincoln said, "Sheriff, I am returning your prisoner to you."

The sheriff looked up from the newspaper he had been reading, saw them and grinned. "You two look like you're betrothed," he said.

"He is much too young for me, Sheriff," Abby said.

"Oh, what is the age difference?"

"I think it is only two years," she said. "But I think Mr. Lincoln is already spoken for, as am I. Not only that, but we have some political disagreements."

Lincoln said nothing but wondered, not for the first time, what it would be like to be married to someone who was so different from Mary Todd. But no less political, he reminded himself. If only... Well, and now he wanted to be president of the United States, and, should he win, Mary would be coming with him into that maelstrom. She would almost certainly bring her emotional problems with her, but the social pressures on her in Washington would be even greater than they were in Springfield. He did not look forward to that.

41

United States District Court
Springfield, Illinois
October 16, 1860

The federal courtroom Lincoln entered on the morning of October 16 was hardly unfamiliar to him. It was not only in the same building his own law firm had occupied earlier in the decade—the courtroom being just one floor down from his old offices—but the ornate room, with its high bench, white railings and green felt-covered tables, had been the seat of the United States District Court for the Southern District of Illinois since 1855.

Lincoln had tried cases in that very courtroom dozens of times. So when he walked into the room that morning, he felt as comfortable there as he did in any other courtroom in the state. He planned to make himself at home in it and show the jury that he owned it.

What surprised him, then, was not the packed gallery he saw, with reporters from all over the country filling every seat, including, in one of them, Clarence (and right next to him, Annabelle). It was instead the man he saw sitting up on the bench. He had expected, as he had told Abby, to find his old friend Judge

Samuel Treat there. Instead, there was a man whose nameplate said *Judge Benjamin Garrett.*

Treat was the only federal judge in the district and a man with whom Lincoln was extremely comfortable. Lincoln had tried hundreds of cases before him back when Treat was a state trial judge, and argued dozens of appellate cases before him when Treat was later promoted to sit on the Illinois Supreme Court. Then, when Treat had been appointed to the Federal District Court by President Pierce back in '55 he had presided over still more of Lincoln's cases.

As for Judge Garrett, Lincoln had never before laid eyes on him. Nor, for that matter, had he ever heard of him.

Garrett had clearly heard of him, however, because before Lincoln could open his mouth to say a word, the judge said, "Welcome to my courtroom, Mr. Lincoln."

"Thank you, Your Honor. I am pleased to make your acquaintance."

"Well, I hate to start out our acquaintanceship on a sour note, Mr. Lincoln, but you are late for this hearing."

"I apologize, Your Honor. I was visiting my client in the jail. She is too ill to attend today, and I was gathering up her wishes on certain motions that may arise."

"Be that as it may, Counsel, you have inconvenienced not only me, but the court's clerk and counsel for the United States of America." The judge nodded his head toward the man sitting at the table to Lincoln's left. Lincoln, who was by then standing behind the counsel table but had not yet taken his seat, leaned his long frame out over the table and swiveled his head so he could read the man's nameplate. It said G.W. Lizar.

Lincoln realized it would be hard to resist making a pun on the man's last name, and he wondered if he could also somehow work the man's initials into it. But G.W. Lizar was another person Lincoln had never before seen in Springfield. The regular United States attorney, the government's principle lawyer in Springfield, was missing from his usual place.

"Let us move quickly forward, Mr. Lincoln," Judge Garrett said. "You are probably wondering where Judge Treat is. I have here his written recusal from this case." He lifted a piece of paper from the desk in front of him. "I will hand it to the clerk to hand to you."

The clerk, a large man named Craig Laurence, whom Lincoln had known for many years, took the paper from the judge and brought it to Lincoln, who read it over and said, "Well, I see that, as is often the case with a recusal, it doesn't say why he is recusing himself."

"I think it's fairly obvious," the judge said. "He told me the two of you are close friends."

"I don't know if I'd say close," Lincoln said. "But however near or far apart we are in our friendship, we've been at the same distance, whether it be measured in feet or furlongs, for many years now, and he's never felt the need to recuse himself before."

"I think the core of it, as I understand it, is that the two of you play chess together frequently," the judge said.

"I would put it more that Treat plays while I have the honor of watching him win."

"That is precisely the point, Mr. Lincoln. He may have felt you were letting him win and thus currying favor with him."

Lincoln paused a moment and said, "That reminds me of the story of the man who took his pig to market..."

The judge interrupted. "Mr. Lincoln, I have heard it said that you like to tell stories in court and that they are often very funny, but I am a judge in Chicago, where we focus on the facts and the law. So we will have to leave the man and his pig behind for the moment."

"I have been to Chicago once in a while," Lincoln said.

"I am aware of that," the judge said. "I know you have had the high honor of being nominated in that city to lead your party's presidential bid. But that is neither here nor there inside this courtroom."

Herndon, who had been sitting in the back listening, raised his eyebrows. The judge might think now that Lincoln's candidacy was neither here nor there, but if Lincoln got himself elected, and the judge hoped for a more prestigious federal job, it would be both here and there. Well, the man was probably a Democrat, so he wouldn't likely be in line for any important job anyway.

Lincoln ignored the judge's remark and said, simply, "Your Honor, I have a motion to bring in this matter that I think is very much both here and now."

The judge peered down at him. "That's fine, Mr. Lincoln. But Mr. Lizar—" Lincoln noticed that the judge had very carefully pronounced the man's name *Lee-sar* "—has let me know he also has some matters to bring to the court's attention. As a matter of courtesy, I think I should permit the government to go first."

"Well, I have no objection to that," Lincoln said and sat down.

The judge had been swiveling back and forth in the high-backed wooden chair that Lincoln knew Treat had had specially built for himself several years before. It squeaked noticeably.

"Did this chair always squeak like this when Judge Treat was presiding?" Judge Garrett asked.

"No, Your Honor," Lincoln said. "Perhaps it needs a little whale grease or something to lubricate it." Lincoln didn't say what he was truly thinking—that Judge Garrett appeared to weigh a great deal more than Judge Treat, which might be the problem.

Lizar rose from his chair and, ignoring the squeak issue, said, "Thank you, Your Honor, and you, too, Mr. Lincoln, for your courtesy. The government moves for a continuance of this matter until after the election."

"On what ground, sir?" the judge said.

"On the ground that Mr. Lincoln is a candidate for the presidency, which will distract the jurors. It is just too bright a light for them to ignore."

"What do you mean by too bright a light?" the judge said.

"I mean that we will have jurors voting by party. Republican jurors will simply vote to acquit Mr. Lincoln's client."

"What do you say to that, Mr. Lincoln?"

"Well, first, Mr. Lizar—" Lincoln made a point of pronouncing the man's name as it was spelled "—has now made the issue of my candidacy either *here* or *there*. I'm not quite sure which. Perhaps both."

The audience tittered. The judge silenced them with a sharp look, and Lincoln continued. "Your Honor, the government's case is so weak I would be happy to have as jurors only those jurors who will swear an oath to vote for Senator Douglas or even that other Democratic candidate who is running." Lincoln scrunched up his brow. "I'm sorry. I have forgotten his name."

"Breckinridge," the judge said.

"That's right," Lincoln said. "Vice President Breckinridge. The only good-looking candidate for the presidency."

There was a burst of laughter in the courtroom.

The judge, apparently deciding that it was best to ignore the humor breaking out around him, said, "I'm going to deny the government's motion. If, during jury selection, it appears that Mr. Lincoln's celebrity is a problem, I will reconsider the government's motion. Now, Mr. Lincoln, I believe you said you had a motion to bring."

"I have two," Lincoln said. "But if the first one is granted I won't need to get to the second."

"Alright, but before we get to your motions, we need to discuss the fact that the defendant is not here."

"As I said earlier, she is feeling poorly."

"I take your word for that, sir. But we do not try people in absentia in this country unless they appear for trial and then flee after the trial has begun or voluntarily absent themselves."

"Your Honor, may I consult with my partner, Mr. Herndon?"

"Yes, of course."

Herndon came forward and whispered in Lincoln's ear.

"Your Honor," Lincoln said, "my more learned partner, Mr. Herndon, informs me that the pretrial motion phase is not considered in this state to be the start of the trial."

"I agree," the judge said. "The trial begins when the first juror is sworn in. Will your client be here for that?"

"I hope so, Your Honor."

"If not, Mr. Lincoln, we will have a problem."

Lizar rose from his table. "Your Honor, the government would be willing to continue the trial until Mrs. Foster is feeling up to it."

The judge smiled. "Why does it not surprise me that the government would be willing to do that?"

Lincoln didn't wait for Lizar to respond. "Your Honor, I don't think we will need to take Mr. Lizar up on his generous offer. I will endeavor to make sure that Mrs. Foster is here when the real trial begins."

"Very well, Mr. Lincoln. Now, let's turn to your motions. What is your first motion, sir?"

"It is one that I think will end this case today," Lincoln said.

"Let's hear it, Mr. Lincoln."

42

"Yes, Your Honor," Lincoln said. "My client has been indicted for violation of Section 7 of the Fugitive Slave Act of 1850, for assisting a captured slave to escape again. The maximum penalty for violating the Act is a fine of $1,000 and six months' imprisonment. The indictment asks for the maximum penalty."

"What is the problem, then, Mr. Lincoln?"

"In a separate section of the indictment, at the very end, the government has asked for a penalty of five years' imprisonment and a fine of $10,000, but without alleging that Mrs. Foster committed any crime that carries that penalty. She is *only* charged with violating the Fugitive Slave Act."

"What is your motion, then, Mr. Lincoln?"

"That the excessive penalty be struck or, in the alternative, that the entire case be dismissed."

"Mr. Lizar?"

"Uh, I think Mr. Lincoln could be right, Your Honor, but only because there is an inadvertent error in the charge. Somehow, the allegation of the other crime, the one that would justify the longer sentence, got left out of the indictment."

"Left out by you?"

"Uh, no, I believe it was an error made by the regular United States Attorney in this District, who is, uh, not here at the moment."

"We have all been wondering," Lincoln said, "what happened to him?" He raised his eyes to the ceiling as if seeking Divine guidance on the man's fate.

The judge seemed not to be offended that Lincoln had interrupted but instead followed his lead and said, "Yes, where is he, Mr. Lizard?"

"He was called back East on an urgent matter," Lizar said, apparently deciding not to notice that the judge had added a *d* to his last name. Or perhaps, Lincoln surmised, it was such a common occurrence that Lizar had simply not noticed. And what *did* the G.W. stand for?

"Well, Mr. Lizar, I don't hear you volunteering to strike the improper request for additional punishments from the charge," the judge said. "So, whosever fault it was, I'm going to grant Mr. Lincoln's motion and dismiss the entire case."

"But, Your Honor…"

"Mr. Lizar, the government can always refile, of course, with the indictment properly drawn."

"The government instead requests that you continue the case," Lizar said. "That will give me time to consult with the, uh, proper people to see what crime was left out of the charge, so it can be put back in."

Lizar kept looking down at a piece of paper on the table, as if the names of the people to consult with were listed there.

"Won't you have to impanel a new grand jury to do that, Mr. Lizar?" the judge said.

Lizar looked back up. "Perhaps," he said.

"Perhaps? Well, my understanding of the law may be limited,

but I don't think you can willy-nilly add a new crime to a filed indictment just because you feel like it."

"Yes, that's right," Lizar said.

"Of course, it's right!" The judge's face was getting red and he was breathing hard. "Here's how it works, Mr. Lizar. The grand jury, after considering the *evidence* put in front of it, decides whether the government has shown probable cause that a crime has been committed by the defendant."

Lincoln had to suppress his laughter because he knew, as every criminal defense lawyer in Illinois did, that grand juries would usually indict whomever the government wanted to indict, for whatever crime the government wanted to indict them for.

Lizar, meanwhile, was trying to recover his standing with the judge. "Your Honor, I didn't supervise the grand jury that brought these charges."

"Charge, Mr. Lizar," the judge said. "And why is dismissing the case while the government fixes the indictment such a big problem? Cases are delayed all the time. In fact, you yourself just moved to delay this one."

"Well, Your Honor, if you dismiss it instead of continuing it, the defendant will no longer be in custody."

"That's not my problem," the judge said. "Mr. Lincoln, do you have anything you want to add before I dismiss the case?"

Lincoln had long ago learned that if you're winning, you should just be quiet, but he couldn't resist. "Your Honor, your question reminds me of the question asked of a pig who was being led to slaughter…"

"No jokes, Mr. Lincoln, remember? Save it for the White House if you get there. Although in all candor, I was hoping we'd have a new president with at least some small sense of poetry to buttress his political rhetoric. Buchanan has been such a disappointment in that regard."

Lincoln shrugged. "Sorry, Your Honor. If I get there I'll see what I can do poetically."

Lizar did have something to add. "Will Your Honor maintain Mrs. Foster's arrest and incarceration while I look into this matter?"

"I would have no authority to do that once the case is dismissed, which is what I *am* going to do today. Even if I did have the authority, I wouldn't keep someone in custody while the government attempts to fix a problem of its own creation."

Lizar turned to Lincoln. "Will your client voluntarily remain in the City of Springfield in the interim?"

"No."

Lincoln tried to suppress his glee. Because if the charge was dismissed for even an hour, he was going to hustle Abby out of town on the first available train East.

The judge was still staring at Lizar. Finally, the judge said, "Mr. Lizar, you represent the United States of America, is that not correct?"

"Yes, sir."

"And the government that has filed this indictment is seeking an impermissible penalty, given the crime charged. Isn't that right?"

"Well, it was the grand jury, but yes, sir."

"The entire grand jury walked over to the clerk's office and filed this? All of them?"

"Well, no, it was the United States attorney's office on their behalf."

"Why can't you, as the *current* attorney for the United States, just strike out the improper part of the indictment? Then we can go forward without a problem. You don't need the grand jury to take something away."

"I may not have the authority. I might have to telegraph Washington. They may want to add additional charges."

"Washington? I thought we were here in Illinois, doing justice as a *local* grand jury thought appropriate."

"Well..."

"Well nothing, Mr. Lizar, if you can't or won't strike the five-year part out and substitute $1,000 for $10,000, I'm about to lift up my gavel and dismiss this case." He put his hand on the gavel.

Lizar said nothing, but just twisted his hands together.

Instead of picking up the gavel, the judge picked up a wooden-handled pen from a pen stand on the bench and held it up. Lincoln could see the gold nib glinting in the light.

"Here's the pen, Mr. Lizar." The judge lifted up a piece of paper that had been lying on the bench. "And here's the charging document. Please make a decision."

Lizar waited a few seconds and, finally, said, "May I approach, Your Honor?"

"Yes."

Lizar walked up to the bench, took the pen, dipped the nib in the inkwell and struck out the offending clause. Then he scribbled some more, clearly striking out $10,000 and adding $1,000 in its place.

The judge examined it and waved the paper back and forth as if to aid the ink in drying. "Alright," he said. "Mr. Lizar has struck out the request for five years' imprisonment and modified the fine, leaving the only penalty demanded a fine of up to $1,000 and imprisonment for up to six months in jail. Is that correct, Mr. Lizar?"

"Yes, sir."

"Now, Mr. Lizar, I know you're a lawyer, but I want to be sure you understand, on behalf of the United States of America, that if we go forward with the trial on this single charge, the government cannot later charge Mrs. Foster with a different, more serious crime based on the same set of facts or related facts. Do you agree with that?"

Lincoln thought Lizar gulped before saying, "Yes, Your Honor." Lincoln wondered what Lizar's superiors were going to say when they heard what he had done. Even if Abby were to be convicted, but was sent to jail for only six months, she'd not equal Frederick Douglass in fame—but she'd be a much brighter star in the abolitionist firmament.

Lincoln had drifted off into his reverie of Lizar being up-braided by his superiors when he realized that the judge was talking to him. "Mr. Lincoln, do you have anything you want to add?"

"No, Your Honor."

Lincoln was getting to like this new judge more and more.

"Now, Mr. Lincoln, you said you had two motions. What is your second one?"

43

"Your Honor," Lincoln said, "I move to dismiss the charge against Mrs. Foster on the ground that it violates the First Amendment to the Constitution of the United States in that it seeks to punish protected political speech."

"What speech do you refer to?" Judge Garrett said.

"In the charge, it says that defendant did willfully violate Section 7 of the Fugitive Slave Act of 1850—which criminalizes attempting to rescue a slave who has escaped—by saying to an audience gathered in the Second Presbyterian Church of Springfield, Illinois, 'Go out and do something about it.' The charge claims that those words caused the enslaved girl known as Lucy Battelle to be torn violently from her lawful owner by a mob and further causing her lawful owner to be injured, and further permitting said slave to abscond with herself."

"Abscond with herself?" the judge said.

"Ah, I can see you have not been much involved with these fugitive slave cases, Your Honor," Lincoln said. "It means she stole herself away from her master. Like a table running away."

"I see. Well, it is an odd locution."

"I want to respond, Your Honor," Lizar said.

"Go ahead, Mr. Lizar."

"Your Honor, speech can of course cause illegal actions. The First Amendment does not protect against inciting to riot."

"We do not concede that that is what happened here," Lincoln said. "But even if there was a riot, the phrase 'go out and do something about it' could mean a thousand things to a thousand people. Indeed, we don't even know if the people in the church who heard the speech were the same people who did whatever they did in the square."

"Mrs. Foster's words clearly meant only one thing here," Lizar said. "Go seize the slave from her lawful owner."

"The phrase 'go out and do something about it' meant go and do something about slavery," Lincoln said. "Under Mr. Lizar's interpretation of the Constitution, *any* words uttered by a person, which are then followed by bad acts by others makes the speaker a criminal. If that is the law, the First Amendment would be the most gossamer of protections. Surely the Founders didn't face down George III, at peril of their very lives, to give us only that."

Lincoln felt good about how he had finished up. The Founders, he had learned, despite most having been dead for nigh on forty years, still played well in courtrooms, to both judges and juries alike.

But not this time.

"I am going to deny your motion for now," the judge said. "Much of what the two of you are arguing is facts, not law. But, Mr. Lincoln, as we develop those facts during the trial, my denial is without prejudice to your bringing your motion again at the close of the government's case."

"Thank you, Your Honor."

The judge might not, Lincoln thought, turn out to be so bad after all, even though he had clearly been sent down from Chicago by someone who wanted either a long delay or a speedy conviction. But judges were like that—hard to order around. Especially federal judges, who were appointed for life. If he were elected president, he'd need to take special care as to whom he appointed to those lifetime positions.

"Let us get started with jury selection," the judge said. "Where is our marshal?" He looked toward the back of the room. "Ah, there you are, Marshal O'Connor."

"Most people call me Red, Judge."

"That's fine. Red, how many potential jurors do we have lined up?"

"I have thirty waiting in various parts of this building—not a lot of room here, you know."

"Good. Would you please put the names of those thirty people in a hat, draw out sixteen at random and have those men come in and sit in the jury box? That's about all we can fit in right now."

"Will do, Your Honor."

"Alright, we will stand adjourned for fifteen minutes while the marshal gets that done."

Lincoln got up from his chair but did not go behind the bar to mingle with the reporters waiting there. They were the last people he wanted to chitchat with. Instead he watched as Lizar went back to talk with them, seeming with all his bonhomie like someone who was running for office. And who knew? Perhaps he was.

Herndon was suddenly beside him. "Well, Lincoln, it looks as if you have yourself a judge you don't play chess with." He grinned.

"Billy, have you ever heard of either this judge or this substitute United States attorney?"

"I've heard of the judge before. He was a Democratic member of Congress from Pennsylvania who was defeated for reelection in '58, and Buchanan made him a district judge. Why in Chicago, I don't know."

"Perhaps it's where they had an opening."

"Perhaps. As for this United States attorney fellow, I have no idea where he came from."

Just then Lizar crossed back over the bar and came up to them to talk.

"Good morning," Lincoln said, putting out his hand. "It's good to make your acquaintance, sir."

"Likewise, I'm sure," Lizar said, pumping his hand vigorously. "And it's an honor to meet a candidate for our country's highest office, even if we find ourselves on opposite sides of a case today."

"I never let politics get in the way of friendly relations," Lincoln said. "And permit me to introduce my law partner, Billy Herndon."

"Pleased to meet you, too, Mr. Herndon."

"Please call me Billy. Everyone else does."

"Thank you, I will."

"Say, how did you end up here today?" Herndon said. "If you don't mind my asking. Our regular United States attorney seems to have disappeared without a trace."

"Oh, my understanding is that he was called back to Washington on an urgent matter."

"Do you know what it was?" Lincoln said.

"I don't think it's a secret. They have an expected opening for a district judgeship in Pennsylvania—the Western District in Pittsburgh, I think—and he's being considered. So it's a job interview."

"Why would they consider a man from Illinois for that?" Lincoln said.

"I don't know."

"Where are you from?" Lincoln said.

"By happenstance, I'm also from Pennsylvania, but the Eastern side. I'm an assistant United States attorney in Philadelphia. I agreed to come out here when they needed someone urgently."

"So you're from the City of Brotherly Love, as they call it," Herndon said.

"No, I was born and bred in a small Pennsylvania town called Cove Gap. Moved to Philadelphia to read law there and then stayed on."

Now, Lincoln thought, the sudden change of personnel in the courtroom all made sense. One way or the other, Buchanan had managed to replace Lincoln's friends with his own loyalists. Indeed, Lizar hailed from the president's birthplace.

They continued to chat until Red's voice boomed out in the courtroom. "Your Honor, I have the first sixteen jurymen."

"Very good," the judge said. "Please seat them in the box and we will get started with voir dire."

A shout came from the very back of the courtroom. A short, thin woman dressed in gray homespun was holding up a hand-lettered sign that said Free the Slaves and screaming, "Where is Lucy Battelle? Where is Lucy?"

The judge, as startled as everyone else, said, "Marshal, please remove that woman from my courtroom."

Red attempted to escort her out by pulling on her arm, but she resisted. He motioned to one of his deputies, and the two of them lifted her up under her arms and carried her, still yelling, out of the room.

A few minutes later, Red reappeared and said, "Your Honor, I have spoken to her and she has promised not to return to this courtroom."

"If she does, arrest her and jail her for contempt," the judge said. "And now, Marshal, let's resume getting the potential jurors in here."

"They are out in the hallway now, so it will only be a moment."

Lincoln turned to Herndon and said, "Do you know that woman?"

"Never seen her before in my life."

Shortly after that, the potential jurors filed in and took their seats.

After the judge had briefly described the case to the jurors, he said to them, "We'll begin now with what we call voir dire. The government will question each juror, then the defense, and then I might have a question or two myself, but not likely.

"Mr. Lizar and Mr. Lincoln, since this is a petty criminal matter, I will give each of you only three peremptory challenges."

Out of the corner of his eye, Lincoln noticed Annabelle Carter leaving the courtroom just as Reverend Hale came in and took a seat. Lincoln didn't have much time to think about why Annabelle had left or why Hale had come in because the judge had begun to address the jurors.

"Gentlemen, the gentleman sitting at the table nearest to you is Mr. G.W. Lizar. He is the United States attorney representing the United States in this case. At the farther table is Mr. Abraham Lincoln, who is representing the defendant, Mrs. Abby Kelley Foster."

After that, Lincoln only half listened as the judge explained the case to the jurors and admonished them to await the evidence before making a decision.

Finally, the judge said, "Now the lawyers will question you to help them determine if they are agreeable to your serving on this jury. If they decide you are not, you should take no offense from it. Lawyers excuse people for—" he cracked a smile "—the strangest reasons. Most of those reasons are without merit, but they have to do something to earn their money."

The judge waited for the laughter to roll in, looked pleased with himself and said, "Alright, let's begin the voir dire. Mr. Lizar, we'll start with you."

44

Annabelle had left the courtroom because she had learned from Pinkerton that, if you were pursuing criminals and had no good leads, it sometimes made sense just to follow your intuition. Her intuition told her that the woman screaming "Where is Lucy?" must have *some* connection to Lucy. Else why would she be asking where she was? On the other hand the woman could just be plumb crazy. Annabelle invited Clarence to go with her, but he chose to stay.

When Annabelle exited the courtroom she feared that the woman might already have left the building. As luck would have it, she was standing at the end of the hallway, peering out a small window.

Annabelle approached her, trying to make as much noise as she could. Early in her career, she had come up quietly behind a man she was seeking and tapped him on the shoulder to get his attention. The man had spun around, grabbed her by the neck and put a knife to her throat. He had not taken it away until she apologized and explained that she just wanted to talk to him, not turn him in to the police.

Annabelle was not about to make the same mistake again even though the woman didn't look physically threatening. On the other hand, even a child could stick a knife in your belly.

When Annabelle was still a couple of yards behind the woman, who had not turned around, she stopped and said, "Excuse me, miss, could I talk with you?"

The woman turned, gave her a wild-eyed look and fled.

Rather than follow her immediately, Annabelle watched through the window, which gave her a view of the street below, until she saw the woman emerge from the building and head slowly down the road. She went quickly down the stairs herself, out the door and looked around to find the woman again.

She spotted her not too far down the street, walking slowly. Annabelle had learned from Pinkerton himself how to follow people without being detected. She employed those skills now, which involved going briefly into stores, stopping to look at things along the way, digging into her bag as if looking for something and saying "Good day!" to people she came upon.

After a while, she saw the woman go up to the front door of the First Presbyterian Church and pound on it, yelling, "Where is Lucy? Where is Lucy?"

In not too long, the door was opened and the woman went in. Annabelle considered going right in herself but as that might scare the woman off, she decided to wait. After perhaps ten minutes, the woman came back out the same door. Annabelle noticed that someone—she could see only the person's outline—had closed the door behind her. Had she been welcomed inside by someone who knew her?

The woman set off down the street again, and Annabelle was torn. Should she follow her or go into the church to try to find who she'd talked with. She could always come back to the church, though, so Annabelle followed the woman, who, in a period of less than an hour, banged on the doors of three more churches plus a cobbler's shop and a millinery store, shouting out the same thing before being admitted. In each case she was ushered back out of the place not many minutes later.

Finally, the woman strolled five or six blocks—and *strolled* was the right word since she seemed in no hurry at all—until she was on the edge of town and headed down a path that led into the woods. Annabelle decide not to follow her. Instead she went back to First Presbyterian and tried to open the door. It was locked, and she knocked, whereupon a tall man in a clerical collar opened it and said, "May I help you?"

"Yes, I'm Annabelle Carter. A little while ago I saw a woman standing in front of this church yelling, 'Where is Lucy?' And then someone let her in through this door."

"That is true." The man said it in a flat voice, not exactly unfriendly, but certainly not with a tone that suggested he was likely to volunteer any additional information. He stood there, and when Annabelle said nothing more, started to close the door on her.

"Wait!" Annabelle said.

The man stopped shutting the door, which left it open by only a crack, through which he now peered at her.

"May I come in?" she said.

"To what end, ma'am?"

"I am seeking information about the woman who was here."

"Why?"

"I'm looking for Lucy Battelle, and I think the woman who was here a little while ago may know where she is."

"That would be right odd, ma'am, since if we're talking about the same woman, she came in asking the same question—where is Lucy Battelle? I would think that if she knows, she wouldn't be asking, now would she?"

He had not opened the door any farther.

"Sometimes people who are…"

He finished her thought for her. "Mad?"

"Yes, mad. Sometimes such people know things without knowing they know."

"Why do *you* want to know where Lucy Battelle is?"

"I'm working for someone who wants to know."

"Who?"

Now she had a problem. Would Lincoln want just anyone to know he was looking for the girl? He had never said he wanted it kept secret. And she had already told Hotchkiss and Clarence. On the other hand…

The man made her decision a lot easier.

"It's rumored about town that Lincoln has hired detectives to find her. Are you one of them?"

Pinkerton had taught her that in detection business, unless you were a spy, honesty usually got better results than subterfuge.

"Yes," she said. "I'm working for Mr. Lincoln."

He opened the door. "Come in, then. Mrs. Lincoln is a member of this church. Mr. Lincoln is not, but he does attend." He smiled. "Whether he truly worships while here is a matter on which there is apparently a variety of opinion. But in any case we are happy to assist that family."

Once she was inside, the man introduced himself as Jed Bottoms, an assistant minister, and invited her into his tiny office. It had only one chair, which he offered her while he leaned against the wall. Annabelle told him what she knew, including about the other places the woman had visited.

"I'm only recently arrived in Springfield," he said. "All I can tell you is that the woman is named Sally VanDerlip and that she comes here perhaps once a week with odd requests for information—whether we've seen her mother's missing necklace, whether we have a cure for gout and so forth. We always let her in for a few minutes, but so far as I can recall, at least in my time here, we have never had any of the information she sought."

"Would you say she is mad?"

"Quite possibly. But more likely the poor woman is simply without the mental capacity that you and I possess."

"How old is she?"

"I'm thinking in her midtwenties. She lives with her parents on the edge of town."

"What did she say about Lucy Battelle?" Annabelle said.

"Nothing. She asked *me* if I knew the girl was missing. I said I did, and then she asked, very politely, if I knew where she was. I said no."

"Did she accept that?"

"In a way, but she also asked if she could look for her here."

"Did you let her?"

"I did. She looked around for a few minutes, including in the basement and the choir loft, then politely thanked me and left."

"Perhaps she thinks Lucy is being hidden in a church," Annabelle said.

"But how would that explain her also visiting the courthouse, a cobbler's shop and a millinery?"

"Four churches in total is a lot, though," Annabelle said.

Bottoms reached under his desk and pulled out a roll of paper, which he unrolled on his desk. "This is a map of Springfield," he said. "On it, I have marked all the churches I know of that have buildings."

Annabelle looked it over. "There are indeed a lot of them," she said.

"More than a dozen. And every month it seems, a new one goes up. But the thing is, some support slavery, some are abolitionist in sentiment, but not strongly so, and some have stepped away from the issue entirely. I doubt very many of them would actually harbor an escaped slave. Too much risk."

"Some might."

"Yes, but I doubt we would. And one of the others Sally visited was her parents' church, and I *know* they wouldn't. They're more likely to turn the slave in and collect the reward."

"What about the last one she visited?"

"When I arrived here a few months ago, I made the rounds of the other churches to meet their pastors. The pastor of that particular church told me that the right to hold slaves is clearly established in Holy Scriptures."

"Alright, I suppose Sally VanDerlip visiting churches to find Lucy doesn't make a lot of sense," Annabelle said. "Or at least not those particular churches."

Then she thought, *If I tell Allan that I got in here and didn't look around, he will think all of his training was for naught.*

"Reverend Bottoms, may I look around, too?"

He laughed. "Of course. We have so few secrets here I don't even need to accompany you. Please just let me know, if you would, when you will be leaving."

She looked everywhere, including the basement, but found no one, nor anything of interest. She thanked Bottoms for his courtesy and let herself out.

Now what? She could, she supposed, if people would permit her to go in, look inside the other three churches, too, plus the cobbler's shop and the milliner's place. But it seemed pointless. If Lucy were being hidden in one of those places the word would by now have gone out that a woman was looking for Lucy. And they could just move her from one place to another, like a pea in a shell game.

She was out of ideas.

45

The trial, in the meantime, had been going forward, and the first potential juror to be questioned had identified himself. "I'm Alexander Humphreys," he said.

"Where are you from, Mr. Humphreys?" Lizar said.

"Taylorsville. That's down in Christian County."

"How far away is that?"

"The part of the county I live in, perhaps fifteen miles."

"That's a pretty far piece to come just to respond to a jury summons, isn't it?"

"No, I always do my duty as a citizen and come, although it's certainly farther to come here than when a case is in the state court in our county seat, which is Taylorsville."

"So you must have really wanted to be a juror on this case."

"No, I wouldn't say that, sir. Like I said, just wanted to do my duty."

"What do you do for a living, sir?"

"I'm a blacksmith. I'm also a part-time miller at a local grist-mill, and I farm a little."

"Do you know Mr. Lincoln?"

"Of course. Almost everyone does."

"Since you've been a juror before, have you been a juror in a case in which Mr. Lincoln was one of the lawyers?"

"Yes."

"How did he do?"

"He lost."

There was a burst of laughter from the audience.

Lincoln laughed with them, but mostly he was looking at Humphreys. He had no recollection of the man. But then again, Christian County had been removed from the Eighth Circuit, the counties where Lincoln practiced, seven or eight years before. So if Humphreys was a juror on one of his state cases way back then, it had been dozens of juries ago.

"Have you ever heard of the defendant in this case, Mrs. Abby Kelley Foster?" Lizar said.

"No, sir." Humphrey paused. "Well, that's not quite right. I read about her in the *Sangamon Times*."

"About the case against her?"

"Yes, and about the speech she gave in church."

"Were you at that speech?"

"No."

"Was anyone you know at that speech?"

"No."

"Sir, if you live in Christian County, why do you read the *Sangamon Times*?"

"Because our own paper in Taylorsville is such a wretched excuse for a newspaper."

There was another burst of laughter in the courtroom.

"Do you have any opinion about this case?"

"I'm not sure what you mean, Mr. Lizar."

"Do you have an opinion about whether Mrs. Foster is guilty of the crime with which she's been charged?"

"Well, I'm not exactly sure what the crime is supposed to

be—" he looked over at the judge "—it wasn't described with a lot of detail. But in any case, I've got no opinion."

"No further questions," Lizar said. "The United States would like to defer any possible challenge to this juror until all have been questioned."

"Alright," the judge said. "Mr. Lincoln, your turn."

"Good morning, Mr. Humphreys. Tell me, are you a church-going man?"

"Well, my wife, Nancy, is a charter member of Second Presbyterian in Springfield. I'm not a member, but I go often enough."

"How often is that, Mr. Humphreys?"

"Well, when it's easy to get there."

Laughter again rolled through the room.

"When is that?"

"You know, in the summer when it hasn't rained and made the roads muddy and it isn't too hot. And in the winter when it's not too cold, and it hasn't snowed and made the roads muddy."

"I see Father Hale is in the room," Lincoln said. "Have you heard him preach?"

"Yes, sir. But, in all candor—and no offense, Father—" he looked over at Hale "—I think the young assistant minister you've got now is better. Doesn't put me to sleep. I'd want him for my funeral."

"Are you ill, Mr. Humphreys?" Lincoln said.

"Oh, no. Not at all. It's just that I'll be fifty-seven next month, and so the funeral reference just meant, well, you know."

"We all know," Lincoln said.

Lincoln wasn't troubled at all by Humphreys. He was looking for jurors who were independent enough to reject the government's case, and Humphreys seemed to be one who would. Lincoln also wanted to communicate to the other jurors-in-waiting that the defense was confident of its case, even if a juror was something of a skeptic.

"The defense accepts Mr. Humphreys," Lincoln said.

The judge looked down at Lizar to see if he wanted to change his mind about reserving on Mr. Humphreys, but Lizar said nothing, and they moved on to the next juror.

They moved rather quickly through the next fifteen jurors, who included a cobbler, a saddler, a farmer, a man who described himself as a large landowner, a baker, a man who had just opened a new hotel and a man who stunned the courtroom by saying he was a "driver" for the Underground Railroad.

Lizar tried to get the "driver" for the Railroad dismissed for cause. To Lincoln's surprise, the judge refused. After that, with sixteen jurors remaining in the box and no more waiting in the hallway, Lizar used one of his peremptories on the Underground Railroad man and his remaining two on two others, but spared Humphreys.

Lincoln used none of his peremptories, leaving them with a jury of twelve and one alternate.

"We are ready to go, it appears," the judge said. "Let's take a fifteen-minute break and then we will have opening statements."

During the break, Lincoln crossed the bar and approached Father Hale, who shook his hand vigorously. After a bit of chit-chat, Lincoln said, "So, Father, did Mr. Humphreys tell the truth about his churchgoing?"

"Well, Mr. Lincoln, let me put it this way. His wife is a good Christian woman and is an anchor of our church. One of the founders, in fact. She attends often, even in inclement weather."

"And Mr. Humphreys?"

"Let's just say that he has found the roads very muddy for the last couple of decades. But I think he will be a good juror for you."

"Is there anything else I should know about him?"

"Hmm. Well, his grandfather was an officer in Washington's personal guard, the Commander-in-Chief Guard. He likes to talk about it. If you can find a way to mention the Revolution, he'd sit up and listen."

"I will keep that in mind."

"There is one other thing, Mr. Lincoln, which I should mention to you. Mr. Lizar came to the church and asked to interview me about what I heard during Mrs. Foster's lecture."

"Did you consent to an interview?"

"No. Generally, I don't think it's appropriate for a preacher to testify."

"I see."

"But I think he plans to subpoena me."

"Will your testimony be helpful or harmful to Mrs. Foster's case, Father?"

"I think neither. But I will make you aware that I met with Mrs. Foster for supper before her lecture, and we did discuss the imminent return to her master of that poor girl who was 'bound to service.'" He smiled. "As Mr. Lizar would put it."

"Would you like to say more?"

"No, but if I am asked about that supper meeting, I don't think what I have to say will be harmful, and it might be helpful."

"Thank you for that."

They were interrupted by a man who approached and, ignoring Hale, looked at Lincoln and said, "May I speak with you, sir?"

"Why, Mr. Artemis, how nice to see you again," Lincoln said. "Do you know Father Hale?"

Clarence turned toward Hale prepared to shake hands, as Hale said, "Oh, Clarence and I do know each other. Not that long ago, I gave him a tour of our church."

"Indeed he did, and I am most grateful," Clarence said. "But what I am here to ask, Mr. Lincoln, is if you might grant me an interview about this trial."

"As you already know, Mr. Artemis—I don't know how many times I have to say it—I am not giving interviews these days for the reason you full well know."

"But this would not be about the campaign. It would be only about this trial."

"I'm afraid I must still decline. Perhaps after the election."

They both watched Artemis walk back to his seat in the courtroom.

"He's persistent," Lincoln said. "I like that in a man."

"Within limits, it can indeed be admirable," Hale said. "And speaking of the election, I wish you the best of luck in that, sir. I cannot in good conscience directly tell my parishioners how to vote, but I have hinted in every way I can that those who have the vote should vote for you."

"Why, thank you, Father. In truth, I will be surprised if I carry Sangamon County, even though I have lived here most of my adult life and am well-known. It is still too Southern a place. But I do hope to carry the city of Springfield and the nation."

"Godspeed, Mr. Lincoln," Hale said.

"Thank you. I will need all the help I can get, especially if I am privileged to be elected. And now I hear the judge calling us back to the trial."

46

The jury was seated, the judge was in his chair behind the bench, and Lincoln and Lizar had taken their seats at their respective tables.

The judge looked down at Lincoln. "Mr. Lincoln, I see that your client, Mrs. Foster, is still not in the courtroom, even though I am about to swear in the jury."

"She is still feeling poorly, Your Honor, but I believe she will be here momentarily. The sheriff has kindly agreed that if my partner, Mr. Herndon, will accompany her, she may come here without handcuffs, and we will return her to the jail at the end of the proceedings."

"How long do you think it will be, Mr. Lincoln, before she arrives here?"

"Perhaps five minutes. Perhaps a little longer."

The judge looked down at Lizar. "Mr. Lizar, do you wish to make your opening statement now or do you want to wait for the defendant's arrival? If you want to start now, I will need Mr. Lincoln's consent on behalf of the defendant."

"I will begin now, Your Honor, so as not to waste the time of our jurors."

It was, Lincoln thought, a nice move on Lizar's part to try to suggest to the jury that Mrs. Foster was somehow about to inconvenience them. Getting jurors to dislike the defendant for reasons having nothing to do with their alleged crime was a common prosecutorial tactic.

In this case, Lincoln had no choice but to consent or the jury would think that *he* was the one about to inconvenience them.

"My client has no objection," Lincoln said.

On hearing Lizar's decision and Lincoln's acquiescence, the judge turned to the jury and swore them in as a group, pledging under oath to decide the case only upon the evidence presented and to follow the law.

After the jurors had finished by saying, "So help me God," the judge said, "Mr. Lizar is going to make an opening statement to you. In it, he will tell you what he expects the evidence in the government's case to show. But what he says is not in itself evidence. For that, you will have to await the actual testimony of the witnesses who will appear here and testify under oath. Then I will tell you what the law is.

"Mr. Lizar, please proceed."

Lizar got up, walked up to the jury box and let his eyes linger on the jurors for a few seconds, as if he were trying to make personal contact with each and every one.

"Good morning, gentlemen," he said. "I am G.W. Lizar. I am an assistant United States attorney. I represent the United States of America."

He paused as if to let the importance of who his client was sink in. Lincoln had been watching the jury, and Lizar's naming of the United States as his client seemed, so far as he could judge, not to have impressed anyone. Lizar, as a newcomer to Illinois, seemed unaware that many people in Illinois, despite the rapid growth of the state, still thought of themselves as pio-

neers settling the frontier. Except in time of war, when patrio-
tism tended to run hot, governments were none too popular
in Illinois.

"Gentlemen," Lizar said, "the government's case is fairly simple. The evidence will show that on Friday, August 24, a federal
commissioner held a hearing here in Springfield to consider a
claim by Ezekiel Goshorn. Mr. Goshorn alleged that one Lucy
Battelle, a woman bound to his service in the Commonwealth
of Kentucky, had run away and been captured near Springfield.
Mr. Goshorn sought the court's order permitting him to return
Lucy Battelle to his tobacco plantation in Kentucky."

Lincoln noted that Lizar had avoided calling the commissioner a *slave* commissioner and had chosen to describe Lucy
Battelle with the evasive legal words the Founders had inserted
into Article IV, Section 3, Clause 2 of the Constitution to describe slaves—"a person held to service." Lizar made the phrase
sound, Lincoln thought, as if Lucy was an apprentice of some
kind, and not a person bound by law to spend the rest of her
life working for Goshorn without pay or any rights of any kind.

Lizar was continuing. "The evidence will show that after Mr.
Goshorn was granted the order of return that he sought, the
United States marshal and the sheriff of this county escorted
Lucy Battelle out of the courthouse..."

"Excuse me," the judge said, "I don't usually interrupt a lawyer's opening statement, and I apologize for doing so. But I want
the jury to understand—" he looked over at them "—that when
Mr. Lizar refers to a court hearing and a courthouse, he is referring to something that took place under federal law, but not
before *this* judge or in *this* courtroom or in *this* building. To my
understanding it was in a hearing room in the Sangamon County
courthouse, not here." He sat back in his chair and said, "Please
proceed, Mr. Lizar."

Lincoln found Judge Garrett's statement quite interesting.
Was the judge, against all odds, a judge who was uncomfort-

able with slavery and the judiciary's role in enforcing it? If so, he would try to make use of that.

Lizar resumed. "Gentlemen, when the marshal and the sheriff escorted Lucy Battelle out of the Sangamon County Courthouse, the evidence will show that they found a mob waiting for them. Wisely, they went back into the courthouse to wait until the mob had dissipated.

"Or so they thought. But what the evidence will further show is that, just as they were about to try again, a radical abolitionist speaker named Abby Kelley Foster—the defendant here—had just finished a speech inside the Second Presbyterian Church. In that speech she riled up the audience about the imminent return to service of Lucy Battelle."

Lincoln had to suppress a laugh. Did Lizar seriously think that no one on the jury knew that *return to service* meant a return to slavery?

Lizar continued. "The evidence will further show that Mrs. Foster knew, in advance of her speech, about the near-riotous situation in the courthouse square and intentionally, at the end of her speech, urged the audience to action by saying 'Go out and do something about it!' She lit the flame."

"Objection," Lincoln said, without getting up, while looking at the jury instead of the judge. "This is argument, not evidence."

"I agree. Gentlemen of the jury you are to disregard the phrase 'lit the flame.' Mr. Lizar, please confine yourself to what you contend the government's evidence will show."

As the judge was speaking, Lincoln wondered if Abby Kelley Foster, a pacifist, had really said that. So far, he had not turned up any witnesses who remembered anything like what Lizar claimed. Lizar must have found *someone* willing to testify that he'd heard her say it.

"The evidence will further show," Lizar said, but he didn't get to finish his sentence because at that moment the courtroom door swung open with a loud creak, and everyone turned to look.

Mrs. Foster appeared in the doorway, holding on to Herndon's arm. She was wearing a white bonnet, her hair put up under it, and a gray dress that covered her from neck to ankles. The outfit had been carefully chosen, Lincoln thought. On the one hand, it was very plain. On the other hand, it was fitted and quite clearly showed that Mrs. Foster still had quite a nice figure. Perhaps some of the twelve men on the jury would find themselves attracted to her.

"Mr. Lincoln, I assume this is the defendant, Mrs. Foster," the judge said.

Lincoln rose. "Yes, Your Honor and members of the jury, this is Mrs. Abby Kelley Foster, the defendant. She is accompanied by my law partner, William Herndon. With the court's permission, Mrs. Foster will come forward and sit beside me at counsel table."

"Yes," the judge said. "And since this courtroom has done away with a separate dock for the defendant, the court has no objection unless Mr. Lizar has one."

"No, Your Honor, I do not," Lizar said.

Mrs. Foster and Herndon walked very slowly down the aisle, making it clear, Lincoln thought, that Abby was not only ailing, but frail. Herndon opened the gate in the bar for her, and when they reached the counsel table Lincoln pulled out the chair for her. She sat down with a sigh, and removed her bonnet, placing it on the table in front of her.

"Please resume, Mr. Lizar," the judge said.

"Just a moment," Lizar said, and looked down at the piece of paper he'd been holding, apparently trying to find his place in the outline of his opening.

"Ah, yes," he said. "Here we are." He looked back to the jury. "Gentlemen, the evidence will show that upon hearing Mrs. Foster's words, 'Go out and do something about it,' numerous people, both men and women, rushed out of the church, poured into the courthouse square and turned over the carriage in which both Lucy Battelle and Mr. Goshorn were by then sitting, badly injuring Mr. Goshorn and permitting Lucy Battelle to escape again from service."

Lincoln was watching the jury. It seemed to him that they were hardly listening. Instead, they were looking at Mrs. Foster. He hoped they were wondering how such a frail-looking woman could possibly have incited a riot.

Lizar was continuing. "The judge will tell you what the law is in this case. But I will summarize what my understanding of it is." Lizar looked up at the judge in case the judge was going to object to Lizar saying a single word about the law.

Apparently seeing no hint of disapproval, Lizar went on. "Section 7 of what we call the Compromise of 1850, makes it unlawful for any person to 'rescue or attempt to rescue a fugitive from service or labor.'" He paused. "It is also illegal 'to assist the person owing service, directly or indirectly, to escape from the claimant.'

"And, gentlemen, as the evidence will show, that is exactly what Mrs. Foster, through her words, did here. After you've heard all of the evidence, the government will ask you to bring in a verdict of guilty."

Lincoln was amazed. Lizar had managed to get through his whole opening statement without once mentioning the words *slave* or *slavery*. He had even avoided calling the Fugitive Slave Act by its real name. Compromise of 1850 indeed! He would correct that when he got the chance.

"Thank you for your kind attention, gentlemen," Lizar said, and returned to the table.

"Mr. Lincoln?" the judge said. "Do you wish to make an opening statement?"

There were times when Lincoln thought defense opening statements were useful, and it was tempting to get up and begin by saying that *the evidence would show* that Lucy Battelle was a girl who had been enslaved from birth, would be rendering her *service* without pay 'til the day she died and that her children and her children's children would also be slaves. Which would be objected to by Lizar, but Lincoln thought he could probably get it said before the judge sustained the objection.

He sat thinking about it. An opening statement would be risky when he knew so little about the facts. His experience had been that if the government, in its opening, got some of its facts wrong, juries tended to be forgiving. But if the defendant's lawyer got the facts even a little wrong, juries tended to think the defendant had personally lied to them. And in this case, he had little idea who the government's witnesses were going to be or what they would say.

Finally, the judge pressed him. "Mr. Lincoln?"

Lincoln rose from his table. "Your Honor, the defense will defer its opening statement to the close of the government's case."

"Thank you. Mr. Lizar, please call your first witness."

47

"The United States calls Wilbur Jenkins," Lizar said.

An elderly man rose from a seat in the back of the room and walked slowly forward. When he got to the bar, Lizar opened it for him and directed him to the witness chair, which was a simple black captain's chair set on a raised platform between the bench and the chairs in which the jurors were sitting. Two steps led up to it.

Jenkins looked at the steps with what was clearly trepidation. Lizar sprang forward and helped him climb up.

Once he was seated, the clerk asked Jenkins to raise his right hand. He raised instead his left hand. "No," the clerk said, grinning, "your other right hand, sir."

Jenkins raised the proper hand and was sworn.

"What is your full name, sir?" Lizar said.

"Wilbur A. Jenkins."

"Does the *A* stand for something?"

"Nothing so far as I know. My parents thought I oughta have one."

"One what?"

"A middle initial. It was popular back around then. I think it was 'cause John Adams done gave his son a middle name. Quincy, you know."

Everyone in the courtroom laughed.

"The Founders didn't need 'em," Jenkins said. "Tom Jefferson didn't have one. But when they got to me, well, there it is. A."

"Thank you for that, Mr. Jenkins," Lizar said. "But if I might turn to another question. Where were you on the evening of August 24 of this year, Mr. Jenkins?"

"Well, I was lot o' places I guess."

"I want to focus you on the evening. Where were you in the evening?"

"Oh, that's what ya want. Sure. Went over to Second Presby."

"Why did you go there?"

"T' hear somebody speak."

"Do you recall who that was?"

"Sure, Reverend Hale. They usually call him Father Hale for some darn reason." He looked at the judge. "Scuse my profanity."

"Did anyone else speak?" Lizar said.

Jenkins paused a moment and screwed up his face. Finally, he said. "Yes! That radical lady, Mrs. Foster."

"Do you recall what she said?"

"Uh-huh, yes."

"Well, what did she say?"

"All kinda things."

"Can you recall any of the specifics?"

"Sure."

Lincoln felt almost sorry for Lizar, who was having that most worrisome of experiences for a lawyer—a witness who, on direct examination, can't remember what he was supposed to say. And on direct Lizar wasn't allowed to lead him.

"Well, Mr. Jenkins, can you tell the jury what you heard Mrs. Foster say?"

"Yes, sir. She said slaves were treated right bad down South, and that there be an escaped Darkie—" he looked up at the judge "—regular, I'd use a differen' word but we is in court, so..."

"Please go ahead, Mr. Jenkins," Lizar said.

"Alright. What it were about was a Darkie what fled is gonna be give back to her owner. Down in the square."

"Did she say what she thought about that?"

"Who?"

"The speaker. Mrs. Foster."

"Oh, her. She was agin it."

Lincoln tried hard to keep a straight face. The jury would draw its own conclusions about the witness, and he didn't want to be seen smiling at an old man struggling with his memory.

Lizar, who'd been standing halfway between his table and his witness, moved closer, so that he was almost on top of the man.

"Did Mrs. Foster say anything specific about what to do?" Lizar said.

"I 'member that real good. Real good. She said go down an' do somethin' 'bout it."

"When did she say that?"

"Who?"

"Mrs. Foster."

"Oh. Right at th' end."

"I have no further questions," Lizar said.

Lincoln was tempted not to ask any questions at all. But the man was presumably the first of a series of witnesses who were going to try to put words in Abby's mouth, so he would try to use a razor on this one instead of an ax.

Lincoln leaned over to Abby, who'd been sitting calmly beside him, her hands folded in front of her on the table, and whispered to her, "Do you recall seeing this man in the church that night?"

"No," she whispered back.

Lincoln walked toward Jenkins until he was only about a foot from him. "Mr. Jenkins, do you have any problems with your hearing?"

"I don' think so. No. I heard you jess' fine there."

"Do you recall where you were sitting in the church?"

"Way back. Was late gittin' there."

Lincoln walked casually back to counsel table, pretending to look at a piece of paper he picked up from the table. It was the oldest trick in the book, but sometimes it worked. In the same tone and level of voice he had used earlier, he said, "Mr. Jenkins, are you *sure* you don't have any problems with your hearing?"

"Like I said, Mr. Lincoln, I was in the back."

"Thank you for explaining that."

Lincoln glanced over at the jury. They seemed quite attentive. One was trying to cover up a snicker.

Lincoln walked back up to the witness and raised his voice. "Mr. Jenkins, did anyone else speak that evening besides Mrs. Foster?"

"Uh-huh. Father Hale."

"What did he say?"

"I don't know."

"You don't recall?"

"Right."

"At the very end, were there women collecting money?"

"Yep. Three or four. Perhaps five."

"Did they say anything?"

"They said a whole lot."

"What about?"

"Givin' money to end slavin'."

Lincoln considered asking him if perhaps it wasn't those women who had said to *do something* about slavery by contributing. But Jenkins might just say no. It would be better to argue to the jury later that Jenkins likely misremembered who said what.

He decided to risk one final question. "Mr. Jenkins, did you contribute any money?"

Lizar was on his feet. "Objection! Irrelevant."

"Overruled."

"Let me ask again," Lincoln said. "Mr. Jenkins, did you contribute any money?"

"Hell no!" He looked up at the judge. "Sorry. Heck no! Hope *heck* is alright here."

"I have no further questions, Your Honor."

The judge looked down at Lizar. "Any redirect, Mr. Lizar?"

Lincoln could almost hear Lizar asking himself: Was there a way to fix this? Certainly, Lizar could try to fix it later with other witnesses who were more certain. Those witnesses, if they confirmed what Abby had said, would give credibility to Jenkins's memory—if Lizar actually had anybody who was more credible.

Perhaps Lizar had the same thought, because he said, "No further questions."

The judge raised his voice. "You may step down, Mr. Jenkins. Mr. Lizar, please call your next witness."

48

"The United States calls George Putnam, Jr." Lizar said. A tall man got up from his seat in the audience and strode up to the bar. Unlike Jenkins, he didn't wait for Lizar to open the gate for him, but pushed it open himself and, without being asked, walked up the steps to the platform and took his seat in the witness chair. Lincoln looked closely at him. He moved like a young man, but his skin, especially around his neck and on his hands, made it clear he was quite old.

The clerk asked Putnam to raise his right hand and said, "Do you, sir, swear to tell the truth, the whole truth and nothing but the truth, so help you God?"

"I do!" Putnam said, in an unnecessarily loud voice.

Lizar began his questioning, "Mr. Putnam, do you recall where you were the evening of August 24 of this year?"

"I sure do. I was at the Second Presbyterian Church."

He was, Lincoln noted, a man with a big, booming voice. Some jurors, he knew, took that kind of thing as showing confidence and credibility. Others thought it made the person a show-off. He glanced at the jury but couldn't tell what any of them thought about the man, although it was early.

"What were you doing at the church that evening?" Lizar said.

"I was attending a lecture by that lady there." He pointed directly at Abby. Abby stared back at him but gave no hint she cared that he was pointing at her.

"Who is that, sir?"

"Abby Kelley Foster, to my understanding."

Lincoln leaned over to Abby and said, in a low voice, "Do you know him?" Abby nodded her head up and down, leaned over and said, "He yelled foul things at me the whole time."

"Were you there for her whole lecture, Mr. Putnam?" Lizar said.

"Every word."

"Do you recall what Mrs. Foster said?"

"Yes."

"Please tell the jury what you remember."

Putnam looked over at the jury and said, "She said a lot, but the meat of it was that slavery is bad, that slaves suffer a lot, that the Constitution is a slave document and a lot of other things abolitionists say along those lines."

"Did she mention politics?"

"Well, she called Mr. Lincoln over there—" this time he pointed straight at Lincoln and then looked over at the jury "—a slave hound." He grinned.

Lincoln decided not to object, even though the man's testimony was quite irrelevant to the subject matter of the trial. He did manage to glance at the jury, but caught no reaction.

"Did she say who to vote for?" Lizar said.

Lincoln had finally had enough. "Objection! This is far from relevant."

"Sustained," the judge said. "Mr. Lizard, please confine yourself to eliciting testimony from this witness that more fits the evidence you told the jury you were going to present."

Lincoln glanced at the jury to see if they'd noticed the judge's latest slip on Lizar's last name. A few clearly had because they were trying to suppress smiles. He thought Lizar had, perhaps, once again not noticed.

"The witness's testimony to this point is just background, Your Honor," Lizar said.

"Background?" the judge said. "Are you proposing to paint a painting, Mr. Lizar?"

"No, Your Honor. It's a recent use of the term, to mean information needed to understand something. I fear I picked up the term in the East."

"I see. Well, here in the West, let's try for more foreground, then."

Lizar turned back to his witness. "Do you recall the end of Mrs. Foster's lecture?"

"Yes.

"What did she say?"

"She mentioned that a recaptured slave was about to be returned to her master in the courthouse square, only a few blocks away."

"Did she say anything else?"

Putnam again looked directly at the jury. "Yes. She said, 'Go out and do something about it.'"

"Are you sure?"

"Yes, because at the time I was quite shocked that she would say such a thing."

"Why?"

"Because my understanding was that she was urging the audience to—"

Lincoln rose to his feet and interrupted, "Your Honor, I object. The witness seems about to give his *interpretation* of what he *claims* Mrs. Foster said. But she is charged here with, in effect, inciting to riot. So the issue here is her intent in saying what she said—if she even said it at all—not Mr. Putnam's interpretation of it."

"The objection is not well-taken," Lizar said. "The reaction of members of Mrs. Foster's audience to what she said is highly relevant."

"Your Honor," Lincoln said, "if Mrs. Foster had said, 'Robins come back in the spring,' would Mr. Putnam's belief about what Mrs. Foster was urging anyone to do as a result of hearing that be worth even a thimbleful of birdseed?"

The judge put his finger on his chin, as if he were thinking about it. Finally, he said, "Mr. Lincoln, your objection is overruled. I think the reaction of a member of Mrs. Foster's audience to her words is relevant." He smiled. "And I'm happy to see you've moved on from pigs."

Lincoln hadn't expected his objection to be sustained. He was simply trying to educate the jury about the importance of intent, and, looking over at them, he sensed that it had worked.

Lizar resumed. "To remind you, Mr. Putnam, my question was, Why were you shocked that Mrs. Foster said, 'Go out and do something about it'?"

"Because I had always heard she was a pacifist, and here she was urging us to go seize the slave girl from lawful authority."

"I renew my objection," Lincoln said. "And request the jury be instructed to disregard the answer."

"Overruled," the judge said, without waiting for Lizar to reply. "Go ahead, Mr. Lizar."

"Mr. Putnam, if you recall, at what point did Mrs. Foster say, 'Go out and do something about it'?"

"At the very end of her lecture. They were the last words out of her mouth."

Lincoln noticed that Abby was shaking her head slowly back and forth, in the negative. He hoped the jury was watching her.

Lizar had noticed, too, and said, "Your Honor, Mrs. Foster is shaking her head back and forth, trying, no doubt, to communicate something to the jury. I ask that she be admonished not to do so."

The judge looked bemused. He had probably, Lincoln assumed, had the same thought he did, which was that Lizar's request had simply called the jury's attention to what Abby was doing. And interrupted the flow of his witness's testimony.

"Mrs. Foster," the judge said, in not too stern a voice, "please don't make head motions indicating your opinion of testimony."

"I'm sorry, Judge," Abby said.

Lizar was resuming. "Mr. Putnam, did anything happen after Mrs. Foster said, 'Go out and do something about it'?"

"Yes. A great many people rushed out of the church. I heard one of them yell, 'Let's go!'"

Abby rolled her eyes. Lincoln didn't think Lizar saw it because he was facing away from her, but he was quite sure the jury saw it because they had been riveted on Abby ever since Lizar's objection to her head turning. If the judge saw it, he said nothing.

"I have no further questions, Your Honor," Lizar said.

Lincoln looked over at Abby, in a way he hoped the judge would interpret as concern for her health. "Your Honor, could we have a few minutes before I begin my cross-examination of the witness?"

"Of course, Mr. Lincoln. Let's take fifteen minutes."

Lincoln turned to Abby. "Let's leave this room. I've arranged for a small room elsewhere in the building where we can meet. We have some things to discuss before I cross-examine Mr. Putnam."

49

The room they repaired to was small, with no windows. In the middle was a scuffed wooden table with four chairs. Lincoln and Abby sat down across from one another, but they had been seated for barely a minute when Herndon came in, carrying a small bag. He sat down next to Lincoln, put the bag on the table and said, "Mrs. Foster, I have brought you some of Dr. Graham's cakes, which, to my surprise, I was able to find here in Springfield. And here is a bottle of spring water, filtered and then boiled."

"Why, thank you, William. But you must call me Abby."

"Alright, but people call me Billy, not William."

"How old are you?"

"Forty-one."

"I still find it odd that someone of your age is called Billy, but I gather you like it, and people should get to choose what they wish to be called, certainly. So Billy it will be."

"Will your husband join us?" Herndon said.

"No. He has been attending the trial, but has abolitionist business of his own to attend to during the breaks. He is in some ways busier with that than I am." She paused and smiled. "And in some ways even more radical."

Herndon raised his eyebrows. "I thought you were the ultimate radical."

"Well, South Carolina and some other Southern states have threatened to secede if Abraham is elected president," Abby said. "Stephen says we should just let them go. I used to think so, too. Now I am not so sure."

"What does he think would happen after they left?" Herndon said.

"Before I answer that, would either of you like to share this Graham cake?" She had taken one of the cakes out of the bag, broken it into several pieces and laid them atop the bag.

Lincoln wrinkled his nose, and Herndon politely declined.

"Alright, then, Stephen claims that the departed states will fail to prosper because the world is more and more opposed to slavery and, more and more, buying cotton from elsewhere, like Egypt."

"We would still buy it to feed our own clothing factories in the North," Herndon said.

"Stephen thinks antislavery voters would soon force the Congress to adopt high tariffs on the import of Southern cotton," she said. "And that more and more slaves would escape from the Border states, and then begin to escape from farther south. The Fugitive Slave Act would of course be gone, and the South would collapse on itself. He believes they would come back with their tail between their legs and beg to rejoin the Union."

Lincoln had listened to the discussion with an amused look on his face. Finally, he broke in. "Abby, would Stephen let the Southern states take federal property with them as they go?" he said.

"Knowing Stephen, he would make them pay for it."

"Aye, there's the rub," Lincoln said. "Some of the Southern

hotheads claim they have already paid for it all with their taxes—federal land, federal forts, the guns in federal arsenals, as well as federal ships in port, among other things. They claim that no payment would be due."

"Well, if you're elected, you'll find a way to deal with it all, I'm sure," Abby said. "Even though I doubt you will deal fairly with the slaves." She paused. "Putting all of that aside, I still find it hard to believe that a man of your importance is representing me in this difficulty I find myself in."

"If I'm elected I will be important for only a short term of years," Lincoln said. "If I am not elected I will fade into the kind of obscurity that has befallen almost all of those who ran for president and lost."

There was a knock on the door. The clerk opened it and said, "The judge has decided to reconvene a little earlier. If you can be back in the courtroom in five minutes, he says it would be appreciated."

"Alright," Lincoln said, and the clerk left.

"Well, that doesn't leave us much time," Lincoln said.

"I'm sorry we wasted it talking about secession," Abby said.

"I didn't find it a waste at all, Abby. But I do want to ask you about Mr. Putnam. You nodded your head 'yes' in the courtroom when I asked if you knew him and you said he yelled at you."

"I recognized him instantly. He is the man who sat in the third row, dead center, and yelled at me throughout my lecture."

"What kind of things did he yell?" Herndon said.

"He was constantly shouting that God had made Negroes slaves and they must stay that way, although he used a different word for Negro."

"So he is biased against what you stand for," Lincoln said.

"Yes. Can I testify about what he said?"

"You have perhaps forgotten, Abby, that in Illinois, as in almost all states—and the court here will follow Illinois law in this—defendants in criminal cases cannot testify under oath in their own defense."

"I thought you told me the judge will let me make an unsworn statement to the jury, telling them my side of the story."

"That's true," Lincoln said. "But I'm not sure he will let you attack the credibility of other witnesses as part of that."

"We could find someone else who heard him say those things," Herndon said.

They all looked at one another and said, almost simultaneously, "Father Hale!"

When the courtroom came to order, with Putnam back on the witness stand, Judge Garrett said, "Mr. Putnam, I remind you you're still under oath. Mr. Lincoln, you may begin your cross-examination."

Lincoln walked up to the witness stand so that he was only a foot or two in front of Putnam. "Mr. Putnam, where were you siting during Mrs. Foster's lecture?"

"Right down in front."

"Third row?"

"Yes, I think so."

"Right in the middle?"

Putnam looked surprised that Lincoln had guessed not only the row he had sat in but his position in it. After a pause, he said, "Why, yes. Right in the middle."

"And you were there the whole time, correct?"

"Yes."

"Who was sitting to your right, Mr. Putnam?"

"I'm not sure of his name. I'd never met the man before."

"An older gentleman?"

"Why, yes."

For Lincoln it had been a shot in the dark. Most people who went to church were older these days, and an antislavery lecture, even by someone as famous as Abby Kelley Foster, was not likely to have attracted the young.

Lincoln took another shot in the dark. "What about on the other side? Also an older gentleman?"

"Yes."

Lincoln asked no further questions about Putnam's neighbors in the pews. He hoped he'd made Putnam think he knew exactly who those people were and that they might show up and testify. Perhaps it would keep Putnam at least a little honest.

"Mr. Putnam, did you say anything during Mrs. Foster's lecture?"

"Not that I recall."

Lincoln looked down at a piece of paper he had been holding in his hand, with copious writing visible on it. Then he said, "Are you sure, Mr. Putnam, that you didn't say anything?"

"Well, now that I think of it, I might have muttered something."

"What did you mutter?"

"I don't really recall."

Lincoln looked down at the piece of paper again. He even squinted at it briefly. "Are you sure, sir? You don't recall a thing you muttered?"

"Well, I probably muttered something about how the abolitionists weren't right about everything."

"So you're not an abolitionist?"

Lizar popped out of his seat. "Objection, not relevant."

"Potential bias is always relevant," Lincoln said.

"Overruled," the judge said.

"Let me ask again, sir," Lincoln said. "Are you an abolitionist?"

"No, I'm not."

"Far from it, right?"

"I guess you could say that."

"You believe slavery is God's plan for people whose skin is darker than ours, don't you?"

Lizar started to get up, no doubt to object, but then apparently thought better of it for some reason and sat back down.

Putnam didn't answer, so Lincoln repeated the question. "You believe slavery is God's plan for people whose skin is darker than ours, don't you?" Lincoln could practically hear Putnam wondering in his head what Lincoln knew and what he didn't know.

Finally, Putnam said, "That's more or less correct. You can read it in the Bible." He looked over at the jury, obviously trying to see if any of them agreed with him. If Putnam read them the same way Lincoln did, none of them agreed with him.

"Didn't you, Mr. Putnam, yell something along those lines— 'God intended Negroes to be slaves'—at Mrs. Foster while she was speaking?"

Putnam's lip was twitching. Lincoln could see him considering his choices. Lie and be exposed if someone was going to testify against him. Or tell the truth.

"I might have said something like that," Putnam said. And then he tried to rescue himself from the implications of his admitted bias. "But what I said about that jez—that woman— saying 'Go out and do something about it' is God's truth. She said it. She did, as God is my witness."

"Well, God *is* your witness, Mr. Putnam, that's what your oath to tell the truth is all about."

Lincoln knew it was time to let that testimony well enough alone. He had one other area to explore, though. "Sir, did you go to the square after Mrs. Foster finished speaking?"

"No."

"Why not?"

"I don't know. Just didn't."

"Well, if she'd urged people to 'Go out and do something about it,' and you thought that meant—" Lincoln looked down at the piece of paper again "—*go seize the slave girl from lawful au-*

thority, wouldn't that sound like it would be exciting to go to the square to watch?"

"I'm not really interested in that kind of thing, Mr. Lincoln."

"You prefer to stay home by your fire with a book?"

"Well, I'm not sure I'd put it that way, but I do like my own home."

"You also said that a lot of people rushed out when Mrs. Foster finished speaking, correct?"

Putnam looked wary, but finally said, "Yes. That's my best recollection."

"Did you ask any of them where they were going?"

"Uh, no."

"And you didn't follow them?"

"No."

"You were just on your way home?"

"Yes."

"When someone said, according to you, 'Let's go,' did you ask that person what he meant?"

"No."

"Because you were just anxious to get home?"

"I guess you could put it that way."

Lincoln looked over at the jury to make sure Humphreys, the first seated juror, was paying attention. He was.

"Mr. Putnam, I just want to make sure we know who was in that church whom you can identify. You are George, Jr. Is that right?"

"Yes."

"So your father is or was George Senior."

"Yes."

"Did he go to the church with you that night?"

"No, that good man has gone to his reward."

"Ah, I'm sorry to hear that. God rest his soul. Do you have a son, Mr. Putnam?"

"Yes. One living."

"Did he go with you to the church?"

"Well, yes."

Lincoln had the sense that Putnam was a vain man, so he took a stab in the dark and hoped to hit his target. "Is he also named George?"

Putnam beamed. "Yes, George Three."

Lincoln had trouble suppressing his glee. He wrinkled his brow in puzzlement and said, "You don't pronounce it George the Third?"

"Objection!" Lizar said. "This is totally irrelevant."

"I withdraw the question," Lincoln said. "George Three or George Third, it obviously makes no difference here." He glanced up at Humphreys, who wore a distinct scowl on his face. No man whose grandfather had served alongside Washington would be likely to think favorably of a man who'd named his son George III, no matter how he pronounced it.

Lincoln looked down at his paper. "I have no further questions."

"Mr. Lizar, do you have any redirect?" the judge said.

"I would like to take a moment to look at my notes," Lizar said.

"Of course."

While Lizar studied his notes, Abby said to Lincoln, "What's on that magic paper you kept looking at?"

Lincoln pushed it in front of her, and she smiled. "Why it's the Lord's Prayer. You wrote out the whole thing!"

"I must get help from whence I can. And it fills the page."

Lizar rose from his chair. "I have nothing further, Your Honor."

"Do you have more witnesses, Mr. Lizar?"

"Yes, two more, both of whom were in the square when the events occurred."

"Mr. Lincoln, how many witnesses are you likely to have?"

"Don't think I'll need a lot, Your Honor." He glanced at the jury, hoping they'd picked up his intent, which was to suggest that the government's case was pathetically weak. "Perhaps only two quick ones."

"Alright," the judge said. "We will break for lunch and return here at 1:30. Perhaps we can finish today."

50

Lincoln, Abby and Billy went to lunch at the Chenery House. The sheriff saw the three of them leave the courthouse together but made no objection to his prisoner being out and about.

After they were seated, Abby said, "It's wonderful to be out of jail, and truly out, not just walked around the square or moved from jail to courthouse."

They had hardly had time to seat themselves when several people came over to their table. They were abolitionists and wanted to thank Abby for her work "on behalf of the slave." They said nothing at all to Lincoln or Billy.

After they had left, Lincoln said, "You are famous, Abby."

"Not so famous as you, Abraham."

Billy rolled his eyes. "The two of you seem to have formed a mutual admiration society. Next thing you know, Abby will announce that she's going to attend one of your campaign rallies, Lincoln."

"He'd have to change his views on abolition," Abby said.

"Profoundly. And, of course, women would need to be permitted to vote."

"You know that I think slavery a monstrous injustice," Lincoln said. "I have said so many times. But..."

Billy interrupted him. "He wants to get elected, where perhaps he can have an ameliorating effect on the peculiar institution, as our Southern friends call it."

"I'm hard-pressed to think of any Southern friends of mine," Abby said. "Except for perhaps the Grimke sisters. And I loathe the expression 'the peculiar institution.' If you were a slave, Billy, you'd find nothing peculiar about it."

"Perhaps we should order," Lincoln said, and picked up a menu.

A few seconds later a waiter came over and said, "There is a woman at the table toward the back—" he pointed "—who wishes to join you, but wanted first to make sure it is alright with you, Mr. Lincoln."

Lincoln followed the waiter's pointing finger and saw that the woman in question was Annabelle Carter. "Yes, please ask her to join us," Lincoln said.

Not long after, Annabelle walked over and said, "My apologies for interrupting your lunch, Mr. Lincoln, but I have some information for you, and you have seemed quite tied up with the trial of—" she glanced at Abby "—Mrs. Foster. I thought this might be my only chance today to see you."

"Won't you join us?" Lincoln said.

"I think it would be best if I don't." She looked at Billy and Abby. "I don't mean to seem impolite."

"At least let me introduce you," Lincoln said. "You know Billy already, and this is Abby Kelley Foster. Abby, this is Annabelle Carter, from Chicago."

Abby and Annabelle exchanged the usual greetings, and Annabelle said, "I'm so pleased to meet you, Mrs. Foster. I have for so long admired your work on behalf of the slave."

"Why, thank you," Abby said. "But please call me Abby."

"I will, and I'd be honored to be called Annabelle."

Lincoln had a hard time suppressing a grin. "Abby and Billy, if you'll excuse us, Annabelle and I need to meet for a moment. Billy, if the waiter reappears—" He ran his finger down a page of the menu. "Ah, here it is. I see they have corned beef and cabbage on offer today. That would be perfect."

"Let's go outside the hotel for a moment," Annabelle said.

Lincoln followed her out to the street, where Clarence was waiting.

"Hello, Mr. Artemis," Lincoln said. "I'm still not granting interviews, you know."

"*We're* not here for that," Annabelle said. "We came to tell you that we think Lucy is here in Springfield, although we're not sure exactly where."

"If you do learn exactly where, I'd prefer you not tell me," Lincoln said. "I don't want to have to worry about what my legal obligations might be. Or perhaps more important, my moral obligations."

Annabelle looked around, as if to be sure no one could over-hear them, and said, "We have now come face-to-face with the problem. We each have different reasons for wanting to find her."

"Which are?" Lincoln said.

She pointed her finger at him. "*You* want to find her for legal reasons. Because, in ways I don't understand, you think finding her will cause people to lose interest in Mrs. Foster's trial and help get the jury to acquit her."

Lincoln looked at Clarence. "If I am to speak candidly, you must promise not to report even a word of what we say here today."

Clarence paused for a long time, but finally said, "Alright, I will not report any of what is said here, or that we ever even met."

"But you are still gripping a pencil in your hand," Annabelle said. "As if you are going to write all of this down as soon as you can. Please give it me."

Clarence handed her the pencil, and she dropped it into her bag.

Lincoln grinned. "I will have to recall that as a way to deal with journalists."

"Now you must answer the question Annabelle asked," Clarence said.

"Very well," Lincoln said. "It is not just for Abby's sake that I want Lucy found. It is for my own sake, too. I am persuaded that, in the mysterious ways of politics, finding her will cool the abolitionists' demand that, if Abby is convicted, I pardon her should I have the honor of being elected."

Clarence turned to Annabelle. "And why are *you* looking for Lucy? Besides looking for her on behalf of Pinkerton, who is looking on behalf of Mr. Lincoln?"

Lincoln gave Annabelle a sharp look.

"I already told him, Mr. Lincoln, that you are Pinkerton's client," she said. "Clarence has promised to keep the secret, and I trust him."

"We are beginning to draw a crowd," Lincoln said, glancing toward the five or six people who had gathered across the street and were staring at them. "These are the wages of running for office. I think we need to finish up here quickly before the number grows even larger."

"Where else can we meet?" Annabelle said.

"Let us meet after court today in my office," Lincoln said. "We can discuss this further then."

Lincoln returned to the hotel and lunch, where his corned beef and cabbage were waiting. The conversation turned to the topic of how the trial was going. They all agreed that it was going exceedingly well. Even Herndon, normally a pessimist, said, "Unless their next witness is a great deal more credible than the first two, we are going to win this with no problem. We might not even need to put on any witnesses."

51

Court resumed promptly at 1:30, as scheduled.

When everyone was seated, Judge Garrett looked
down and said, "Mr. Lizar, please call your next
witness."

"The United States calls Herbert Winkler."

A man who looked to be in his forties, with a large shock
of hair, still mostly black with only a few flecks of gray, rose
from his seat in the audience and walked to the witness chair.
Where most of the other people in the courtroom were infor-
mally dressed—some men in sack coats looked as if they'd come
directly from farm chores—the new witness was decked out
in an expensive silk suit, a vest with gold buttons and a high-
collared white shirt.

He looked to Lincoln like a man who'd complete his outfit
with a tall silk hat and, sure enough, when Lincoln looked, the
man had left behind just such a hat on the chair he'd been occupying in the audience.

Once Winkler was sworn, Lizar asked, "Mr. Winkler, what
is your occupation?"

"I'm a banker. Specifically, I'm the majority shareholder of Winkler Bank."

"Is that here in Springfield?"

"No, it's in Chicago, but I hope I will soon be able to open a similar bank here." He smiled out at the audience, displaying a mouthful of perfect white teeth. Lincoln noticed that Winkler was looking out at the audience, probably imagining each and every one as a potential depositor or borrower. But he was not looking at the jury. Perhaps he thought they looked too poor to do either.

"Do you recall where you were on August 24 of this year, Mr. Winkler?" Lizar asked.

"Yes, I was here in Springfield. I had arrived the day before."

"Why were you here, sir?"

"To talk to potential investors in the bank I plan to open here."

"Do you recall what you did on the evening of August 24?"

"Yes. I attended an abolition lecture given by Abby Kelley Foster."

"Do you see her here in the courtroom?"

Lincoln had half a mind to object. It was not as if Abby was an accused robber whose identity was at issue. But he decided not to interrupt Lizar's attempt at theatrics. He hoped it would just irritate the jury.

"Yes," Winkler said. "She's right there, sitting next to Mr. Lincoln." He pointed at her.

Abby, instead of sitting stiffly as some people on trial might have done, acknowledged Winkler with a nod of her head, then turned slightly to the jury and nodded at them, too, as if acknowledging her celebrity and taking pride in it. Lincoln thought it was a perfect reaction.

"Did you attend Mrs. Foster's lecture?"

"Yes, the entire thing. From start to finish."

From start to finish? That was not a phrase that fell naturally from a man's lips. The witness had obviously been rehearsed and, unlike Lizar's earlier witnesses, had learned his lines. It worried Lincoln.

"Where were you seated, Mr. Winkler?"

"About halfway back."

"Were you able to hear what Mrs. Foster said?"

"Oh, yes. Very clearly. I didn't miss a word. Even though she is a woman, she has obviously learned to make herself heard in a big room."

"Do you recall what she said?"

"Yes. First she talked about the election and said that if you were an abolitionist, there was no point in voting, and even if you were going to vote, she did not recommend voting for Mr. Lincoln."

Lizar looked over at Lincoln, as if to direct the jury's attention to him. Lincoln just shrugged—he hoped in a way that said to the jury, "Doesn't matter a lick to me."

"Did Mrs. Foster say anything else, Mr. Winkler?"

"Well, she said many things, mostly about the terrible condition of the slaves and the horrible unjustness of it all."

Lincoln thought that the witness had begun to drone on a bit, and he noticed that Judge Garrett's head was nodding—perhaps too big a lunch? If he were Lizar, he'd get to the point before he lost the jury, too.

"What else do you recall that Mrs. Foster had to say?" Lizar asked.

"Well, she even quoted the Declaration of Independence— the part about all men being created equal."

A woman in the audience suddenly shouted, "What about women? Aren't they equal, too?"

The judge snapped his head back up. "Madam, if you shout out again, I will have the marshal remove you from the courtroom and hold you in contempt. Mr. Lizar, please continue."

Lizar finally got to the point. "Mr. Winkler, did Mrs. Foster mention anything about what was going on in the courthouse square that evening?"

It was technically a leading question, but Lincoln let it go. He knew that Abby had in fact mentioned something about it to her audience.

"Yes. She said there was a young slave girl who had escaped but been caught, and that she was about to be returned to her master."

"Did she say anything else about that?"

"Yes. At the very end, Mrs. Foster shouted out, 'Go out and do something about it.'"

"Did you have an understanding of what Mrs. Foster meant by that?"

Lincoln was on his feet. "Objection! Even assuming Mrs. Foster said that, which we will dispute, and even assuming Mr. Winkler imagines he knows what she meant, it's irrelevant. Only Mrs. Foster knows that."

The judge folded his hands over his midsection and squeaked his chair back and forth for a moment, seeming to think about how to rule.

Finally, he said, "I'll allow the question. Let's see if Mr. Winkler even has any understanding of what Mrs. Foster—assuming she said it—might have meant."

Lincoln could hardly contain his joy. The judge saying "assuming she said it" was a major victory. It would suggest to the jury that the judge himself had his doubts whether Abby had in fact said anything of the kind.

"Let me repeat the question," Lizar said. "Mr. Winkler, did you have an understanding of what Mrs. Foster meant by that?"

"Yes."

"And what was that understanding?"

"I renew my objection," Lincoln said.

"Overruled."

"I understood her to be urging the audience to go and inter-fere with the return of the slave girl to her owner."

"Thank you, Mr. Winkler," Lizar said and glanced up at the judge. "I have no further questions." Whereupon he sat down, with a self-satisfied smile pasted on his face.

The witness started to get up, but the judge said, "Please sit back down, Mr. Winkler. I suspect Mr. Lincoln may want to have at you." He paused. "Cross, Mr. Lincoln?"

"Yes, indeed," Lincoln said, strode up to the witness chair and peered down at Winkler. He did not plan to treat him gently.

52

"Good afternoon, Mr. Winkler," Lincoln said. "I'm Abe Lincoln, counsel for Mrs. Foster." Lincoln had seen no benefit to using 'Abraham.' He wanted the jury to think of him as plain folks, just like them. Unlikely as they were to think of him that way now.

"Good afternoon," Winkler said.

"Mr. Winkler, you testified that Mrs. Foster said, 'Go out and do something about it.' Do you recall her saying that?"

"Yes."

"And you've got that clearly in your memory, word for word?"

"Yes."

"Were you paying close attention?"

"Yes."

"Both before and after she said it?"

Winkler paused. Lincoln could tell the man was trying to figure out where this was heading.

After a few seconds, Winkler said, "Could you repeat the question?"

"Certainly. The question was, 'Both before and after Mrs. Foster said, according to you, 'Go out and do something about it,' were you paying close attention?"

"Yes."

"Well, what did she say right before that?"

"I don't recall exactly."

"What about right after that?"

"I don't recall exactly."

"Did Mrs. Foster accompany what she said by any kind of hand gestures?"

Winkler blinked, and Lincoln could see that he was having the problem all liars have. His lie was woven of thin cloth, and he was in fear that his misrecollection of any detail that others knew and could testify to might shred the fabric of it.

Winkler didn't say anything for several seconds.

"Mr. Winkler, shall I repeat the question?" Lincoln said.

"Uh, no. To the best of my recollection, Mrs. Foster didn't use any hand gestures when she said it."

"Wouldn't it have been logical for Mrs. Foster, if she was urging people to go to the square, to point to the church doors?"

"Objection," Lizar said, rising from the table. "It's improper to ask this witness what is logical. He's here to testify only about what he saw and heard. It's up the jury to consider what's logical and what's not."

"Sustained," the judge said. "Mr. Lincoln, why don't you rephrase that?"

"Alright, Your Honor. Mr. Winkler, did Mrs. Foster point to the church doors as she said it?"

"No."

"Are you sure?"

Instead of immediately saying he was sure, Winkler hesitated again—a fatal mistake, in Lincoln's view. A witness in Winkler's position needed to be firm about his memories or they'd be doubted. Finally, Winkler said, "Well, I don't think she did."

Lincoln looked over at the jury. At least two of them were staring at Winkler with what Lincoln took to be distaste.

Now Lincoln intended to make it worse for the man. "Your Honor, I need to refer to a note I left in my hat. With the court's permission, I will return to my table for a moment to fetch it."

"Go ahead," the judge said. He made no remark about Lincoln's hat-based filing system, presumably because he was aware that it was common for lawyers in Illinois to keep papers inside their stovepipe hats.

Lincoln walked back to the table and picked up his hat from under his chair, where it had been sitting on the floor, brim down. He turned it over and extracted a small note from the inside hatband. He looked it over, and finally said, almost to himself, but loud enough for everyone to hear, "No, I don't need to pursue that right now."

"Alright, Mr. Lincoln, let's try to get this over with," the judge said.

Lincoln hoped that the hatband trick had had its intended effect, which was to make Winkler think that Lincoln knew things that Winkler couldn't be sure about. In fact, the piece of paper had been a note from Mrs. Lincoln asking him to pick something up on his way home from court.

Lincoln considered asking no further questions. He had made excellent progress in piercing the witness's air of certainty. Trying for still more risked ruining what had already been won. But what was motivating the man to lie? It seemed unlikely he'd been bribed in such a high-profile matter. That was probably beyond even the Buchanan administration.

Lincoln walked back up to the witness and said, "Mr. Winkler, are you an abolitionist?"

"Objection," Lizar said, without bothering to get up.

"Goes to bias, Your Honor."

"Overruled."

"I am a gradual abolitionist," Winkler said.

"What does that mean, sir?"

"Well, it means I hate slavery," Winkler said. He paused. "Like you claim you yourself do, Mr. Lincoln. But I don't know how it can easily be ended."

"Unless, for example, slave owners are compensated by the government for what they call their property?" Lincoln said.

"Yes. Or something like that."

"Or like transporting them to Africa?"

"Yes."

"All four million of them?"

This time, Lizar stood up. "I must object, Your Honor, this is well beyond any possible relevance to this trial, which is about whether Mrs. Foster aided and abetted a riot."

Lincoln had to admire Lizar's attempt, in the guise of an objection, to redirect the jury's attention to the main thrust of his case.

The judge cocked his head and squeaked his chair back and forth again. To Lincoln's surprise—because the question was well beyond relevant—the judge said, "I'll allow you a little more leeway, Mr. Lincoln. But you need to wrap this up soon."

Lincoln hoped one last question would show Winkler's bias against Abby. But he tried to toss it off as a casual introduction to a new line of questioning.

"By the way, Mr. Winkler, you're from the South, right?"

"Well, yes, Kentucky. Back when I was young."

And then Lincoln, an inveterate card player, tried to fill an inside straight. "Do you own any slaves, Mr. Winkler?"

Winkler sat silent.

"Do you, sir?"

"Objection!" Lizar said.

Lincoln couldn't tell if Lizar was genuinely angry or just pretending.

Lizar stood up. "Completely irrelevant!"

"Sit down, Mr. Lizar," the judge said. "This strikes me as

highly relevant to bias against Mrs. Foster and her views. You may answer, sir."

"No, I don't own any slaves," Winkler said. "And never have. My father owned two, but I persuaded him to emancipate them without requiring them to buy their own freedom. Five years ago, I think it was."

And so, Lincoln thought, he had demonstrated once again the risk of asking a hostile witness a question to which he didn't know the answer in advance. He tried to suppress a grimace and said, "Thank you, Mr. Winkler. I have no further questions."

"Any redirect, Mr. Lizar?"

Lizar gave the jury a look clearly intended to be one of victory, and said, "No further questions."

"Alright," the judge said. "Do you have any more witnesses, Mr. Lizar?"

"Just one quick one."

"Let's hear from that witness and then we'll take a break."

Lizar then called Robbie Culp, the boy from whom Clarence had bought the drawings of the overturned carriage.

He proved a no-doubt disappointing witness for the government. He admitted he had been in the square for the large gathering that had seen the marshal take Lucy back into the courthouse. And he said he'd been there, too, for the gathering of the smaller, but more violent crowd that later overturned the carriage. But he wasn't able to provide Lizar with any helpful detail about who was in the crowd.

Worse, he didn't know or claimed not to recall who had overturned the coach (although he watched it being overturned), who had injured Ezekiel Goshorn (although he did see him lying on the ground, bleeding), nor who had unlocked Lucy's handcuffs and fetters (although someone "musta," he said, because she'd "had 'em on" when they brought her out of the jail the second time).

Nor could Culp, under continued close questioning, say exactly how Lucy had escaped or where she had gone. All he could say for sure was "that girl got herself away clean."

As for the origins of the new, more violent crowd, he could only say that it had arrived suddenly, "out of nowhere."

As a last resort, Lizar tried to get away with leading his own witness. "You saw people coming into the square from the direction of the Second Presbyterian Church, didn't you, Mr. Culp?"

Lincoln decided to gamble and not object. He had a sense the answer wasn't going to hurt.

"I don't 'member that neither, Mister," Culp said.

"Didn't a man say to you that he was in the square because Abby Kelley Foster told people to go there?"

"I don't 'member that neither. No, sir, not at all."

"I have a newspaper article I want to show you," Lizar said.

Lincoln practically jumped out of his chair. "Your Honor, I believe I know what newspaper article Mr. Lizar is referring to, and I object to it being shown to this witness—who did not write it. It's hearsay and it's completely, utterly false."

"Why don't you gentlemen approach the bench?" the judge said.

Lincoln and Lizar walked up to the bench. The judge leaned down and said, "What's this all about? The jury is close by, so please keep your voices down."

"Your Honor, Mr. Culp is quoted in a newspaper article published the day after the riot," Lizar said. "In it, he says that the mob came from the direction of the church."

"Is that it, Mr. Lizar?" the judge said.

"The article specifically quotes Mr. Culp as saying, 'One of them guys that come to rescue the slave girl said Abby told 'em, "Go do somethin' 'bout that poor slave girl."'"

"Are you trying to introduce that article into evidence?" the judge said. "That would be improper because there's not yet any foundation for it, not to mention at least two layers of hearsay."

"No, Your Honor. I just want to use it to refresh Mr. Culp's memory."

"Which it might or might not do," Lincoln said. "In the meantime the jury will have heard it, which will improperly prejudice them against my client."

"The rule is that you can use *anything* to try to refresh someone's recollection," Lizar said. "Even a frying pan if it would serve the function."

Lincoln laughed. "The difference, Your Honor, is that a frying pan isn't allowed to say what it saw and heard after it's been used to refresh."

"I'm going to bar you from using that newspaper article to refresh your witness's recollection," the judge said.

"In that case, Your Honor, I plan to call as a witness the man who interviewed Culp and then wrote that article. Then I will try to introduce it in evidence."

"What Mrs. Foster said to someone might be admissible," Lincoln said. "But not what she allegedly said to someone who repeated it to someone else who then said it to the writer of that newspaper article. It's inadmissible hearsay."

Ignoring him, Lizar continued on, "The writer's name is Clarence Artemis. He's been sitting in the courtroom since this trial began." As he said it, he turned as if to point Clarence out to the judge, but where Clarence had been sitting only a few moments earlier, there was only an empty chair.

"You'll have to find him and subpoena him," the judge said.

"I suspect he might end up being a tad hard to find," Lincoln said.

"Will you delay the trial while the government tries to find him?" Lizar said.

The judge looked, Lincoln thought, downright bemused and said, "Mr. Lincoln, here's your chance. Do you know any good jokes that speak to Mr. Lizar's question?"

"Well, yes I do," Lincoln said. "It goes like this. What's the best way to catch a pig that's on the run?"

"What the answer?" the judge said.

"Try to be in front of it when it starts to run."

The judge laughed loudly and said, "Well, there's your answer, Mr. Lizar. If you'd been at the courtroom door when Mr. Artemis started to leave, I'd delay the trial a few moments while you snared him. But since you weren't, there will be no delay."

Lizar looked, Lincoln thought, a bit downcast and said only, "Alright."

"Do you have any more questions for this witness or any more witnesses?"

"No."

"Does the government rest its case, then?"

"Yes, sir. The government rests."

"Mr. Lincoln, we will take a fifteen-minute break now. You deferred your opening statement. Do you wish to make one when we return?"

"No, we will waive it."

"Very well, then. How many witnesses do you think you will have for the defense case?"

"Just one, Your Honor. And I expect that one to be quick."

53

Lincoln, Herndon and Abby went to the same small room they'd used before.

"We don't have much time to talk," Lincoln said. "I think I need only a single witness whose credibility is beyond doubt. And I need him to say only that he heard Abby's entire speech—clearly—and that she never said anything even close to 'go do something about it.'"

"Do you have one?" Herndon asked.

"Yes."

"Who?"

"I'd like you to be surprised," Lincoln said.

Herndon looked over at Abby. "Lincoln likes secrets and surprises."

"I see," she said. And then, "Abraham, how did you know Herbert Winkler was from the South?"

"I wish I'd not figured it out, for obvious reasons."

"Yes, I could see it turned out not to be the best question. But I would still like to know how you knew."

"Well, Abby, Mrs. Lincoln, as everyone in the country seems to know by now, given how that's been used against me in the campaign, grew up in Kentucky."

"Does she sound like that man?"

"Not at all. But she has what sometimes seems to me like dozens of brothers and sisters, aunts and uncles, cousins, and nieces and nephews. And one or two of them, in order to do business in the North more easily, have tried to Yank-ify their accents. They sound just like Winkler."

Herndon looked at him. "Really? I've met some of Mrs. Lincoln's relatives, and I never heard anyone who sounded like Winkler."

"Well, Billy, you'd be the first to admit that you and Mrs. Lincoln don't get along so well, and she's not often invited you to the house to meet any of her relatives. So you've just not met enough of them.

"Now let's turn to the most important thing," Lincoln said.

"What is that, Abraham?"

"Closing argument. This judge is not likely to adjourn until tomorrow for that. I'm guessing he will make us give our closings today."

"Do you know what you're going to say?" Herndon said.

"I will simply point out that the government has the burden of proof here, and that it can't possibly meet it with a man no longer of sound mind and two lying scoundrels."

"That sounds persuasive," Abby said.

"Yes, but what you say is the linchpin, Abby. You can't testify under oath in your own defense. But you can make an unsworn statement."

"How do I do that?"

"Just tell your story as best you can and be persuasive that you never said what they say you said."

"You've said the judge may not let me say certain things."

"I think you need not worry about that. If you step over the lines he draws he will stop you."

"You don't want to rehearse, then?"

"In the few minutes we have left, I want to go over what you want to say in broad strokes. I don't want you to seem as if you are an actor reading rehearsed lines from a play."

"There is no risk of that, Abraham. I speak from an un-rehearsed heart."

"Good, let's spend a few minutes finding out what your heart has to say."

With the lawyers and Abby back at their tables and all the jurors back in the courtroom, Judge Garrett seemed anxious to finish up. "Mr. Lincoln, you have only one witness, is that correct?"

"Yes, Your Honor. Before I call him, though, I have the usual motion to bring."

"Why does that not surprise me?" the judge said, smiling.

Lincoln had half expected that the judge would ask the jury to leave while he made his motion. The fact that he did not could be read in one of two ways; the most logical one was that the motion was going to be denied.

Lincoln rose from his table and said, "Defendant Mrs. Foster moves to dismiss the government's case on the ground that the United States has not met its minimum burden of proof in the case. I will now specify the ways in which that is true and cite the relevant law to Your Honor." Lincoln glanced over at the jury, to be sure the judge was really wanting them to stay.

"That won't be necessary, Mr. Lincoln," the judge said. "First, I'm familiar with the procedural law that is applicable to these sort of motions here in Illinois because I've been a federal judge in Chicago, where the same law applies. Second, I've listened to the witnesses and while some might say the matter is close, I believe a reasonable jury could go either way. So I'm going to deny your motion."

Lincoln breathed an internal sigh of relief. The judge had practically given the jury permission to acquit Abby if it felt like doing so.

Lincoln looked over to Lizar to see if he was going to say something or protest, or ask for a mistrial on the grounds that the judge had prejudiced the jury. But he said nothing.

Abby leaned over to Lincoln and whispered, "Was that good?"

"It was wonderful," Lincoln whispered back, then said aloud, "The defense calls Reverend Albert Hale."

There was an audible gasp in the courtroom as Hale pushed through the bar and took his seat in the witness chair. Men of the cloth were not usually called to testify in court.

After he was sworn—saying "So help me God" in a particularly strong voice, Lincoln asked his first question.

"Father Hale, do you recall where you were the evening of August 24?"

"Yes, I was in the church of which I have been privileged to be the pastor these many years. Second Presbyterian."

"Why were you there?"

"I was there to introduce a speaker I had invited to the church, Abby Kelley Foster, a noted abolitionist."

"Did people attend?"

"Yes, except for the last few rows in the back, the sanctuary was full, and when filled it holds three hundred people."

"Did you introduce Mrs. Foster?"

"Yes, I did. And then she gave what we call an abolition lecture. So she spoke at some length on the need to free the slaves in this country."

"Did she talk about anything else, Father?"

"Well, Mr. Lincoln, at the start she went out of her way to say that she was not supporting anyone for president, and certainly not *you*." He smiled.

"Do you recall her mentioning anything else, Father?"

"Yes, she mentioned that nearby, a young, enslaved girl was about to be returned to her master."

"Did she say anything else about that?"

Hale paused, as if searching his memory. "She said that the girl was about to be returned to bondage in Kentucky."

"Anything else?"

Hale paused again. "Oh, yes. She asked for a show of hands of those who had been to a protest about the matter that had taken place there earlier."

"*There* being where, Father?"

"Oh, in the courthouse square, but I don't think she mentioned the place by name. I recall that she just said something like 'several blocks from here.'"

"Did she urge anyone to take any kind of action?"

"No. Not at all." He paused again. "Oh, later on she urged people to contribute money to help spread the word about the need to abolish slavery. That was at the very end. There were even women there walking around in the aisles and near the doors with collection plates, taking up contributions as Mrs. Foster was finishing up."

"Did you stay for the entire lecture?"

"Yes."

"Every minute of it?"

"Yes."

Lincoln considered asking Hale straight-out if Abby had said anything like "Go do something about it," but decided against it. What he'd gotten from Hale was good enough without making it seem as if he had put words in his mouth. He would instead let Hale deal with it if Lizar was foolish enough to go near it.

"I have no further questions," Lincoln said. He glanced over at Lizar. The man looked like someone who had just taken a bite out of a bitter apple. "Mr. Lizar, cross-examination?" the judge said.

54

"Yes, Your Honor." Lizar rose and walked over to Hale, but stood not nearly as close to him as he had with the other witnesses.

If I were Lizar, I'd start with bias, Lincoln thought.

Which is what Lizar did.

"Good evening, Father," Lizar said. "I don't think we've had the pleasure of meeting."

"No, we haven't," Hale said. "But if you're staying awhile in town, you'd be very welcome at our church this coming Sunday."

Nice shot, Lincoln thought. Hale had managed to remind the jury that Lizar was from out of town.

"Thank you, Father," Lizar said. "You are an abolitionist, am I correct?"

"Yes. Although something of a moderate one by most people's standards, I'd say."

Good, Lincoln thought, Hale has positioned himself where most of the jurors are likely to be, politically. Probably half of their wives say the same thing at the supper table. Let's see if Lizar is inept enough to ask Hale to elaborate.

But he didn't. Instead he asked Hale what Lincoln thought of as a good *yes/no* question.

"Father, did you meet with Mrs. Foster before her lecture?"

"Yes, in fact we had supper together beforehand."

"At that supper, did you tell her about the enslaved girl?"

"Yes, I told her there was such a girl—only twelve years old, can you imagine? A girl who was about to be handed back to her so-called owner."

"Did you tell her there was going to be a protest?"

"Either that there was going to be or had just been one. I don't recall the timing."

Lizar should stop now, Lincoln thought.

"Did she express any desire to 'do something' about the situation of the slave girl?"

Well, Lincoln thought, perhaps Lizar was continuing down his perilous path because he trusted a minister to be honest, but if any of the jurors were inclined toward abolition, they would not like that Lizar had slipped and called Lucy a "slave girl" instead of "enslaved."

"Not at all," Hale said. "She said only that she might like to go herself to such a demonstration but was far too weary from her trip to do so. And then she said she needed to rest in her room for an hour before her lecture."

Lizar didn't pursue it further, but looked down at some notes he'd apparently taken during Lincoln's direct examination.

Lincoln wondered if Lizar was going to risk asking an even more direct question of a witness he knew nothing about and hadn't interviewed. Lincoln felt sorry for him. He was a man sent from afar to do a job in a midsize town he didn't know. If they'd left the regular United States attorney in place, he would surely have gone and interviewed Hale. Or perhaps the regular man had simply refused to participate in this outrageous charade of a case.

Lizar took a deep breath, and said, "Father Hale, during her lecture, did Mrs. Foster urge anyone to do anything?"

"Oh, yes," Hale said. "Toward the very end of her lecture, she urged people to go forth and oppose slavery and to please contribute to the collection plates that were circulating, both in the aisles and near the front door. I think she may have pointed toward the doors."

"Father Hale, do you carry a pocket watch?"

"Yes, in fact my wife recently gave me as a gift the new Waltham Model 57. It even has interchangeable parts, so it can be repaired more easily!"

Ignoring Hale's enthusiasm, Lizar said, "Do you look at your watch frequently to check the time?"

"Yes, although at times my wife says I do it too much and it makes people think I'm impatient with them."

"I see. Did you happen to check the time Mrs. Foster finished speaking."

"I did."

"Do you recall it?"

"I do. She finished at precisely 9:00 p.m. And I remember that because I recall thinking that she had not droned on forever, as some speakers do."

He glanced over at Abby and said, "Apologies, Mrs. Foster, I can't imagine you ever droning on."

Abby nodded slightly in response, but didn't crack a smile.

"One final question, Father Hale. Did you put up posters advertising Mrs. Foster's lecture?"

"I didn't personally, but I did ask some of our parishioners to do that."

"I have no further questions," Lizar said.

The judge looked at Lincoln. "Any redirect, Mr. Lincoln?"

Lincoln thought about it for a second, considering where Lizar was likely going with the time issue, but he couldn't immediately think of any way to defang it. "No, Your Honor. I don't have any redirect."

"Does the defense have any other witnesses, Mr. Lincoln?"

"No."

"In that case, we'll have closing argument now," the judge said.

"Excuse me, Your Honor," Lizar said. "I request leave to reopen my case to call one additional witness."

"Who?" the judge said. "And on what grounds?"

Lizar turned and pointed toward the back of the courtroom. "To question that man." He pointed directly at Clarence, who to Lincoln's astonishment, had apparently been unable to restrain himself from returning in order to hear the end of the trial.

Clarence, who'd been sitting in the last seat in the row closest to the door, jumped up and started walking rapidly toward the exit.

"I ask that the marshal restrain him," Lizar said.

Red, without being asked, moved into the middle of the doorway, where Clarence, who was not a big man, bumped up against him and stopped dead in his tracks.

"Please move to the witness stand, sir. Since you are in the courtroom, Mr. Lizar does not need a subpoena to call you as a witness." The judge paused. "Unless, Mr. Lincoln, you have some objection to Mr. Lizar reopening his case. Do you?"

Lincoln could tell by the tone of voice in which the judge had said "Do you?" that he ought not to have an objection.

"It's fine with me, Your Honor."

Clarence walked up to the witness chair and sat down. After he was sworn, and had given his name and profession, Lizar said, "Sir, were you in the courthouse square the evening of August 24."

"In late afternoon and evening, yes."

"Were you there more than once?"

"Yes, twice."

"What did you observe happening the first time?"

"A large crowd was threatening to interfere with the transfer of an enslaved girl back to her so-called master."

"Did you see any physical violence?"

"Threatened, but it hadn't happened when I left. At that point they had announced they weren't moving the girl that night— I think it was Red who said that. Most of the crowd was dispersing."

"You went back a second time, right?"

Lincoln had decided not to object to leading questions. He was most anxious to get Clarence off the stand and out of there as quickly as possible.

"Yes, I did."

"Why did you go back?"

"I was back in my office, a couple of blocks away, when someone shouted to me that they were bringing the carriage around again, presumably to try a second time to move the girl."

"Did you do anything in response?"

"Yes, I grabbed what I needed—pencil and paper—and raced back to the square."

"What did you observe when you got there?"

"The carriage was on its side and the man I'd seen sitting in it before was gone. I didn't see the girl, Red or the sheriff. I had the sense it had all just happened, seconds or minutes before I got there."

"Did you see anything else?"

"There was a small fire burning in a room inside the courthouse, and a small fire that had been built in a hole in the ground."

"Did you note the time that you got back to the square?"

"Yes."

"Is it your normal practice to note the times of important events?"

"Yes."

"What time was it when you got back to the square?"

"Exactly 9:15."

"By your watch?"

"Yes."

Lizar smiled. "Is it by chance a Waltham Model 57?"

"No, it's a much more exp—beautiful one."

"I see. Are you sure of that time?"

"Yes."

"I have no further questions."

Lincoln breathed a sigh of relief. He had thought Lizar was going to try to move Clarence's newspaper account of the riot into evidence, including the part that speculated about the possible role of Abby's lecture in fomenting what happened. For whatever reason, Lizar had decided against it.

"Mr. Lincoln, cross-examination?" the judge said.

"No, Your Honor."

"Do you have any further witnesses?"

"No," Lincoln said. "The defense rests, while reserving the usual post-trial motions and the right of Mrs. Foster to make a personal statement."

"Very well, then," the judge said. "We shall have closing argument. Mr. Lizar, are you ready?"

"Yes, Your Honor."

The judge addressed the jury. "Gentlemen, we will now have closing argument, in which the lawyers will sum up the evidence and tell you why they believe you should find the defendant either guilty or innocent. After they are done, the defendant will make an unsworn statement. I will explain that procedure later. And then I will instruct you on the law you are to apply."

Lizar rose from his table. "Your Honor, I request that Mrs. Foster go first with her statement. Then I will know, in my closing, what I am up against."

"Her statement is unsworn, Mr. Lizar, so you aren't up against anything, the way I see it. Your motion is denied. You said you were ready, so let's not keep the jury waiting."

55

Lizar stood directly in front of the jury. "Gentlemen, the evidence is quite clear here. Mrs. Foster stands accused of violating the Compromise of 1850 by feloniously assisting the fugitive Lucy Battelle, who was bound to service in Kentucky, to escape after she was recaptured.

"The government, as the judge will tell you, has the burden of proving beyond a reasonable doubt that Mrs. Foster committed that criminal act. I put to you that there is really no doubt at all here.

"To convict Mrs. Foster, we must prove two things—first, that Mrs. Foster spoke words intended to interfere with Lucy Battelle being moved to a carriage so that she might be returned to her owner. Second, that Mrs. Foster's words caused a riot to happen that prevented that return.

"You might think it logical to start with the first—the words Mrs. Foster spoke. But I think it is in fact more logical and more useful for you to start with the second question. What happened in the square?

"You heard Mr. Culp testify that, earlier in the evening, a large, hostile crowd had gathered, but that it had dispersed, and that it had *not* attacked anyone or anything. You then heard him testify that much later, a smaller crowd gathered, seemingly out of nowhere, and that it overturned the carriage to which the marshal was attempting to move Lucy Battelle. That allowed her to escape and apparently also injured Mr. Goshorn, Lucy's legal owner. As we all know, he later died of his injuries."

Lincoln leapt to his feet. "Your Honor, I have rarely interrupted another man's closing argument, but I must object, and strenuously. Whatever we all might know or not know, there is no evidence in this trial that anything at all happened to Mr. Goshorn. And even if it did, Mrs. Foster is not on trial here for anything other than what she is charged with in the indictment."

"Mr. Lincoln is right, Mr. Lizar," the judge said. "There has been no evidence adduced here about what happened—if anything—to Mr. Goshorn. Nor does it matter to this trial."

He looked at the jury. "Gentlemen, you are to completely disregard what Mr. Lizar has just said about Mr. Goshorn. The charge against Mrs. Foster, while it may be referred to as a felony, is much, much less serious than anything involving a death, and Mrs. Foster is charged with no such thing."

Lincoln saw that Lizar had hung his head and was doing his best to look abashed. But Lincoln had no doubt that Lizar was happy. He had managed to remind the jury that, even though the judge had told the jury to ignore Goshorn's death, the riot wasn't just about the return of an enslaved black girl. It was also about the murder of a white man. As the saying went, you can't unring the bell once someone's heard it sound.

Lizar resumed. "As I was saying, the evidence is that a crowd came suddenly out of nowhere, overturned the carriage and allowed Lucy Battelle to escape again from her lawful owner.

"Now, when did that happen? Mr. Artemis, by his own testimony, a journalist who says he is careful about time, has told you that he rushed back to the square immediately after hearing what must have been the start of the riot. And that he consulted his watch. He has told you that it was 9:15 p.m.

"Now ask yourself, please, what happened just before that? We know from Reverend Hale's testimony and that of several other witnesses, that right before that, Mrs. Foster finished her lecture. And what time was that? According to Reverend Hale she finished at precisely 9:00 p.m.

"I put it to you that even if we did not know anything about what Mrs. Foster had said in her lecture, it would be at least suspicious that not long before the start of the riot, a radical abolitionist lecturer had just finished her lecture in a church only blocks away—a church filled nearly to capacity with people presumably angry about slavery."

Lincoln considered objecting again since there was no evidence about the nature of the audience, but it was probably true, so he let it go.

"We would be suspicious that she said something to that crowd that caused them to go over to the square and riot."

Lincoln had been watching the jury closely. They seemed rapt on what Lizar was saying. As Lizar finished saying "We would be suspicious," several of the jurors were nodding in apparent agreement.

"But we don't have to be satisfied with mere suspicion," Lizar said. "Because we know what Mrs. Foster said. We have had three witnesses to tell us that. First, Mr. Wilbur Jenkins. He told you quite clearly that right at the end of her lecture, Mrs. Foster, right after talking about Lucy Battelle, told the audience, 'Go out and do something about that.' He may have repeated it in a slightly country way, but he remembered it, and he testified to it."

Lincoln had to admire the way Lizar had gone about that. He wasn't going to apologize for the weaknesses of his own witness. He'd leave that to Lincoln if he wanted to do it.

"There was also Mr. George Putnam, Jr. Another credible witness who was there and heard Mrs. Foster say exactly the same thing—'Go out and do something about it.' And that something was the transfer of Lucy Battelle back to her owner. The fact that Mr. Putnam may have been hostile to Mrs. Foster doesn't change the very precise nature of his recall, particularly when supported by the recall of two other credible witnesses."

Lincoln noted that Lizar had done what Lincoln himself sometimes did—bring up something negative about his own witness so that the opposing lawyer wouldn't be the first to bring it up and accuse Lincoln of having hidden a bad fact. He looked again at the jury and was pleased to see that a couple of them, who had been paying rapt attention a minute ago, were starting to nod off. Lizar taking too long.

"And there was, finally, Mr. Herbert Winkler, an upstanding citizen of this state. He also heard clearly what Mrs. Foster said, 'Go out and do something about it.' And he was able to say with great precision what he understood Mrs. Foster to be asking of her audience." Lizar looked down at a piece of paper in his hand. "He said, 'I understood her to be urging the audience to go and interfere with the return of the slave girl to her owner.'

"Gentlemen, the evidence shows that Mrs. Foster knew exactly what was about to happen in the square with Lucy Battelle. She told her audience to go and do something about it and they did.

"And through riot they did exactly as she intended—prevented the return of Lucy to her proper owner and allowed her instead to escape.

"Mrs. Foster's actions in so doing obviously feloniously violated Section 7 of the Compromise of 1850, which forbids anyone to assist a person bound to service from escaping if they are in the custody of the United States marshal.

"The United States asks you to bring in a verdict of guilty as charged. Justice requires no less. The government thanks you, as I do, for your time spent as jurors in this matter."

"Mr. Lincoln, we will now hear from the defense," the judge said.

56

Lincoln had always believed that if you were representing a defendant it was important to make your argument brief and uncomplicated, so that it would seem a simple task to acquit. With that in mind, he began.

"Gentlemen, I will not keep you long. I am in favor of short and sweet.

"As for the timing of the events in the square, I suppose you could imagine that a speech blocks away somehow caused the events the government complains of—the rescue of an enslaved girl in this free state of Illinois. But the simple explanation of things is usually the best. And here we have a much simpler one.

"Earlier that evening, as Mr. Culp testified, the United States marshal found the mob in the square so threatening that he took the enslaved girl back into the courthouse. Most of the crowd then dispersed.

"But there's the rub—the word *most*. Because, as Mr. Culp also said, some people remained. And so, when the government tried again to move the girl, it is logical to assume those who remained quickly notified others, and the mob reformed, with the result that we know.

"If you then ask what caused the riot the government complains of, the answer is simple—the government!

"The fact that, at the same time that the government tried a second time to move the enslaved girl, Mrs. Foster was finishing up a speech somewhere else is no more than a coincidence. Like most coincidences in our lives, it has no meaning.

"If you conclude, as I urge you to, that the government's actions were the cause of the riot, you need not, I suppose, worry overly about what Mrs. Foster did or did not say over at the Second Presbyterian Church.

"But if you do examine that evidence I am confident you will find no *credible* testimony to suggest that Mrs. Foster urged anyone to go and do anything other than, perhaps, contribute to the collection plate.

"With regard to the three witnesses the government dragged in to try to remember to the contrary, you can no doubt judge their reliability for yourselves, without the need for my assistance. We all heard what they said, and we all heard them, one by one, admit their bias.

"I would also remind you that in judging the credibility of a witness, you may judge not only a man's words, but the way in which he spoke them, including his pauses and stumbles as he purported to remember. I am speaking of course, of Mr. Winkler.

"I would also call to your attention that there was but one witness who testified on behalf of Mrs. Foster—Father Hale. Now I didn't ask him if Mrs. Foster had urged people to 'go out and do something' about Lucy Battelle. It was Mr. Lizar who, in effect, asked him about that. Father Hale swore under oath that Mrs. Foster did not say that.

"Well, who to believe? I ask you to consider which of the four was most likely to take seriously the phrase 'So help me God' in the oath they all swore."

Lincoln paused, and then said, as if he'd had a second thought, "Oh, and there is one more thing. The government presented not a single witness who said he heard Mrs. Foster speak and then went over to the square. Not one.

"You would have thought, out of all the people who were in the church and all the people who were in the square, the government, with all its resources, could have found at least one such person. After all, they went all the way to Chicago to find one of their other witnesses. Couldn't they have found just one person who went from church to square? The fact that they didn't speaks for itself about what or who caused the riot in the square.

"Far from proving beyond a reasonable doubt that Mrs. Foster assisted a slave to escape, the government has proved not a single thing that supports the charge. I urge you to find Mrs. Foster not guilty.

"Thank you for you kind attention today."

"Mr. Lizar, do you wish a rebuttal?" the judge said.

"Yes, Your Honor. I certainly do."

"Please proceed."

Lizar walked toward the jury and said, "I, too, will try to be short and sweet, but also willing to look at the detailed evidence.

"We all have our biases. But biases are not necessarily disabling. Most of us, when charged with a solemn legal duty, can put our biases aside.

"Each of the government's witnesses took an oath to tell the truth. Let's look at them."

"First, Mr. Jenkins, who said he heard Mrs. Foster say, 'Go out and do something about it,' referring to the recaptured slave. And yes, he is hard of hearing, and yes, he apparently is not someone who wishes to contribute to the abolitionist cause.

"If he were the only witness, perhaps there would be reason

to doubt him. But he was not. There were two more who said the same thing.

"Next came Mr. Putnam. And yes, Mr. Lincoln might consider him biased, but remember what Mr. Putnam said under oath—that not only did Mrs. Foster say, 'Go out and do something about it,' but that he, Mr. Putnam, clearly understood her to mean, 'Go seize the slave girl from lawful authority.'

"Please don't forget that Mr. Putnam also saw a crowd rush out of the church when Mrs. Foster finished speaking. And he heard a man say, 'Let's go.' Mr. Lincoln didn't mention either of those things.

"There was also, of course, Mr. Winkler. He, too, heard Mrs. Foster say, 'Go do something about it.'" He paused. "And there was not a single indication of any bias on his part. None. Indeed, it is just the opposite. He has actually caused his father to free slaves.

"Please also remember that all three of these witnesses support each other on the key point. Are we to believe that two of them are so biased that they lied under oath, and that the third one, Mr. Winkler, where no bias at all was shown, simply forgot what he heard?

"Finally, while we are on the subject of bias, the only witness the defense put forward was Reverend Hale."

Here it comes, Lincoln thought.

"If you want to talk about bias, Reverend Hale is the picture of bias. He is not only an abolitionist, but he invited Mrs. Foster, a known radical abolitionist, to come to his church to lecture. And he had his parishioners put up posters to advertise Mrs. Foster's lecture. So he could fill the hall.

"Now I ask you to consider, why is the testimony of the government's three witnesses to be compared negatively to the bias of Reverend Hale? Why is he to be judged more truthful than all *three* of them?"

Lincoln wondered if Lizar was actually going to accuse Hale of lying. Perhaps he would find a less direct way.

"Far be it from me to accuse a man of the cloth of lying," Lizar said. "But perhaps, in his zeal for his cause, the good reverend, without meaning to, misremembered what Mrs. Foster said."

Nicely done, Lincoln thought.

"Now let's talk about coincidence," Lizar said. "If you believe that the three men who testified about what they heard Mrs. Foster say—'go out and do something about it'—testified accurately, then what happened in the square was no coincidence. It was cause and effect. If you believe it was just a coincidence, I have some gold-laden land in California I want to sell you.

"The United States of America asks you to return a verdict of guilty."

Lincoln admired Lizar's effort. The case was going to be closer than he had hoped. Abby's statement would be key.

"Mr. Lincoln, I believe you said Mrs. Foster would like to make a statement," the judge said.

"Yes, she does."

"May we approach the bench, Your Honor?" Lizar said.

The judge sighed. "Yes."

57

"What is it now, Mr. Lizar?"

"Your Honor, instead of making an unsworn statement, the government has no objection to Mrs. Foster being sworn so that I can cross-examine her after her direct testimony."

Lincoln said nothing. He preferred the law the way it was, at least for this case, but didn't want to appear afraid to have Abby cross-examined.

The judge seemed exasperated. "Mr. Lizar, the law in this state and, I believe, all states, is that criminal defendants may make an unsworn statement but may not be sworn and cross-examined."

"But, Your Honor, many legislatures are even now considering changing the law."

"So I have heard. But considering changing is not the same as changing. And the reasons that have been given over the centuries why defendants may not be sworn seem persuasive. For one thing, defendants may lie to protect themselves, cheapening the oath. For another, if they are permitted to testify and choose not to, the jury might conclude that they refused because they are guilty."

"What is wrong with that inference?" Lizar said.

Lincoln answered. "It erodes their Fifth Amendment right not to be a witness against themselves."

"Thank you, Mr. Lincoln, for your Constitutional erudition," the judge said. "But whatever the arguments, until the Illinois legislature changes the law—and in federal courts we still follow state law on these things—I'm not at liberty to let Mrs. Foster be sworn and cross-examined."

"Thank you, Your Honor," Lizar said.

"Please return to your tables, gentlemen," the judge said. "I will then explain the procedure to the jurors."

The judge then addressed the jury. "Gentlemen, our law, for sound reasons, does not permit a criminal defendant to be sworn and testify, even if she were to want to do so. We do permit a defendant to make an unsworn statement—*not* under oath—to the jury. Mrs. Foster wishes to make such a statement."

He looked at Abby. "Mrs. Foster, you may proceed, but please do so while standing at your table so that the jury will not misunderstand and think you are a sworn witness. Also, you may tell your story, but you may not directly attack the testimony of those who have testified under oath. Do you understand?"

Abby stood up. "Yes, Your Honor."

"Good." He looked to the jury again. "Gentlemen, with regard to Mrs. Foster's statements, you may choose to believe all or none or believe some but not others. Mrs. Foster, please begin."

Abby hung her head for a second, as if seeking God's blessing, and said, "Brothers—for that is how we address people—I was raised a Quaker in rural Massachusetts, near Lynn. We lived on a farm. For many years, my father and mother had no sons, and I was my father's farmhand." She smiled. "Which I loved.

"But there was one thing I would not do. I would not kill the chickens when it was time for that. And yes, I ate their meat, but with regret.

"When I left our family home in my midtwenties, I became a schoolteacher in Lynn. I went to an abolition lecture and found my calling. Since then, for well over thirty years, I have traveled this land saying to all who would listen that slavery is evil and must be abolished. I have founded two abolition newspapers. I have been the general agent for the American Anti-Slavery Society. I have done all I could do on behalf of the slave."

Lizar rose and said, "Your Honor, I object that this is irrelevant."

"It is well within bounds, Mr. Lizar. Sit down."

Abby continued. "I am a radical abolitionist. Which means I think the slaves should be freed now, not later. Nor do I believe the slaves should be freed in exchange for compensation, or sent to a foreign land that they have never known. I believe they should be freed because of what it says in our Declaration of Independence—that all men are created equal.

"I am also a come-outer. If your church doesn't wholeheartedly oppose slavery, you should come out of it and join some other church. We are not lacking in other churches to join.

"I am also a lifelong pacifist. I abhor war and violence. When it has been suggested to me that the slaves ought to be freed by an army, I have opposed it. When more times than I can count things were thrown at me at abolition lectures—including things from the outhouse and the barn I regret to say—I refused to seek the arrest of those who attacked me.

"I was aware, before I spoke at the Second Presbyterian Church here on August 24, that an enslaved girl was to be transferred back to her so-called owner that day. In my younger days, I might have attended a rally in support of her. I am now much too old and too tired to do it, and I did not go. I am embarrassed to say I took a nap instead.

"Even had I gone, I would never have urged anyone to go do

something about the transfer because I would have known that it could lead to violence. I am opposed to violence in all its forms.

"In my lecture, I did urge people to go forth and oppose slavery, and I may well have said to do something *about* slavery by contributing to the cause, so that we might publish more newspapers, send out more mailings and dispatch more abolition lecturers like myself to go forth and tell our fellow citizens the truth about the horrors of slavery.

"I am not guilty of the crime with which I am charged.

"I thank you, my brothers, for your time in listening to my story. I hope soon to return to my husband, my daughter and my colleagues in the cause."

She sat down.

Lizar stood up. "I move that the court instruct the jury that everything the defendant said starting with 'I would never have urged anyone' be disregarded. It is in direct contradiction to what the sworn witnesses testified to, which is not permitted in unsworn defendant statements."

Judge Garrett seemed to think about it for a moment, then said, "Your motion is denied."

Lincoln thought that Lizar had made a mistake because all he'd done was remind the jurors that Abby was contradicting what his witnesses had said.

"Are there any motions?" the judge said.

Lincoln stood. "I move to dismiss the government's case on the ground that it has not met its burden and that, when considered together with the evidence the defendant has proffered, it is woefully short of the mark."

"Your motion is denied, Mr. Lincoln. Unless there are other motions, I will now instruct the jury."

Which he did.

After instructing the jury on various aspects of evidence and how to weigh it, as well as the meaning of "beyond a reasonable doubt," the judge said, "Gentlemen, in order to convict Mrs.

Foster in this case you must conclude that the government has proved, beyond a reasonable doubt, each of three entirely separate things, all of which together would constitute, in the language of the statute, 'assisting a slave to escape.'

"First, that during her lecture Mrs. Foster uttered the words *go out and do something about it* or very similar words.

"Second, that she uttered those words with the intent to persuade members of the audience to go to the square and assist the enslaved girl, Lucy Battelle, to escape by physically interfering with her transfer to her owner.

"Third, that at least one member of her audience who heard those words went directly to the square and interfered with the transfer of Lucy Battelle to her owner or otherwise assisted her to escape.

"To convict Mrs. Foster in this case, you must determine that *each and every one* of those acts was proved by the government beyond a reasonable doubt."

Then he added, "If you find, for example, that only the first two of those items have been proved beyond a reasonable doubt, but not the third, you must acquit the defendant.

"I also instruct you that although it may in some circumstances be a crime to urge someone to commit a particular criminal act even if they do not go forward and commit the act, that is not the case with the Fugitive Slave Act. Someone hearing Mrs. Foster's words must have acted in some direct way to assist the escape. You may, however, also consider whether acts such as shouting encouragement to someone who was trying directly to free the enslaved girl constituted assisting a slave to escape."

Lincoln could hardly contain his joy at the narrow interpretation of the Act that the judge had just embraced. There had been no testimony by anyone that after they heard Abby's words they went to the square and assisted the escape. Nor was there testimony that anyone had shouted encouragement to someone else. Lincoln didn't see how the jury could do anything but acquit.

Which is what he told Abby as they headed to their usual room, but without Clarence and Annabelle, who had gone elsewhere.

Before they arrived at the room, Lincoln said, "Many people would look askance at a man and a woman who are not married being alone together in a private place. Would you be more comfortable if I asked Herndon to join us?"

"Ha! I am a woman who has served on committees made up only of men except for me, and spent time alone with them on multiple occasions. I have also ridden long distances in carriages with men to whom I was not married. Certainly my husband would make no objection. What about Mrs. Lincoln?"

"I'm going to assume she would be alright with it, but I don't plan to ask her."

Abby laughed again. "Now, Abraham, let us return to your prediction that I will be acquitted because there is so little evidence. But one could have said, before this all began, that there was not remotely enough evidence even to indict me. Yet it happened."

"Well, the trial is over, and it will do no good to try to predict the outcome. I should not have started down that path. Perhaps we should talk about something else while we wait."

And so they did. Lincoln was quite interested to hear more about Abby's thoughts on abolition, and she turned out, to his surprise, to be quite conversant with national politics. When they ran out of politics to discuss, she also told him more about her husband, Stephen. She explained that Stephen Foster was even more radical than she and had been thrown bodily out of churches and other places when he tried to speak about abolition.

58

After the jury was sent out, Clarence had wanted to stay in the courthouse until the verdict came back. Annabelle had wanted to leave and spend more time trying to find Lucy. She was still convinced the girl was being hidden in Springfield. Eventually Clarence agreed to pay a young man to remain behind and come to notify him straightaway the instant the jury came back. They had repaired to Clarence's tiny office, when he said, "I think I know where she is."

"Where?"

Despite their cooperation agreement, Clarence felt compelled to say, "Before I tell you, I want your assurance that if we go there together and find her, that whatever happens, you will tell no other journalist before I have the chance to put out a special edition of my newspaper."

Annabelle looked him in the eye and said, "Clarence, if we find her, what are we then going to do?"

"I don't know, which is probably why I haven't pursued my idea."

Annabelle walked to the window. "It's getting dark. So, even if you were willing to tell me, evening is probably not a good time to go looking for anyone. This city seems to have ruffians about at night."

"I thought you were a detective."

She laughed. "Clarence, being a detective doesn't mean putting myself at risk when I don't need to. Whatever place you have in mind to visit will likely still be there in the daytime."

He came and stood beside her at the window, and they looked out together. "I will protect you, Annie."

"Don't call me…"

"I meant it with affection."

She bristled. "I don't need protection."

After that, the two of them just stood there together, looking out, but not looking at each other, until Clarence finally said, "Alright, I'll tell where I think Lucy is if you'll agree to my condition."

"I agree, unless it's necessary to tell someone else to assure the girl's safety. And her freedom."

"That's agreeable. When I first came to Springfield, I visited the pastors of all of the churches to introduce myself. Father Hale gave me a tour of his church. At my request, he even took me up to see the bell tower and the bell."

"Go on."

"One of the things Father Hale told me is that the bell is rung only for weddings, funerals and for worship on Sundays. Oh, and to notify the citizenry of fires."

"What has that got to do with Lucy?"

"This past Sunday the bell didn't ring."

"There are a lot of possible explanations."

He turned to look at her. "What would you think if I told you that there was a wedding there the Sunday before, and I've learned that the bell didn't ring for that, either."

"A seriously ill bell ringer and no replacement easily available?"

"I think Lucy is being hidden there by Father Hale."

She raised her eyebrows. "Really? I've heard Father Hale is what people call a moderate abolitionist. Hiding her would seem out of character."

"Perhaps the prosecution of Abby Kelley Foster has radicalized him. Anyone can see that it's being managed from Washington by the Buchanan administration."

Clarence turned and began to walk around the room, hands behind his back. "I'm wondering if I should tell you what I've done."

She laughed. "As a detective I've learned that when people say things like that it means they're getting ready to tell you. So tell me."

"Earlier this week, I went to investigate."

"I thought that was my job."

Clarence ignored her and continued. "The church is heavily used Friday through Sunday. The rest of the week, it is not, especially in the evenings. There is usually no one there. And there is an unlocked back door, so one evening I just went in. After I went in, I looked carefully around. I suspected she was in the bell tower, but the door was locked and I couldn't find a key.

"There is another solution."

"What?"

"I'll show you when we get there, Clarence."

"For now, let's go back and wait for the jury verdict," he said. "If it's an acquittal, there will likely be a small victory party, and we can sneak away to the church since it's a weeknight, and Father Hale will likely be at the party."

"And if it's a conviction?"

"The party will turn into a wake, and we can sneak away even more easily."

59

There was a knock on the door of the room in which Abby and Lincoln had been meeting, and the clerk stuck his head in. "Jury is back with a verdict," he said. "Please return to the courtroom."

"That was quick," Abby said.

Lincoln checked his pocket watch. "A little over an hour."

"Is that a good omen, Abraham?"

Lincoln pursed his lips. "Well…all I can say after almost twenty-five years of doing trials and waiting for verdicts is that there is no real way to tell."

Abby let out a sigh. "Alright," she said. "Let us go and find out."

"Yes."

"Before we go, Abraham, whatever the outcome, I want to thank you. I cannot imagine having had a better lawyer. Despite that, I still cannot bring myself to urge white men—sadly, the only ones who can legally vote—to mark their ballots for you on November 6. It's a matter of principle, I hope you understand. But I do promise to stop calling you the slave hound of Illinois." She laughed. "At least in public."

Perhaps it was because she had spent so many years agonizing over the fate of the slave that Abby had never had much chance to worry about her own fate. That had changed during the weeks she spent in her cell, where she had been provided with plenty to read, but where she found herself also thinking about her own future.

She had steeled herself to the idea that she was going to go to jail. But it would only be for six months, and she could, through letters and visitors, continue to promote the cause— as a kind of martyr. As for jail, she would just have to endure it. And surely, women would be treated better in prison than men. Or would they?

She was still having those thoughts as the jury, led by the clerk, filed in and everyone took their seats.

The judge looked to the jury and said, "Gentlemen, the clerk has informed me you have a verdict. Who amongst you is the foreman?"

"I am," Alexander Humphreys said.

"If you have a verdict form, please hand it to the clerk."

The clerk walked over to Humphreys and took from him a folded piece of paper. The clerk unfolded it, looked at it and handed it to the judge, who glanced at it and handed it back to the clerk.

"The defendant will please rise and face the jury."

Abby rose and turned to face them. Lincoln and Lizar rose, too.

"Please read the verdict, Mr. Clerk," the judge said.

Abby felt her hands shaking. She tried to suppress it by closing her fists.

The clerk seemed to puff himself up and said, "We the jury, in the case of *United States vs. Abby Kelley Foster, Southern Dis-*

trict of Illinois, Case No. 392, find the defendant not guilty of the crime with which she has been charged."

Abby felt a wave of relief wash over her and felt, more than heard, Lincoln congratulating her.

The clerk turned to the jury. "Is this your verdict, so say you one, so say you all?"

There was a chorus of yeses and Abby noticed that almost all of the jurors wore broad smiles.

The judge addressed Lizar. "Mr. Lizar, do you wish the jury to be polled individually?"

"No, Your Honor."

The judge looked again to the jury. "Gentlemen, thank you for your service to your country. You are dismissed with the court's thanks. You are free to talk to counsel, the defendant and the journalists, who I see at the back of the courtroom hankering to talk to you. But you are also free not to talk to any of them. The marshal will escort you out if you wish to escape without talking to anyone."

Turning to the sheriff, he said, "I know that you have been holding the defendant in your jail on behalf of the United States. By order of this court, the defendant is to be released from custody forthwith.

"Are there any other matters or motions that need to be brought to the attention of the court?"

No one spoke up.

"Very well, we are adjourned."

Abby felt the tension drain from her body.

Lizar came over and extended his hand, muttered something—Abby couldn't quite hear it—and she shook his hand in return. Had he been a slaveholder, she would have refused. But it seemed the thing to do.

Then she noticed that the judge had come down from the bench and was approaching them.

He first turned to Abby and said, "Mrs. Foster, I am not

supposed to say this kind of thing, but I think justice was done here."

He next turned to Lizar, extended his hand and said, "Mr. Lizar, thank you for so competently representing the United States in this matter. I'm sure you have a bright future ahead of you—in the East." They both laughed.

Finally, he turned to Lincoln and said, "Congratulations, Mr. Lincoln. You know, I was originally going to vote for Senator Douglas, but I think I may change my mind and vote for you."

"Why, thank you, Judge."

"The election isn't very far off, is it?"

"November 6, Your Honor. Just over three weeks."

"Well, I dare say that may well be the most important one in our history." He then turned back to Lizar and said, "Mr. Lizar, before we part, I have been wondering, what do your initials, G.W., stand for?"

"George Washington, Your Honor."

There was a small silence as they all took that in.

"I hope it hasn't been a burden to bear that name," the judge said, "in that he was so famous…"

"It has been an honor," Lizar said.

Well, perhaps so, Abby thought, but Washington was a slave-holder who treated humans as property. She considered saying it out loud but for once in her life decided not to spoil the festive occasion with the truth. Also, most of the jurors were crowding around her, waiting to talk, and she spent the next little while thanking them, and then talking with Billy and Annabelle.

Lincoln invited them all to his office, including Clarence, for a celebration, but Clarence and Annabelle begged off, saying they had something else they had to do first and would come by a little later.

60

When Annabelle and Clarence approached the church, there were no lights showing. After waiting awhile and seeing no one, they tried first the front door and then the back door, but both were locked.

"The back wasn't locked the last time," Clarence said.

"One of the things I've learned as a detective is that last time usually doesn't matter," Annabelle said. "It's like saying as you lay dying, 'Last time I didn't get shot.'" She grinned at him. "Luckily, Clarence, I think I can pick this lock."

"I thought you needed a piece of metal or a pin."

"I do, but I think I have some hat pins in my bag." She rummaged in her bag and pulled them out.

"Clarence, you keep a lookout while I see if I can still do this." She leaned over and got to work.

It had been quite a long time since Annabelle had picked a lock, and Pinkerton had remarked on one occasion that she was not, among his detectives, the most skilled at it.

As she thought back to that conversation, she felt the tumblers give way. She leaned on the door and it opened.

"I'm impressed," Clarence said.

"It's not that difficult. If you think it would be useful for a journalist, I'll teach you."

They walked into the church, with Clarence leading the way. Annabelle heard the door swing shut behind her. It was suddenly pitch-black. After a few steps they stopped, letting their eyes try to adapt to the tiny bit of light.

Annabelle wondered if she should tell Clarence her secret. Well, she needed to, really.

"Clarence, I know this is very odd for a detective, but I'm afraid of the dark. I need you to take my hand if we're going to go farther."

She heard him chuckle and felt him take her hand in his.

"That feels rather nice," she said.

"It's for purely professional reasons," he said. "It wouldn't be helpful to our mission if you were to scream."

"Of course. Although I don't scream. Ever."

The two of them stood there in silence for a moment until, finally, Clarence said, "Annabelle, don't you have a candle and flint in that bag of yours?"

"I do, but it would be imprudent to light a candle here. Someone might be able to tell someone is here. And it would leave a smell long after we're gone."

"Alright. I know where the entrance to the bell tower is. I'll lead us there."

They walked very slowly, Clarence leading her by the hand, until they came to the bell tower door. When Clarence tried it, he found it, as he expected, locked. "Do you need to see to pick a lock?" Clarence said.

"No, it's done by feel."

She unclasped her hand from his and found the lock by feel.

She rummaged again in her purse for the pins, inserted them and managed to spring the lock in only a few seconds.

Clarence tilted his head back and yelled up, "Is there anyone up there?"

There was no answer. But seconds later there was a rustling noise up above, and they both jumped.

"Probably a mouse," Annabelle said. "Now one of us needs to go up the ladder and make sure no one is hiding up there."

"Well, just as you've admitted you're afraid of the dark, Annabelle, I'm afraid of heights," Clarence said.

"I can't possibly go up the ladder, Clarence. My dress is much too tight to climb a ladder in, and being on the rungs with you standing down below would be immodest."

"Even in the dark?"

"There is enough light now to see. You go, Clarence."

There was a long silence as Clarence contemplated what to do. Finally, he began to climb, although Annabelle could tell from his rapid breathing that he was genuinely afraid.

She heard him reach the top and climb into the room above. After a while, he shouted down, "There's no one up here. Nor any sign that anyone has been living here. I'm coming back down. Please hold the ladder firmly."

When he got to the bottom, he was breathing heavily.

"Are you alright?" Annabelle said.

"Mostly."

"Even in this light, I can see you're shaking," she said.

"No, I'm not."

Annabelle wrapped her arms around him. "I can feel that you are." She held him tighter, then leaned in and kissed him full on the lips. He kissed her back, and when they finally broke apart, he said, "This was unexpected."

"Yes, Hopper, I suppose that it was. But I wouldn't mind expecting it again the next time we're together in the dark."

"Neither would I, Annie."

"Let us return to business," Annabelle said. "So Lucy's not up there?"

"No. Or if she was, she's gone."

"Is there a basement?"

"Yes, there is," a voice behind them said.

They both jumped.

In the dim light Annabelle could make out that it was Father Hale.

"Good evening, Father Hale," she said.

"I assume you children—and you are both young enough to be my children—were looking for Lucy Battelle," he said.

"I don't suppose you will accept that we were just admiring the bell tower," Annabelle said.

"Ha! No, I won't. But I am impressed that Clarence went up the ladder. He was terrified of it last time he had to climb it."

"You watched me go up?" Clarence said.

"Yes, I did. Up and down."

"Then you saw…" Clarence felt his face redden, but hoped it couldn't be seen in the near dark."

"Do not be concerned," Hale said. "I was young once myself."

"I'm not concerned at all," Annabelle said. "I would like to ask, though, do *you* know where Lucy is, Father Hale?"

"I will tell you, but, first, you must both swear an oath, in the name of God, that you will not tell anyone else, and also that you, Clarence, will not publish a word of it."

They both agreed.

"She was here for a number of days," Father Hale said. "Several days ago, a brave conductor from the Underground Railroad came, and they went away together. He pledged that she would reach Canada safely."

"Did you arrange it?" Clarence said.

"I think the best way to put it, Clarence, is that it was arranged."

"I had hoped to find her and buy her freedom," Annabelle

said. "Amasa, Ezekiel Goshorn's son and heir, has been in Springfield looking for her. I met with him and he agreed that if I found her he would let me emancipate her in that way."

"Where were you going to get the money?" Clarence said.

"I had put it aside to try to emancipate Polly, the slave who raised me. Right before I left the plantation, I offered to free her in that way and support her in her freedom. I was in the process of trying to arrange it—my mother had agreed to it—when my sister sent me a telegram with the bad news. Polly died a month ago."

"I offered to do the same for Lucy with my own money," Hale said. "Although it was in truth my wife, Abiah, who first suggested it. Lucy thanked me, but said no. She said it would still make her feel like property that had been bought and sold."

"She used the term property?" Clarence said.

"No. She said she it would make her feel like a cooking pot or a pair of boots."

"Can I use at least that in my paper?" Clarence said.

"No."

"Now, if you don't mind, I need to lock up my church again," Hale said. "I suppose I need to get more secure locks, too. And if you will both leave now, I have a party to go to."

"I think we are going to the same one," Annabelle said.

Hale smiled. "Yes, and after we celebrate Abby's acquittal, we must all turn our efforts to trying to assure that on November 6, Abraham Lincoln is elected the sixteenth president of these United States."

61

The next day, Lincoln and Herndon were back at their law offices, in their usual places, although Lincoln's stack of newspapers and magazine was taller than ever, and more of them than usual had already spilled onto the floor.

"Well, Lincoln, looks like you just might get yourself elected on November 6," Herndon said. "I'm still trying to cotton what that will be like, having a law partner who's president of the United States."

"Don't count your chickens before they're hatched, Billy."

"I can hear them picking at their shells already, Lincoln. And if they do hatch, and you're president and way off in Washington, I suppose I'm going to have to get myself a new law partner."

Lincoln didn't respond immediately, but, after a while, said, "Billy, if I'm lucky enough—or cursed enough, depending on how you look upon it—to be elected, I hope you will keep this partnership just as it is and leave the Lincoln and Herndon sign hanging on the building just where it is."

"I don't know if I will be able to afford the rent here as well as our other expenses, if I'm the solitary lawyer bringing in cases. I might need a partner."

"If you want one you should certainly get one. You could also come to Washington, of course, and I'm sure there'd be a place for you in the administration. Is there something you'd want?"

"I will think on that and appreciate your confidence in me, but I'm doing pretty well now and have a family to support. I will probably want to stay here."

"I understand," Lincoln said, and went back to reading the *New York Herald Tribune*, edited by Horace Greeley, who was sometimes his friend and sometimes not.

Lincoln was in many ways relieved that Herndon was inclined to stay in Springfield. Despite his great energy, Herndon could at times present a political problem because he didn't know how to contain his views when they needed containing. And yet, except when Lincoln had been in Washington during his one term in Congress, or out on the circuit or, in more recent years, off somewhere giving political speeches, he'd seen Herndon almost every day since 1844, when they'd formed their partnership. He would miss him.

His musings on that subject and others were interrupted by a perfunctory knock on the door and the arrival of John Hay, who was wearing a bowler, a white shirt, a sporty bow tie and a corduroy jacket. There had been an unusually early-in-the-season dusting of snow that morning and Hay, on coming into the office, shook it off his shoulders and brushed it off his bowler.

"Good morning, Mr. Lincoln, Mr. Herndon," he said. "I am just off the train, having started yesterday in Pittsburgh. But I wanted to come here immediately, seeing as the election is so near."

"I've appreciated the telegrams you've sent," Lincoln said. "But now I am most anxious to hear the detail. Let's all gather at the table."

At the table, Hay began by reading from a small piece of paper.

"Mr. Lincoln, I have a report, I don't think you'll fall short, nor need to abort...the election."

Lincoln and Herndon both looked at him as if he'd lost his mind.

"Oh," Hay said, seeing their reactions. "I thought you knew that I studied poetry at Brown and was the class poet."

"It sounds more as if you studied doggerel," Lincoln said.

"Sorry, I thought it was kind of funny and that the pause before the word *election* made it work rather well. In any event, I spent two weeks in Pennsylvania and Indiana. Went to a lot of taverns and political meetings, and just talked to everyone I could find."

"Did you avoid women?" Herndon said. "As we suggested?"

Hay turned red in the face. "Mostly."

Herndon laughed, "Well, where were you mostly other than with the ladies?"

"A lot of small towns, but some big cities as well, including Pittsburgh, Scranton and Philadelphia."

"What was the talk?" Lincoln said.

"Mostly, people have picked up on what the editors in Republican newspapers have been promoting—if a lawyer is asked to represent someone who's been falsely accused, the lawyer has a duty to take the case."

"So the abolitionists have forgiven me for refusing to promise I'd pardon Abby if I'm elected?" Lincoln said.

"Yes, but mostly because you mooted the question by getting her acquitted. And as for the Republicans who aren't abolitionists, those people don't care at all about Mrs. Foster. They're Republicans because they hate Democrats and Southerners."

"What about Democrats?" Lincoln said.

Hay rummaged awkwardly in an inside pocket of his jacket, finally found what he was looking for, flattened a piece of paper out on the table and consulted it.

"Some Democrats still are inclined to vote for you because

you're not Buchanan, with all the corruption that has come with him. Others wouldn't vote for you even if you could walk on water."

"Can I see your notes?" Hendon said.

"Of course." Hay handed the sheets of paper over to Herndon.

As Herndon was looking them over, Lincoln said, "What groups did you talk to in terms of the kinds of work they do?"

"Farmers, small artisans like cobblers, blacksmiths and tanners, and grocers, bakers and people like that. In big cities I also talked to a few bankers, landlords and one man who owns a countinghouse."

Herndon gave the notes back to Hay. "You didn't write down the last names of the people you talked with. So I can't tell if any were immigrants."

"Oh, I talked to lots of those, including both Protestants and Catholic German immigrants."

"What about Quakers in Phil-del, Johnny?" Lincoln said. "They are usually strong abolitionists."

"Most were not that anxious to talk to me."

"About me?"

"Correct."

Lincoln got up, went over and looked over Hay's shoulder at the notes, which Hay had placed back on the table. Lincoln laughed. "Was it a Quaker who said, 'He does not have God in him'?"

"Yes. He said if you did, you would have immediately agreed to pardon Mrs. Foster if she were convicted."

Lincoln got up and began to pace the room, hands behind his back. Finally, he said, "None of that is good news, Johnny. Quakers make up a very large part of the population in Eastern Pennsylvania. We could be in trouble in that state."

"How much trouble?" Hay said.

"Pennsylvania, which has 27 electoral votes. That's 18 percent of the 152 I need to be elected."

There was again a brief silence in the room.

"What about Quakers in Indiana?" Herndon said. "That's also a center of Quaker life."

"I didn't find many Quakers in Indiana to talk with," Hay said. "But Quakers don't frequent taverns a lot."

"Don't worry, Johnny. You've done well," Lincoln said. "Now that we know the problem we can try to fix it." He grinned. "We won't do to you what the Greeks did to their own messengers who returned with bad tidings."

"That's good to hear."

"What this means to me is that in the time we have left before November 6, my supporters in Pennsylvania need to get busy talking more to the Quaker community there. Very busy."

As Hay was about to leave, Lincoln said, "By the way, Johnny, if you go and get yourself a silk top hat, like mine, you can store your important papers in the inside hatband. Then you wouldn't have to struggle to find things in your pockets."

"I'd look ridiculous in a hat like that. I'm too short for it. I look better in a bowler."

"You should try it," Lincoln said.

"Alright. Perhaps I will."

62

Election Day
November 6, 1860

etween John Hay's return and Election Day, hundreds
of telegrams had gone out, sent by both members of the
Republican National Committee and Lincoln himself.
They had been dispatched to local Republican officeholders, supporters and speakers in small towns and big cities alike, urging
them to try to create more enthusiasm for Lincoln among certain
groups in certain states. The telegrams warned that two states
in particular—Indiana and Pennsylvania—had once seemed safe
but were now at risk.

On November 6, Lincoln had not wanted to cause a commo-
tion when he voted. He waited until a time when he was told
that there were not too many people at the polls, and only then
went to vote. The word soon spread, though, that he was voting,
and he was soon joined by dozens of his friends and neighbors,
clapping, whistling and shouting encouragement. At least for
that one day, he was the local hero even, he suspected, among
those who didn't intend to vote for him.

Lincoln did cast votes for local and state offices, but carefully avoided voting for the electors for president. Whether he refrained because he thought it untoward to vote for himself or because he thought it bad luck, he didn't say.

After voting, Lincoln returned home. As evening fell, he sighed and said, "I might as well go and see what the American people have in store for me." He gathered up Herndon, Hay and several others and walked over to the governor's office in the statehouse, where the acting governor, the mayor of Springfield and other notables were awaiting early returns.

The numbers were brought in to them, city by city and county by county, by a runner from the local office of the Illinois and Mississippi Telegraph Company. The returns from nearby places naturally arrived first. Every time Lincoln won a city or county in Illinois, all of the people cheered. When Illinois looked to be won, Lincoln, ever phlegmatic, said only, "Had it been otherwise, we would be in trouble." Later, growing anxious to hear the results more quickly, the group walked over to the offices of I&M itself, on the second floor of a building on the north side of the square.

The telegraph room held several wooden desks, the telegraphers' swivel chairs, and a couple of wooden file cabinets. On each desk sat a pad of three-by-five mustard-colored paper on which the telegraphers could translate the incoming dots and dashes of the Morse code into English. Each desk also held a brass telegraph key, set atop a polished wooden block.

The chief telegrapher on duty greeted them, then turned back to transcribing incoming messages and tapping out those being dispatched elsewhere.

Lincoln stared at the small rolls of paper tape—called registers—that sat next to each telegraph key, on which incoming dots and dashes, heard audibly in the room as beeps, were reduced to small spots of ink. By the next day, he thought, those inky dots would let him know one of two things—that he would be the next president of the United States or that his dreams would be consigned to the dustbin of history. Lincoln assumed Douglas, Breckinridge and Bell were watching similar returns elsewhere in the country. Douglas, he knew, was still in Alabama, where he had been campaigning.

Somewhat later in the evening, when the New England states had unanimously moved into Lincoln's column, along with Iowa, Michigan and Minnesota, Herndon said, "Lincoln, Pennsylvania and Indiana are almost certainly going to go for you, and I am quite confident about New York. I think we are going to win the whole thing."

"You know how I feel about counting your chickens, Billy..."

"I do, but I'm hungry. The Republican ladies of Springfield have set up refreshments in front of the ice cream parlor across the square. Let's go there, eat and drink and come back here later to savor the final victory."

And so they went, although Lincoln shrank away—as politely as he could—from those who wanted to congratulate him even though the final result was still unknown. Mary was there, too, of course, and he tried to assure her that victory was in hand. He could tell, though, that Mary, who had lived politics since she was a small girl in a political family, was not persuaded. "I am not going to bed until we know for sure," she said. And yet, even without final victory in hand, but only anticipated, he could already feel the weight and formality of the office he might assume begin to come between him and these good men and women of Springfield, many of whom he had known all of his adult life.

In late evening, Lincoln and the others returned to the telegraph office. But it was in the early hours of the morning that the results came in from New York, with its trove of thirty-five electoral votes—more than 20 percent of the 152 needed for victory. Finally, New York was declared won, and a boisterous cheer went up in the room. But even assuming Lincoln were to win California and Oregon, with their combined 7 electoral votes, he would only be at 140, still 12 short. Either Pennsylvania, with 27, or Indiana, with 13, could put him over the top.

The results from Pennsylvania and Indiana, though, had still not come in, by early morning of the next day. No one understood why, since those states were not very far away. Lincoln spent the night sleeping on a couch in the telegraph office.

He was awakened by Hay saying, "Mr. Lincoln, the Indiana and Pennsylvania results are coming in." Lincoln sat up, heard the cacophony of two separate keys beeping and watched them as they moved up and down.

"Is one telegraph key bringing the results from Indiana, and the other from Pennsylvania?" he said.

"Yes," said one of the telegraphers.

"Hay, you tally the results from the Indiana key," Lincoln said. "I'll take Pennsylvania."

"I need a pencil," Hay said. One of the telegraphers started to hand him one. Instead of taking it, Hay, who'd worn a bowler into the office earlier in the evening, lifted it off the hat rack on which he'd hung it and, bowing, extracted a pencil from the hatband. Lincoln laughed hard.

Over the next half hour, one telegrapher handed Lincoln the Pennsylvania results as they came in. Using his own pencil, Lincoln tallied them on one of the mustard-yellow sheets.

Lincoln finished his total first. "Johnny, I've lost Pennsylvania by almost 7,000 votes." He said it without emotion.

Hay paused in his own count of Indiana and said, "Before considering Pennsylvania and Indiana, you had already garnered 133 electoral votes from the other states. Pennsylvania, with its 27, would have put you way over the 152 you need to win. But now you're not going to have those 27 Pennsylvania votes. So even if you get California and Oregon, you'll only be at 140. Not enough."

"Well, Johnny, there's still Indiana," Lincoln said. "It may have only 13 electoral votes, but assuming we land the 7 that are out there in California and Oregon, Indiana would get me to 153. Which would be enough, if only by one."

After a few minutes, Hay said, "Mr. Lincoln, I'm sorry. I think you've lost Indiana by about 5,000 votes. So, even if we assume California and Oregon have gone for you—which we won't know for sure for days, or even weeks—without Indiana you'll still end up with only 140 electoral votes, 12 shy of the 152 that you need." He paused. "And there are no other states left to count." He looked over at Lincoln, who was still sitting on the couch, staring at the floor.

Lincoln looked up and said, "Well, Johnny, we've lost. No, *I've* lost. There's no one to blame but myself."

Herndon, who'd come back into the room at some point and had been listening quietly said, "No, Lincoln, you've simply failed to win this round. But no one else has won it either. The next round will be in the House of Representatives."

63

Washington, DC
United States House of Representatives
November 8, 1860

William Pennington looked around him and marveled at the situation in which he found himself—ensconced behind an elegant desk in the opulent Speaker's Room of the United States House of Representatives, complete with high ceilings, a large fireplace and carved marble pediments. He was there because, in a situation he could not have imagined in his wildest dreams, he *was* the Speaker of the House, and had been since February. Even more amazingly, he had been elected to that high position despite the fact that he was only serving his first term in Congress.

One of his two clerks, a man named Jeremiah Jarvis, came in and said, "Excuse me, Mr. Speaker. There is a man to see you name of Horace Trenton. Here is his calling card. Like most such these days it bears only his name."

Pennington turned the card over in his hand but said nothing.

Hearing no response from Pennington, Jarvis said, "He says he has come as a representative of Senator Douglas. As it is almost evening, should I ask him to come back tomorrow?"

"No, I am expecting him, Mr. Jarvis. Please show him in."

The man who entered a moment later looked to be in his midfifties and was tall, with muttonchop whiskers, perhaps intended to set off the fact that he was quite bald up top.

Pennington rose to greet him. After they had introduced one another and shaken hands, Pennington directed him to one of the two black horsehair couches that faced each other across a low table, and took a seat on the other one.

"Thank you for seeing me on such short notice, Mr. Speaker, and with no formal introduction."

"It is not a problem. Well, what can I do for you, sir? When your appointment was arranged I was told you were coming on behalf of Senator Douglas."

"Yes, I was Senator Douglas's campaign chairman in Philadelphia, and he has entrusted me with a special errand."

"Congratulations on a successful campaign there. Along with whoever ran the senator's campaign in Indiana, you have managed to deny Mr. Lincoln the presidency. For now at least."

"That is what I wanted to talk with you about—the *for now* part. As you know, the electoral votes, cast by the electors in each state, will be counted in early March here in Washington, as provided by the Twelfth Amendment to the Constitution, before a joint meeting of the Senate and the House."

"Yes, but the counting of the ballots will be presided over by the president of the Senate, our current vice president, Mr. Breckinridge. I will have no role in that process."

"Do you mind, Mr. Speaker, if I get up and walk about a bit? Or lean against something? I have a very bad back, and sitting is hard for me."

"Not at all. If you want to lean against a wall, try the wall right next to the three marble heads over there." He pointed to them. "They came with the room."

Trenton got up and walked over to them. "Washington and Jefferson are easy to identify." He peered down at the final one. "Who is the third man? I can't make out his name on the plaque."

"That is Frederick Augustus Conrad Muhlenberg, the first Speaker of this House, back in 1789."

"I've never heard of him."

"I'm afraid he's faded into history. As I soon will, too, since I was defeated for reelection to my House seat a few days ago."

"I have heard that, and I'm sorry. Perhaps you'll find something equally interesting to do in government when your term is finished."

So there it is, Pennington thought. Whatever it is Mr. Trenton wants, he has subtly hinted, in an eminently deniable way, that if I do whatever it is Senator Douglas wants me to do, the good senator, if elected, will make sure I have something "interesting" to do in the next administration. He decided to avoid playing the game and just ask straight-out what they wanted.

"Mr. Trenton, this next May I will turn sixty-five years old. Many years ago now, in a time that seems almost beyond recall, I was a member of the New Jersey Legislature for several terms and subsequently, way back in the forties, governor of New Jersey for six years. So I am far too old to dance around things. What does Senator Douglas want?"

"He wants both you and Vice President Breckinridge to assure a fair count of the electoral votes."

"How could it be unfair?"

"By allowing faithless electors to vote for a candidate other than the one they are pledged to."

"You are worried that Mr. Lincoln, who looks to have 140 electoral votes if we assume he'll also get California and Oregon, will find 12 faithless electors to vote for him, thus bringing him to a winning 152, even though they are pledged to vote for someone else?"

"Yes."

"Doesn't it bother you, Mr. Trenton, that you are scheming

to defeat the man who got both the most electoral votes and the most popular votes?"

"No. Politics is my business."

"As it is mine, I suppose. But the issue of faithless electors is a matter for the states, Mr. Trenton. State law determines whether an elector may vote for a different candidate than the one to which he's pledged."

"Perhaps so, but if the states take no action, the Senate and House, acting together, could refuse to accept the votes of faithless electors."

"Isn't this a moot issue, Mr. Trenton? I see no way Lincoln can find 12 faithless electors, which is what he'll need, assuming he also gets California and Oregon with their combined 7."

"It nevertheless concerns us."

Well, Pennington thought, I'm not going to find out today what Senator Douglas really wants. I will have to wait on that. He got up from the couch, where he'd been sitting the entire time and said, "Mr. Trenton, thank you for coming. I will keep your concerns in mind."

"Thank you for hearing me out. If I might ask you a personal question, how did you come to be elected Speaker?"

"As a first-term member of this House?"

"Yes."

"Well, as I'm sure you must know, the Republicans have a plurality in the current House, but, due to third parties, not a majority. So they and the Democrats went through forty-three ballots without being able to choose a Speaker. I was selected on the forty-fourth."

"How did your selection solve the problem?"

"I was seen by both parties as a moderate Republican who wouldn't do anything important while in office. Meanwhile, the Republican Party—which is my own party, of course—expects to have a firm majority in the next Congress. It can then replace me with someone they really want."

"And you have obliged them by failing to be reelected."

"Yes. Considerate of me, don't you think?"

Trenton, no doubt sensing that Pennington wasn't looking for an actual answer to his question, thanked him again and left.

After Trenton departed, Pennington walked over to a fourth bust that sat by itself in a niche on the opposite wall. It was of John Quincy Adams, the sixth president of the United States.

Pennington remembered very well the election in which Adams had been chosen. It was 1824, and neither Quincy, as Adams was universally called, nor his opponent, Andy Jackson, had garnered enough electoral votes to be elected. Under the procedures set forth in the Twelfth Amendment to the Constitution, the election had been thrown into the House of Representatives, where each state, no matter its size, had only one vote.

Pennington, like most people, had been shocked when the House elected Quincy, despite the fact that in the election itself Jackson had received both more electoral votes *and* more popular votes than Quincy.

Pennington had been only twenty-nine when that happened, but he still remembered the anger and bitterness that followed Adams's ascension to the presidency. It had been known ever-after as the "corrupt bargain"—corrupt because it was widely believed that Henry Clay of Kentucky had thrown the votes of the three states he controlled—Kentucky, Ohio and Missouri—to Quincy Adams in exchange for being appointed Secretary of State.

Now, he thought, thirty-five years later, the presidential election was going to end up in the House again, with the same Twelfth Amendment rules. But there would nevertheless be a lot of parliamentary maneuvering before the vote, which, as the Speaker, he would control.

What would he be offered for his support? What did he want? Perhaps nothing?

He expected someone from the Lincoln campaign would be coming by soon.

64

Law Offices of Lincoln and Herndon
Springfield
November 10, 1860

"Billy, I have been reading the Constitution," Lincoln said. He was stretched out in his favorite chair and, as usual, surrounded by heaps of newspapers and magazines. "In particular, the Twelfth Amendment."

Herndon, who had been pacing back and forth across the office, hands behind his back, said, "By which old John Quincy Adams got himself selected as president?"

"Yes, back in '24."

"I actually remember that." Herndon grinned. "I was six years old, and my parents were outraged. I think it was the first time I ever heard the word *corrupt*."

"You know, Billy, I met Quincy Adams when he had returned to the House after finishing his supposedly ill-gotten presidency, back in '48, when I was a first-term congressman."

"Your only term, as I recall."

He nodded. "That is true."

"Lincoln, did you ever ask Quincy about the corrupt bargain he supposedly put together back in '24?"

"Ha! I was a greenhorn first-termer. I felt honored he even deigned to speak with me. I certainly did not ask him about *that*."

Herndon stopped pacing and sat himself down in a chair at the end of the big table. Lincoln grabbed a few newspapers from his stack, came over and joined him.

"The way I figure it is this," Lincoln said. "We now have a new campaign in front of us."

"To find twelve so-called faithless electors so you'll move from 140 to 152 electoral votes. Assuming you garner the 7 out on the Coast. Otherwise you'll need 19 faithless souls."

"No, I have been over at the statehouse for three days arguing with the Republican National Committee about that. They are going to pursue that idea. I am not. It's a fool's errand. Most of the Douglas and Breckinridge electors—and Bell's, too, really—despise me and think that even a whiff of me anywhere near the White House will drive Southerners to immediate disunion."

"I'm not convinced, but you're the man running."

"Also, we may have difficulty hanging on to all of our *own* electors." He walked back over to the chair he'd been sitting in, sifted through the pile of newspapers he'd left behind, found the one he wanted and brought it back to the table.

He passed it to Herndon. "Look at the top article in the *New York Herald*." Herndon read it, grimaced and handed it back without comment.

"So as you can see, the *Herald* is urging what is, in effect, an electoral college coup. Suggesting all of my electors abandon me and vote for someone—according to them—less destructive to the Union."

"Well, that editor has never supported you," Herndon said. "So it's hardly surprising."

"That is so. But now look at this, too, Billy." Lincoln passed him another newspaper.

Herndon studied it and said, "My God. This says Alexander

Hamilton's son, John Church Hamilton, is urging your pledged New York electors to desert you. And he's a *Republican*."

"Yes. But aside from his name, he's never had any power in New York politics, and that will not happen no matter who urges it. And in any case this whole business of chasing after faithless electors is a waste of time. No one is going to win that way."

"What's your plan, then?"

"Congress is required by law to count the electoral votes on February 13. After none of us gets the needed 152 votes, the House is required to move immediately to a contingent election. Voting state by state, where each state gets only one vote, the House will choose a winner from among the top three electoral vote-getters. I plan to win that contingent election."

"What if no one gets a majority of the states?"

"In that case..."

Lincoln's answer was interrupted by a knock on the door, and Herndon went to answer it. It was Clarence Artemis.

"I'm sorry, Clarence," Herndon said. "We're having a private meeting and..."

"I invited him, Billy. Show him in, please."

Herndon raised his eyebrows, but did as Lincoln asked.

After they were all seated at the table, Lincoln said, "Clarence, I am prepared to give you another interview, even though I have not reached the White House quite yet. But some topics are not to be covered, and I will let you know what they are when and if you get to them."

"Alright, my first question is what do you plan to do if you lose the electoral college vote on February 13? By my calculation no candidate will get the 152 votes needed to win."

"I don't want you to publish this, Clarence, but I agree with you about that."

"I apologize for being blunt, Mr. Lincoln, but when the House then moves to a contingent vote state by state, I don't see how you win that election, either."

"Well, Mr. Artemis, by the time that contingent vote happens there will be 34 states, since Kansas will come into the Union in January. Is my count correct?"

Clarence had brought with him a pad of paper on which he had apparently written down the vote counts he'd been studying. He looked down at the top page and said, "Yes, after Kansas is added, there will be 34."

"And in the House, I will need a majority of all the state delegations to vote for me, correct?"

"That would be 18," Clarence said. "How many are you confident of, Mr. Lincoln?"

"Mr. Artemis, I'm sure an enterprising journalist like yourself has already calculated that number. So you tell me." He smiled a broad smile.

Clarence looked down once again at his papers and said, "I count 16 House delegations, by state, that have a majority of Republican congressmen. Those states will almost certainly cast their votes for you."

"I am therefore 2 states short."

"What are you going to do to get 2 more?"

"Good old Illinois persuasion. All I need to do is convince a few congressman to switch parties and throw their states to me so I might be elected. I think I already know who they are."

"Are you gonna promise them appointments, as Quincy Adams is said to have done in 1824 to get the three additional states he needed?"

"Certainly not. Particularly in this time of a crisis of the Union, doing that would destroy the presidency of any man who does that even before he takes the oath of office."

While Clarence was writing that down, word for word, Lincoln looked over at Herndon, who had been sitting at the table, grim-faced, arms folded. Lincoln had learned, belatedly, that

Herndon had made promises of cabinet posts at the Republican convention back in May in order to secure Lincoln the nomination. And Herndon was aware that Lincoln knew and was not pleased.

Still looking at Herndon, Lincoln said, "Nor is anyone else going to make such promises on my behalf. Please write that down, too, Mr. Artemis, and put it in your newspaper."

"I need to go out for a spell," Herndon said. "I need coffee," he added, and left abruptly.

"I'd appreciate it, Mr. Artemis, if you did not report Mr. Herndon's departure in the middle of this discussion."

"Well..."

"It will help assure you of future interviews."

"Alright. But there is another important question I'd like to ask you."

"What is it?"

"Three states, South Carolina, Mississippi and Florida, are threatening to secede even before the matter comes to a vote in the House."

"Even without waiting to see if I come out on top?" Lincoln said. "I am apparently poisonous even as an almost-winner. But what is your question, Mr. Artemis?"

"If those three states leave the Union—and they are certainly not states whose Congressional House delegations are ever going to vote for you—that will leave only 31 states in the Union. The 16 states whose delegations will almost surely vote for you will then make up a majority and can elect you to the presidency."

Lincoln stood up, stared down at Clarence and said, "Mr. Artemis, the Union is perpetual. No state may leave it without the consent of the others. I will not permit anyone to assure my victory in the House by claiming those three states have left." He paused. "You can put that in your paper, too!"

"I will."

As Clarence was about to leave the room, Lincoln said, "Oh, there's one more thing, Mr. Artemis."

"Yes, sir?"

"Give Mrs. Carter my regards." He winked.

65

Washington, DC
The Speaker's Room
November 17, 1860

Before November 6, Pennington, despite being Speaker, had not had a lot to do. As he had explained to Trenton, he had been elected as a consensus caretaker and was not expected to have to make any important decisions. As Speaker, he had, of course, presided over the House and swung the gavel as needed. He had also, without complaint, dealt with the slew of paperwork—proposed bills and committee reports—that came with the job. But there had been a lot less legislating than he had anticipated. The Pacific Telegraph Act had been the only major bill. It was almost as if everyone was waiting to see who would be chosen as the new president. In any case, he had two clerks to handle the bulk of what there was.

That changed after Election Day. Within a few days, a horde of people had descended on his office. It seemed that almost all of them assumed that no candidate for president would win the needed majority of the electoral votes, and that there would be a contingent election in the House, presided over by him.

Some of the people who came proffered advice on how to go

about the process. Some asked for a prominent role in the proceedings. And a few, like Mr. Trenton from the Douglas campaign, wanted assurance that their candidate would be treated fairly—or perhaps even a bit more than fairly. A representative of the Breckinridge campaign suggested, for example, that there should be only one ballot and, later, in what he hoped seemed an unrelated matter, had asked if Pennington had ever wanted to be attorney general.

Pennington knew why the man was suggesting there be only one ballot. Under the peculiar provisions of the Twelfth Amendment, while the House was choosing the president from among the top three electoral vote-getters, the Senate would be choosing the new vice president from only the top *two* vice presidential electoral vote-getters.

He had expected someone from the Lincoln campaign to arrive sooner, but was not surprised when William Herndon, Lincoln's law partner in Springfield, had that morning made an appointment to see him.

Herndon came into the Speaker's Room riding on what seemed a burst of energy, striding across the room, extending his hand, and saying, "It is an honor to meet you, Mr. Speaker! I think you were a delegate to the convention in Chicago last May that nominated Abe Lincoln, were you not?"

"Yes, I was. And it was an honor to be there."

"I wasn't a delegate, but as Lincoln's law partner, I was there, too, of course. I think we may have met briefly."

"I apologize for not recalling it, Mr. Herndon, but, then again, there were over six hundred delegates and a lot of other people, as well."

"Of course."

"Won't you be seated?" Pennington said.

Herndon sat down on one of the couches, declined an offer of something to eat and said, "I come on behalf of Abe Lincoln."

"I've already seen men who came on behalf of Douglas and Breckinridge, so your visit is not unexpected."

"To go directly to the matter, Lincoln respectfully makes two requests."

"Which are?"

"First, he wishes the process to be scrupulously fair to all, and for it to be understood that no promises of office will be made to any man."

"Lincoln doesn't want to end up in a presidency like that man's?" Pennington pointed to the bust of Quincy Adams.

"Precisely."

"That is the kind of request I would expect of Lincoln," Pennington said. "I can assure him of fairness, but of course I don't control who makes what offer of what office to whom."

"We appreciate that."

"What is the second thing?"

"That when the contingent election is inevitably held in the House, that you assure that there are at least three ballots before the matter is closed."

"Before I ask the reason for that, is Mr. Lincoln so sure the contingent election will be needed? That no man will have a majority of electoral votes when they're counted?"

"Lincoln, with a likely 140 if we assume he gets California and Oregon, too, does not have the required majority of 152, and none of the other three even come close," Herndon said.

"Perhaps so," Pennington said. "Yet everyone, so far as I can tell from what my various visitors have had to say, is shopping for faithless electors."

"The Republican National Committee is casting about for those. Lincoln himself is not. He calls it a fool's errand."

"Well, I agree with Mr. Lincoln about that. And at my request, the Architect of the Capitol has gone and found some old ballots left over from the Quincy Adams contingent election in the House back in 1825."

Pennington walked over to his large desk, unlocked a drawer and pulled out two yellowing pieces of paper. He gave the pages to Herndon, who looked them over.

"I see that the first ballot had the expected three names," Herndon said. "Clay, Jackson and Adams. With a box to check next to each, plus a space for the name of the state casting the vote."

"Correct."

Herndon looked next at the second piece of paper. "It's blank," he said. "Except for a place where a state's name can be written in."

"That is for states whose House delegations were tied," Pennington said. "An equal number of Whig and Democratic congressmen in the state's delegation. In which case, no candidate got that state's vote. To indicate that, the state was asked to hand in a blank ballot that had no candidate names on it."

"So no one could surreptitiously check off a candidate name on that ballot even though the state delegation had not voted for that candidate?"

"Correct," Pennington said. "What the Architect of the Capitol tells me is that when the ballots were counted, those were announced as blank votes."

Pennington took back the two pieces of paper from Herndon and locked them away again.

"Now, let me ask," Pennington said. "Why does Lincoln want at least three ballots to be held?"

Herndon took a piece of paper out of his vest pocket and unfolded it. "We have done some calculations," he said. "As you know, when Kansas comes into the Union in January that will create a country of 34 states. To win the contingent election, Lincoln needs a flat majority—18 states—to vote for him."

"And?"

"Right now, there are 16 states whose House delegations are

solidly Republican, 16 that are solidly Democratic, and 2 that appear, one way or another, tied."

"I have made my own list," Pennington said. He removed a piece of paper from his own coat pocket and he and Herndon compared their lists.

When they were done, Pennington said, "Alright, we agree. Now, how do you plan to get the 2 additional states you will need to make 18 for Lincoln?"

Herndon named them and went over the strategy for each.

"I wish you luck," Pennington said. "It might work. Although what Lincoln did in representing that radical Republican woman in her trial will make it hard to bring the Democratic congressmen you want on board."

"You may be right, Mr. Speaker, but we will try."

"Again, why at least three ballots?"

"It's similar to the strategy at the Republican Convention that got Lincoln the nomination," Herndon said. "We will need multiple ballots to gain strength. No one will win on the first ballot, but Lincoln will hope to gain at least one state on the next one and win with more added on the third. But if there is only one ballot…"

Pennington finished the thought for him. "No one will win for president. And then the vice president, who will be chosen by the Senate from among the two top finishers in the earlier-counted electoral vote for that office, will become the acting president for the next four years."

"Who could well turn out to be Senator Douglas's running mate," Herndon said. "Herschel Johnson, the slave-owning former governor of Georgia."

"How could that happen?" Pennington said. "There are many more senators from the North than from the South. Won't those Northerners vote instead for Lincoln's vice presidential running mate, Hannibal Hamlin of Maine?"

"Some will, some won't, Mr. Speaker. Some Northern Democratic senators will vote for Johnson over Hamlin simply because they are pro-slavery. As for those who aren't pro-slavery, if they thought Lincoln might win the presidency here in the House, they will want to balance Lincoln out with a pro-slavery Southerner as his vice president. Senator Hamlin is strongly antislavery, while Governor Johnson owns more than a hundred slaves."

They both sat for a few seconds and contemplated what a Herschel Johnson presidency would mean for the country.

Pennington spoke first. "A President Herschel Johnson would likely let the Southern states who want to secede go their way in peace. He would be worse than that drunkard Buchanan."

"Then, if I had to guess," Herndon said, and paused, "Georgia would wait a year or two to secede as the final state to go, Johnson would resign the presidency, go with them, and become the president of some kind of Southern confederacy."

"You could be right."

"We are counting on you, Mr. Speaker, to be fair," Herndon said. "But not so fair as to permit anyone but Lincoln and Hamlin to be elected."

66

Law Offices of Lincoln and Herndon
November 18

Lincoln was in his office and, for the first time in many days, alone. The weather had turned suddenly colder, and there was hickory wood burning in the fireplace.

He had sent Herndon to Washington, and banished the law clerks who were usually working and studying in the office. Hay had gone to spend time with his ailing mother, and his correspondence secretary, Nicolay, was over at the statehouse.

Lincoln had spent hours and days with members of the National Committee, who were still convinced they could find 12 faithless electors and thus provide him the necessary 152 votes (California and Oregon had been confirmed for him) he needed to be elected when the votes were counted in Congress on February 13.

He had tried to persuade them to concentrate instead on winning the contingent election in the House that would follow when no candidate garnered a majority of the electoral votes. They had said that effort could come later. But there was nothing to stop him starting work on the problem himself.

One of the states that looked likely to cast a vote for Senator Douglas instead of Lincoln in the contingent election was, embarrassingly, Illinois. Five of its nine congressmen were Democrats, but only four were Republicans.

Lincoln was to a large extent a self-made politician. Which meant that when he really wanted something, he often went directly to the person involved instead of sending an emissary. And living right there in Springfield was a Democratic congressman from Illinois whose mind and vote he could try to change.

His name was John McClernand—a lifelong Democrat and one of Senator Douglas's strongest supporters.

McClernand and Lincoln had been, at the same time, both political enemies and good friends for more than twenty-five years. They had served side by side in the Illinois legislature in the '30s and in the Congress in the '40s. They were both lawyers, and had tried cases together as cocounsel, and on other occasions opposed each other in court. Eighteen years ago, the man had also married Sarah Dunlap, one of Mary Lincoln's closest friends.

When the knock on the door came, it was, as he expected, McClernand, a wiry man who seemed, as usual, to be brimming with energy.

They shook hands and Lincoln said, "I know Sarah has been ill with consumption. How is she faring? Better I hope."

McClernand looked down at the floor, and the energy with which he came in seemed to drain out of him. "Not well. I fear the worst, but perhaps God will see to her recovery."

"I fervently hope that will come to pass," Lincoln said and, sensing that his friend wished to move on to a less painful topic, said, "John, I don't think we've seen each other since the patent case we tried together as cocounsel last year."

"Well, we've both been busy campaigning, albeit on different sides of the aisle, as we'd say in the House."

"That's true," Lincoln said, as he cleared a space for them both at the table, pushing aside the usual piles of newspapers.

"I had expected to be calling you Mr. President the next time we met," McClernand said.

Lincoln laughed. "Perhaps so, although you have been working hard to provide Senator Douglas with that title."

"Yes, but now it's almost in your hands. The rumor is that your National Committee is searching for errant electors who will come over to you and give you the electoral college win when the votes are counted in February."

"It is devoutly to be hoped that that will happen. Would you like some tea, John?"

"I would indeed."

In anticipation of McClernand's arrival, he had made a pot of hot water, using a special grate that hung out over the fire, and then steeped the tea leaves in it. He poured a cup and said, "It's something new, imported to England from China and then brought here. A gift from a supporter. I have unfortunately forgotten the name of it." He handed the full cup to McClernand. "Sugar or milk?"

"No, thank you," he said and sipped it. "Quite good."

"I was surprised to hear that you were in Springfield," Lincoln said. "What with the Congress still in session."

"Not much is happening there at the moment, legislatively speaking. Mostly men talking incessantly about faithless electors. Although we did pass the Pacific Telegraph Act, and the lines should reach all the way to California by sometime next year."

"That's welcome news. We heard the election results from California and Oregon only two days ago, and that quickly only due to that new outfit, the Pony Express."

"Congratulations on that!"

Lincoln decided to get to the point. "I asked you to come by today, John, because I wanted to discuss the contingent election that may take place in the House on February 13."

"You're assuming you will not win the electoral vote."

Lincoln hedged and said, "I expect to win, but I am making some plans in case I do not."

"What does that have to do with me?" McClernand said and smiled, as he knew full well what the answer would be.

"If we get to a contingent election in the House, I must have the votes of 18 states to win. I am assured of 16. I am searching for 2 more."

"Let me guess. You want me to cast my vote for you when the Illinois House delegation votes, so that it will be 5 to 4 for you, instead of 5 to 4 against? Putting Illinois in your column."

"Yes."

"Why should I do that for you?" McClernand said.

"Because if you add it up, as it now stands I will get 16 states, Douglas will get the 5 states in the North that have clear Democratic majorities in their delegations and Breckinridge will most likely get 11, mostly in the South and Border states. At least 2 states will probably be tied."

"Perhaps some of the delegates will change their votes after no one wins on the first ballot."

"If you study the states involved and the congressmen who currently represent them, you will see that it can't possibly happen for Douglas, and is very unlikely for Breckinridge."

"I will have to analyze that for myself, Abe."

"I expect you to. But keep in mind that if no one of the three of us gets a majority after several ballots, the Senate's choice for vice president will become acting president for the next four years."

"You fear Johnson, the former governor of Georgia?"

"Wouldn't you? He is a slaveholder. The Southern senators will vote for him, and because he is Douglas's running mate, a lot of Democratic senators from the North may well do so, too."

"I can't promise you my vote, Abe. I am bound to Senator Douglas in every way."

"I am not asking for it on the first ballot. I am asking you to consider it on the second and third, when it will have become clear that Douglas cannot win."

"I seem to have finished my cup of tea quite rapidly," Mc-Clernand said. "May I trouble you for another?"

"Of course." Lincoln took McClernand's empty cup from him and refilled it. Lincoln had learned over the years that people, and especially politicians, used the excuse of pausing to take a sip or two of some beverage to give themselves time to think something over before speaking.

Lincoln waited for McClernand to drink his fill and said, "We were talking about whether I could count on you to vote for me after the first ballot, John."

McClernand put his cup back down on the table and said, "Abe, why should I do that rather than vote for Breckinridge on a subsequent ballot? He says all the right things about keeping the Union together."

"Because we are both for the Union come hell or high water, and he is for it only so long as the streambed is dry enough to walk across. And because we both abhor slavery yet are not abolitionists, whereas Breckinridge would see slavery expand into the territories and beyond."

There was a knock at the door.

"I have no idea who that could possibly be," Lincoln said. "But as I am the doorman this morning I will go and find out."

67

When he opened the door, Mary Todd—as he still on occasion, and with affection, called Mrs. Lincoln despite eighteen years of marriage—was standing there.

"Why, Mary, I am surprised. You never come to the office."

"I heard that John McClernand is here and I want to inquire after Sarah."

"John," he said, in a voice loud enough for McClernand to hear, "Mrs. Lincoln has come to see you."

McClernand rose from the table, and he and Mary Lincoln greeted each other like old friends, which they were. Lincoln retreated to another part of the big room so that Mary and John might be left alone to discuss Sarah's grave condition.

When they were done, Mary had a long face and said, "Mr. Lincoln, I have a few things to discuss with you later. While you gentlemen complete your business, I will just pick up one of your newspapers and busy myself until you are done."

Lincoln and McClernand returned to the table and Lincoln

said, "We were discussing why I am a much better choice for your second ballot vote than Breckinridge."

"Yes, but you were also claiming you are not an abolitionist."

"I am not, as I have said many times."

McClernand took another sip of his tea, sighed and sat silent for a few seconds. Finally, he said, "Abe, not long ago, I would have told anyone who asked that I believed you when you said that. Now I am not so sure."

"Why is that, John?"

"Because you chose to represent Mrs. Foster in her trial."

"She was a defendant—unjustly accused I might add—in need of a lawyer. Don't you agree that we lawyers are obligated to undertake a case like that when asked, without regard to the politics of the defendant?"

"You are not just any lawyer and she was not just any client. Taking that case called into question whether your denial of holding abolitionist sentiments is sincere."

"It is quite sincere."

"Well, it is not only I who tend now to doubt that but, apparently, many voters in Pennsylvania and Indiana who might otherwise have voted for you."

Lincoln laughed. "Some people have told me that I lost abolitionist voters because I did not immediately say I would pardon Mrs. Foster were I elected. And now you are telling me I lost anti-abolitionist voters, too."

"Perhaps it was both."

"Well, John, all I ask is that before that contingent vote is taken—and it's still almost three months away—that you will consider voting for me after the first ballot."

"I will think on it, certainly."

"Thank you."

After he had seen McClernand out, Mary, who was sitting in the far corner leafing through one of the newspapers, put it down and said, "I told you that you should not represent that woman."

They argued about it briefly, as they had when he made the decision to do it, and then she left.

After Mary had gone, Lincoln returned to a list he had made of other congressmen he might approach, both in and out of Illinois. No sooner had he settled in than there was, to his great annoyance, still another knock on the door. When he opened it, there stood Clarence.

"Mr. Artemis. What brings you here?"

"I would like to interview you once again, sir."

"I already gave you an interview—just about a week ago if I recall correctly. And promised you the next one only if I reach the White House."

"True. But your perspective as we get ever-closer to the vote in the House could prove even more informative for our readers. And I'm leaving tomorrow for Washington, where I hope to talk to people."

"Sorry, Mr. Artemis. I cannot give you another interview today. But it's a cold day. Come in and have some hot tea. I'm interested to hear whom you plan to see on your trip."

After Clarence had taken a cup of tea, Lincoln said, "May we have our usual agreement? Nothing I say today can be published or repeated to anyone?"

"Of course."

With that agreed, Lincoln explained to Clarence the mechanics of the upcoming electoral college vote. And told him he expected to win that vote and become president. But then Lincoln explained that *just in case* he didn't win that way, he had to be concerned about the contingent election in the House that might follow.

Clarence seemed unaware of the details of the Twelfth Amendment because, after the explanation, he said, in some wonderment, "And therefore, if neither you, Douglas nor Breckinridge get the vote of a majority of the states in the contingent election in the House, the vice president, who is chosen by the

Senate from the top two vice presidential candidates, would become president?

"That is how it works."

"I am amazed," Clarence said.

"Well, the Amendment was adopted in 1804, when our politics was quite different."

Clarence finally seemed to understand and said, "So how the state Congressional delegations vote will be the important thing."

"Yes, and in particular how certain Democratic congressmen from certain states plan to vote, which might change the outcome in a particular state, which could change the overall outcome. Talking to certain ones of them—I will give you a list—could help you write a very interesting story."

Lincoln wrote out the names on a piece of paper and handed it to Clarence, who looked it over and said, "Democratic congressmen from Oregon, California, Delaware and Illinois?"

"Yes."

"Why them?"

"Those delegations are either split fifty-fifty between Democratic representatives and Republication representatives or are one- or two-congressman states. So if even one Democratic congressman in such a state votes for me, I will have the votes of a majority of the delegation's representatives and win the state's vote."

"Do you expect me to report back to you?"

"Of course not. But if we should happen to see each other and you think it might help you to ask me some questions about what you've learned, you are certainly welcome to do so."

Lincoln stood up. "Now, Mr. Artemis, if you will excuse me, I have some work to do." Clarence rose, too, and they shook hands. As Clarence lingered in the doorway, he said, "You know, some of the Southern states are still threatening to secede even though you've not yet been elected. Is that troubling?"

"Of course. Deeply."

Clarence hesitated, then said, "Mr. Lincoln, when *exactly* can I expect another interview?"

"Mr. Artemis, if I am chosen as president, I will provide you the interview immediately after the electoral college vote is final, or if it comes to it, as soon as the House contingent election is final."

"If you can promise me that interview immediately after the vote, that must mean you plan to go to Washington yourself."

"Indeed I am—probably in the week before the counting of the electoral votes in the Senate on February 13. But those plans are not to be printed or repeated to anyone." He paused a moment. "Well, you can tell Mrs. Carter since she has no doubt already learned the plan from Pinkerton."

"I am having dinner with her tonight. I have been wondering, though, why she is still here in Springfield. She is being quite secretive about it."

"She is part of the group protecting me. From what I am not quite sure, but Pinkerton insists on it."

"I have not noticed her doing much protecting because, well, she has been spending a lot of time with me."

"Pinkerton has given her some time off from her job. She requested it as I understand it." Lincoln grinned. "Specifically, I believe, so she could spend more time with you."

"Oh, I see. I...well, I..."

"Why, Mr. Artemis," Lincoln said, laughing. "You are at a loss for words. Very unusual for you. Please sit back down." Lincoln pointed to the two chairs in front of the fireplace. After Clarence had taken one, Lincoln picked up a small log and tossed it on the fire, where it kicked up a flurry of sparks.

Lincoln took the other chair, stretched out his legs and said, "Mr. Artemis, if I may be so bold, I think you may be in need of advice. Of the sort a father might provide to a son, and I am, I believe, old enough to be your father."

"About?"

"Mrs. Carter."

"Ah, yes. She has been on my mind, certainly."

"A woman of such beauty and intelligence would make a fine wife to you, don't you think?"

"Yes. But, you know, she is a detective. What in God's name would it be like for a man to be married to a detective?"

"Interesting, I would think," Lincoln said.

"What about children?"

"Pinkerton has children, despite being a detective."

"That is different!"

"Is it? I would wager that two intelligent, worldly people like you and Mrs. Carter would be able to find your way through that problem."

"I will need to consider it carefully."

"You should. Children, I might add, are quite a joy to have in your life, even though a burden at times. Which reminds me…"

Lincoln got up, walked over to a high cabinet, opened a door and pulled out a wool cap. "Here is your hat, Mr. Artemis. I'm sorry it took so long to return it. Tad had hidden it well. And this time he assures me it is the correct one."

Clarence took the cap and laughed. "It is the correct one, but perhaps a bit the worse for wear."

Lincoln furrowed his brow. "Oh? It didn't originally have a small hole in the top?"

"Not so small a hole," Clarence said, putting his hand through the hole and wagging his fingers.

"I'd be happy to buy you a new hat, Mr. Artemis."

"There is no need, Mr. Lincoln. I will treasure this as a souvenir of your campaign for president."

"Well, you will at least need a new one for a wedding."

"I don't know if there is going to be a wedding. Even were I to ask her, I'm not sure she would accept. She is rather independent-minded." He got up from the chair. "Thank you for the return of the cap, Mr. Lincoln." He placed it on his head, then tipped the brim. "And the advice."

68

Washington, DC
The Speaker's Room
February 12, 1861

The train trip to Washington had proved uneventful. It had not snowed, no engine had broken down and no stretch of track had been found cracked by the cold. Thus, the trains had run on time and the trip from Springfield took Lincoln just a little over two days and nights.

Pinkerton had insisted on arranging protection on the trip, although Lincoln had doubted anyone would make an attempt on his life until after he was sworn in. Assuming he ever was.

He had finally consented to Pinkerton putting several incognito guards in his carriage, including Annabelle Carter, who sat uncomfortably behind him throughout the entire trip. And *uncomfortably* was the proper word because he had refused to travel first-class, preferring to sit with ordinary people in the less expensive cars, whose seats were worn and in places threadbare.

At some point during the trip, he had learned that Senator Douglas was traveling on the same train, although Douglas and his entourage were said to be in a special first-class car far to the rear of the train, well away from the smoke spewing out of the steam engine. Lincoln and Douglas had not set eyes on each other during the entire campaign, and Lincoln had at first thought of going back to greet the senator. Hay, who was traveling with him, had talked him out of it, arguing that it would seem like the loser calling on the victor.

After a night at the Willard Hotel to rest up, Lincoln had gone up to Capitol Hill to meet with Pennington in the Speaker's Room. Pennington had greeted him cordially and shown him the schedule of meetings he had arranged for the day. Lincoln had spent most the day in those meetings, as various luminaries, including most of the members of the Republican National Committee, the Republican Caucus chair in the Senate, and various senior congressmen and Committee chairs paraded in and out, all with their own procedural suggestions and electoral vote headcounts.

Finally, they were all gone, and Lincoln and Pennington were alone, sitting on the couches, facing one another.

"Are you sure I can't offer you a libation, Mr. Lincoln?" Pennington said.

"Thank you, but no. I don't partake. Although at times like this I wish I did. But I do want to ask you, Mr. Speaker, after all we've heard today, how do you think the electoral college vote count will go?"

Pennington got up and walked over to the bust of Washington. "My predecessor told me, when he handed over the Speaker's gavel, that if you rub the head of Washington, he will speak and tell you what you want to know. Shall I try it?"

Lincoln laughed uproariously. "Why not? Do you think you need some kind of incantation while you do it?"

"I'll try the first few words of the Preamble to the Constitution," Pennington said. He began rubbing the top of Washington's head while chanting, "We the people of the United States, in order to form a more perfect union," and then repeated it twice more.

"Nothing," Lincoln said. "Perhaps you are rubbing the wrong

head. Washington pretended to be above politics, but Quincy Adams certainly did not. Try him."

It was Pennington's turn to laugh, but he did as Lincoln suggested. Adams, too, remained silent. "Well, Mr. Lincoln, I guess we are stuck with our own prognostications. I am the first to admit I have little idea what will happen when they count the electoral votes tomorrow. And, apparently, the journalists who have been trying to sniff out faithless electors also have no idea."

"It didn't help that, when the electors caucused out in the states in December, many states made their electors meet in secret," Lincoln said. "And…"

Pennington finished his thought, "Then mailed in their ballots to the president of the Senate in sealed envelopes. Which won't be opened until tomorrow! Are you sure you don't want a drink, sir?"

"Perfectly sure."

"I hate to say it, Mr. Lincoln, but I think you will not win a majority in the electoral college. Let us, therefore, turn to the contingent vote here in the House that will follow, where the odds may be better."

"Better in some ways," Lincoln said. "But not in others. There used to be 33 states, and I needed the votes of only 17 delegations to have a majority of the states. With the admission of Kansas to the Union two weeks ago, there are now 34, and I need 18."

"Correct," Pennington said. "You have 16 states definitely in your column, but now you will need to add 2 more instead of just 1 more."

"I am hopeful that Illinois will swing my way," Lincoln said. "Others have been working on the Democratic congressmen from California, Oregon and Delaware, who could swing their state to me if they would switch their vote."

"Well, Mr. Lincoln, we will just have to wait and hope. But now we have three procedural matters to discuss."

Lincoln glanced over at the busts on the wall. "Will we need to consult the heads again?"

"I think not."

69

"Let me address the first matter," Pennington said. "Assuming the electoral college vote yields no majority winner for president, do we want to let the Senate hold its contingent election for vice president first or let the House hold its contingent election for president first?"

"Shouldn't we, in fairness, consult Senator Douglas and Vice President Breckinridge as to their preferences?"

"Senator Douglas's representatives have told me that I should decide. They added that despite the fact that I was chosen as a consensus Speaker, I am a lifelong Republican, and no one will be offended if I act as a partisan in this particular matter."

"What about Vice President Breckinridge?"

"As the current vice president, he will be presiding over the Senate, despite the fact that he is himself one of the three electoral college candidates for president. He has also left the choice on this matter to me. He described it as a courtesy."

Lincoln rose and began to pace the room, hands behind his

back. Finally, he stopped and said, "Let us have the Senate's contingent vote for vice president held first."

"May I ask why?"

"That will force the senators, particularly the Democratic ones, to choose for vice president between my vice presidential running mate, Hannibal Hamlin of Maine and Douglas's running mate, the pro-slavery, slave-owning former governor of Georgia, Herschel Johnson."

"I don't quite see…"

"Mr. Speaker, the senators will have to vote *before* knowing whether the House will later be able to choose a president. Which means that in choosing a vice president they will be staring a potential acting president in the face. I hope that will cause them to come to their patriotic senses and avoid picking a man who owns slaves and will, if he becomes acting president, likely take the Union down, no matter what he says now."

"I will inform the vice president of our choice of timing, then," Pennington said. "But now there is a second question from someone else who wishes to see you."

"Who?"

"The Sergeant at Arms of the House, who is, as you know, the protector of all of the members of the House as well as our guests." Pennington leaned out his office door and said, "Mr. Jarvis, please send Mr. Hoffman in."

A large, burly man entered the room, and Pennington said, "Mr. Lincoln, this is our recently appointed Sergeant at Arms, Mr. Henry Hoffman. He is former member of this House from Maryland and has now returned as our protector."

"It is a pleasure to meet you, Mr. Lincoln," Hoffman said. "May I say, I hope you will be our next president!"

"It is a pleasure to meet you, sir, and thank you for the thought. To what do I owe the pleasure of your company today?"

"I am concerned about protecting you while you are our guest in the House tomorrow."

"Do you think I will need protection?"

"Yes. There have been many threats against you. Most are probably exaggerated, but I have been talking with Allan Pinkerton, who shares my concerns."

Lincoln smiled. "Ah, Mr. Pinkerton. My guardian angel."

"He thinks of himself that way, I believe," Hoffman said.

"I assume you have some advice for me, Mr. Hoffman, in regard to these threats."

"I do. First, I must ask a question. I understand the electoral college votes will be counted tomorrow in the Senate, with the entire Congress in attendance."

"That is indeed what the Twelfth Amendment mandates."

"That will be a very large crowd gathered in a very small space. And we have had, as you know, bad experiences on the Senate floor not so long ago."

Lincoln knew he was referring to an episode several years before in which an irate Southern congressman had beaten radical Republican Senator Sumner of Massachusetts nearly to death at his desk in the Senate, using a metal-tipped cane.

Hoffman was continuing. "I understand that since you are a candidate, Vice President Breckinridge, who will preside over the Senate in his capacity as vice president, has extended you an invitation to attend the counting of the electoral ballots."

"He has very kindly issued me that invitation, yes."

Hoffman glanced at Pennington, as if seeking permission to say what he was about to say. Then he plunged ahead, "I'd request that you not go."

"Even though I am the candidate most likely to win if anyone wins in the electoral college vote?"

"Yes, and to make you more comfortable about that, I have also persuaded Senator Douglas to forgo attendance, despite being a sitting senator, and he has agreed."

Lincoln raised his eyebrows. "And Douglas will not attend even the contingent vote for vice president that follows in the

Senate in the event there is no electoral vote winner for that office?"

"Correct. Unless there is a tie in the contingent election and his vote is needed to break it."

"I will need to think on that," Lincoln said. "I will let Speaker Pennington know my decision."

"Thank you. There is more, however. I assume you will want to attend the contingent election in the House if there is one, since it might elect you as our next president."

"Yes, that I must attend."

"I understand, sir. But because you are a former member of this House, you have the privilege of the floor and could be on the House floor during the vote."

"I intend to do that," Lincoln said.

"I would ask that instead you sit in the House gallery during the vote. Both Senator Douglas and Vice President Breckinridge have already agreed to do so."

Lincoln grinned. "So we will be like three peas in a pod."

Hoffman laughed, albeit nervously. "I plan to drop the pod and keep you all as peas some ways apart. And the press will be kept well away, of course."

"Alright," Lincoln said. "I will let you know my decision on that by this evening."

"Thank you."

"Thank you, Mr. Hoffman, for coming and letting me know your concerns," Lincoln said. "And thank you for your hard work on this."

"You are most welcome."

After Hoffman had left, Lincoln said, "Mr. Speaker, you said there were three procedural questions. What is the third?"

"It is simple. Five Southern states have seceded."

"No, they have announced they are seceding, but they have no right to do so. The Union is perpetual."

"Agreed. But they have nonetheless announced and many

of their representatives and senators have resigned, or in some cases, just left. Indeed, last month Senator Jefferson Davis gave a formal farewell speech."

"Please get to the point, Mr. Speaker, as it is growing late."

"The point is this. I have met with the parliamentarian of the House, who for reasons I have not been here long enough to understand, is called the Messenger to the Speaker."

Lincoln chuckled. "And he has spoken to you about something. As if from on high."

"Yes, for purposes of the contingent election only, the House could declare, so long as the Senate concurs, that there are now only 29 states with the right to vote in the contingent election, even if representatives from the seceding states are still here."

Lincoln got up and walked over to the bust of George Washington. "I don't suppose I need to ask George here to calculate it for me. If the supposedly seceded Southern states were ruled no longer present in the Congress, those resolutions would pass."

"Yes."

"And then, with only 29 states left my 16 states would easily be a majority, and I would be elected president."

"Yes."

"Mr. Speaker, if I were to countenance that, I will have conceded the right of the Deep South states to depart, and I suspect the other Southern states and the Border states would quickly follow."

"It guarantees you the presidency," Pennington said. "And avoids the possibility that the slaveholder Herschel Johnson of Georgia, would become acting president of our Union."

"It would be a Union not much worth having."

"You will not countenance it, then?"

"No, and if I am elected in that fashion, I will decline to take the oath of office. There is only one Union, which has 34 states, and that is the one I intend to lead."

There was a long silence.

Finally, Pennington said, "Alright, I will not do it."

"Thank you. And to make your task at least somewhat less of a burden, I will accede to the wishes of the Sergeant at Arms and not attend the counting of electoral votes in the Senate to-morrow, nor the contingent election for vice president that will follow."

"Will you agree to sit in the House gallery, rather than on the floor, for the contingent election for president?"

"Yes. So long as Douglas and Breckinridge are both there."

"I will guarantee it."

70

February 13
The House of Representatives

The counting of the electoral votes had been scheduled for 10:00 a.m. Lincoln had arrived in the Speaker's Room around 9:00 a.m. and had met briefly with Pennington, who left shortly thereafter. From time to time Jarvis came in and inquired if he wished something to drink or eat. He had politely declined each time.

It was now noon.

Lincoln noticed a small pendulum clock on a table in one corner of the room. He stared at it for a while, watching the pendulum move back and forth through its arc. He wondered whether the clock was ticking away the end of his political career or heralding the start of something he'd long strived to achieve. He hadn't realized until recently that he might achieve it only to confront the young republic's greatest crisis.

He finally dozed off.

Jarvis's voice awakened him. "Mr. Lincoln, there is someone here to see you who claims to know you."

"Who is it?"

"A Mrs. Foster."

Lincoln blinked, decided to ignore the potential adverse political consequences of seeing her again—the popular election was over—and said, "Show her in, please."

"That will leave you alone with a woman," Jarvis said. "Would you like me to stay lest people say things?"

"People have already said I am the spawn of the devil, so it will hardly matter. I will see her alone."

A moment later, Abby walked in and said, "Abraham, I found myself in Washington on another matter today, and the congressman I called on earlier this morning told me you were likely to be with the Speaker."

Lincoln smiled "As indeed I am. It is a pleasure to see you again, Abby. Will you please have a seat?"

"I thank you, but I would prefer to stand. What I have to stay will take not long."

Lincoln laughed. "Ah, because you have come simply to wish me a quick good luck?"

Lincoln thought he detected a trace of a smile on her face, but it quickly vanished, and she said, "No, for as you know, I have no preference in this election."

"As you have said many times."

"I came to see you because it seems likely to me that you will soon be the most powerful man in the United States. If that comes to pass, I beseech you to use your powers to help the slave."

"I hate slavery as much, I think, as you do, Abby. I will try to do what I can."

"Abraham, there is a gulf as wide as the ocean between trying to do something and actually doing it."

"I know," he said. "I know."

"Goodbye, then. Perhaps the next time I see you, I will call you Mr. President."

"If that transpires, Abby, you may always call me by whatever name you wish. Although I think the odds are that I am going to leave here today the same way I came in—as plain Abe Lincoln, a lawyer from Springfield, Illinois."

After she left, Lincoln returned to watching the clock. In not too long, a voice behind him said, "The electoral vote count is completed."

It was Pennington, accompanied by the Sergeant at Arms.

"Who won?" Lincoln said.

"No one polled a majority of the electoral votes," Pennington said.

"What was my actual count?"

"You were first with 140 electoral votes. The remaining 163 were split four ways, exactly as expected, with Douglas in second place, Breckinridge in third and Bell in fourth."

Lincoln rose from his chair and stretched his lanky frame. "So, there were no faithless electors."

"Not a single one," Pennington said.

"I guess faithless electors are a bit like leprechauns," Hoffman said. "Oft talked about but rarely seen."

They all laughed, and Lincoln said. "Who won the contingent election for vice president in the Senate?"

"Herschel Johnson," Hoffman said. "If you are elected president, what will you do about him?"

"Endure him, I suppose," Lincoln said. "As one must endure so many things in life...and in government."

Pennington glanced at the clock, whose dial read one o'clock. "The House will convene at 2:00 p.m.," he said, "to conduct the contingent election for president of the United States. Mr. Lincoln, Mr. Hoffman will escort you to the House gallery."

"Thank you both."

"Godspeed, sir," Pennington said. "Our country needs you."

Not long after, inside the House chamber, Hoffman assisted Lincoln down the steep gallery steps to his seat, which was in the third row back from the front. The rows immediately in front of him were empty, as were the seats immediately to his left and right.

Lincoln looked to his left and saw Senator Douglas sitting three seats over. Three seats to his right was Vice President Breckinridge. They both avoided looking at him.

Behind Douglas there was an entourage of seven or eight people, and about the same number behind Breckinridge. He turned and looked behind his own seat and saw an equal number. Amid the crowd, he spotted Annabelle, sitting at the very back, next to the entry door. His face broke out in a broad smile. He gave her a special wave, and she waved back.

Lincoln looked toward the floor of the House and tried to count the number of representatives gathered there. A full complement, now that Kansas had been added, would be 238. But he could tell from the many empty desks that a lot of Southern state representatives had departed. Looking at the desks—each a small wooden writing desk with a hinged top and scroll legs— brought back to mind the two years he had spent on that floor in the late '30s. Congressmen didn't have offices, so the desk, and whatever a man could get inside it, on top of it or on the floor around it, made up his entire work space.

At 2:00 p.m. sharp by the clock on the wall, Pennington, standing on the rostrum beneath two crossed American flags, with a large portrait of Washington to his right and one of Lafayette to his left, banged his gavel and said, "The House will come to order. I am informed by the president of the Senate that he has caused to be counted the electoral votes forwarded to him by the presidential electors, and that no candidate for president or vice president has received a majority of the electoral votes."

He took a deep breath, looked out at the gathered congressmen, over whom a hush had fallen, and said, "Now, accordingly, pursuant to the procedures required of us by the Twelfth Amendment to the Constitution of the United States, we will conduct an election for the office of president of the United States from among the three candidates in the election who received the most electoral votes. He looked down at a piece of paper and said, "Those three candidates are, in order of the total electoral votes received, Abraham Lincoln, Stephen A. Douglas and John C. Breckinridge."

He looked up at the gallery as if to acknowledge the presence of the candidates. "Let the record reflect that each candidate is present in the gallery of the House."

There was a scattering of applause from the floor and the gallery.

Lincoln noticed that a large camera and tripod had been set up in the far left wing of the gallery, aimed squarely at him and the other two candidates. With the three of them sitting in one place, the photographer must hope to get an unblurred picture. If he succeeds, Lincoln thought, it will become a very famous photograph.

As if reading his thoughts, Pennington said, "Gentlemen of the House, we are about to take a photograph." He then motioned up to the photographer, who looked at Lincoln and the two others and shouted, "Gentlemen, don't move!"

To Lincoln's amusement, none of them did—photographers seemed to have been granted the right to freeze life. After what seemed an eternity, the photographer finally yelled, "We are done!" and everyone relaxed.

After that, Lincoln watched as the clerk of the House, assisted by two burly men, carried in an old wooden box with a hinged top with a small slit in it. Two metal straps ran down from the top of the box onto the front, where each was fastened to the front of the box by a padlock run through a hasp. Pennington described the procedure to be followed, explaining that each state's delegation would take a secret vote and then record on a white card distributed by the clerk the name of the state and the name of the candidate who had won the votes of a majority of its delegation. If a state delegation proved unable to find a majority for any candidate, a member of the delegation should deposit a blank card in the box, bearing only the name of the state.

"For those five states whose delegations are not among us today, I will deposit a blank card on behalf of each," Pennington said.

"To win election as president a candidate must receive the affirmative votes of a majority of the states. Accordingly, there being 34 states in this Union, a winning candidate must receive the affirmative vote of at least 18 states."

A congressman in the front row rose. "May I be recognized, Mr. Speaker?"

"The Chair recognizes the gentleman from Illinois."

"Mr. Speaker, there being no still extant house rule with regard to this procedure, I move that, given the absence of five states from this chamber by alleged secession from the Union, that your announced procedure be revised to consider, for this purpose only, that there be only 29 states still in the Union and that a majority of those—15 states—be considered sufficient to select a president."

Lincoln stiffened. The congressman who had made the motion was a Republican from Illinois whom he did not know. Was Pennington attempting to do what Lincoln had specifically asked him not to?

Pennington looked down at the man and said, "I had anticipated that such a motion might be made. Before we convened I consulted with the Messenger to the Speaker on the issue, and your motion is out of order. Please be seated. The chair will not entertain any similar motions."

As Lincoln felt his body relax, there was a loud noise in the back of the gallery, and someone shouted, "Death to traitors!" Lincoln instinctively turned his head to see what had happened, and was just in time to see three soldiers wrestle a man to the ground and drag him back out the door. Lincoln had not realized there were soldiers there, guarding them. He wondered which of them the man had called a traitor. All of them perhaps? Only him?

On the floor, delegations seemed to have caucused quickly because men were already lined up, ready to slip white cards into the ballot box.

"Are there any more states still to vote?" Pennington said. When there was no response, Pennington said, "The tellers will count the ballots." Two men who'd been sitting to the side of the dais came down and removed the ballot box to another table. Each one, carrying a separate key, opened one of the two locks and one man removed the white cards and counted them.

"Mr. Speaker, I count cards from 34 states," he said in a loud voice. He handed the cards to the other man, who counted them again and said, in an even louder voice, "Mr. Speaker, I also count 34."

Each man went separately through the cards, marked down his count on a tally sheet and signed it. They compared their two tally sheets, nodded their heads, sealed the cards into a large envelope, and passed it and the tally sheets up to the Speaker.

Pennington reviewed them and said, "We have the vote."

Lincoln looked down and saw that he was gripping the handles of his chair. He glanced at Douglas who was doing the same. When he looked at Breckinridge, the man looked almost asleep.

"I have reviewed the tally sheets and found them to match," Pennington said. "The vote is Abraham Lincoln 16 states, Stephen Douglas 6 states, John Breckinridge 5 states, with the cards of 7 states left blank." He paused. "Unless there is a protest, we will commence in thirty minutes to have a second ballot. The clerk will distribute another set of cards."

Lincoln noticed that Pennington had chosen not to announce how each state had voted. Lincoln supposed the tally would be recorded in the formal record and he could examine it there later.

As he waited for the next vote to take place, he looked again at the floor of the House. Where everyone had been orderly, indeed almost tense, during the first vote, now congressmen were milling about, talking and laughing.

He felt a presence beside him. It was Annabelle.

"May I join you for a moment?" she said.

"Of course. But how can you protect me if you're down here with me instead of up there by the door?"

"There is now practically a whole battalion of soldiers out in the hallway. There had been only two to start with, but after that first man got in, someone sent more."

"Who was that man?"

"All I can tell you is that he was white, middle-aged and had a graying beard."

"Could you tell where he was from?"

"He had a Southern accent I associate with Mississippi."

Lincoln looked at her and saw that she had a big smile on her face. "Why the big smile?" he said.

Annabelle reached into her ever-present bag and handed him a telegram. He pulled his reading glasses out of his pocket and read it aloud in a whisper. "Lucy safe in Canada. Allan."

Lincoln looked at her and grinned. "How wonderful."

After that, they chatted for a while, until Lincoln looked closely at her and said, "There is something different about you today, Mrs. Carter. You look...well, I can't quite figure out what it is."

Her face reddened and she said, "Hopp...I mean Clarence, has asked me to marry him."

"Did you accept?"

"Yes."

"Congratulations!"

"Why, thank you, Mr. Lincoln."

"We will need to celebrate," he said. "And soon."

"That would be wonderful. But for now I do need to return

to my post in the back, where I can see you and those around you." She left abruptly.

Annabelle had not been gone long when Douglas got up from his seat, came over and said, "I know I am a poor substitute for the beautiful woman who just left, but may I join you?"

"Of course, Senator. It will be an honor."

Lincoln rose, they shook hands and then sat back down, next to one another.

71

"Senator, should we invite the vice president to join us, too?" Lincoln said.

Douglas pointed to Lincoln's right. "He has left."

Lincoln looked and saw that Douglas was correct. "Where do you think he's gone?"

"A guess? Now that he'll no longer be in office—he must have concluded he can't win here today—I assume he'll go back to Kentucky. And if it secedes, he'll go with it."

"And if it doesn't?"

"He may go south anyway."

"We didn't see each other at all during the campaign," Lincoln said. "It is perhaps unusual to come together like this, at the very end."

"We've known each other almost all of our adult lives," Douglas said. "And said some bitter things about each other perhaps."

Lincoln thought about it for a few seconds. "Yes, that, too. But our disputes have been about policy at least, which is what I have lived for all my life, as have you."

"They are starting the count again," Lincoln said. "I fear neither of us is going to win and then Herschel Johnson will be
president."

"If that happens, I fear the Union is gone," Douglas said.

"Yes, I fear the same, although you are the one who chose
him as your running mate."

Douglas didn't respond.

They sat in silence for a while as the tellers once again tallied
the vote and handed their tally sheets up to the Speaker.

Pennington began to read from the tallies. "The totals are, on
this second ballot, Lincoln 16, Douglas 6, Breckinridge 5, Blanks
still 7. No candidate for president has achieved the needed majority, and therefore no president has been selected."

People who had been milling about on the floor seemed suddenly frozen in place and an eerie silence descended momentarily, then broke into loud exclamations and shouting.

Pennington banged his gavel. "The House will come to
order!"

After the members had quieted, Pennington said, "We will
now have a third ballot. In order to encourage the members to
consider their votes carefully, I intend to make this the last ballot."

"Do you think that is a good idea or a poor idea?" Lincoln
said.

"I don't know," Douglas said. "But I hope there will be movement on this last ballot."

Suddenly, Douglas stood and shouted, "Mr. Speaker, as a
member of the other body, I ask consent to speak here in this
honorable House."

Pennington looked shocked.

Lincoln wondered whether Douglas was going to make one
more argument as to why he ought to prevail. If he did, would
Lincoln need to respond? Would this be the Lincoln–Douglas

debate redux? Would they have to do it here, shouting from the balcony?

Finally, Pennington, after a moment of silence, said, "Unless there be objection, Senator Douglas may have the privilege of speaking here."

He waited a few seconds. "There being no objection, Senator Douglas, please proceed. And if you would prefer to come down to the floor, you are of course most welcome. And we will extend the privilege as well to our former member, Mr. Lincoln."

Douglas remained standing and, raising his voice in order to be heard, said, "I can say what I wish to say from here. I will be brief. Gentlemen, the Union is at stake. If we fail to elect a president here today from among the three of us—the people who were put forward for the office by our parties—I fear it will be the end of the Union as we know it. And, I believe, the end of our prosperity and ultimately the end of democracy in this hemisphere."

Lincoln wondered where Douglas was going. It seemed an odd beginning if he intended to tout his own candidacy.

Douglas drew in a great breath, and said, "Therefore, to the extent any member of this great House feels any obligation to vote for me because I and they are both members of the great Democratic Party, to the extent it is within my power, I release them from that obligation. And with all my heart I urge a vote for Abraham Lincoln of Illinois."

He sat down, amid a great murmur that rose up from the floor.

"Mr. Lincoln, do you wish a reply?" Pennington said.

Lincoln rose and said, "I need no reply and I thank the great patriot from Illinois, Senator Douglas, who has devoted his life to our country."

"We will have the third ballot now," Pennington said.

As the members were caucusing and lining up to slip their

white cards into the ballot box again, Lincoln turned to Douglas and said, "I am most appreciative. But why did you do that?"

"It is simple," Douglas said. "You had the most popular votes *and* the most electoral votes. Therefore, among the three of us, you most deserve to be president."

"Thank you."

"And there is one more thing. Much as we have had our policy differences, I know you love this Union as much as I do and will move heaven and earth to preserve it."

"Thank you again. Now we will find out if your gesture has had the effect you—and I—hope for."

The balloting and the tabulating were quicker this time. Pennington looked over the tallies and paused before starting to read them. Lincoln looked at his face to see if he could discern anything. He thought Pennington looked grim and braced himself for the worst. He gripped the arms of his chair and saw that Douglas had done the same.

Pennington began to speak. "The tabulations are Lincoln 20, Douglas 3, Breckinridge 6, blank ballots 5. Abraham Lincoln has been chosen as the next president of the United States."

The House erupted in cheers. Lincoln stood and acknowledged them.

Douglas rose, extended his hand and said, "Congratulations, Mr. President-elect."

"Thank you, Senator."

Lincoln was about to say something further to Douglas when a giant of a man in an army uniform, with three stars on his epaulettes, appeared beside him and said, "Mr. President-elect, I am General Winfield Scott, Commanding General of the United States Army."

"I know who you are, General."

"I believe you are in need of protection. I have brought troops with me who will escort you back to your hotel and protect you there until your inauguration, which is only three weeks hence."

Lincoln followed Scott up the gallery steps, nodding his head at the applause that followed him, thinking that his life would never be the same.

At the top of the steps, he saw Annabelle standing a few feet away, looking out from behind one of the soldiers. He caught her eye, grinned and said, loud enough for her to hear, "White House wedding!"

And with that, he walked into history.

★ ★ ★ ★ ★

Historical Notes

Abraham Lincoln won the presidential election of 1860. Although he had only 39.9 percent of the popular vote nationwide, he had a majority of the electoral vote—180 out of 303, as well as a plurality of the popular vote at approximately 1.9 million votes. Unlike in the novel, he handily won both Pennsylvania and Indiana, as well as Oregon and California. The other three candidates all had many fewer electoral votes, although Douglas was second in popular vote (while being fourth in electoral votes) with approximately 1.4 million votes.

HISTORICAL CHARACTERS WITH MAJOR ROLES IN THE NOVEL

Abraham Lincoln was inaugurated as the sixteenth president of the United States on March 4, 1861, and took the oath of office on the East portico of the United States Capitol. Forces in South Carolina fired on Fort Sumter on April 12, 1861. Three days later, Lincoln called for seventy-five thousand volunteers to help put down the rebellion. Several days later, Senator Stephen Douglas met privately with Lincoln at the White House and urged that the call-up be expanded to two hundred thousand men. Lincoln was shot in the head at Ford's Theater in Washington, DC, on April 14, 1865. He died in the early morning of April 15. He was fifty-six. More than sixteen thousand books have been written about him.

Stephen Douglas, who had served two terms in the United States Senate, died of typhoid fever on June 3, 1861. He was forty-eight.

Abby Kelley Foster was a nationally known radical abolitionist lecturer whose many fervent followers were known as Abby Kelleyites. Her fiery speeches were so feared by those who wished to push the issue of slavery aside that many towns tried to ban her from coming to speak. She founded two influential abolitionist newspapers and was a prodigious fundraiser for the cause. She was also an early suffragette, but fell out with other suffragettes over the issue of the Fifteenth Amendment, which gave the vote to all male citizens. Many suffragettes opposed the Amendment because it did not also give the vote to women. Abby supported the Amendment despite that egregious flaw. She was married to Stephen Symonds Foster, himself a radical abolitionist who was on occasion thrown bodily out of churches where he'd gone to speak on abolition. The Fosters' home (Liberty Farm) in Worcester, Massachusetts, is a National Historic Landmark. So far as I know, Abby never went west of Indiana. I have brought her to Springfield, Illinois, for purposes of the novel.

Reverend Albert Hale was the pastor of Second Presbyterian church of Springfield, Illinois, (now called Westminster Presbyterian) from 1839 to 1867. He was a strong abolitionist from an early age, as witnessed by a letter he wrote in 1838 supporting the need to support an abolitionist agent in Illinois. The letter is archived at the Lincoln Presidential Library in Springfield. The historical record on Reverend Hale is thin, but I have filled it in a way that I think honors his life and work. And although he was apparently a serious evangelist with a somewhat dour and stern demeanor (leavened by his wife, Abiah Hale), I have read several things about him that suggest to me that he on occasion had a twinkle in his eye. I hope he would be pleased by the way in which I have depicted him and the major role I've given him in the novel.

President James Buchanan was the fifteenth president of the United States. After his term ended, he returned to Wheatland, his home near Lancaster, Pennsylvania, and wrote a memoir, *Mr. Buchanan's Administration on the Eve of the Rebellion*. In it, he defended his conduct in office. He died in 1868. Most historians rate him the worst US president. Jeremiah Black served as attorney general for much of Buchanan's term.

John Breckinridge, who served as Buchanan's vice president from 1857 to 1861, fled south during the Civil War, joined the Confederate Army, eventually becoming a major general and, ultimately, the Confederate States Secretary of War. After the Union victory, he fled to Cuba in a small boat, then to England, and eventually to Canada. He was pardoned by President Andrew Johnson in 1868 in a general amnesty and returned to Kentucky, where he died in 1875. In a continuing claim to familial fame, Breckinridge's great-grandson, John "Bunny" Breckinridge, starred as the alien ruler in Ed Wood's classic 1959 cult science fiction movie, *Plan 9 from Outer Space*.

William "Billy" Herndon was Lincoln's law partner from 1844 until Lincoln's death in 1865. After Lincoln's assassination, Herndon interviewed many people who had known Lincoln. With coauthor Jesse Weik, he produced a two-volume biography of Lincoln: *Herndon's Lincoln: The True Story of a Great Life (The History & Personal Recollections of Abraham Lincoln)*. That work has provided historians with a wealth of information about Lincoln's life, particularly the period before he came to national prominence.

John Hay served as Lincoln's assistant secretary during Lincoln's presidency. Together with the secretary, John Nicolay, he lived and worked in the White House during Lincoln's entire term. After Lincoln's death, he and Nicolay later published, in ten volumes, a massive biography of Lincoln titled *Abraham Lincoln, A History.* Hay later became Secretary of State under William McKinley and Theodore Roosevelt and served in that position for seven years.

Harriet Lane was President Buchanan's niece and the hostess of his White House. She was the first woman to be referred to as the First Lady. Some have compared her style and influence to that of Jackie Kennedy. In later life she became a philanthropist, including founding the Harriet Lane Children's Health Clinic at Johns Hopkins Medical School, which is still in operation today. The cutter *Harriet Lane,* the third ship to be named for her, is currently in service with the United States Coast Guard.

Allan Pinkerton founded the Pinkerton National Detective Agency and sought to protect Lincoln from harm both before and after he was inaugurated. He hired women detectives starting in the 1850s, the most famous of whom was Kate Warne.

John McClernand was a Democratic congressman from Illinois and later a general in the Union Army.

William Pennington was the Speaker of the House of Representatives for one term, from 1860 to 1861. Henry Hoffman was the Sergeant of Arms of the House in 1860.

Frederick Douglass was born in Maryland in 1818. An enslaved man, he escaped to New York City at the age of twenty and eventually settled in Massachusetts and still later, Rochester, New York. A powerful orator, he became one of the most prominent and effective abolitionists in the United States as well as one of the most powerful speakers on a variety of social causes, including women's suffrage. He wrote three autobiographies. He died in 1895. Cedar Hill, his final home, in Washington, DC, is a National Historic Site.

Acknowledgments

I think the typical image of a novelist is someone who sits alone in a small room, writing. And there is some truth in that. But once the writing is done in rough form, it takes a village to make the novel into something good enough for a reader to want to read it.

The residents of the village for this novel, to all of whom I owe a debt of gratitude, include my terrific agent, Erica Silverman, who encouraged me to write a second alt-history novel (departing once again from my original legal thrillers), and my editor at Hanover Square, Peter Joseph, who acquired the novel and suggested after reading the first draft that Clarence and Annabelle might well have a mutual attraction (despite seeming to dislike each other) and perhaps something might be made of that. So Peter, in addition to his many other good suggestions, thus encouraged me to write my first-ever romance amidst the politics of the 1860 presidential election.

I must also thank, as well, the entire "crew" at Hanover Square, including Natalie Hallak, Grace Towery, the production staff and the terrific copy editor, Anne-Marie Rutella (who picked up an important factual error that I had somehow missed), and the excellent proofreader, Canaan Chu.

As with all of my earlier novels, I am indebted to my wife, Sally Anne, who read every chapter as it came hot off the printer and provided an early edit of each that improved the novel immensely. The usual pattern was I'd finish a chapter, she'd read it and make suggestions, I'd grumpily reject them and then return a few hours later to admit that she was right and go on to make most of the changes she had proposed. I must also thank my son Joe, who took time away from his job to read the early drafts and provide extremely insightful advice on both characterization and the overall arc of the story.

Many others helped with the research. Along those lines, I want to acknowledge, first and foremost, the assistance of Westminster Presbyterian Church of Springfield, Illinois (previously Second Presbyterian), and especially of its pastor, the Reverend Dr. Blythe Denham Kieffer, and its Historian (and Music Director) Dale Rogers and the volunteer archivists, Carol Bloemer and Sue Cull, who assist him, as well as the late Kathie Nenaber, who initiated the archive project and set up the current files. In the summer of 2018, my wife and I spent a wonderful afternoon in the superbly well-kept and organized archives of the church, with Dale guiding us through materials about both the history of the church in the 1850s as well as material regarding the ministry of the Reverend Albert Hale. Dale also located an 1838 letter from Hale, currently archived in the Abraham Lincoln Presidential Library, stating the urgent need for an abolitionist lecturer in Illinois. Dale also helped us with his knowledge of the provenance of the original church bell, still in use today as one of three, and mentioned prominently in the novel. A history of the church (along with a sketch of the church as it was circa 1860) can be found here: http://www.wpcspi.org/history-of-westminster.html.

I also want to acknowledge the resources of three institutions and thank them for the materials they make available: (1) The Abraham Lincoln Library and Museum in Springfield, Illinois. The museum is one of the best historical museums focused on a particular individual or historical period that I have ever been to (it is well worth a trip to Springfield just to see it). http://lincolnlibraryandmuseum.com/ (2) The American Antiquarian Society in Worcester, Massachusetts, which has a substantial collection of Abby Kelley Foster materials, including a large trove of her letters, many of which it has made available to read online, for the benefit of historians, researchers and general readers. Reading some of those letters was very helpful because it gave me a good sense of Abby's intensity, especially her letters from the period when she was feuding with William Lloyd Garrison. Thomas Knoles, the Curator of Manuscripts at the Society, was especially helpful. https://www.americanantiquarian.org/ (3) The New Jersey Historical Society in Newark, New Jersey, and particularly James Amemasor and Greg Guderian, who helped me find information there about William Pennington. https://jerseyhistory.org/

And I must thank my trusty beta readers and consultants, who have, as always, via their comments and suggestions and general support, made the novel much, much better than it would otherwise have been. They include Daniel Wershow (including for the great research assistance he provided on several arcane matters of legal history), Melanie Chancellor, Dale Franklin and Barbara Wong, Marty Beech, Roger Chittum, Deanna Wilcox and John Shelonko, Linda and John Brown, Gayle Simon, Clint Epps, Carolyn Denham, Mark Morris and Francoise Queval, Prucia Buscell, Mi Ahn, Tom Stromberg, Hwa Kho and Ping Lee, Annye Camara, Elizabeth Friedman, Don Warner, Brinton Rowdybush, Mike Haines, Tom Reiber, Stan Goldman, Jeff Davison, Elaine Jarvik, Mary Lane Leslie and Tyson Butler.

And a big thank you is due to Diana Wright for the design and support of my website and social media accounts.

Last but not least, I am grateful for the availability of Wikipedia. Although at times flawed in various ways (like all such sources), it is a great resource for starting research—it is often both deep and wide in its coverage—including its end-of-entry footnotes, which sometimes make reference to obscure books and articles that would otherwise be difficult or more time-consuming to find. My thanks to the Wikimedia Foundation, which supports it, and to the many volunteers who do the work that make it possible.

Of course, any errors or infelicities in the novel are solely my own.